THROUGH THICK OR THIN

It seemed as though everything was stacked against him and Gloria. She was his love, his life. He wanted to make his marriage work.

Josh looked out the window as the plane pulled up to the gate. He knew Gloria would be waiting for him and he wondered what kind of greeting he'd get.

He saw her as soon as he walked through the gate door. She looked happy to see him, though the question in her eyes was obvious. She walked toward him and he opened his arms. They held each other for a long time, gathering strength and love from the other. Gloria broke the embrace, pulled away, and looked up at him. There was a smile on her face and the question in her eyes was dimmed by tears.

Josh lifted a finger to wipe the tears. "Happy tears, I hope?"

Gloria nodded. "I missed you, Josh."

He squeezed her to him. "Where do you want to go for dinner?"

"It doesn't matter," she answered. "As long as we're together."

He believed her and felt relief. They just might make it through this.

ANGELA BENSON

FOR ALL TIME

PINNACLE BOOKS
KENSINGTON PUBLISHING CORP.

PINNACLE BOOKS are published by

Kensington Publishing Corp.
850 Third Avenue
New York, NY 10022

Pinnacle and the P logo Reg. U.S. Pat. & TM Off.
First Printing: August, 1995

Printed in the United States of America

Chapter 1

Fired. Joshua Martin couldn't believe it. After nine years of dedicated service to General Electronics, he was being fired. "When will you make the announcement?" he asked Marvin Callahan, his boss and friend. At least, he had thought Marvin was his friend.

Marvin looked away. "I'm meeting with the managers Monday morning. We'll tell the staff Monday afternoon."

That's fast, Josh thought. Too fast. "When's our last day?"

"Two weeks, Josh. They're giving everybody two weeks."

Marvin continued talking, but Josh didn't hear him. I can't believe this is happening to me, he thought. Not to me. I've done everything right. I've worked hard for General Electronics, done more than was required of me. And what do I get? Two weeks' notice.

Josh shook his head. Nine years to build a career and *two weeks to watch it die.*

"The severance package isn't what it should be,"

Marvin was saying, "but I'm sure you won't have a problem finding another job. I'll give you an excellent recommendation."

Josh could think of nothing more to say. He straightened the tie that was now feeling tight around his neck. He needed to get out of Marvin's office. He was suffocating.

As if Marvin had heard Josh's thoughts, he stood and extended his hand. Josh took it.

"It was great working with you, son," Marvin said. "You deserve better than this."

Josh dropped Marvin's hand and headed for the door. After he opened it, he turned and faced Marvin, "You're right, Marvin. I do deserve better than this."

Josh made the long walk back to his office, not quite believing what had happened. He had gone into Marvin's office expecting to discuss his upcoming promotion. Man, had he been wrong. He couldn't have been more wrong.

When he reached his office, Grace, his secretary and the one person who still had a job, was still at her desk. "That was a short meeting," she commented.

Josh gave her a grim smile. "Why don't you knock off for today? I'll see you Monday."

Not waiting for Grace's response, Josh walked into his office and closed the door behind him. He sat at his desk, threw back his head, and stared at the ceiling. You're no better than your father, he thought.

"Wait up a minute, Gloria."

Hearing her name, Gloria Martin turned to see her friend Portia rushing down the hallway in a swirl of flowers. Gloria shook her head. Portia and her clothes, she thought. The solid navy jacket lessened the effect, but the rainbow of colors in the drop-waist dress was still eye-catching. "Hi, Portia. I haven't seen you all week. You must be very busy."

Portia tugged at the button of her jacket as if she were uncomfortable in it. "I am, girl, but no more than you. I've been trying to reach you all morning. Dexter and I are planning a dinner party two weeks from today and we want you and Josh to come."

Gloria smiled. "No can do. Josh and I will be on our second honeymoon in two weeks."

"Second honeymoon, huh? How long have you been planning this?"

When Portia reached Gloria's side, they strolled together down the hall toward their offices. "A year."

"A year?" Portia rolled her eyes. "You've only been married a year."

Gloria nodded her head. "That's right. Before Josh and I got married we decided we would celebrate every anniversary as another honeymoon."

Portia wrinkled her nose. "Whose idea was this? Yours or Josh's?"

"Josh's."

"I knew it," Portia said. "Josh is such a romantic. I've told Dexter he needs to spend more time with Josh. I'm hoping Josh will rub off on him. Dexter is about as romantic as a lamp post."

Gloria laughed at Portia's exaggeration. She knew Portia and Dexter had a good marriage and they were deeply in love with each other. "You'd better stop putting Dexter down. One of these days you're going to hurt his feelings."

A soft expression came across Portia's face. "The big lug knows I love him, but that doesn't mean he couldn't bone up a little in the romance department. All the romantic ideas are mine and that gets to be tiring."

"I can imagine."

"No, you can't," Portia said, "but thanks for saying it."

When they reached the point where they would have to part company to go to their respective offices, Gloria looked at her watch. "I have to call Josh about our dinner date tonight. Why don't you come by my office? We can catch up on the office gossip."

Gloria led the way to her office. She motioned Portia to a seat at the conference table next to her desk, then she picked up the phone.

"Hiya, handsome," she said when Josh answered.

"Hi, yourself."

Gloria noticed that Josh's voice didn't hold the contained excitement that usually marked their conversations. "Is everything all right?" she asked. "You sound funny."

"Odd you should ask that question," Josh said in a resigned voice so unlike himself. "Things could be better."

"What's wrong?" Gloria was concerned. It wasn't like Josh to be down.

"Nothing that can't wait until I see you. How about Mick's at six?"

His words didn't reassure her. "Mick's is fine, Josh. Are you sure everything is all right?"

He paused and she heard him release a deep sigh. "It's nothing that can't wait," he said. "Now get back to work. I'll see you at six."

Gloria held the phone after Josh hung up.

"Something wrong?" Portia asked.

Gloria looked up. She had forgotten Portia was in the room. "Josh is upset about something."

Portia stood and moved toward the office door. "Call him back. We can do lunch next week and catch up on the news."

Gloria waved Portia back to the table. "There's no need for that. I'm not meeting him until six. He wouldn't tell me what's wrong over the phone anyway."

Portia remained standing. "Are you sure?"

Taking a seat at the conference table, Gloria smiled. "I'm sure. Josh will tell me over dinner. Whatever it is, we'll work it out."

Portia sat next to her. "In that case, I have some news for you."

"What did you hear?" Gloria leaned forward, eager to hear the latest gossip.

"I'm up for a promotion," Portia said, a satisfied grin on her face.

"A promotion? Portia, that's wonderful. Which department?"

Portia hesitated, then whispered, "That's where the news is. I'm not sure yet, but it'll be either Trusts or Commercial Lending."

Gloria sat back in her chair and straightened her back. "Commercial Lending? That's my department. How can you get promoted into my department? That would mean you'd get my job."

Portia's grin grew wider. "That's right. I'd get your job."

Gloria didn't say anything. She didn't know what to say.

Portia laughed then. "Don't look so confused, you goose. The word is that you or Bob in Trusts will be promoted to Commercial Investments Second Vice-President."

Gloria breathed a relieved sigh. "Where did you hear this?"

"I have my sources."

Gloria studied her friend. Portia was well connected

in the office grapevine so she was usually right on the money with her news, but this news was too good to believe.

"Nothing's final," Portia cautioned her. "So don't decorate your new office yet."

Gloria laughed because Portia knew her so well. "If this news of yours is true, when will we know?"

"Two months, tops."

"Two months, huh? Well, I hope you're right. This really would be good news for us. Josh is up for a promotion, too. Wouldn't it be great if we both got promotions? We sure could use the money."

Portia rolled her eyes. "You and Josh have more money now than you can spend. What do you mean, you need the money?"

"Josh and I want to start a family soon," Gloria confided. "And when we do, I want to stay home with the kids for a few years. We need the money so I can do that without changing our lifestyle."

"You—a stay-at-home mom? That I can't picture."

"And why not?" Gloria knew Portia too well to be peeved by her comment, though it did rankle just a bit.

"You're too much of a career woman. I thought you'd have the baby Wednesday and be back to work Friday."

Gloria laughed at that. "At one time, maybe, but Josh and I have talked a lot about it. We both grew up in households with working mothers. Mothers who worked a lot. We don't want that for our children. Besides, I can always return to work if I change my mind or if I get bored. What about you? Have you and Dexter been talking about babies?"

Portia slid her chair closer to Gloria's. "We've been trying to get pregnant for the last six months."

"And you haven't told me?" Gloria asked with a smile. "I'm insulted."

"Don't be. We haven't told anybody. We don't want to talk about it until I'm pregnant."

Gloria saw uncertainty in Portia's face. "There aren't any problems, are there?"

Portia shook her head. "I'm getting anxious, but the doctor says there's nothing to worry about yet. I've stopped taking the pill and my body has to adjust."

"You guys will get lucky soon," Gloria said, touching Portia's hand. "So, will you continue working or will you stay home?"

"That's another reason we aren't talking about it. I knew a promotion of some sort was in the works for me and I didn't want my manager to know how immediate our plans for a family were. It might make him think I'm not serious about my career."

Gloria nodded. It was the nineties, but corporate America still functioned as though it was the Dark Ages when it came to women and pregnancies. "I know what you mean. You still haven't answered my question, though. What will you do after the baby is born?"

Portia's slight shoulders drooped and her usually bright eyes dimmed. "We haven't decided. Dexter wants me to stay home. I want to stay home for a while, but I'm not sure I could do it for more than a year. I'd miss work too much. We're considering the part-time option."

"Good for you," Gloria said. "You'll find a solution that works for both you and Dexter. All the books say the best environment for a baby is a happy home, whether that's with a working mom or a stay-at-home mom."

"I'm glad you said that. Sometimes I feel guilty

about not wanting to stay home, as though I'm putting my baby second.''

"Don't think that way, Portia," Gloria said. "If you stay home, stay because it makes you happy, not because you think it's expected. If you're happy, your baby will be happy.''

Portia reached over and hugged Gloria. "You're a good friend. Even with all the work we have, we should make time to talk more often.''

Gloria pulled back and smiled at her friend. "You're right. Let's do that.''

"I'm leaving now," Portia said, getting up from her chair. "You'd better go too, if you want to make your date with your husband.''

Gloria looked at her watch. "You're right. I have a couple of things to do first and then I'm out of here. I hope you and Dexter have a good weekend.''

When Portia left the office, Gloria returned to her desk and began reviewing contracts. After about an hour, she stopped and pushed her chair back from the desk. "There's nothing here that can't wait until Monday," she said to herself. "I'm going to meet my husband.''

When Gloria walked through Mick's bright orange doors, she scanned the after-work dinner crowd for her husband. Her eyes found him seated at a table near the windows. He was staring into his glass, apparently deep in thought.

As she walked toward him, her heart swelled with pride. Joshua Martin was everything a woman could want. He was a handsome man, her husband. And he was hers. All of him. His close-cut, wavy, black hair. His smooth, clean-shaven, brown, almost black, skin. His beautiful brown eyes. He lifted those eyes to her when she reached him and she saw that they were troubled.

"Hiya, handsome," she said as she leaned down to give him a kiss on the jaw. "Have you been waiting long?"

"Not long," Josh said. He stood, pulled out a chair for her, and gave her a long, wet kiss before he took his seat again. "Do you want a drink?"

Still reeling from that kiss, she pointed to the glass in front of him. "Whatever you're having."

Josh beckoned the waiter and ordered Evian for Gloria. Since she knew what she wanted, they also placed their dinner orders. When the waiter left, Gloria asked, "Do you want to tell me what happened?"

When Josh looked at her, Gloria saw the debate in his expression. "Not yet. Why don't you tell me about your day first?"

Something is terribly wrong, she thought. It's unlike Josh to hedge my questions. Maybe good news will help. "I talked to Portia today."

That brought a smile to his face. "How is she? It's been awhile since we've seen her and Dexter."

Gloria smiled because Josh was smiling. "Portia's Portia. She and Dexter invited us to a dinner party, but I told her about our anniversary trip. Have you decided where we're going?"

Josh's smile widened into a grin as he pulled airline tickets from his pocket. He waved them toward her, but when she reached for them, he pulled them away and put them back in his pocket.

"So, we're flying?"

Josh put a finger to his lips. "I'm not saying any more."

Gloria pouted. "If you don't tell me where we're going, I won't know how to pack."

"It doesn't matter. You won't need clothes. We'll spend most of this vacation inside anyway."

Josh's grin was now a leer. Gloria began to relax. Maybe nothing was wrong after all, she thought. "Maybe so, but I have to know what to wear to the airport."

"I'll do your packing for you."

Gloria laughed and shook her head. "I don't think I'll risk that. If I leave it to you, I'll have nothing but lingerie and probably very little of that."

Josh clutched at his heart. "You wound me!"

"Wound me, nothing. I know you, Joshua Martin."

Josh's look turned serious and he reached for Gloria's hand. "I love you, Gloria. More each day."

Gloria saw the troubled look in his eyes return. "What is it, Josh? You can tell me."

"I know, Gloria, but I don't know how to tell you."

"Start at the beginning," she said in what she hoped was a calm voice. Josh was making her nervous, afraid even. *Please, God, don't let it be something terrible.*

Josh applied pressure to her hand. "Marvin gave me some news today," Josh began, but before he could continue the waiter returned with their salads and Gloria's drink. Josh released her hand and picked up his fork.

"Marvin gave you some news today," Gloria prompted after the waiter was gone. "What news?"

Josh took a bite of his salad before answering. "The company has decided on more cuts. This time my department."

Gloria didn't know how to respond to this news. The last time downsizing affected Josh's department, he was promoted. Obviously that wasn't the case this time. "What's going to happen?"

Josh placed his fork on the table and sat back in his chair. "Everybody has to go but one person."

Gloria lifted the glass of Evian to her lips. She didn't say anything. That one person had to be Josh. He was the best thing to happen to General Electronics in years.

"That person is Grace."

Gloria spilled her drink on the front of her dress. "You can't be serious." She placed her glass on the table and picked up a napkin to dab at the water spot expanding on the front of her dress.

Josh gave a wry grin. "Do I look like I'm joking?" He didn't wait for an answer. "Marvin told me this afternoon. He'll make a general announcement Monday. We have two weeks to clear out."

Gloria stopped dabbing at the water spot and lifted her eyes to Josh. "Two weeks! That's criminal, Josh. This doesn't happen to professionals."

"That's what I thought too, but apparently we're wrong. There are no rules of etiquette when it comes to salvaging the corporate bottom line."

Gloria picked up her glass and took a long swallow, wishing she had ordered something stronger. "Marvin could have told you sooner. Surely, he knew something. You deserved to know when the talk first started."

Josh returned to his salad, as if they were discussing inclement weather. "Don't be angry with Marvin. He's doing his job. He's out too. Forced retirement."

"I don't believe it," Gloria said, picking at her salad with her fork. "Everybody but Grace. What saved her?"

Josh shrugged. When he finished chewing, he said, "They used some service formula and Grace met the criteria. Marvin and I were pushed out on opposite ends of the spectrum. He had too much service; I had too little."

"Is there any chance you can find work someplace else in the company?"

Josh shook his head. "That's not an option. They want us off the payroll."

Gloria wished they were home now instead of in a public restaurant. She wanted to be comforted. And she wanted to comfort her husband. She knew him well enough to know that even though his demeanor said "calm," he was shaken up. She reached for his hand and squeezed hard. "I love you, Josh. We'll make it through this. Together."

Josh returned pressure to his wife's hand. "I love you, too. This thing blind-sided me. I walked into Marvin's office expecting to talk about my upcoming promotion. This was the farthest thing from my mind."

Gloria's thoughts went to the promotion she and Portia had talked about. She decided now was not the time to mention that to Josh.

Chapter 2

The moonlight shone through the bedroom window, giving Gloria a clear view of her sleeping husband. His relaxed expression gave her a sense of peace. He looked like a carefree little boy. But he wasn't a little boy. He was a man. Six-feet-three inches of gorgeous, black man. And he wasn't carefree, at least not this morning. This morning he had more than his share of worries. She wanted to reach out and caress his face to reassure herself that everything was going to work out, but she knew her touch would wake him.

She was still steamed about his treatment from General Electronics. It wasn't fair. Josh had done everything right—more than right. This shouldn't be happening to him, to us.

She studied his face. From the look he wore, she assumed his dreams were pleasant, peaceful. Maybe pictures of the two of them on some secluded island filled his mind. She lifted her hand again to touch him and withdrew it a whisper from his cheek. She wasn't going to wake him.

Gloria turned to lie on her back, her eyes focused on the ceiling, her mind on her marriage. She and Josh were a good team. They were best friends as well as husband and wife. They brought out the best in each other. She knew Josh would need her to make it through this job ordeal just as he had needed her tonight. Their lovemaking had taken on an ethereal quality. Josh was doing more than making love to her. He was claiming her, making sure that she was real and that she was there.

"Two dollars." The smooth silkiness of Josh's voice interrupted her thoughts. She turned her head in his direction to see him leaning on his elbow looking at her.

She turned fully toward him. "My thoughts are worth more than two dollars this morning."

Josh gave her a quick kiss on her mouth. "How much more?"

She returned his kiss, giving him one that was longer and wetter than the one he had given her. "Money's not everything, Josh."

"I love you, Gloria Martin."

Gloria saw the sincerity in his eyes. She never doubted his love for her. When he said it like this, though, it brought out something primitive in her. She rolled toward him until her body was flush with his, her lips so close to his that she felt his breath on her face. "I love you, Joshua Martin."

Josh wrapped his arms around her and pulled her atop him as he rolled over onto his back. "You're a beautiful, sexy woman, wife."

"I feel like a beautiful, sexy woman in your arms."

Josh rubbed his hands up and down her buttocks

and thighs. "You probably say that to all your husbands."

Gloria moved so her breasts feathered across his chest. "What did you say?"

Josh groaned. In retaliation, he pushed his hardness more firmly against her. "I can't remember."

Gloria moaned as she met his hardness with her softness. "Fortunately, you remember the important things."

Josh met Gloria's gaze and held it. "You know you're in trouble, don't you?"

Gloria pressed her breasts flat against his chest and kissed him fully on the mouth. "When are you going to stop talking?"

Josh pushed up off the bed and rolled over until Gloria was under him. He stared into her eyes and saw a reflection of the love and desire he felt. "I've stopped."

Gloria placed her arms around his broad shoulders and pulled him to her. Josh reveled in the kiss she gave him, a kiss that made him feel she wanted to devour him. God, that was a heady feeling. This was his woman. With all the uncertainty in his life right now, he could be sure of this woman who purred so sweetly beneath him. She was his and she would be his forever.

She was his. That was the last thought Josh had before he erupted inside her.

Later, Josh smiled at his sleeping wife sprawled across the bed. Her normally well-coiffured hair was a mass of disarray around her face. Her lips were curved in a sensuous smile. The small, black mole above the right side of her upper lip was so enticing that he leaned over and kissed it. She stirred, but she didn't awaken. He pulled away and let his gaze wander down her naked body. He only got as far as her maddeningly sexy, full, round breasts before he was fully aroused. That didn't surprise him since simply talking with Gloria could awaken his arousal. It had been that way since he had first seen her strolling along McCosh Walk at Princeton.

"Who's that?" Josh had asked his friend Walter.

Walter looked in the direction of Josh's stare. "I can't believe you're even interested, Mr. Iceman."

Josh continued to stare at the tall, slim beauty with curly black hair that waved around her face. She was talking to Gwen, a fellow student. Even from a distance, he could see her happy smile and feel its warmth. "Are you going to tell me who she is or will I have to have Gwen introduce me?"

"Someone has finally gotten to the Iceman. I don't believe it," Walter said, shaking his head and laughing. "She really has your number, doesn't she, Josh?"

Josh began to walk away from Walter and toward Gwen and the beauty. "Her name, Walter. All I want is her name."

Walter called after him, "Gloria. Her name is Gloria."

"Thanks for nothing, buddy," Josh responded without looking back.

Gwen greeted him when he reached her and Gloria. "Hi, Josh. Have you met Gloria?"

Josh directed his smile to Gloria. "Not yet."

"Now you have," Gwen said. "Gloria Adams, Josh Martin."

Josh felt fortunate to have that brilliant smile and those bright eyes focused on him.

"Hi, Josh."

He knew he was staring, but he couldn't help himself. That black mole against her warm, brown skin mesmerized him. "Will you have dinner with me tonight?"

Gloria's eyes registered her surprise.

Gwen laughed, then said, "You don't waste much time, do you, Josh?"

Josh's gaze didn't leave Gloria's face and he didn't answer Gwen. "Tomorrow night?" he offered when Gloria didn't answer.

The twinkle in her big, brown eyes told him that she was laughing at him, but he didn't care. He wanted a date with her. He had to have a date with her. "Okay, you pick the night."

Gloria laughed, a happy, full, feminine laugh that made him want to laugh with her. "I think I like you, Josh Martin. Tomorrow night is fine."

Actually, they went out ten nights in a row. On the tenth night, Josh surprised himself. "Will you marry me, Gloria Adams?"

From her look and her answer, the question didn't surprise Gloria. "When?"

"June, seven years from now."

Gloria didn't hesitate. "Yes, Josh. I'll marry you."

Josh remembered the day as if it had been yesterday. He and Gloria had been so young, so arrogant and so full of dreams. Walter had laughed when Josh had told him of their engagement.

"Seven years? You expect that gorgeous woman to wait seven years? You're crazy. Some other guy will come along and snap her right up."

Josh was undaunted. "You're wrong, Walter. Gloria and I *will* marry in seven years. She'll date other men and maybe I'll date other women, but in seven years you'll be the best man at our wedding."

Walter shook his head. "I believe in planning as much as the next guy, but you take it too far, Josh.

You can't fit everything into your Day Planner for life. Some things won't fit. I don't want to see you hurt, man.''

"You don't understand. Gloria and I want it this way. She has things she wants to accomplish before we get married, and so do I.''

"But seven years is such a long time,'' Walter countered.

Josh shook his head. "Not when you think about it. Gloria has two years of school and then five years of work to accomplish her goals before we get married.''

"What about you? How are you going to handle seven years?''

"Working. I'm taking that job with General Electronics in San Francisco. I'm up to my eyeballs in debt. Seven years should give me more than enough time to get established financially. By that time, I should have arranged a transfer to Atlanta.''

"Atlanta? I thought you wanted to live on the West Coast.''

"Hey, buddy, I'm in love, remember? Gloria wants to move back to Atlanta. You know she went to Spelman.''

"I don't know, man. Seven years is a long time.''

"It'll work for us. I'm sure of it.''

Josh still remembered Walter's skeptical look. He had reminded Walter of that look many times over the last two years. "Surprised'' didn't adequately describe Walter's reaction when Josh had asked him to be best man at his and Gloria's wedding. Of course, Walter had agreed. And on June tenth, seven years after she had accepted his proposal, Gloria Adams became Gloria Martin.

Everything had gone according to plan for them. They'd had their time apart and they had begun their time together. Their goal for their first year of marriage had been to save for a substantial down payment on a house large enough for the family they wanted to start by their third year of marriage. They had accomplished that first-year goal with the recent purchase of a five-bedroom contemporary in Atlanta's South DeKalb area. Their second year's goal was to save enough money for Gloria to leave work to raise their children. The size of their portfolio suggested they were well on the way to accomplishing that goal.

Thinking about their goals brought Josh's job situation to the forefront of his mind. For a while last night and this morning Gloria had helped him forget. But Josh knew he couldn't spend the entire weekend making love to his wife to forget his troubles. No, Josh Martin needed to do what he did best. He needed to make a plan.

Gloria reached for Josh, but he wasn't in bed with her. She opened her eyes and looked around the room. He sat at the desk in the alcove of their bedroom, writing intently. It was a familiar sight.

"Working, Josh?" she asked.

Josh looked up then. "No need for that now."

Gloria ran her hand through her hair and sat up fully in the bed. Had she really forgotten that Josh had lost his job? "What are you doing?"

Josh placed the pad on the desk and walked over and sat on the bed. He pulled Gloria into his arms and kissed her forehead. "Planning to find a new job."

"Have you come up with anything?"

"Not much," he answered. "I've been thinking more than anything else."

"You were writing up a storm a few minutes ago."

"Just getting my thoughts together. Writing helps."

"What were you thinking about?" she asked.

"How naive I've been. Given the churn at General over the last few years, I should've had a contingency plan."

Gloria responded immediately to the self-directed guilt she heard in his voice. "There was no way for you to know, or even suspect, you'd be terminated."

Josh winced. "Ouch. I guess I'd better get used to that terminate word."

Gloria was instantly contrite. "I'm sorry, Josh."

He squeezed her to him. "It's not your fault. You have nothing to be sorry for." Josh was silent for a while. Finally, he spoke. "I started a list of contacts to explore. It doesn't look too promising, though. Most of the companies I listed are downsizing, too."

"You know as well as I do, Josh, that companies hire with one hand while they're laying off with the other. We'll have to use our inside contacts to find out what's really going on."

Josh gave a hollow laugh. "I sure hope that our contacts, as you call them, know more about what's happening in their companies than I knew about what was happening at General."

"Stop talking like that," Gloria said, pinching him on the arm. "There was no way for you to anticipate this. God, Marvin had been talking to you about a promotion."

A promotion, Josh thought. It was almost laughable now. Almost. "I'll start making calls Monday. All I want this weekend is to be with you. Is that all right?"

"Let me see," Gloria teased, glad that Josh was coming out of his doldrums. "Do I want my husband's full attention this weekend? Surely, I can find something better to do with my time."

Josh patted her bottom. "You can, can you?"

She felt him relax. "Easily. But since you need me,

I'll put those plans on hold. What do you want to do today?"

"We could spend the day in bed." He reached out his hand and tweaked her left nipple. It immediately puckered.

Gloria pushed away from him, though she was tempted to go along with his suggestion. Very tempted. "We could, but we're not. Let's do something wild. How about Six Flags? I love amusement parks. We haven't been in ages."

Gloria got up from the bed and paraded to the bathroom. Josh called after her, "There's probably a good reason for that. I hate amusement parks. Let's take the boat out instead."

Gloria stepped out of the bathroom, her toothbrush in her mouth. She didn't want to spend the day on the boat that General Electronics made available to its executives. "That's not true, Josh. You hate the idea of going to the Park, but once you get there you enjoy it as much as I do."

"But I want to be alone with you and Six Flags will be so crowded."

Gloria pulled the toothbrush out of her mouth, relieved Josh hadn't mentioned the boat again. "Sure, there are lots of people there, Josh. It's a park, for God's sake. Now get up and get dressed. We can spend the whole day there."

Josh got up from the bed and went to his closet. "I don't believe we're doing this. Where has the romance gone in this marriage when the wife prefers Six Flags to a quiet, private day on the lake with her husband?"

Gloria put her hands on her hips, knowing that since Josh was in his closet, the trip to Six Flags was a done deal. "We're going to Six Flags, Joshua Martin, and you're going to love it."

* * *

The relaxed feeling Josh had experienced over the weekend wore off as soon as he walked into his office Monday morning. He dreaded the morning meeting with Marvin to discuss the specifics of the "termination," but more than that he dreaded the afternoon meeting when he had to tell his staff they'd be out of work in two weeks. Everybody but Grace.

"What's wrong, Josh?" Grace asked after he was seated at his desk.

"What makes you think something is wrong?"

"Well, for the first time in the three years I've worked for you, I beat you into the office. Second, there was no new work on my desk this morning."

Josh smiled. He usually worked on weekends, leaving work on Grace's desk for Monday mornings. Things were changing already. "Close the door, Grace, and have a seat."

Josh gave Grace the news.

"I don't believe it, Josh. I'm the only one staying on. How can that be?"

"They're doing this strictly by service times. You're the only one who meets the criteria. Everybody else will be terminated or forced to retire."

"Not you too, Josh?"

"Yes, me too." The stricken look on Grace's face only made him feel worse. If Grace took it this way and she was keeping her job, he didn't want to think about how the others would take it.

Josh stood, a signal for Grace to do the same. "The managers are meeting with Marvin this morning to discuss the details. Call a staff meeting for one this afternoon. I'll tell everyone then. I want you to be prepared, Grace. This won't be easy. Our people have a lot invested in this company and they aren't going to take the news well. I'll need your help to deal with them."

Grace nodded. "Just tell me what to do."

"Don't mention our conversation to anyone. I don't want the rumor mill to get this before this afternoon's meeting. And don't make a big deal out of the meeting; just make sure everybody's there. I'll handle the rest."

Josh walked to the door and opened it. Grace followed him. Before she left the office, she said, "I should feel relieved for myself, Josh, because I do need this job, but it doesn't seem fair."

Josh agreed. But nobody had ever said business was fair. "Fair or not, Grace, you have a right to be happy. It's my job to deal with the fairness issue, not yours."

Josh closed the door and returned to his desk. He knew Grace was still upset, but there was nothing more he could say. He was upset himself. Though he had only worked with these people for three years, he felt close to them. He knew they had families. Jack Johnson's wife had been hospitalized for the last six months. What would this news do to him? Lora Taylor was a single mother with two children in college. How was she going to cope?

Josh turned around in his chair and faced the windows. It was a clear day and he could see Stone Mountain. The thoughts he had kept at bay since hearing the news flooded his mind. How had his father felt when he had been laid off? Josh remembered very well the two years of his childhood that his father had been out of work. He tried not to think about that time since the memories brought pain. One memory was more painful than all the others.

The sounds of his parents arguing had wakened him. He had gone part of the way down the stairs and peeked through the rails to the living room. His father had been yelling and his mother was in tears. It had happened so fast. Josh had stood up to say something, to stop his father, but before he could open his mouth, his father had slapped his mother so hard that she had fallen to the couch.

Josh never told anyone what he had seen that night, but it had changed him. He had gone from a carefree child to a young man who had failed to take care of his mother. That night, he had promised himself he would never let her down again. He became his mother's protector. His father became a nonentity to him.

When Josh was away for his second year of college, his parents were killed in a car accident. Josh blamed his father and himself. Again, he had failed his mother. It's easier not to care, he had reasoned. That's when he'd gotten the nickname *Iceman*. He had never dated much, but he had stopped altogether after the death of his parents.

Things had changed when he met Gloria. Something about her caused the gates of his heart to open. Beyond a doubt, it had been love at first sight for him. He had promised himself that he would take better care of Gloria than he had taken of his mother, better than his father had taken of his mother.

I'm not going to be like him, Josh thought. I love Gloria. We're not going to end up like my parents.

Josh turned around to his desk. He pulled out a pad and began to make notes for the meeting with his staff. He knew that words wouldn't make it easy, but maybe they could keep things from being too painful—for him and for them.

Nothing could have prepared Josh for how painful it really was. The meeting started as any other staff meeting. Then he dropped the news. The immediate reaction was silence or maybe stunned disbelief. Then came the questions.

"Why?"

"Why didn't you tell us before now?"

Next, the accusations. "You knew before now and you didn't tell us."

"I bet you aren't losing your job."

Then, worst of all. "I have three kids—how am I supposed to make it?"

"My husband has already lost his job. How will we live?"

Josh had no answers for them because he had no answers for himself. He repeated the company line. "This is the last day . . . This is the severance package . . . These are the reasons I've been given . . . I'll write each of you a personal recommendation . . ."

When Gloria met Josh for dinner at Mick's later that evening, she immediately saw the change in his attitude since the morning. "Bad day?"

"That's an understatement."

"Want to talk about it?"

"Not now. Maybe later."

Though Gloria wanted him to talk about it, she followed his lead and didn't push. "Okay."

"Are you ready for our anniversary trip?"

Gloria had wondered if Josh still wanted to go. She had mixed feelings about it. Though it was a perfect opportunity for them to get away and clear their heads, she wondered if it was the right time for a trip, given the change in their finances. "I'd understand, Josh," she said, "if you didn't feel up to the trip."

"No. I still want to go. Don't you?"

If he wanted to go, she thought, they needed to go. The time away would be good for them. "I do."

Josh nodded. "My last day of work coincides with the beginning of our trip. Ironic, don't you think? A celebration of beginnings and endings."

Gloria winced at the dry laugh that Josh gave. "Celebrating our first year of married life should be a happy time, Josh. We're not turning it into a wake because you're losing your job. When we married, we promised to use these trips to celebrate the past year and to plan for the next year. Finding a new job for you will be a challenge that we'll face together, but it won't overshadow our relationship or this trip."

"You're right, Gloria, and I'm sorry. I promise not to let what's happened ruin our anniversary trip."

"We can work this out, Josh. I know we can." She reached for his hand. Even though she believed her words, she knew that Josh didn't. "Did you make any calls today?"

Josh shook his head. "I was in meetings all day. Tomorrow I'm having lunch with Dexter. He should know something. Have you told Portia yet?"

"No, I thought you'd want to tell Dexter first."

"Thanks for that," Josh said. "You know, I'm thinking about giving Walter a call. He may be able to help."

"I wouldn't think Walter had many contacts in Atlanta. He's been in San Francisco since you graduated."

"I know, but maybe there's something in San Francisco. How do you feel about relocating?"

Gloria thought about the promotion Portia had mentioned. "How do *you* feel about it, Josh? We've always planned to plant roots in Atlanta. We've bought a house. Atlanta is home for us.''

"We need to keep all of our options open. What if I can't find a job here?"

"You'll find a job here," Gloria said with confidence. "Let's not talk about moving until we've exhausted all possibilities here. Call one of those executive search firms. They should know about openings at your level."

"I may do that later. Dexter and Marvin will be my first steps. Marvin has contacts in the city. He's making some inquiries."

"He owes you that much, Josh. I still believe he knew about this long before he told you. He could have given you more notice."

Josh shook his head again. "I disagree with you on that. These decisions are made at levels a lot higher than Marvin's or mine. They come down and everybody is affected. I don't blame Marvin."

Gloria still didn't buy it. Marvin was a department head; he had to have known. "Who is Marvin talking to?"

Josh told Gloria of his discussion with Marvin. Her thoughts wandered as he talked. Josh's job loss was already affecting their relationship. She wasn't being straight with him about her feelings. She hadn't told him about her possible promotion. And she was sure there were things he wasn't sharing with her. The idea of moving unsettled her. She didn't want to move. She loved Atlanta. She loved their life here in Atlanta. She loved her job. Everything was perfect. Correction. Everything had been perfect until Josh lost his job.

"You haven't heard a word I've said, have you, Gloria?"

His question brought her thoughts back to him.
Thoughts she didn't want to share with him. She
handled it the way she was handling a lot of her
feelings these days. She lied.

Chapter 3

Grace closed the bottom drawer of the file cabinet in Josh's office and stood up. "I still don't believe this is happening. It's been two weeks since you told me and I still don't believe this is happening."

Seeing the strain on her face, Josh walked over to her. "Grace, you have to get over this. It's not that bad. We'll find other positions."

Her eyes registered disbelief. "I know you will, Josh, and so will some of the engineers, but what about the others? It's a tough market out there now. The more education you have, the better off you'll be. Some of these people don't have the education you do. I don't know what will happen to them."

Josh hoped Grace was right about his finding a job with ease, but he doubted it. He knew she was right about one thing though—it was a tough market now. For everybody. "You can't worry about everybody, Grace. It's not your fault."

"But I feel so guilty. Why do I get to keep my job when nobody else does?"

Josh looked at the gray-haired woman who had been his secretary for the past three years. She worried about him. She worried about all the workers. He pulled her into his arms for a big hug. "One of the saddest things about leaving this job is that I won't see you every day." He pulled back from her to see her teary eyes. "You've been more than a good employee, you've been a good friend and I'll miss you."

Grace wiped at the tears in her eyes. "I'll miss you too, Josh."

Josh tapped her on her nose. "Gloria and I will make sure that we continue to see you."

Grace nodded as her tears fell more freely. "You're all packed up here. I'd better get to my desk and finish my packing."

Grace turned and walked out of the office. Josh closed the door behind her, then walked back to his desk. He remembered the day he had moved into this office. He and Gloria had come in over the weekend to decorate. She had wanted the office to say "Josh." He had laughed at her, but her excitement had been contagious.

"I'm so proud of you, Josh," she had said from her seat at his desk.

He sat on the edge of the desk, facing her. "I'm proud of you too," he had responded.

"Josh, I'm serious. You've accomplished a lot in a short time. The youngest Chief Engineer in General Electronics' history. One of only four African-Americans. That's something to be proud of. Aren't you excited?"

Josh smiled at her. "I'm excited, but I don't express my excitement the way you express yours."

"You can say that again. That's why you need me. You need someone in your life to express emotions. That way you can maintain your macho exterior."

Josh leaned toward her and kissed her. "I do need you."

Gloria pulled away. "You're so bad. That's not the kind of need I'm talking about and you know it."

Josh smiled at the memory. He had known what she was talking about. And he knew she was right. She *was* the emotion in his life. She saw joy and made him see it. She felt pain and made him feel it. She had a courage that left him in awe. She was proud of him. Josh gave a wry laugh. *No, Gloria, I'm proud of you.*

Gloria had been proud of him then, but he wondered how she felt now. He knew she loved him. That wasn't the question. He also knew this job thing had her worried. He had seen fear in her eyes the day he had mentioned moving, but he hadn't responded to it. How could he? He didn't have the answers. All he could do was find another job. Fast.

Marvin's entry into his office brought Josh out of his thoughts. "Do you have a few minutes?"

Josh gave a grim smile. "I've got nothing but time."

Marvin took the chair in front of Josh's desk. "Have you made any plans yet?"

"I've put out some feelers, Marvin, but no responses yet. It's short notice to find another job."

Marvin winced. "I guess I deserved that."

Josh stood up and stretched to relieve tension. "I'm not blaming you."

Marvin waved his hand. "No matter. I'm not here to talk about that. I have some news for you. I've made a few calls."

Josh sat on the corner of his desk and faced Marvin. "What did you find?"

Marvin handed him a slip of paper. "There are four names on that list. No promises have been made, but they're all willing to talk with you."

Josh looked at the list of names. He recognized all of the companies, but only one of the names. He put the list in his wallet. "Thanks, Marvin."

"No thanks needed. What are friends for? We are still friends, aren't we?"

Josh extended a hand to him. "We're friends, Marvin. I know you couldn't have prevented this. It just came as such a surprise that it threw me off balance."

"I know, Josh. I had planned to stay around another year or so before retiring, so I wasn't ready to leave either. We'll both have to make adjustments, though I won't be in the market for another job."

Josh nodded.

"How's Gloria handling all this?"

"As expected, she's being a trooper. She's positive we'll find something better. I hope she's right."

"I know she's right," Marvin said. "It may take awhile, but you'll land on your feet. You're like me in that respect. We rise to the challenge every time."

"Especially when there's no other choice."

Marvin laughed. "When are you leaving?"

"Around three. Gloria's picking me up. We're going straight to the airport."

"Oh, yes, your anniversary trip."

"We're off to Aruba. The trip couldn't have come at a better time. Since we found out about the termination, there's been a black cloud hanging over our heads. This trip will give us a chance to focus solely on each other."

Marvin stood. "I'm happy for you, Josh. And I wish you the best. If you need me for anything, just call. Martha and I will be there for you."

"I appreciate the offer, Marvin." Josh patted his coat pocket. "You've done more than enough by giving me this list."

* * *

Portia drank the last of her coffee. "I'm so envious."

"You have no reason to be. You and Dexter travel a lot," Gloria reminded her.

"Never to some romantic place Dexter has picked out. I can't believe you haven't found out where he's taking you."

Gloria pushed her plate away, placed her napkin on the table and looked away. "Well, I . . ."

"You found out, didn't you?"

Gloria laughed. She knew Portia wouldn't stop until she had an answer. "I found out. We're going to Aruba."

"How did you find out?"

"I . . . ah . . . sorta . . . went through his closet. He has a box where he 'hides' things. The tickets were in the box."

Portia laughed. "You've only been married a year and you already know Josh's secret hiding place? Shame on you."

Gloria shrugged her shoulders. "Shame on Josh. He ought to stop using the same place. He puts everything in that box."

Portia nodded her head knowingly. "That's the difference between men and women. A woman would never use the same place twice."

"I'm glad Josh does. Thinking about this trip has kept me sane these last two weeks."

Portia sobered then. "Do you want to talk about it?"

Gloria shrugged again. "What's there to say? Josh lost his job."

"There's more to it than that, isn't there?" Portia probed.

38 *Angela Benson*

"I don't know how to talk about it, Portia. Josh is different, but he's not really different. He says the right things but I know there's a lot he's not saying."

"You can understand that, can't you?"

"Of course, I understand, but I feel shut out and helpless."

Portia reached across the table and touched Gloria's hand. "All you need to do is be there for Josh. He loves you, Gloria. He needs your reassurance that you love him."

Gloria squeezed Portia's fingers. She needed her friend's reassurance now. "I'm trying, Portia, but it's hard. It's only been two weeks and I already feel a breach between us."

"You're blowing this out of proportion," Portia said softly. "This is the first real trial you've had in your marriage. You'll deal with it."

Gloria removed her hand from Portia's and needlessly adjusted the napkin she had placed on the table. "Josh doesn't trust me as much as I thought he did."

"What makes you say that?"

Gloria placed her hands in her lap. "Sometimes he just sits and stares. When I ask what he's thinking, he shrugs and says nothing."

"You already know what he's thinking, Gloria. The man has lost his job. Give him a break, will you? You can't expect him to act as if nothing has happened."

Gloria picked up her napkin and placed it in her lap. She was feeling sorry for herself and she knew it, but she couldn't stop her feelings. "I know that, and I understand it, but it doesn't change the way I feel. Josh and I have always talked about everything."

"You need to wake up, Gloria. You can focus on how things *were* or you can adjust to how things *are*."

"Maybe that's it, Portia. My marriage, my life, is changing and I'm not adjusting very well."

"But you will."

Gloria nodded because she knew Portia was right. She had to adjust to this new situation. "I will because Josh loves me and I love him, but I don't like this feeling of helplessness. I didn't want my marriage or my life to change. Things were great the way they were."

"And things will be great in the future," Portia finished for her. "They'll just be different."

Gloria could feel the tears puddle in her eyes. "I feel so stupid and so selfish. I should be concerned about Josh and all I can think about is me."

"There's nothing wrong with that, Gloria. One thing I've learned in five years of marriage to Dexter is that you have to know what your individual needs are as well as those of your marriage. Any time you need to sound off, I'm here for you."

Gloria smiled at her friend while managing to keep her tears at bay. "Thanks, Portia. I'm going to need a friend through this. You see, Josh isn't the only one holding back these days. I've been holding back my feelings as well."

"That's probably for the best. Honesty may be the best policy, but there's something to be said for timing. Josh may not need you to be honest now. Just be supportive. You can be honest with me."

Portia's words sounded right. Gloria hoped they were. "I've always told Josh everything. I feel dishonest not telling him everything."

"Growing pains, that's all. You're not telling Josh things that Josh can't handle right now."

"That's the problem. How do I know he can't handle them if I don't give him a chance?"

"I don't know," Portia answered. She put her hand across her heart. "You feel it somewhere deep inside. You know Josh better than anybody. Do you think he's ready to hear what you have to say right now?"

Gloria thought about it. How would Josh respond if she told him her fears? He would probably want to protect her, to ease her fears. Would that put additional pressure on him? Gloria nodded slowly. It would. And Josh didn't need any more pressure right now.

"Is that nod in answer to my question?"

"What? No. I'm sorry, Portia. I was thinking about your question."

"What's the answer?"

"You're right. What I want to say to Josh now wouldn't help at all. I'm going to take your advice and ride it out. I'll be there for him. And you'll have to be there for me."

Portia smiled. "That's what friends are for. Now tell me more about Aruba."

Gloria welcomed the change to a more pleasant topic. She told Portia what she knew of the plans for the trip. "My major concern now is putting on a believable performance when we get to the airport. I'm supposed to be surprised."

Portia laughed. "You'll pull it off. And if you don't, Josh will have a good laugh at your, ah . . . inquisitive nature."

Gloria laughed too. "That's my incentive to put on a good performance. If Josh finds out what I've done, he'll never let me forget it."

Gloria arrived at Josh's office a little before three. He was standing before the window, his back to her. She watched him and wondered what his thoughts were. She hoped they were happy thoughts, thoughts of them and their life together. She quietly walked over to him and placed her arms around his waist.

"I didn't hear you come in," he said with a smile.

"Lost in your thoughts?" she asked.

Josh turned, keeping her arms around him. "Thinking about you."

Gloria smiled up at him, pleased to see the sparkle in his eyes. "Those are words a wife likes to hear."

"For the next fourteen days, Mrs. Martin, all you're going to get are sweet words and even sweeter actions."

"Promises, promises."

"What do I have to do to convince you?"

"How about a preview of coming attractions?"

Josh moved until his lips were almost touching hers. She felt his breath on her face. "Consider it done."

Before Gloria could give a retort, Josh captured her lips with his own for a kiss that left them both wishing they were somewhere other than his office.

When Josh pulled back, Gloria saw the passion in his eyes. "We've never . . . ah . . . christened . . . your office," she said.

Josh looked at his desk. Gloria knew the thoughts running through his mind. When he turned back to look at her, he said, "If only we had more time."

"As I said, promises, promises."

Josh playfully swatted Gloria's bottom and pushed her away from him. "Get away from me, woman." He picked up the packed box on his desk and headed for the door. Gloria didn't move. "Are you coming?"

She debated asking how he felt about leaving his office for the last time. Remembering her conversation with Portia, she decided not to. If Josh wanted to talk, she'd be there for him, but she wasn't going to force it.

"Are you coming?" Josh asked again.

"Almost," Gloria answered as she sashayed past him and out the door.

His laughter covered the sound of the office door as he closed it.

The moonlight on the water made the white sand beach sparkle. This is as close to heaven as I'll get while I'm alive, Josh thought. What more could a man want? A beautiful night. A private beach. A beautiful and loving wife next to him.

After making love on their private beach, neither of them had the desire or the strength to go back to their cabana. He knew Gloria was awake but he didn't feel the need to speak to her. There were really no more words to say. The important things had been said. Though he had been afraid his joblessness would cast a pall on the trip, their two weeks in Aruba had been a healing balm for them, for their marriage. "All I need to do is find a job."

"You'll find one, Josh."

Josh didn't realize he'd spoken aloud. He turned on his side to face Gloria. "It may take some time, though."

"We have plenty of time. All of our lives."

Josh smiled. "I hope it doesn't take that long."

Gloria leaned on one arm and playfully slapped Josh across his chest. "You know what I mean."

"Yes, I do. I feel better now that I have a plan. Monday, I'll call the contacts Marvin gave me and follow up with Dexter."

"Sounds like a good start to me. I'm glad Marvin made the effort."

Josh had been thinking about Marvin's list. It was unlikely any of those companies were looking for a

Chief Engineer. "I may not get the position I want, so I may have to settle for something less."

"What do you want, Josh? A position like your last one?"

"I enjoyed being Chief Engineer, but I'd have to be very fortunate to find an equivalent position."

"If not management, would you go back to engineering?"

Josh shrugged. He preferred using his management skills; he was a natural planner and negotiator. That was his passion. "That's not my first choice. An engineering position would pay a lot less than a management position. How would you feel about that?"

Gloria squeezed his hand. "I want us to be happy. If you want to go back to engineering, that's fine with me. With both of us working, money shouldn't be the deciding factor."

"What about the baby?" he asked. Though he had been thinking about their plans for a family, this was the first time in weeks he'd had the courage to voice his thoughts.

"Baby?" She had been thinking about babies lately, but she wasn't ready to share those thoughts with him. She wasn't sure he was ready to hear them either.

"The baby we were planning for next year," he answered. "You were going to stop working after we had the baby."

"I don't have to stop work to have a baby, Josh. There are alternatives."

Josh stood up. "There may be alternatives, but our plan was for you to stay home."

Gloria looked up at his back. "Maybe we need to reevaluate that plan. Is it a wise idea for us to put all of our financial eggs in one basket? If I keep working, we'll have more options."

Josh walked to the water's edge. "You don't trust me to support us, do you, Gloria?"

I'll have to watch what I say to him, Gloria thought as she went to him. "That's not it, Josh. I trust you. I don't trust the economy. I don't trust corporate America. We have to learn from this experience and what I've learned is that we can't depend on anything. There's no need for you to carry our financial burden alone. I won't be the first working mother and I certainly won't be the last."

Josh continued to stare out over the water. He needed the calm that smooth waves provided. "It's amazing how much can change in four short weeks. Four weeks ago, you never would have said what you just said. You didn't want to be a working mom like your mother. You wanted to be there for our children."

Gloria had thought about her mother a lot lately. Maybe she had been too hard on her. "My childhood wasn't all that bad," she said. "Things have changed, Josh, and we are affected. Maybe we'll change a little, too, but we'll change together. We won't let adversity separate us or distance us. Our love is stronger than that. You do believe that, don't you?"

Josh turned to face her. She was the most beautiful woman he had ever seen. Her eyes shone in the moonlight and his heart expanded at the love he saw in them. "I want to believe it, Gloria. I love you more than you'll ever know, but I worry that I'm not keeping the promises I made to you when we married."

Gloria's eyes flashed her annoyance. "Don't you dare say that, Joshua Martin. You've given me everything any woman could want and a hell of a lot more than most women have. Do you know that my friends are envious of me?"

"Because of me?"

Gloria gave an annoyed sigh, but when she spoke, her tone was soft. "Yes, because of you. Because of the ways you show your love for me. This trip is a perfect example. Portia is practically green with envy because Dexter never does anything like this. You go out of your way to make me feel special, to make me feel loved. You *are* keeping your promises. We both made promises. We promised to love forever. I'm still holding up my end of that promise and you'd better hold up your end."

Josh pulled her into his arms. "Is that enough?"

"It's more than enough," Gloria said as she snuggled in his arms. "Sometimes I worry about us, Josh. We're both so practical and logical."

"What's wrong with being practical and logical?"

"There's nothing wrong with it, but it's not always right. I don't want us to allow our logic to make decisions that may not agree with our hearts. Our love may force us to go against logic sometimes and we have to be open to that."

Josh knew that logic and practicality had gotten him where he was today. "That might be hard for me, but I'll try."

Gloria hugged him tighter. "That's good enough for me."

When Josh didn't say anything more, Gloria asked, "Are you all right?"

"I'm better than I've been in the last few weeks. I'm beginning to see some light at the end of the tunnel. Maybe this will turn out to be a good thing after all."

Gloria pulled away from him and looked up into his eyes. "I've been thinking, hoping, the same thing. Our relationship will be stronger because we'll have faced a trial together and you may even end up with a better job."

Josh turned, put his arm around Gloria's waist, and led her back to the cabana, stopping only to pick up their blanket. "I've been having thoughts like that myself, but I've been a little afraid to voice them."

"I'm not. I feel it, Josh. This will all work out for us. Just wait and see."

Later that night when Josh and Gloria were in bed, Josh asked, "So, Portia's jealous?"

"Yes, she is. She says Dexter could take lessons from you in planning surprise romantic getaways."

Josh was silent for a while. Gloria heard the smile in his voice when he asked, "How long have you known about my secret box in the closet?"

Chapter 4

"You have an outstanding résumé, Mr. Martin," Thomas Williams, Vice President of Operations at Micro Systems Limited, said.

Josh merely nodded but had a sinking feeling.

Williams closed the résumé folder, pulled off his glasses, and placed them on his desk. "I'm sorry we don't have a position open for a man with your experience. Of course, we'll keep your résumé on file."

Josh was numb. Williams was the last name on the list of contacts Marvin had given him. As such, he was Josh's last hope. But Josh didn't have any hope these days. He'd had hope two months ago when he had started his job search with Marvin's contacts and his friends' support. He'd had hope on the first interview, then the second interview and then the third interview. Each time, the message was the same. "You're great, but we can't hire you." Josh had hoped, prayed to hear something different today.

"The openings we have would be an insult to someone with your expertise and the pay would be a drastic comedown from your previous salary.''

Josh had heard that before, too. He had priced himself out of the market. It was a Catch-22. On one hand, his salary at General Electronics had been so substantial that few positions could match it. On the other hand, if he took a position at a salary less than that, his negotiating powers for a higher salary elsewhere would be severely hampered. What was he to do?

Josh stood. He no longer waited for the interviewer to stand first. Extending his hand, he said, ''Thank you for your time, Mr. Williams.''

Taking Josh's outstretched hand, Williams stood. ''Good luck, Mr. Martin.''

Josh walked out of the office to the elevator. He stood there a few minutes before realizing he hadn't pressed the button. He pressed it and the doors opened immediately. He stepped into the empty car, selected the button for the first floor, and leaned against the back wall. He studied his reflection in the mirrored walls of the car. Anyone looking at him would think he was a busy executive on his way to a power lunch. He still had the look. The close-cut haircut, the strong, hairless face, the power suit, the expensive attaché case, still named him a man to be reckoned with. He had the look, but now he didn't have the power to go with it.

The elevator doors opened and Josh stepped off. He stopped in front of the bank of telephones, then moved on toward the revolving doors. He couldn't talk to Gloria right now. He knew she was waiting to hear about his interview. He needed her support and she was giving it, but he still felt pressured to be as successful in finding another job as he had been in everything else. Gloria believed in him and he needed that, but each time he gave her bad news, he saw the light dim in her eyes. Sure, she covered it up with words like, "Next time" and "Their loss," but he saw it.

He understood her feelings. The money he had received in his severance package was gone. They were no longer putting Gloria's salary in the bank. Instead they were living on it. Since her salary was less than his, soon they would have to dip into their savings. Josh didn't even want to think about that. Their savings represented their plans for a family. What if they had to use it all?

No, Josh told himself, we will not use that money. There has to be another way. He looked up to find himself in front of Dexter's office building. He walked in.

"I'm glad you dropped by, Josh," Dexter said as they settled themselves at a picnic table in the park a couple of blocks from his office. "I needed to get out of the office for a while. The fresh air feels good."

"It sure does." Josh had pulled off his suit coat so he could enjoy the cool breeze.

Dexter took a huge bite of the submarine sandwich he had purchased. "What are your plans now?"

Josh took a long swallow of beer. Being out of work meant he could have a drink in the middle of the day. "That's a good question. I have to do something so we don't end up spending all our savings."

Dexter nodded between bites. "Be glad that you have savings to fall back on. What's the money for, if not for when you need it?"

"The money isn't for this, I can tell you. The headhunter says I should be prepared to wait nine months to a year to find a job. That's a long time to skim off your savings.''

"Whew," Dexter said. "Why does he think it will take that long?"

Josh mimicked the headhunter's coached voice as he repeated the reasons to Dexter. "It's a tight market, Mr. Martin, especially for middle managers like yourself. You're going to have to wait this one out if you want to find a comparable position here in Atlanta. If you would settle for less pay or if you were open to relocating, we could reduce the time."

"Are you?" Dexter asked.

"Am I what?"

"Willing to settle for less or to relocate?"

Josh wiped the sweat from his beer can with his napkin, then wadded up the napkin and tossed it in a garbage can about five feet from their table. "That's a good question. The truth is, I'm not ready to do either yet."

"Which one do you think you'll be ready to do first?"

"I'd rather relocate for a comparable position with comparable pay than take a pay cut."

"What does Gloria think?"

That was Josh's concern. Gloria didn't want to move. "Gloria thinks I'll find a job here."

Josh saw Dexter's eyebrow raise slightly. "And if you don't?"

"We don't discuss that. We keep hoping I find something." When Dexter didn't comment, Josh added, "We've got to get a better handle on our money. I don't want to use all of our savings."

"Have you talked with your financial planner?"

Josh shook his head. "Not since the news with the job. We probably need to."

* * *

Gloria placed the fluffy, white towel around her neck and stepped on the treadmill next to the one on which Portia stood. "It's been awhile since we've done this."

Portia was out of breath. "Too long. I think my heart is about to burst. How do you do it?"

"I'm consistent, Portia. It would help if you came more than once or twice a month."

Portia started walking again. "How do you find the time? On the days that I don't work through lunch, I usually have some errand to run."

Gloria upped the speed on her treadmill. "Exercise is important to me so I make time."

"Now that Dexter and I are working on a baby, I need to get started on something that I can continue after I'm pregnant. Walking seems like the answer."

Preparation for pregnancy had been one of Gloria's reasons for exercise too. She wanted to give her baby a good start and a healthy body was part of that. But as she was learning these days, her baby also needed a happy and stable home life. Once she would not have questioned her and Josh's ability to provide that. Now, she wasn't as sure.

"Did you hear what I said, Gloria? You look as though you're a million miles away."

"What? Yes, I heard you."

"Come on. Let's have it. What's on your mind?"

Gloria slowed her pace. "Josh."

"What about Josh?"

"It's taking longer than I thought for him to find a job."

"And . . ."

"To talk to Josh, you'd think we were destitute or something. He wants to put our lives on hold until he finds a job. I'm working. We're getting by. And we're far from being destitute."

"Have you told him about the promotion yet?"

Gloria shook her head. "I'm not going to bring it up until it's a sure thing. I never thought I'd say this, but I don't know how Josh will react."

"Come on, Gloria. He'll be happy for you."

Gloria wished Portia were right. Keeping secrets from Josh was not fun. "I'm not so sure. Josh is turning out to be a little chauvinistic in his attitude. He doesn't look at the money I bring in as our money. It's my money. When he was working and we were saving my salary, it was our money. Now that my salary is all that we have, it's my money. It doesn't make sense."

"Did you two talk about money before you got married?"

"Of course we did. But any time we talked about us being a one-paycheck family, it was always Josh's paycheck."

"Does it bother you that much?"

"Yes, it bothers me. What does Josh think I am? I have an education. I'm capable. I don't need him to take care of me. I thought we were taking care of each other. Now, Josh won't allow me to enjoy sharing this burden with him. I know it's hard for him, but he needs to think about me."

"What do you want him to do, Gloria?"

Gloria shrugged her shoulders and reduced the speed on the treadmill. "I just want him to acknowledge that our marriage is a partnership. We support each other. He's making it seem so one-sided."

When Portia didn't comment, Gloria looked at her. "You don't have anything to say?"

"I wonder if there's something else bothering you."

"Like what?"

"Maybe your talk with Eleanor this morning. Did she mention the promotion?"

If anyone but Portia had asked this question, Gloria would have thought they were being nosy. But how could Portia be anything other than nosy? Well, it wasn't really nosiness, it was friendly concern. "How did you know about Eleanor? God, you and office gossip. Does anything get by you?"

Portia laughed. "Not much. What did she say?"

"You don't know?"

"I couldn't put a glass to the door, now could I?"

Gloria laughed at that. "We talked about changes at the bank."

Portia straddled the belt of her treadmill. "You got the promotion?"

"No, I didn't get the promotion. Yet. Eleanor and I had an unofficial career planning session. She talked about possibilities."

"Did she give specifics?" Portia turned off her treadmill and leaned against one of the handrails.

"Not really. Nothing's final. But she did talk time-frames and numbers."

"Come on, Gloria. Don't keep stringing me along. What did she say?"

"Everything should be final in four weeks. If things work out, I'll get the promotion and a thirty-five per-cent raise."

"Thirty-five percent? That's great. You should be ecstatic. Why aren't you?"

Gloria had asked herself that same question. A year ago, she would have been planning a party. But not now. "I've learned that nothing is sure until it's done. I'm not celebrating until it's official."

"You're thinking about what happened to Josh, aren't you?"

"How can I not think about it? Josh was expecting a promotion and look what happened. Nothing is certain."

"You're becoming cynical, Gloria. It doesn't sound like you."

"Not cynical. Realistic."

"*Not me,* I'm making Dexter take me out tonight as sort of a precelebration," Portia said. "Good news for you is good news for me. Hell, I may even start planning to redecorate my new office."

Gloria shook her head. "You're one of a kind, Portia."

"That's what Dexter says. Are you going to give Josh the news?"

"Not now. I told you, I'm waiting to celebrate and I don't know how Josh will react to the news." And the way Gloria figured it, there was no need to stir the pot until something was definite.

"I think it's funny."

Gloria turned to Portia. "Enlighten me, then, because I could use a laugh. I don't see anything funny about the situation."

"Not funny ha-ha, but funny interesting. If Josh were content to sit on his butt while you worked, you'd be furious. You'd think he was using you. But when he wants to be the provider and feels badly because he can't be, you're furious. I'm beginning to wonder if Josh is in a no-win situation."

"It's not like that at all. Sure, I want Josh to find work. I'd be pissed if he didn't look for a new job and he expected me to support us indefinitely. But I need to know that we're a team. I want to be there for Josh in all ways—including financially. Why can't he just accept it? It won't be forever."

"If you feel this strongly about it, you need to talk to him."

"I know that and I've been putting it off. After Aruba, I thought we had crossed the biggest hurdles, but they don't seem to end. There's one thing after another."

Portia laughed and shook her head. "I have to keep reminding myself that you're a newlywed."

"What's that supposed to mean?"

"It means you haven't learned yet what marriage is all about. Somehow you think it's a straight road to a predetermined destination, but it's not. There are no guarantees where you'll end up, what roads you'll follow to get there or that you'll make it there together."

"And you call me a cynic?"

"I'm not saying marriage isn't great. I love being married, but I also know that it's a day-by-day commitment to stay together and follow the road wherever it leads."

Josh was in the kitchen when Gloria came home from work. "In here," he called when he heard the front door open.

Gloria walked into the kitchen and greeted him with a kiss. "How you doing, handsome? Let's go out to dinner tonight."

Josh smiled at her before turning to set the temperature on the oven. "Are you getting tired of my cooking?"

Gloria took a seat at the table. "I love your cooking, but it's been ages since we've gone out."

Josh nodded. They hadn't been out once in the

last couple of months, but he didn't feel comfortable going out. All he thought about was how much things cost and how much they could save if they stayed home. "I've already prepared dinner. We can go out another night."

"But I want to go out tonight," Gloria cooed.

Josh took the salad fixings out of the refrigerator. "What's so special about tonight? We can go out another night."

"You've been saying that for a while, Josh, but we never go."

Josh pulled a huge salad bowl from the cupboard. "We need to watch our money. The headhunter said nine months to a year."

"But does that mean a year without going out?"

"No, but we can't go out as much as we did before."

Josh turned on the faucet to wash the lettuce. They were not going out for dinner.

"I know that, Josh, but we never go out anymore. We can afford this. I'm working. We have savings."

I'm working. I'm working. Those words echoed in Josh's mind. She had finally said it. He didn't know why he was surprised. He knew it would finally come to this. Leaving the water running, he turned to face her. "So, it's your money and you should be able to spend it any way you want to? Is that what you're saying, Gloria?"

He heard her frustrated sigh before she said, "It's our money. We should be able to enjoy some of it."

Josh turned off the water and slammed the salad bowl on the table. "If you want to go out, then we'll go out." He walked out of the kitchen. "I guess you'll pick up the check?"

Gloria rushed after him. "Don't be like this, Josh."

Josh turned around unexpectedly and she bumped

into him. He grabbed her by both arms. "Like what, Gloria? You don't want me to be concerned about money because you've got it covered. Okay, I won't be concerned about the money. You happy?"

Gloria jerked away from him. She rubbed her arms as if he had hurt her. "What's wrong with you, Josh? Why are you talking to me like this? I'm trying to continue our lives and you want to curl up and wither away. It's not going to work."

Josh knew he was wrong, but he couldn't stop himself. "Since you seem to know everything, then you tell me what will work."

"I can't talk to you when you're like this," Gloria said. She grabbed her purse from the couch. "I'm going out. You stay here and think about what's happened. You owe me an apology." With that, Gloria raced out of the door, leaving it open behind her.

Josh heard her car start as he slammed the front door. "Good riddance."

Josh stormed to the couch and flopped down. He grabbed a pillow and punched it repeatedly. He stood up, still holding the pillow, and paced back and forth in front of the couch. *I'm working,* she had said. *Well, I know she's working. There's no need for her to rub it in. Damn! Who the hell does she think she is? I'm trying my damnedest to find work and she throws it up in my face that she has a job. To hell with her.*

Josh threw the pillow on the couch and pounded into the kitchen. He jerked open the refrigerator door and pulled out a beer. After popping the tab, he threw his head back and took a long swig. "Now, that was good." He closed the refrigerator door, leaned back against the sink, and opened his mouth to down the rest of the can. As he lifted the can to his lips, he remembered another beer can in another hand. How could I have forgotten that? he wondered. His dad had held a beer can in his hand the night he had struck his mother.

Josh turned around and poured the contents of the can down the drain. He was not going to be like his father. He was not going to try to drink away his troubles and he was not going to take his frustrations out on his wife.

Is that what I did tonight? he asked himself. Was the fight all about me and my problems?

Josh walked slowly back into the living room. Memories of the evening flashed through his mind. How had things gotten out of hand so quickly? One minute he was preparing a romantic meal for his wife and the next she was storming out of the house. He flopped down on the couch again. Why had he forced his wife to leave like that? Why had he done it? What if she hurts herself? Oh, God, where could she have gone? She shouldn't be driving in her condition.

He stood up again, went to the door, and looked out the side panels. What if she had an accident? He felt fear rise up in him. *No, I won't think like that. She's fine.* She probably went to Portia's. I'll call and see. Josh stalked over to the phone, picked up the receiver, and dialed Portia's number. He hung up before the first ring. I'm blowing this way out of proportion, he reasoned. Gloria is a grown woman, more than capable of taking care of herself. He looked at the phone. He moved to pick it up again but changed his mind and went back to the couch and sat down. *Where the hell is she?*

"What the hell is Josh's problem?" Gloria asked aloud as she floored the Beamer down the street, no destination in mind. "I've bent over backwards to be supportive and he treats me like this. Just who the hell does he think he is?"

Gloria pulled into the parking lot of Viner's Diner, less than a mile from her home. She walked in, smiled briefly at the waitress, and took a table near the back.

Their first real fight. She and Josh were having their first real fight. They had argued before but never like this. Never with her storming out. Never with Josh yelling at her, grabbing her. Never with them being unable to talk.

Josh had scared her tonight. The things he had said and the way he had said them. Things had gotten out of control. She hadn't liked what she had seen. It was a glimpse of a side of Josh that she hadn't known existed. No, her Josh was controlled and direct. Their arguments were more along the line of debates. Their only major fight, until now, had been over the car.

"It's not practical, Gloria," Josh had said, leaning against the powder blue Corvette.

"You mean, I'm not practical, don't you, Josh?"

"That's not what I mean at all. It's not practical for both of us to buy sports cars. One of the vehicles has to be general purpose."

"But why does it have to be my vehicle? Why don't you get the general-purpose vehicle and let me get the sports car."

"Let's be reasonable about this. We'll be keeping this car for at least six years. During that time, we'll have two or three children. We need to buy a car now that will hold those children."

"We can trade in your car and get a 'reasonable' car. You don't need a Turbo Saab."

"Be reasonable, Gloria. Who'll stay home with the children? Who'll drive this car most?"

Gloria had eyed Josh then. She hated when he was right. "We could buy the sports car now and trade it in when I get pregnant."

"That wouldn't make sense and you know it. We'd lose money. If you get a new car now, it should be the Volvo wagon. There's nothing wrong with the Beamer that you have now. Why not keep it a few more years?"

"But the Corvette is . . . it's me."

Josh had laughed at that. "If you really want the car, of course, we can get it. But it'd be a waste of money."

"I knew I should have bought my convertible before we got married. My friends all said things would change. I didn't know how right they were."

Josh laughed again. "I'm not keeping you from getting the car, Gloria. Get the car. I want you to get the car."

"You know you've won, Josh. I'm not getting the car. How could I after all your practical arguments? I'd never be able to drive it and have any fun. I'll keep my 325."

Josh had hugged her to him and laughed again. "I knew you'd make the right decision."

She had pretended to be piqued. "I want you to know, Joshua Martin, that you won't win all our arguments so easily."

As Gloria thought about it now, she realized Josh had always controlled the money. We'd probably be fighting about money even if he hadn't lost his job, she reasoned. I should have gotten that Corvette.

Gloria requested a diet Coke when the waitress took her order. She would drink the soda and then she would go back home. She and Josh needed to talk.

By the time the waitress returned with the Coke,

Gloria's appetite had returned. She was hungry enough for two dinners. Hungry enough to stay in the restaurant for a good three hours. She smiled to herself. That should give Mr. Martin enough time to put together a decent apology.

Chapter 5

When Josh saw the headlights in the driveway, he stood and faced the door. After what seemed to be more than an hour, he heard the car door open and close. Next, the click of heels against the walkway. The clicking stopped right outside the door. There was a period of silence before he heard the key turn in the lock. He rushed to the door.

"Gloria . . ." he began when she walked through the door. She met his eyes, then brushed past him. He turned and watched her flop down on the couch, dropping her purse on the floor next to her. She leaned her head back and closed her eyes.

"Gloria," he began again. "I'm sorry about what happened."

"What did happen, Josh?" She spoke without opening her eyes.

Josh sat on the cocktail table in front of her and placed his hand on her knee in supplication. She moved and his hand fell away. "I've said I'm sorry. What more do you want?"

She opened her eyes and sat up straight. Her eyes were red and he knew she'd been crying. "Why won't you say something?" he asked.

He stood up and walked away from her, frustrated by her unwillingness to talk to him, to forgive him. "To hell with it, Gloria. Why did you come back if you're not going to talk to me?"

"I asked you a question," she said softly.

He walked back to his seat on the cocktail table. He didn't know what had happened, so he stalled. "What did you ask?"

"Oh, Josh," she said, as if it were some major calamity that he didn't hear or didn't remember the question.

"Ask me again," he said, placing his hand on her knee once more. He was relieved and encouraged when she allowed it to remain there.

"What happened here, Josh? Why were we fighting? It's more than my wanting to go to dinner."

Josh moved to sit next to her on the couch. He placed his arm around her shoulder and attempted to pull her into his embrace. She pulled away. "This isn't helping," she said. "We need to talk."

"Can't I hold you while we talk?" Josh needed the physical contact of her body against his to assure him that everything would be all right.

She got up from the couch and stood in front of the fireplace, her back to him. "You don't need to hold me in order to talk."

Josh heard the pain in her voice. She was hurting but she was wrong. He did need to hold her. And, he decided, she needed him to hold her. He followed her steps to stand behind her. He reached his arms around her waist and pulled her back against him, resting his head on top of hers. "I love you, Gloria," he said softly. "I'm sorry for the things I said earlier."

She turned in his embrace so that she could face him, but she didn't pull away. "Why did you say them then?"

He wiped away a tear that was about to fall from her eye. "I don't know, but I'd never deliberately hurt you. You have to know that." Josh felt his heart contract with pain at the disbelieving look in her eyes. *What's happening to us?* he wondered. *What more can I say?*

Before he could say anything, she moved as if to leave his arms. He relaxed his hold on her and she stepped out of his embrace. She continued to stand in front of him, but they were no longer touching. "You don't have to protect me, Josh. I'm a big girl. You have to talk to me. We can't go on like this."

Fear welled up in Josh. "Go on like what?"

Gloria shook her head in dismay. "Not talking. Pretending everything is okay."

Josh wasn't ready for this discussion. He didn't want to talk about the problem until he could provide the answer. But actually, he argued with himself, he knew the answer. The answer was for him to get a job and return their lives back to the way they were. Unfortunately, he couldn't do that just yet. What was the point in talking about it until he could? He looked away from her. "I know things are different since I've been out of work, but they'll get back on track once I find a job."

"That could be months. Do you think we can go on like this for much longer?" When Josh didn't answer, Gloria replied for him. "I can't."

What does that mean? Josh wondered. "What do you want from me, Gloria? I'm doing the best I can."

Gloria smiled sadly. That was the problem. Josh was doing his best, but it wasn't enough. She looked at this man she had loved since she had first met him over eight years ago. She had thought he could handle anything, do anything. Now, she wondered if she was wrong. Was Josh one of those men who functioned well as long as things were going well, but who fell apart at the first sign of adversity? No, that wasn't it. Josh was strong; Josh was sure. Josh's problem was that he kept his emotions bottled up inside. She had known that from the beginning. If she wanted him to open up, she had to open up first.

She took a step toward him, put her arms around his waist, and lay her head on his chest. She opened the flood gates and let the tears she had been holding in flow freely. She felt his arms pull her even closer, as if he wanted to pull her into his body. She heard his words of comfort, but her tears wouldn't stop. She hadn't realized how much she needed this. How much she needed to cry in Josh's arms. She stood there, in his arms, her tears falling, for what seemed to be hours, but was probably only minutes.

"It's going to be all right, Gloria. I promise you. Our lives will be back to normal soon."

If only that were true, Gloria thought, then we could keep up this charade. But it's not true and we have to face reality. "It's been almost four months, Josh, and the headhunter says it could be up to a year."

She felt him stiffen at her words, but she knew she couldn't back down now. She pulled back to look at him. "We have to accept that for the next few months we'll be living off my paycheck." At Josh's chagrined look, she added, "That's not a bad thing. I'm happy to help out. We've been living off your salary since we married. We ought to be glad we have a second salary to fall back on."

Josh tried to pull away from her, but she refused to release him. "It's not that easy for me," he finally said. "I'm the man, I should be supporting you."

She touched her hand to his face. "Support is more than money, Josh. I need your emotional support as well."

Josh gave that dry laugh that was becoming his trademark. "I never thought of myself as chauvinistic, but I'm showing tendencies, aren't I?"

Gloria nodded. "It's endearing in some ways. I'm glad you want to protect me, to provide for me, but it's not necessary."

Josh pulled away and this time Gloria let him do so. He took her hand and led her to the couch, where he seated himself before pulling her onto his lap. "I know it's not."

"If that's true, why can't you accept my being the breadwinner for a while?"

Josh gave a long sigh. "What do you want me to do?"

"I want you to have some fun. We have enough money to do most of the things that we want to do, Josh. It won't break us to go out once in a while."

"But what if we have to use all our savings?"

"That's why people have savings. If we have to use it, we will."

"If we use the money, we'll have to delay our plans for a baby. How would you feel about that?"

Gloria had other ideas on the subject of babies, but now was not the time to discuss them with Josh. "Maybe we will, Josh. Then again, maybe we won't. We won't be extravagant with our money, but we won't be tightwads either."

When Josh didn't respond, Gloria asked, "What are you thinking about?"

"Money. We need to see Jerry Thomas. If we have to dip into our savings, I want professional advice before we do it."

"If that's what you want, we can do it."

"That's what I want."

They were both silent for a while, then Josh said, "I don't want what happened tonight to ever happen again. It scared me, Gloria."

She heard the fear in his voice. "It scared me too."

He hugged her to him. "I shouldn't have touched you like that. Did I hurt you? I swear it'll never happen again."

Gloria shivered, remembering his action. "You didn't hurt me physically. Your words hurt me."

"I'm sorry, sweetheart. This job thing has me in knots."

Gloria was glad Josh was opening up. She decided to remain silent and let him talk. She wasn't going to push.

"I've tried to be big about the whole thing," he continued, "but I'm so angry. And the irony is I have no one to be angry with. I can't be angry with Marvin, it wasn't his fault. I can't be angry with General Electronics, a company. That's senseless. I can't be angry with the companies that won't hire me. So then I'm left being angry with myself for not seeing what was coming."

"You have valid reasons to be angry, Josh. Just don't turn that anger inward or toward me. Use it to find another opportunity."

"I've been trying to do that. Not very well, I guess. The more I look, the more it seems that there's no opportunity. At least, not here in Atlanta."

They were back to that again. "Well, I'm not ready to give up on Atlanta just yet. I know you'll find something."

"You want me to do what?" Josh slammed his fist on Jerry Thomas's desk.

"You have to sign up for unemployment benefits, Josh. It's a reasonable move to make."

"We came here for financial planning advice, not advice on how to 'milk' the system."

"Jerry is offering a suggestion, Josh. We should consider it," Gloria said.

Josh turned on her. "You can't be serious, Gloria. You want me to apply for unemployment benefits . . . social security . . . welfare? Never."

"It's not welfare," Gloria clarified.

"The hell it's not."

"Josh," Jerry Thomas interrupted, "Gloria is right. Unemployment benefits are not welfare benefits. Every working American pays into the Social Security system through FICA taxes. Unemployment benefits are provided through those taxes."

Josh looked at Jerry as if he were a two-headed monster. "I know how unemployment benefits are funded and I don't care. I won't go that route."

"That's your decision, Josh. You came to me for advice on making the best use of your savings while you're unemployed. One way to do that is to bring in more income. A source of such income is unemployment benefits. If you choose to ignore that source, then you'll reduce your savings that much faster. You won't get rich on unemployment benefits but every penny that you get in those benefits will be money that you won't have to take from your savings. The choice is yours."

"Why did we go if you're not going to take the man's advice?" Gloria asked later that evening. They had eaten dinner at home and were seated on the couch.

"I thought he'd give us some fresh insights on managing withdrawals from our savings and investments. All he did was tell me to get unemployment."

"It's not a bad idea, Josh," Gloria said. "It is your money."

Josh gave her a skeptical look. "You really want me to do this? You don't find the whole idea degrading?"

"No, I don't, and I don't know why you do. What is it?"

Josh gave a pained expression. "My dad was out of work often when I was a child. We went on relief a couple of times. I swore I would never do that. You don't know how it felt to stand in those lines and have people talk to you like you're the scum of the earth."

Gloria was amazed. This was news to her. She knew Josh came from a modest background, that his parents had been simple, working-class people, but she never guessed that they had slipped into poverty. "Why didn't you mention this before now?"

"I've tried to forget, Gloria. I've worked hard to build a life far above the life I lived as a child. I can't go back to that. I won't."

Gloria knew Josh was adamant. "It's not the same thing. It's not a handout."

"My mind knows you're right, but my heart can't see the difference. To me, it's all the same."

"Well, you can let your benefits sit there while we go through our savings or you can overcome your fears. Like Jerry said, it's your decision."

Josh drove around the unemployment office four times before pulling his Saab 9000 Turbo into the lot. I should have borrowed a car, he thought as he watched the other cars pull up. His gaze followed the people who entered the office. He made a game of giving backgrounds to everyone who entered the building. The woman with the three children had been deserted by her husband. The well-groomed man with the attaché case was the program director. Josh looked down at himself, glad he had dressed casually in slacks and a sports jacket. He opened the car door to get out, but closed it when he saw another man walking toward the entrance door. The man was also dressed in slacks and a sports jacket. Josh wondered whether he was an employee or a claimant.

Josh opened the door and stepped out of the car, closing the door behind him. He walked to the entrance of the building, took a deep breath, and opened the door. He walked through the door, but he didn't enter the room. He was not one of these people. He was different. Wasn't he?

He wanted to turn around and leave, but he couldn't. He had driven by the office for the last three days and today was the first day he had mustered enough courage to come in. It wasn't really all courage; Gloria's urging had a lot to do with it. He couldn't let her down in this. He had to do his part.

"May I help you?" a uniformed guard asked, interrupting his thoughts.

"Uh . . . yes. I'm here to file a claim for unemployment benefits."

The guard pointed to his left, to a line of about twenty people. "Over there."

"Thank you," Josh said. He moved slowly toward the line. Perspiration beaded on his brow, though he knew the room was cool.

"Hello." It was the guy in the slacks and sports

jacket Josh had seen when he was outside. "This must be your first visit."

Josh was surprised that he was able to smile. "Is it that obvious?"

The guy grinned. "You do have the look of a first-timer." He extended his hand. "I'm Elliot Wells."

Josh took his hand. "Josh Martin."

"I'm a veteran here now," Elliot said. "I've been out of work for almost a year. How about you?"

"Almost four months, but it seems longer."

"I know the feeling. I never guessed it would take so long to find work. What business were you in?"

"Electronics manufacturing. You?"

"Automotive manufacturing. Fifteen years. Worked there since high school. Worked my way through college. Never even thought about being laid off."

Josh gave a relaxed grin. "We have a lot in common."

"I know it seems impossible now, but you can make it through this. I'm living proof."

Josh nodded. "What do I do now? How do I sign up for these benefits that are going to make me a rich man?"

Elliot laughed outright at that, which was Josh's goal. The conversation had turned too serious too quickly. "Here." Elliot handed Josh a form. "Fill this out and then get in line."

"What are you going to do?"

"I'm going through the jobs digest. I'll wait around until you're done. We can go for coffee and share war stories."

"Sounds good to me," Josh said. "Now, I'd better get to filling out this form."

* * *

"I see you made it through the interview," Elliot said when Josh walked out of the door.

"Talk about war zone," he said. "You would think the woman was paying the money out of her own pocket."

Elliot shook his head in what Josh guessed was disgust. "I know. It takes all the courage we can muster to even walk in there. Then they try to make us feel that we're the dregs of society. Just remember we've paid into the fund. The money is ours."

"Somebody needs to tell Mrs. Hitler that," Josh said with a suppressed laugh. "I finally had to tell her that I paid her salary so she should treat me with more respect."

Elliot's eyes shone with respect. "You didn't? What did the old bitty say then?"

"She gave a 'humph.' Only after I suggested that I talk with her superior did she get her act together."

Elliot clapped Josh on the back. "You did good for a first-timer. It took me three visits to get enough courage to demand some respect. Now, how about that coffee?"

The two men walked to a nearby café. Seeing Elliot's wedding ring, Josh asked, "How's your wife handling all this?"

"It was tough there for a while, but I think we're on track now. Marilyn has been very supportive. I don't know how she does it and I know I don't deserve her."

Josh thought about Gloria. Did he deserve her? "Gloria, that's my wife, has been supportive too. Almost too supportive. Do you know what I mean?"

Elliot nodded vigorously. "Do I ever? There were times when I wished she would scream at me, curse me, leave me. That I could handle. The constant support and positive thinking almost drove me crazy."

Josh was glad to find someone who finally understood. "How did you get past it?"

Elliot shrugged. "I allowed Marilyn to help me through it."

"Sounds simple enough, but I know it wasn't. Gloria and I are at that stage now. I didn't know I was a male chauvinist until this came up."

"I know what you mean. A lot of your stated opinions on marriage and women's roles are put to the test. I came up short, too."

"Has Marilyn been supporting you two the entire time?"

Elliot nodded. "She's trained me not to say it like that. I'm supposed to say we're a single-paycheck household. She says she'll get her turn when my business takes off."

"You've started your own business? What is it?"

"I've been tinkering around with a formula to improve fuel efficiency in automobiles. I have a small lab set up in my garage. We've done some testing, but not enough. It takes money, more money than I have, to do the kind of testing that's required. So, now I'm looking for seed money. I've talked to some investors, but nothing yet."

"I'm impressed. I wish you luck finding an investor."

"Thanks. There's no need to be impressed though. It's amazing what a man can do when there's nothing else to do. After I was unemployed for six months, Marilyn encouraged me to pursue this. She says it makes her supporting us seem more like an investment in our future."

"So, you've always had an entrepreneurial spirit?"

"I guess I have. Being wrapped up in Corporate America doesn't leave much time nurturing that spirit though. Marilyn said being out of work took away all my excuses. I had to take my shot."

"I want to meet Marilyn. She sounds a lot like Gloria. Why don't you two come over for dinner one night?"

Elliot pulled out a business card with his number on it and handed it to Josh. "Give us a call and we'll be there."

Chapter 6

Gloria watched Portia dance into the bathroom ahead of her, checking each stall. "Looking for somebody, Portia?" she asked.

"No, girl," Portia answered, walking away from the last stall. "I just wanted to make sure no one else was here. I'm so excited, I could scream."

"Why don't you? Nobody's here but us. I'll even guard the door to make sure no one comes in."

"Oh, God, this is the best news I've had in years. I called Dexter's office, but he's out. I'm about to burst. Hey, why aren't you excited?"

Gloria leaned back against the vanity. "I'm excited, Portia. This is good news."

"What did Josh say?"

Gloria looked away. "I didn't call him yet."

"You didn't call him? Why didn't you?"

"I don't know what to say. I don't know how he'll react."

Portia froze in her tracks. "I thought you and Josh

had worked through the money issue. What's wrong?''

"We've made strides, but we still have a ways to go. Josh accepts that I provide enough for us, at least for the time being. But I know it's painful for him. I just don't know how he'll react when I tell him about the promotion.''

"What are you afraid of?''

"I'm scared Josh will fake excitement. I'm afraid this will send him back to the doldrums. I'm afraid of everything.'' Gloria covered her face with her hands. "Oh, Portia, what am I going to do?''

Portia pulled Gloria to the settee and they sat down. "What makes you think it will be so bad?''

"When I get home, Josh will tell me about his first day at the unemployment office. How can I tell him about my promotion?''

"You make it sound as though you and Josh are in some kind of competition.''

"I don't know what we're doing, but I do know that my promotion reinforces just how much our lives have changed. Josh was supposed to be getting promoted.''

"I don't think you're giving Josh enough credit. He'll support you in this. He may feel a tinge of envy, maybe even some hurt, but he'll support you in this and be happy for you.''

"I hope you're right,'' Gloria sighed.

"I know I'm right. Now, when are you going to tell him?''

Gloria hedged. "I'll tell him.''

"Tonight?''

Gloria smiled through her tears. "You don't give up, do you?''

"Not when it comes to my favorite couple. Now,

why don't the four of us get together tonight for a celebration?''

"I'm not sure tonight is a good night. Not with Josh's visit to the unemployment office today."

"Why don't you give Josh a call and see what he thinks? Maybe a night out is what you both need." When Gloria would have restated her refusal, Portia added, "You don't have to decide right now. Call me at home before seven and let me know. We'll probably do dinner and dancing. Wouldn't that be fun?"

Before Gloria could answer, the door opened and a woman walked into the bathroom. Gloria took that opportunity to walk over and check her face in the mirror. She expected to look like a raccoon, but her makeup was still intact. "We'd better get out of here, don't you think?"

Portia grinned. "Why not? I've done all my screaming."

Portia got up from the settee and they left the bathroom. Before they parted for their respective offices, Portia said, "Don't forget to call me. You and Josh will have a great time. Trust me."

"I'll call you, Portia. Promise."

When Gloria got back to her office, she sat at her desk. This should be one of the happiest days of my life, she thought. Under normal circumstances, it would have been. But circumstances aren't normal. They haven't been normal for a while. God, when will things settle down? When will I stop walking on egg shells around my husband?

A knock on her office door brought her out of her thoughts. "I hear congratulations are in order," Foster Dixon said.

Gloria smiled. She had known Foster for over five years. He was both a competitor and a friend. Once he had wanted more than friendship, but she was already in love with Josh. "Thanks, Foster. You didn't have to drop by, you could have called. How did you hear?"

Foster walked fully into the office and took a seat. "I've known for a couple of weeks now. Thought I'd wait until you knew before I told you."

"And you were able to keep a secret that long?"

"That's me. Tight-lipped Dixon. I'm known far and wide for my ability to keep a confidence."

Gloria chuckled. "You're known far and wide for a lot of things, but I don't think being tight-lipped is one of them. What's the real reason you didn't tell me?"

"Eleanor threatened me."

"My boss told you before she told me?"

Foster nodded, smiling all the while. "How does it feel, Madam Vice President?"

Gloria gave a slight smile. "Quite honestly, I don't feel anything right now, Foster."

"That doesn't sound like the Gloria I know. My guess was that you and Portia would be bouncing off the walls by now. I bet Portia is."

Gloria laughed again, feeling more relaxed than she had felt in a long time. "You're right. Portia is bouncing off the walls."

Foster laughed then, a rich, full, male laugh, something Gloria had not heard around her house in a long time. "What's keeping your feet firmly planted on the ground?" he asked.

"I'm excited, even if I'm a tad more reserved than my usual self."

"I know about Josh."

The statement surprised her. "It's not a secret."

"I was sorry to hear about it. He got a bad break."

Gloria moved an inch away from him. She didn't

buy Foster's sympathy. He and Josh were not friends.
"Since when have you been concerned about Josh?"

"I'm not. I'm concerned about you and I know
that you love Josh. I know that really well."

If anyone knew of the depth of her love for Josh,
it was Foster. He had tried everything thinkable to
win her away from Josh, but nothing had worked.
"There's no need for you to be concerned about us.
We're both fine."

"Your lips say that, but your eyes tell another story."

Gloria debated discussing this with Foster. Maybe
getting a man's perspective would help. It took only
a second for her to dismiss that idea. Another man's
perspective, maybe, but not Foster's. She didn't want
to confuse things with them. As if sensing her
thoughts, Foster said, "I want to be your friend, Gloria. Nothing more. You chose Josh and I've accepted
that."

"Josh and I are fine, Foster." Seeing the skeptical
look in his eyes, she added, "Really."

"I don't believe you, but I care enough about you
not to push it. Let me take you to lunch to celebrate
your promotion."

"No thank you. That wouldn't be wise."

"Are you afraid to have lunch with me?" Before
she could answer, he added, "If you need a chaperon, Portia can come with us. I know she won't
turn me down. How about it? Give a guy a break,
will you?"

Gloria couldn't resist his puppy dog expression.
"You win. If Portia is free, we'll go to lunch."

Foster ginned then. "Who said Christmas comes
but once a year? Having lunch with two gorgeous
women makes any day Christmas for me."

* * *

Gloria looked at her watch. Six-thirty. Josh was late. Today was the first day she had beat him home since he lost his job. How much things had changed! A few short months ago, six-thirty would have been early for Josh to get home. No use thinking about that now, she thought. I just hope everything is all right.

She had already called Portia and told her that she and Josh wouldn't make the celebration. She wanted to be alone with Josh when she told him anyway. If things went well, they could have a private celebration.

"Gloria," she heard Josh call when he opened the door. "Where are you?"

She hadn't heard his car. "I'm in the kitchen."

She pulled off her apron and walked out of the kitchen to meet him. She was taken aback when she saw him. He practically beamed at her.

"Sorry, I'm late," he said, gathering her in his arms. "I had a good day today."

"I can tell. What happened? You look like you won the lottery?"

He kissed her on the lips. "I said I had a good day. If I had won the lottery, I think the word would be great."

He brushed her lips with his again.

"Whatever happened today sure has you in a good mood," she said. "You didn't go to the unemployment office?"

Josh palmed her bottom and pulled her tighter against him. "Of course I went. I told you I was going, didn't I?"

Gloria licked Josh's lips. "But you weren't too happy about it. It must not have been as bad as you expected."

Josh wrapped his arms around her waist and walked

her to the couch where they sat down. "It was worse. God, you'd think I was the scum of the earth."

"You say that, but you don't sound upset about it. What gives?"

"I met a guy in the unemployment office. We really hit it off. His name's Elliot and he's been out of work for almost a year."

"What's so special about this Elliot guy?" It was unlike Josh to be so excited over meeting someone.

Josh shrugged. "It just felt good talking to someone in the same situation as me. Someone who understands how I feel."

I've tried to understand, Gloria thought. "I'm glad for you."

"Elliot was a middle manager at Welco Automotive. He lost his job when they shut down his division. That was eleven months ago."

"And he hasn't found a job yet? He can't be too happy about that."

"Of course he's not happy about it, but he's making the most of it. He and his wife, both. I told him that we'd have them over for dinner soon. His wife's name is Marilyn. From the way he talked about her, I'm sure the two of you will hit it off."

"You think so?" Gloria was skeptical. Josh had just met this Elliot guy and he was already inviting him over.

"I *know* so. You have something in common—out-of-work husbands." Josh hugged her to him, adding, "I know this hasn't been easy for you, Gloria. You probably need someone to talk with as much as I do."

"You make it sound as if I've been suffering, Josh. It hasn't been that bad." At Josh's skeptical look, she added, "Maybe a little."

"It's been more than a little, Gloria. You've said it

before. Our lives are changing and we've had no power over it. Talking with Elliot today, I realized the feelings I'm having are normal."

"Of course they're normal. I've told you that."

Josh caressed her shoulders. "I know you have, Gloria. You've been very supportive, but today with Elliot was different. We talked about fears, fears that only another man in the same situation could understand."

"You can share your fears with me, Josh. I want you to," Gloria said, her voice rising.

"I know you do and sometimes I've wanted to share them with you, but I was afraid. Afraid that you would think I was weak. Hell, I was afraid that I was weak. That's why talking with Elliot helped so much. As I listened to his story, I accepted that he wasn't weak, that he wasn't a failure. Accepting him gave me room to accept myself. Can you understand that?"

Gloria nodded in understanding. Josh had found someone to share his deepest thoughts with and that someone was not her. She was happy for him, but she was also a little hurt that he hadn't felt secure enough to share those things with her. "Of course I understand. I'm glad you and Elliot hit it off. When do you want to invite them over?"

"How about next week? I really want you to meet his wife. Did I tell you Elliot is starting a business?"

Gloria shook her head. "What business is he in?"

Josh proceeded to tell her about Elliot's business. She heard his words, but she focused more on him than the words he was speaking. It had been a long time since she had seen him this excited, this animated.

"Marilyn knew about his dream, and when he couldn't find work after looking for a while, she encouraged him to follow the dream."

"She sounds like a remarkable woman. What kind of work does she do?"

Josh laughed. "You know, Elliot didn't say and I didn't ask. We'll find out when they come over. Why don't I call him now?"

"Sure. Call them. It won't take much to prepare a small dinner party."

Josh kissed her on the lips and got up from the couch. "Don't worry about the preparation. I'm doing the cooking. All you have to do is show up. You can do that, can't you, sweetheart?"

Gloria smiled at Josh's lightheartedness and her jealousy toward his new friend vanished. She knew she was going to like Marilyn and Elliot. She already liked them. She'd never be able to repay Elliot for what he had done for Josh.

While Josh was on the phone, Gloria remembered that she hadn't told Josh about her promotion. He was so happy tonight. Why bring that up now? she reasoned. I'll tell him later. When we're in bed. After we've made love.

It was six o'clock before Gloria arrived home Thursday night. "I'm sorry I'm late, Josh."

"No problem, sweetheart. Everything is under control. They won't be here for another hour. Why don't you change and relax?"

Gloria dropped down in one of the kitchen chairs. "God, I'm tired. Do you know what I'd like? A nice, hot, relaxing bubble bath."

"Why don't you do it? You have plenty of time. Relax. I want you to have a good time tonight."

The promotion, Gloria reminded herself, tell him about the promotion. "There's something I want to talk to you about first. It's important."

"Not so important that it won't wait until you're out of the bath. Now get to it."

"But Josh . . ."

Josh took Gloria by both arms and pulled her from her chair. "No buts allowed. Tonight is for fun and relaxation."

Gloria didn't resist because she didn't want to. She should have told Josh about her promotion last night, but the right moment had never come. It had probably been the right moment all night, but she hadn't wanted to chance spoiling their interlude. She had given herself that same excuse since she'd learned of her promotion a week ago. Josh had been his old self again and she had reveled in it. He was still like his old self now. "Okay, Josh, I'm going to my bath now, but we'll talk when I'm out."

"Fine. We'll talk when you're out. Now get out of here."

Josh walked into the bedroom and found Gloria standing in the doorway of her closet, dressed in her bathrobe. "Sweetheart, they're here. Why aren't you dressed?"

Gloria pulled dress after dress out of the closet. "I know they're here. I heard the bell. Why didn't you wake me?"

"How was I supposed to know you were asleep? I thought you were taking a leisurely bath."

"That's the problem. It was too leisurely. I fell asleep in the tub. Now I'm not ready and I don't have a thing to wear."

Josh looked from the pile of dresses on the bed to the full closet and shook his head. "Well, I'm sure you'll find something, but hurry it up, okay?"

Gloria dropped another dress on the bed. "Go back

down and entertain them, Josh. I'll find something to wear."

He walked to the door. "Don't be too long. They're waiting to meet you."

Josh walked down the stairs to the living room and his guests. "You'll never guess what happened? She fell asleep and now she's scrambling to get dressed."

"You're probably going to get in trouble for telling us that, Josh," Marilyn said from her seat on the couch.

"That's only if she finds out," Josh responded.

"You know women, Josh, they stick together. Marilyn will tell her."

"I will not, Elliot. You're so bad."

Josh watched the couple's playful interchange. Once again, he told himself that meeting Elliot had been a good thing for him. For them. He could see the two couples' lives intertwined for a while. He smiled at the thought.

"What are you thinking about, Josh?" Marilyn asked. She looked as though she knew.

"He's probably wondering where his tardy wife is," Gloria answered from the doorway. "I'm sorry I'm late, everybody. It's all Josh's fault."

Elliot laughed first, then Josh joined him. "How is it my fault?"

Gloria gave Marilyn a "you know men" look, then extended her hand. "I'm Gloria and I'm glad to finally meet you. Josh has done nothing but talk about you and Elliot since they met."

Josh walked up behind Gloria, placing his arm around her waist. "And that guy over there is her worse half. Elliot, meet my better half, Gloria."

Elliot shook Gloria's hand. "Josh talks a lot about you, too," he said. "I see he didn't exaggerate your beauty."

At Gloria's blush, Josh added, "We're fortunate men. How did a couple of ugly mugs like us get such beautiful women?"

Marilyn spoke to Gloria. "Only men secure in their looks talk like that. Sometimes it's burdensome being married to such an attractive man."

Gloria agreed. Marilyn and Elliot were an attractive couple. The petite Marilyn was much shorter than Elliot. She fit under his arm perfectly. Elliot was an inch or two taller than Josh, but in Gloria's opinion, he was nowhere near as attractive. Though he was good-looking in his own right. "I know what you mean, but let's not tell them we've noticed that they aren't exactly a pair of dogs," Gloria whispered loud enough for the men to hear. "We don't want their heads to swell."

Josh released Gloria and motioned to Elliot. "Since our women are talking about us like we're not here, why don't you follow me to the kitchen. I prepared the dinner; you can help me serve it."

Gloria and Marilyn watched their husbands leave the room. "They're good guys, aren't they?" Marilyn said.

Gloria smiled. "I think I'll keep mine. You know why they left us alone, don't you?"

"Yes, I know. Elliot has done nothing but talk about Josh since they met. It's very important to them that we like each other."

"I know. Josh has never taken to anyone the way he's taken to Elliot."

"It's the same with Elliot. You'd think he and Josh had known each other for years."

Both women were silent for a minute. "It's the job loss, isn't it?" Gloria asked softly.

Marilyn nodded. "In all the time that Elliot has been out of a job, I never considered his need for a support group. I thought I was enough support for him. I thought he was doing fine, but I've seen the difference in him since he's met Josh."

"The same with Josh. I never thought it could make such a difference."

"I admit to feeling a twinge of jealousy when Elliot first began talking about Josh, but now I'm beginning to understand."

"I was jealous too." Gloria smiled at Marilyn, then added, "He said you and I would get along and I think he's right."

"Has it been hard for you?"

Gloria didn't have to ask what Marilyn was talking about. "The hardest thing I've ever faced. If there were something I could do, we could do, to change the situation, it wouldn't be so bad. It's the help-lessness that kills me."

"Don't I know it. When Elliot was first out of work, I kept trying to fix things, to make them better. I finally realized there was nothing I could fix. Life didn't stop. I had to go on."

Gloria thought about her promotion. "That's so easy to say. How do you do it? How do you share your professional accomplishments with him without making him feel bad about his situation?"

"I learned the hard way. I can't make Elliot feel bad. That's something only he can do. I finally stopped caring for his feelings and started caring for my own. And guess what? It didn't kill him."

"Then why does it feel like it will?"

"It's us. We have to take care of everybody's feelings at the expense of our own. That doesn't help the marriage. I found myself resenting Elliot and hating the sacrifices I was making."

Gloria nodded. She understood very well the things Marilyn was saying. "I got a promotion last week and I didn't tell Josh." The words surprised Gloria. She hadn't planned to tell Marilyn.

"Why didn't you tell me?" Josh asked. He and Elliot stood in the doorway.

Chapter 7

Josh closed the door behind Elliot and Marilyn. He didn't know how he had made it through the evening. He couldn't believe it. Gloria hadn't told him about her promotion. What was happening to them? God, things were getting out of hand.

"We need to talk," Gloria said, interrupting his thoughts. She walked hesitantly toward the couch. "Shall we do it down here?"

Now she wants to talk. "What's there to talk about? Everything has already been said." He knew he was being a bastard, but he couldn't stop himself. "Congratulations again on your promotion. You deserved it."

Gloria sat on the couch, looking at her hands. "I wanted to tell you." She looked up at him. "I tried to tell you."

Josh didn't want to hear her excuses now. He wanted to get out of this room, out of her presence. Instead, he walked over and sat next to her on the couch. "Why didn't you tell me?"

He saw the tears forming in her eyes when she looked up at him. "I didn't know how you'd take it," she said.

He looked away, not wanting to see her tears, wanting to hold on to his anger. "What's that supposed to mean? You didn't think I'd be happy for you?"

"I had my doubts," Gloria whispered.

He jumped up from the couch and began pacing in front of her, careful not to look directly at her. "Doubts? You had doubts? Why didn't you tell me how you were feeling? You're a good actress. I thought things were good between us."

"They are."

He stopped pacing for a moment and stared at her. "The hell they are." He shook his head and resumed pacing. "My wife gets a promotion and how do I find out about it? An overheard conversation with people we barely know. Things are definitely not good between us. What the hell is going on here, Gloria?"

"Nothing is going on. I only found out about the promotion last week. I didn't want to give you the news on the same day that you went to the unemployment office, so I put it off. And I kept putting it off. No time seemed like the right time. Portia kept after me to tell you and—"

"Hold on a minute," Josh interrupted. "Portia had to convince you to tell me? I don't believe what I'm hearing."

"Listen to me, Josh," Gloria pleaded. "I had planned to tell you the day I found out, but you were so happy about meeting Elliot. We were having such a good time. I didn't want to risk bringing you down. My actions may have been wrong, but my intentions were sincere."

Josh never thought Gloria would ever deliberately do anything to hurt him, but she had hurt him tonight. It wasn't only that she had kept the news of her promotion secret. It was the way he had found out. He had felt like a fool. Elliot probably thought him a fool.

"Aren't you going to say something?" Gloria asked when he didn't respond.

"I've said congratulations. What more do you want?"

"I want to know how you feel. Talk to me."

Josh shook his head. "There's nothing to talk about. I'm okay." Josh stopped pacing and walked toward the kitchen, effectively ending the discussion. "I'd better do the dishes."

Gloria got up from the couch. "I'll help."

Josh lifted a hand in her direction to stay her. He didn't want her company right now. "There's no need. I can do it. Why don't you go to bed?"

Gloria looked at the clock. Two o'clock and Josh still hadn't come to bed. She had known he was angry, but she hadn't known how angry. A part of her wanted to go down and talk to him, but another part, a larger part, saw no reason to beg for Josh's forgiveness. She had apologized. He'd have to get over it. She was getting tired of Josh and his feelings. She had feelings, too.

She looked at the clock again. Two-oh-two. When was he coming to bed? What was he doing? She was tempted to tiptoe downstairs and see. Maybe he was sleeping on the couch or in a guest room. She turned over on her stomach.

*   *   *

Josh drank his second beer. He wasn't going to get drunk, but he needed to relax. These incidents, fights, were happening on a regular basis. When will the arguing stop? he wondered. Will things ever get back to normal?

Josh took the last swig of beer, crushing the can before throwing it into the garbage. He walked out of the kitchen and up the stairs. As he got closer to the bedroom door, he softened his steps. The door was open and he saw Gloria lying on her stomach. If she got any closer to the edge of the bed, she'd fall out, he thought. Even in her sleep, she pulls away from me. The hell with it. He took one last look at her and walked past the open door to one of the guest rooms.

Gloria heard the water running in the shower. Not their shower, but the shower down the hall. At least he had spent the night at home. Not much, but these days she was thankful for anything she could get. Well, Josh might put it off, but he'd have to face her before he went to work. All his clothes were in their bedroom closet. Gloria shook her head at the direction her thoughts were taking. Would she ever get used to it? Josh wasn't going to work today. She had no idea what he planned to do. She hoped he'd look for work. She hoped he'd find another job. A good job. They needed some good news.

She heard the water go off in the shower. A little while later, she heard the sound of Josh's footsteps coming down the hall. When he walked through the bedroom door, she was amazed at her reaction to him. God, her husband was an attractive man. The towel he wore this morning showed off his narrow waist and broad shoulders. His legs, strong like a swimmer's legs, weren't bad either. No, Josh Martin was an excellent physical specimen.

Josh lifted a brow in her direction and she knew he knew where her thoughts were. Their physical attraction to each other was never something they denied. Far from it. They celebrated it. Often. The physical side of their marriage was strong. Or it had been. Even though she hadn't wanted to acknowledge it, even that had changed. They still aroused each other, but their lovemaking had taken on a desperate tone as if it were the only thing that held them together. Yet it wasn't working. Instead of bringing them closer, it amplified their distance. She wondered if Josh felt it too. Now was not the time to ask, though. She wondered how to play the morning— should she bring up last night or wait for him to make a move?

"I'm going to visit Walter," he said. Turning to look at her, he added, "We can use some time apart."

Maybe he was right. "So you're running away. We need to talk. Your leaving won't help."

"It'll help me. I'm going because I need to go. Seeing Walter will do me good." He pulled a suitcase from the closet. "He may even be able to help me with a job."

She couldn't believe it. "In California? A job in California? I thought we decided you'd limit your search to the Atlanta area."

He began pulling clothes from the closet. "Not we. You. I knew I had to keep my options open. I've looked. There's nothing for me here in Atlanta. I'm reduced to unemployment. Do you have any idea how that makes me feel?"

Before she could answer, he continued. "I need

to feel like a man again, Gloria. I'm losing my edge. I've got to get it back before it's too late. For us. For me."

"California isn't the answer. Don't give up yet."

With the suitcase packed, Josh dropped the towel he was wearing and began to get dressed. "My flight leaves at ten."

She recognized that tone. There was nothing she could say to change his mind. "Does Walter even know you're coming?"

"I called him last night."

She should have known Walter would welcome Josh on a moment's notice. He would love for Josh to move back out there. "How long will you be gone?"

"At least a week."

She was surprised at the length of the trip, though she shouldn't have been, given the amount of clothing he had packed. "Does Walter already have an interview lined up for you?"

Josh looked at her from the mirror as he straightened his tie. "A couple."

"You've already decided, haven't you, Josh? If they make you an offer, you're going to take the job."

"I don't see that I have any choice. Unless you know something that I don't."

"What about me, Josh? I just got promoted."

"They have banks in San Francisco. You could find something."

Something. Sure she could find something. But she didn't want something. She wanted what she had. "That's your answer—I'll find something?"

He turned to look at her for the first time since he had heard about her promotion. "I don't want to fight about this. I'm going to California to see Walter and to check out some job possibilities. Let's just leave it at that."

* * *

"You're coming, aren't you?"

Gloria opened her eyes. The sauna was so relaxing that she had almost fallen asleep. "I'm sorry, Portia, I was a million miles away. What were you saying?"

"The party next weekend. You and Josh are coming, right?"

Gloria didn't feel like a party right now and she had no idea what Josh would think. "I'll have to see what Josh says."

"Well, I'm not taking no for an answer. We deserve a celebration for our promotions and we're going to have it."

"I don't even know if Josh will be back by next week," Gloria said. "He may decide to stay longer in California."

Portia would not be put off. "You'll just have to call him and tell him to get his butt back here. I'm not kidding, Gloria. You have to be there. This party is for you, too."

Gloria looked at her friend in the multicolored, striped towel and smiled. Portia had done it again. She'd made Gloria feel good about herself. "We'll be there."

"That's more like it. This party might light a fire under Josh. Remind him what a treasure you are."

Gloria laughed outright then. "And just how are you going to do that?"

"I won't have to do anything. Foster will do it all by himself." Portia nodded. "That should knock some sense into Josh."

Gloria knew Foster would attend the party. And she knew that he would flirt with her. "There was never anything between Foster and me and Josh knows that."

"Yeah, he may know it, but when he sees Foster mooning after you like some star-struck teenager, he'll wise up. Nothing like a little territorial struggle to get a man back in line."

Gloria wasn't too sure she agreed with Portia's thinking, but she didn't feel up to debating. Portia was giving a party, and if her other parties were any indication, it would be great. "Do you need me to do something for the party?"

"Do?" Portia laughed as if that was an outrageous idea. "I've already called the caterers and everything is taken care of. The only thing you have to do is find a dress that'll knock both Foster and Josh off their feet." With a twinkle in her eye, she added, "I have a new outfit myself and I can't wait to see what you think of it."

Josh's flight didn't get in until two hours before the party. He rushed home from the airport and dressed quickly. Gloria took his breath away when he saw her in the black *thing*. He wasn't sure he should call it a dress. There didn't seem to be that much to it. It was cut square across the top of her breasts, just high enough to make you wonder if you would get a glimpse of heaven if you looked down at her. It hugged her body from her breasts to just above her knees, showing off every perfect curve. Then there was the back, or where the back was supposed to be. The spaghetti straps led to a balloon-looking drape that fell in swirls at her waist. No way was she wearing a bra with that dress. Not that she needed one. No, Gloria had firm, round breasts. They jiggled when she walked and her nipples jutted out when she was aroused. God, Josh was jutting out himself just watching her put the finishing touches on her makeup.

She turned around to face him. "Are you ready? We're running . . . ah . . . late."

He knew she saw his erection and he saw her reaction. Those perfect nipples immediately puckered against that perfect dress. "We could be later," he said, with a casualness he didn't feel.

Gloria couldn't seem to pull her eyes away from him. Her tongue slipped out to moisten her lips, damaging the lipstick line that she had so patiently constructed.

He walked over to her and bent his head to kiss her. "Since you started it, I'll finish it." At her puzzled look, he added, "Your lipstick. You started removing it. I'll take the rest of it off and then you can reapply it."

Josh kissed her then and he felt some of the tension between them fall away. He hadn't told her about his trip to California and he knew she was worried, though he couldn't tell it by her kiss. She had given him what he wanted in that kiss.

Her eyes were glazed when he pulled away from her. In them, he saw desire and love. That made him happy. "Let's talk when we get back tonight. We have a lot to talk about."

Gloria didn't know what had happened in California, but the trip had done Josh a world of good. She liked him like this, but she didn't want to think what a job in California would mean. Somehow they'd work it out, but not now. Now she just wanted to enjoy. She looked around for Portia, who was conspicuous by her absence. It wasn't like her to be out of the action. She was a world-class hostess and saw to each of her guests, but Gloria hadn't seen her tonight. She had asked Dexter about her, but he had only said she was "around somewhere."

Gloria turned and finally saw the face she had been looking for. Portia was coming through the patio doors. She looked different somehow. What was it? she wondered. Her dress. That's it. Why was Portia wearing that shapeless dress? It wasn't her style at all. Typically, Portia's dress made Gloria's look like schoolmarm attire. Gloria remembered Josh's reaction to her dress and smiled. He certainly hadn't been thinking "schoolmarm."

Portia walked up to Gloria and took her arm, but before Gloria could say anything to her, Dexter swished Portia away and moved to the center of the crowd. He tapped fork to glass to get everyone's attention. "Tonight we're celebrating Gloria's and Portia's promotions. So let's drink to the ladies of the night."

Gloria saw Foster Dixon lift a glass in her direction and wink, all the while wearing the biggest grin.

"That guy needs to get his own woman. He's been making eyes at you all night."

Gloria hadn't known Josh was nearby until he spoke. His words sent a shiver down her spine. "Jealous?"

Josh placed a possessive arm around her waist and lifted his glass to her. They drank together, never losing eye contact, thinking of the way this night would end.

They were brought back to the present when Dexter spoke again. "We have a second item to celebrate tonight." He hugged Portia to him. "We're pregnant."

Everyone in the room seemed to flock to Dexter and Portia. Everyone but Gloria and Josh. Gloria felt

Josh's arm drop from her waist and she knew he was thinking what she was thinking—if things had worked according to their plan, she'd be pregnant now, too.

Realizing she hadn't congratulated her best friend, Gloria walked away from Josh and moved through the crowd to get to Portia.

She had tears in her eyes but she was genuinely happy for her friend. "Why didn't you tell me?"

Portia had tears now, too. "Dexter made me promise that I wouldn't. He wanted to make the announcement. We only found out two weeks ago. I'm three months along." Portia pulled back from Gloria and turned around slowly, holding out the flared skirt of her dress. "How do you like it?"

Gloria laughed. "Oh, Portia. That's it. You're wearing a maternity dress. It's beautiful."

Portia lifted a questioning brow. "Not exactly my style, though, is it?"

"It's not that bad."

"I don't know, girl. I may have to start my own line. But I couldn't resist wearing it tonight. I'm not showing or anything but I had to wear this dress."

Gloria knew exactly what Portia meant. Wearing that dress made it real and announced it to the world. Portia was having a baby.

"How was the trip?" Gloria asked, after a quiet ride home. It seemed Portia and Dexter's announcement had taken the shine off her and Josh's evening.

"I didn't turn up anything concrete, but I did get some leads."

"That's good," Gloria answered.

Josh wondered if she'd even heard what he'd said. From the lazy way she was undressing, he knew her thoughts were far away. He had a good idea where her thoughts were. She was thinking about the baby. Not Dexter's and Portia's baby. No, Gloria was thinking about their baby. The baby they didn't have. More than anything, that showed how much his job loss had changed the course of their lives. He might as well bring it up. "That's good news for Portia and Dexter, isn't it?"

"Yes, it's good news. She told me a couple of months ago that they were trying. They deserve this."

He heard the unspoken "And we don't." "We'll have children."

"Don't, Josh, not now. Let's not talk about it now." As if to soften the words she had spoken, she added, "Let's talk about your trip. What were you saying?"

Josh hesitated, then decided to follow her lead. "I talked with Walter's AVP. They didn't have any openings out there, but the AVP gave me the name of a manager in Raleigh. It seems they're looking for someone with my qualifications and experience."

"I don't see why you don't concentrate your efforts here, Josh. What good will a job in North Carolina do us?"

"You can't be serious. All our problems are because of my job situation. Once we get that back in line, everything will be all right." Josh prayed that he spoke the truth. "Once I get a job, we can start our family. Continue with our lives."

"How was Walter?"

Josh recognized the change in subject for what it was. She didn't agree with him, but she didn't want to argue. Things had just gone from bad to worse.

Gloria lay on her side facing away from Josh. She could feel his eyes on her back willing her to turn to him for comfort. But she couldn't. Not yet. Not until she reconciled her feelings. God, what was she feeling? There was the initial envy. Next came the great relief. She was glad she wasn't pregnant. Glad. How could she tell Josh that? She couldn't. He'd want to know why and she just couldn't bring herself to tell him.

She felt more than heard him turn away from her, giving up on comfort tonight. She knew she had hurt him. Tonight had shown all the signs of being a fresh start for them, but it was not to be. It seemed that every time they were about to turn a corner, something else came up. Would they ever again be able to just enjoy each other?

Gloria admitted to herself that she feared for her marriage. She and Josh were not handling this problem well. Instead of pulling together to get through it, they were pulling apart. A lot of the fault rested at Josh's feet, but she shared a part of the blame as well. She laughed softly to herself, in most situations identifying the problem meant you had crossed the biggest hurdle. Unfortunately, that didn't seem to be working for her and Josh. They both knew what the problem was. They even agreed on the solution. It was just the path of getting from the problem to the solution that was causing all the havoc.

Josh couldn't sleep and he knew Gloria wasn't asleep. He could feel her turmoil. She wanted a baby. If he had a job, they could have a baby. But he couldn't find a job. At least, not here in Atlanta. And every time he even hinted that he was considering a move, Gloria pushed him in another direction. He wasn't going to find a job here and Gloria had to realize that. They were going to have to relocate.

Chapter 8

Just as Josh was leaving the unemployment office, he saw Elliot walking in his direction. Elliot had called a few times and Josh, embarrassed over the dinner party fiasco, had begged off each of his invitations.

"Just wanted to thank you again for having us over the other week," Elliot said when he reached Josh. "Marilyn and I want to return the favor."

Josh felt duly chastised. "I'm sorry, Elliot, but Gloria and I have been pretty busy lately."

"Don't sweat it, Josh. What happened the other night didn't bother me or Marilyn. You have to remember that we've been through a lot of the things that you guys are going through."

Josh knew Elliot was trying to make him more comfortable, but it wasn't working. "Let's say the evening opened my eyes to some things."

"Sounds like you're having an ego problem, my friend. How about a cup of coffee while we do some male bonding?"

Josh looked at his watch but his decision was already made. "Let's take separate cars. I have an appointment in about ninety minutes."

Once they were seated at the coffee shop, Elliot asked, "What happened when you talked about it?"

"We didn't exactly talk about it."

"Not good, man."

You're telling me. "It doesn't matter now. Things are starting to look up."

"You've found a job?"

Josh shook his head. "Not quite, but I have a lead."

Elliot slapped Josh on the shoulder. "Congratulations. What's the deal?"

"An old college friend hooked me up. I have an interview in two weeks. Comparable in position and pay to my old job." Josh didn't see a need to mention that the new job was in North Carolina.

"Good for you. Seems the bad stretch is over. And I was just thinking of asking you to consider a partnership with me."

"Doing what?"

"Management, general business. Right now I'm working out of my garage, but after the papers are filed with the Commission, things will start rolling. I thought we'd make a good team. We hit it off so well."

"Well, you're right about our hitting it off, but I don't think I have the stomach for entrepreneurship. At least, not while this job possibility is in front of me."

"From where I'm sitting, I think you need just as strong a stomach to work in Corporate America."

"You have a point there. Nothing is stable these

days. Anyway, tell me more about what's happening with your business. Maybe I can help out even if I'm not ready to be a partner."

"What are you so afraid of, Gloria? I don't see how my interviewing for this job will make anything worse."

Gloria took the basket of laundry from Josh and began stuffing clothes in the washer. "I can't believe how selfish you are."

"Selfish?" he responded, his voice rising. "You call me selfish. What's selfish about a man wanting to take care of his family? What's selfish about a man wanting to get his life back on track? Tell me how that's selfish."

Gloria dropped the basket on the floor and turned to look at him. "What about me, Josh? What about my job? Have you thought about that? I don't want to move. I've just been promoted. I want to stay here."

"I hear what you're saying and you have a point, but we can't go on like we are. This is tearing us apart. Something has to change. Do you have any better ideas?"

"You can continue to look for work here."

Josh lifted his hands in the air. "What kind of answer is that? Where have you been for the last six months? I've looked. There's nothing here for me. When are you going to face that?"

Gloria knew he was right, but she was afraid. Her life wasn't supposed to be like this. Josh wasn't supposed to be like this. They weren't supposed to be like this. "So, you expect me to quit my job and move to North Carolina if you get this job?"

"I expect you to do what's best for our marriage, for us. I know about your promotion. I even remember the night I found out about it. We both have to compromise in this situation. You've got to decide what's more important—keeping this marriage together or keeping your job. I can't make that decision for you."

"Are you saying that our marriage is not as important to me as it is to you?"

"I'm not saying that at all, Gloria. It's just that right now something has to give. You'll admit that my being out of work is not working for us?" After Gloria's slow nod, Josh continued, "Well, I have to do something about that. Right now my best opportunity is in North Carolina. If I get the job, we'll have to figure out how to handle it. But I can't not try. I have to go. Can you understand that?"

She knew he was right, but she was right too. Why did it all have to be so complicated? "It makes sense, Josh, but it's so scary. I just wish things were back like they were."

"That wish is *not* going to come true. You have a lot of thinking to do while I'm gone. I'm open to discuss any ideas that you may come up with, but we've got to do something."

"He's right," Portia said from her seat on the floor next to the treadmill Gloria walked on.

Gloria looked down at her. "You're supposed to be my friend."

"I am your friend, but the truth is the truth. You and Josh have got to make some changes if you're going to work this out. Girl, you're changing in ways that I never would have imagined."

Gloria straddled the belt, turned off the treadmill, and sat on the floor next to Portia. "You told me that we would change because of this. I'm proof that you were right."

"Don't put that on me. I don't know what's going on with you these days. I could tell my pregnancy threw you, but you haven't even wanted to talk about it."

Gloria looked away, embarrassed. "I didn't know I was being so obvious."

"I'm your friend. Your best friend. You can't hide something like that from me. I know you. Do you want to talk about it now?"

Gloria looked around the gym. There weren't many people out tonight. A couple of guys lifting weights, she and Portia. One of the guys caught her eye and smiled. She looked away. "Hearing about your pregnancy made me realize how much my life had gotten off track. If things had gone according to plan, Josh and I would be pregnant by now. But now I don't even know if I want to have a baby."

"Sure you want to have a baby. What are you talking about?"

"You're right, I do, but I don't know when. I just know now is not the time. Josh has it in his mind that when he gets a job we can just pick up with our original plans. I don't know if those plans still apply for me."

"Have you told Josh this?"

Gloria shook her head. "All we've been talking about lately is this trip of his to North Carolina."

"Not good."

"That's an understatement. Josh is sleeping in the guest room."

"You didn't tell me that. How long has this been going on?"

"He moved out the night of our dinner with Elliot and Marilyn. He came back to our bed the night of your party but that only lasted for a couple of nights. We haven't made love since before that dinner."

When Portia didn't say anything, Gloria said, "What? You're speechless. This I don't believe."

"I didn't realize how serious things were between you. Are you two going to be able to work this out?"

Gloria couldn't count the number of times she'd asked herself that same question. "I don't know. I just know I don't want to move to North Carolina."

"Do you love Josh? Do you want your marriage to work?"

If it was only that easy, Gloria thought. "I love him, but it's more complicated than that. There's no guarantee I'll find a job in North Carolina. What am I supposed to do then?"

"If you feel that strongly about it, you won't go. You and Josh will find another option."

Gloria laughed. "Like what? Josh will live in North Carolina and I'll live here? What kind of marriage would that be?"

"You're laughing, but it's not so uncommon these days. With both spouses needing to work, sometimes they end up in commuter marriages."

Gloria shook her head. "That doesn't seem right to me. How can the relationship survive the distance? Marriage is about togetherness."

"Of course it couldn't go on indefinitely, but until you find something there or until something else turns up for Josh here, you could give it a try.''

"I don't know, Portia," Gloria said, but she didn't dismiss the idea.

"You don't have to decide now, but it's an option for you to consider. Don't count it out yet." Portia got up then. "Time for a shower. Come on."

"I'll be along in a minute," Gloria said, but she didn't move. A commuter marriage, she thought. She and Josh in a commuter marriage. Would it work?

"We're preparing for our descent into the Atlanta area," the pilot's voice announced on the intercom. "We should arrive at the gate in twenty minutes."

Josh relaxed in his first-class seat. The interview had gone well. He was pretty confident he would get an offer soon. He felt better than he had felt in months. This was his shot and he had to make good on it. He liked everything about the job. He already liked his prospective boss, Carla Stevens. It would be the first time he'd worked for a woman but he didn't think that would be any problem at all. He and Carla had hit it off. She was only a couple of years older than him and she was already Plant Manager. Josh could see himself as her Chief Engineer. He knew that she could see it too.

Carla was an attractive woman. Not as attractive as Gloria, but attractive. And single. Not that it mattered to him. He was happily married. Happily married. Ha! These days he knew he couldn't describe his marriage as happy. He and Gloria fought too much.

Originally, he had thought finding a new job would

put an end to the fighting, but it seemed that it had only introduced a new topic to fight about. He didn't know how Gloria would react when the job offer came. He had talked to Carla about helping Gloria find work. Unfortunately, the company had a policy of not hiring couples, so a job for Gloria with Carolina Microelectronics was out. But they did have a relocation counselor who helped spouses find work. Josh's talk with the guy had been promising, but tentative. He hoped this was enough to pacify Gloria. If it wasn't, he didn't know what else he could do.

There was no way he could pass on this job. He just couldn't. He couldn't give up his marriage either. But he knew his marriage couldn't take much more of his being out of work. He wondered if the marriage could handle his taking an out-of-town job.

It seemed that everything was stacked against him and Gloria. She was his love, his life. And he wanted to make his marriage work. It seemed it had been ages since they'd made love. He ached for her sometimes, but she pushed him away. Never with words though. She was just never there. When he wanted to reach out to her, he could feel her pull away. That scared him.

Josh looked out of the window as the plane pulled up to the gate. He knew Gloria would be waiting for him and he wondered what kind of greeting he would get.

He saw her as soon as he walked through the gate door. She looked happy to see him, though the question in her eyes was obvious. She walked toward him and he opened his arms, almost afraid she wouldn't walk into them, but she did. They held each other for a long time like that. Gloria broke the embrace, pulled away, and looked up at him. There was a smile on her face and the question in her eyes was dimmed by tears.

Josh lifted a finger to wipe the tears. "Happy tears, I hope."

Gloria nodded. He wasn't sure whether she was answering his question or acknowledging it. Being in a positive mood, he chose to believe the former. He smiled at her, put an arm around her waist, and began the walk down the concourse.

"How did the interview go?" she asked.

"I impressed the hell out of them." He felt her stiffen at his words, but he continued. "We'll probably get an offer in the next few days."

"Josh . . ."

"I know you have reservations about it and we'll talk about them when we get home, but let's celebrate tonight. We need to celebrate."

"Okay," she said hesitantly.

"I missed you while I was away. Did you miss me?"

He felt her smile. "I missed you, Josh."

He squeezed her to him. "Where do you want to go for dinner?"

"It doesn't matter. As long as we're together."

He believed her and he felt relief. They just might make it through this.

"It was fun tonight, wasn't it?" Josh asked.

"Uh-hum." Gloria snuggled closer to him on the couch in front of the fireplace. It had been a glorious night. After dinner, Josh had taken her to BE's in Underground to listen to some jazz.

"Ready for bed?" Josh asked.

"Uh-hum, bed would be nice."

"Tired?"

"No." Gloria wasn't tired, but she was ready for bed.

Josh stood and lifted her in his arms. "I can take a hint."

"I kinda figured that, loverboy."

When Gloria was seated on the bed watching Josh disrobe, she began to feel nervous. It had been so long since they'd made love. She wanted him, but she was scared.

"What are you thinking about?" Josh was standing beside the bed now.

"You. Us."

"Good thoughts, I hope."

"It's been a long time, Josh. I was just thinking how long it's been since we've made love."

He put his hands to her face and looked into her eyes. "But I've wanted you every day, every minute." At the surprise in her eyes, he added, "I love you, Gloria. I've never stopped. I've been scared a lot lately about what I've seen happening to us. I don't want to lose you."

"I don't want to lose you either. We're going to make it through this. We'll compromise and we'll go on. Is that good enough for you?"

Josh shook his head. "I need more than that."

He saw the light in her eyes fade. "I don't know that I can commit to more than that."

"Do you love me?"

The light returned. "Of course I love you."

"Well, I haven't heard you say it in a long time. I need to hear it."

Her relief was obvious. "I love you, Joshua Martin. I think I've loved you forever."

He kissed her then. A kiss that said he loved her too. A kiss that said he cherished her. A kiss that said she was important to him. A kiss that said this was a beginning for them. A kiss that was only the beginning of their night of love.

"I love you in white," he said, tracing a finger around the lace at the neck of the white bodysuit she wore. "When did you buy this?"

"Yesterday, in anticipation of your return."

Josh fingered the lace from the collar to the waist of the suit. "Too bad you spent all that money for nothing."

"If you like it, it was worth the money."

"I like it, all right. You're just not going to get much wear out of it."

"Why not? If you like it, I'll wear it a lot."

Josh pushed the straps down her shoulders. "Somehow I don't think so. Even though white is great, I prefer you in brown—as in skin." He felt her shiver when her breasts were exposed. He touched them both with the tips of his fingers and their nipples puckered. He rubbed his fingers back and forth across their firm tips. Soon his mouth replaced his fingers. He felt electricity when his mouth touched those peaks. He was home.

When she was fully naked before his eyes, he studied her every curve. It had been so long since they'd been together. Too long. He vowed never to let anything keep them apart again. This, being with her, making love to her, was too important. It was life-sustaining for him.

He captured her gaze with his own and maintained it as he entered her. His look spoke words that were too voluminous to be spoken now. It spoke of his love, his need, his desire to protect her and keep her safe. She was his haven and he wanted her to know that he was hers.

She responded beautifully as she always did, arching against him, meeting him thrust for thrust, her concern and care for his pleasure obvious. When she lowered her eyelids, he kissed her. A kiss that sealed their bodies and hearts together in all the places that mattered. It seemed right that at that moment they shattered together.

Chapter 9

Josh smiled. His wife was working her magic in the early morning hours. It had been awhile since she had welcomed the morning this way. He kept his eyes closed while his hands moved to her waist to help with her movements and they fell into a rhythm of their own. When he knew he couldn't take it anymore, he opened his eyes and pleaded with her to come with him. She looked as if she was going to deny him, but in the end, they went together to that place of warmth and peace. He pulled her to him, kissed her sweaty brow, and fell back asleep.

When he awoke the second time, she was propped on an elbow looking at him. "Good morning, sweetheart," he said.

She stroked a finger down his chest to his waist. "Just good? Surely it was better than that."

Josh stopped her finger before it moved into dangerous territory, and he placed it to his lips for a kiss. "Maybe that was an understatement. How about earthshaking?"

She placed a finger between his lips, pulled it out, and pushed it back in again. "Better."

Josh sucked on her finger, moving his tongue up and down its length. "Maybe you need to refresh my mind."

Leaving her finger in his mouth, she moved to straddle him once again. "Remember anything now?"

Josh groaned as she pushed her pelvis against his. "My memory seems to be coming back."

She laughed a carefree laugh that he hadn't heard in a while. "Seems to me more is coming back than your memory."

Josh raised his hands to touch her nipples while he returned her thrusts. "It's getting warm in here, isn't it?"

Gloria covered his hands with her own, encouraging him in his ministrations. "I don't feel warm."

Josh took that statement for the dare that it was. He rose up and pulled her down so he could take her breasts in his mouth. At her first moan, he asked, "Not warm?"

She groaned again, all the while undulating against him. "Maybe a little warm."

Josh moved from one breast to the other, his hands all the while massaging down her back to her hips and thighs. "Getting warmer?"

Gloria groaned again, a sexy sound from the back of her throat.

Josh rolled so that he was poised over her while she lay on her back. "I thought so."

"Now, Josh. Now."

He rolled off her, onto his side, and drew circles around each breast with his fingers. Her skin was hot to his touch. "What's the hurry? We've got all day."

"Josh . . . I can't wait."

Josh moved his hands from her breasts to her flat stomach and drew more circles around her button navel. When he moved to kiss her there, she moaned and lifted her hips.

"Just a little while longer," he said. His kisses moved lower until he touched the wet covering of her mound.

"Josh . . ."

Josh moved until he was fully between her legs, his mouth never leaving that wet place. He was able to maintain his control, at least partially, until she heaved against his mouth. Then he lost it. He pushed her thighs farther apart and sank into her warmth.

Gloria met him thrust for thrust. They were one. Together. Soon they were soaring.

It was heaven to wake with Josh's head on her breasts, their bodies entangled, the smell of sex all around them. She wished they could stay like this forever, but she knew they couldn't. They hadn't talked about his trip to North Carolina and she knew they had to. Thoughts of the talk didn't scare her as they once had. She knew they'd work through it. Together.

"What are you thinking about?"

Josh's question surprised her. She thought he was still asleep. She smiled and answered, "You."

He gave her a quick kiss. "Good try, but what were you really thinking about?"

"Us."

His look told her he knew there was more. "How about us and North Carolina? Do you want to talk about my trip now?"

She nodded. As if sensing her need, Josh pulled

her into his arms before he began talking. "They're going to make me an offer."

That part she had figured out. "Are you going to take it?"

"I want to. What do you want?"

She pulled out of his arms and looked at him. "I want all our mornings to be like this morning, with our only concern being how to pleasure each other."

"But what do you want me to do about the job?"

"I want you to be happy. I want us to be happy."

This was harder than Josh had expected. "It's a great opportunity for me. The position is better than the one I had at General Electronics. They haven't given any specific salary numbers, but I know it'll be a significant increase over my old salary."

"I don't want to leave my job." There. She'd said it.

"They have a relocation counselor who helps with placing spouses. The company has a policy against hiring couples, but they've promised to help find something for you in the Raleigh area."

"But I was just promoted. How will I ever find a job as good as the one I have?"

"Believe me, Gloria, I understand," Josh said, his hand caressing her shoulders. "This isn't something that I ask lightly. I just don't see that we have many options. Either we stay here or we go to North Carolina. I've pretty much exhausted all my resources here. I just don't think I'm going to find a job in Atlanta."

"And you think I'll find something in North Carolina?"

Josh nodded. "I think you will. There are some big banks there. With your track record, you'll find something."

"I don't doubt I'll find something, but I don't want something." Gloria knew she was whining, but she couldn't stop herself. "I want what I've established here."

"I don't know what else to say."

Gloria silently thanked God for Portia. "I have another option for us."

"Well, don't hold back. Tell me what it is."

Gloria spoke slowly and softly. "You could go to North Carolina and I could stay here."

Josh felt his muscles tighten. Were his worse fears actually coming into being? "You mean separate? You want a separation?"

She pulled back and looked up at him with widened eyes. "No, Josh, that's not what I want at all. I'm talking about a commuter marriage."

"A commuter marriage?"

"Yes. You go to Raleigh and I stay here. I'll look for work in Raleigh and you'll continue to look here. The first one that finds something will move."

"A commuter marriage? Isn't that a contradiction in terms? Marriage means together."

She lay her head back on his chest and tightened her arms around him. "We'll be together in spirit and we'll see each other often. We just won't go to the same home each night."

"Or to the same bed. Is this what you really want? You want a commuter marriage?"

"No, it's not what I want, but what other choice do we have? It would be a mistake for me to move without having a job lined up as much as it would be a mistake for you not to take this job. This is only a temporary solution."

That was the first mention of the word *temporary*, Josh thought. Maybe they could make it work temporarily. "How temporary? How long will we have this commuter marriage?"

"We could set a time limit. Six months, nine months, a year. If, after that time, neither one of us has found work in the spouse city, we'll decide who'll give up their job."

"Seems like we're just postponing a hard decision."

"That's a defeatist attitude, Josh," she said, hugging him tighter. "You just said you thought I'd find work in Raleigh. If you really believe that, you shouldn't be so upset."

She had him there. She was right. Though he didn't put too much stock in his finding work in Atlanta, he felt pretty confident she would find something in Raleigh. "I want to go on the record as saying I don't think this is a good idea, but I don't see any other option. We'll try it, but only for a specified amount of time. How about three months?"

"Come on, honey, that's not reasonable. We'll need more time. How about nine months?"

"Let's compromise. Six months?"

"Okay, six months."

Josh felt as if he had made a pact with the devil. How would they make this work? Married people were meant to be together. He understood Gloria's position, but a part of him was disappointed that she wouldn't even consider leaving her job to follow him.

"They made the offer. I start the new job in two weeks."

Elliot looked up from the workbench in his garage. "You aren't wasting any time at all, are you?"

"I've been out of work for almost eight months. I think that's enough waiting."

"Point taken. Have you figured out how you're going to manage the separation?"

He and Gloria had talked the issue to death. Josh knew she was as afraid of doing this as he was. Neither one of them had voiced the one concern that hung between them. What if their marriage, their love, couldn't handle the separation? "Yeah. We have a plan. We'll be together each weekend, and of course, holidays and vacations. One weekend, she'll go to North Carolina. The next weekend, I'll come here. It'll work out."

Josh saw the skepticism in Elliot's glance. "Are you trying to convince me or yourself?" Elliot asked. "Are you having doubts about this?"

Josh knew Elliot thought he and Gloria were crazy to even consider a commuter marriage. "It'll only be for six months."

"And what if neither of you finds anything? How will you decide who should quit their job and relocate?"

Josh shook his head. He and Gloria had come close to discussing this more than a few times, but they never had. Instead, they focused their energy on positive thoughts about one of them finding suitable work. "We'll work it out."

"If you say so, man."

Josh knew Elliot wanted to talk more about it, but since Josh didn't, he changed the subject. "Have you found a partner yet?"

"Not looking for one," Elliot said. "After you turned me down, Marilyn and I decided to go it alone. Now, if you were to change your mind, I might reconsider. What do you say?"

Josh shook his head. "Not this time. See me in six months. You might be the answer to all my problems."

Elliot laughed. "If you ever want in, just let me know. Did you get to look over that proposal I gave you?"

"It's in the car. I made a few changes and reworked the numbers. It looks good. Really good. Gloria looked it over, too. You should call her at the bank. She might be able to help you out."

Elliot's eyes lit up. "She really thinks I have a shot at getting the money?"

"From her response to your proposal, I'd say your odds were better than that."

Elliot grinned then. "What do you know? Maybe I should ask Gloria to be my partner?"

"I'm glad you two came over tonight," Marilyn said, pouring coffee for herself and Gloria.

Gloria felt guilty about the times since that first fateful dinner that she and Josh had turned down their invitations. "I'm glad, too. I'm embarrassed it's taken us so long to get over here."

Marilyn handed Gloria a cup. "Elliot knew Josh was out of sorts because of what happened that night. We didn't want you two to be embarrassed. We've been where you are and we know what you're going through."

"I guess that's why it was so easy for me to talk with you. I've wanted to call a couple of times since that night, but I never did."

"Well, you're here now and that's what's important. Let's not worry about the past. When are you and Josh leaving for North Carolina?"

"I'm not going this weekend." Josh had suggested she go up with him, but her work schedule wouldn't allow it. "I'm in the middle of a closing and I can't take time off right now. Josh is driving up Sunday and he'll be back Friday night. I won't be able to go up until the following weekend."

"Has he found a place to live yet?"

Gloria shook her head. "He's staying in a hotel. He'll look at some places but we'll make the final selection the weekend I go up. That way it'll seem more like our place."

"Well, it seems like you're getting off on the right foot."

Gloria put down her coffee cup. "I hope so, Marilyn."

"Having second thoughts?"

"Not second thoughts. It just doesn't feel right. Josh shouldn't be leaving like this."

"He's not leaving. He's going to work and he'll be home in a week."

"That's what I keep telling myself. Sometimes I'm convinced this will all work out, but sometimes I wonder if we're putting our marriage at risk."

"Are you and Josh having problems?"

Gloria shrugged and stood up. "No new problems. I just don't know if we've worked through the old ones."

"I'll listen if you want to talk about it," Marilyn encouraged. "Just remember our husbands are in the garage."

Gloria laughed softly, thinking of the last time she'd shared a secret with Marilyn. "I won't say anything that I don't want Josh to hear."

Marilyn smiled with her. "Just wanted to remind you. Now what's going on?"

"We're relying so much on this new job. Almost like it's going to get us back on track, but I know that Josh has as many reservations as I do. If things were good between us, it wouldn't matter. But things aren't."

"You aren't getting along?"

"Recently we've started to put the pieces back together, but now we're going to be separated. Is this separation going to bring us closer or pull us farther apart?"

"You want to know what I think?"

"Of course."

"I think this will be a good time for the two of you. A break will do you good. Josh needs this, Gloria. Elliot has his fuel. Josh needs this to feel like a man again. You have to let him go and you have to be happy about it."

At the sound of the men coming in from the garage, Gloria sat back down on the couch. "Thanks for saying that. I needed to hear it."

Chapter 10

"Two bottles of your best champagne, please," Josh said into the telephone.

"Josh, you're being too extravagant," Gloria said. "We don't need champagne."

Josh sauntered over to her, happy this trip was turning out so well. When he and Gloria had boarded the plane five days ago, he had told her they were going to Raleigh. He had failed to mention the stopover in Bermuda. Her response and their time together made the entire trip worth it. "I'm hosting this party and I think we need champagne." He pulled her from her seat on the bed and into his arms. "Nothing is too extravagant where you're concerned. I love you and I don't want you to forget it because I'm not going to be around much."

Gloria looked up at him, the love in her eyes plain for him to see. "I'm going to miss you so much."

"I'll miss you too. We have to make the best of this

situation until one of us finds another job. I'll try my best to make your weekends in Raleigh special."

She smiled then. "You're so good at making me feel special, Josh. Thanks for this weekend."

"There's nothing to thank me for. We've gone over a rough patch and we made it. A little worse for the wear but we made it."

"It was rough going for a while there, wasn't it?"

He squeezed her to him. "That's all behind us now."

"I hope you're right, Josh. I'm nervous about my interview next week."

He pulled back to look at her. "I don't see why. You're going to knock them dead, sweetheart."

"I don't think that's an objective evaluation," Gloria said.

"It may not be objective, but it's true. You know as well as I do that there's not much in a bank that you can't do."

"That's another thing that has me so nervous. I have no idea what position I'm interviewing for."

"I can hardly believe that myself, but it must be something similar to what you do now. Why else would they want to interview you?"

"I hope you're right, Josh," she said.

"I know I'm right. But even if I'm wrong, it won't matter. We have time for you to find the job that you want. Not just anything that's available. We're going to make this commuter marriage seem like the best thing since our honeymoon."

She pulled back then and looked up at him, her eyes full of skepticism. "Huh?"

"I'm planning some special weekends for you in Raleigh. This trip is just the beginning of what I have in store for you, Mrs. Martin."

"Is that a challenge, Mr. Martin?"

He shook his head. "A challenge means you have a reasonable chance of outdoing me. I can tell you now that's not possible."

"I think that's a challenge and I'm taking you up on it. The weekends I plan for us in Atlanta will rival anything that you plan."

"I doubt it, but if you want to try, by all means, do so."

"You think you're hot stuff, don't you?"

He nibbled at her ear. "Hmm . . ."

So this is Carla Stevens, Gloria thought. Under ordinary conditions she was the kind of woman Gloria would naturally gravitate to. Self-assured, aggressive, no-nonsense. A woman who knows where she is and where she's going. A woman on her way to the top.

But there was something about Carla that caused unrest in Gloria. Carla Stevens was also the kind of woman that caused envy to well up in other women. The woman was drop-dead gorgeous. She couldn't be more than five-four and probably didn't weigh one hundred and fifteen pounds soaking wet. The pounds were, Gloria noticed, well distributed. No, Ms. Stevens wasn't lacking in any endowments. Gloria was grateful for one thing though. Carla didn't play up her good looks. On the contrary, she played them down. The severe cut of her suit, the hair pulled back in a bun, only a hint of makeup. Clearly, Carla was all about business.

"It was good meeting you," Carla said in a voice that sounded caring and friendly. Gloria could imagine this woman as a caregiver—a doctor or a nurse. "We're happy that you and Josh decided to join the Carolina Microelectronics family. If there's anything we can do to help you get settled, just let us know.''

"Thank you," Gloria said. She knew she should have gone on more about how they were so happy to be here, but she couldn't.

"We're looking for temporary housing this afternoon," Josh added, "so we'd better get moving." With that, he and Gloria said their goodbyes and headed for the elevators.

"Good going, Gloria," Josh said when they were out of Carla's earshot. "What's the matter with you? You could have shown a little more enthusiasm."

Gloria knew Josh was right. She was being a bitch and she had been since the interview yesterday. It had turned out to be a total waste of time. To say she was overqualified for the position was an understatement. And then to come here and see this woman that her husband was going to be spending more time with than he spent with her, well, that made her angry. "What did you want me to do? Kiss her feet?"

Josh punched the button for the elevator and put his hands in his pockets. "You know how important first impressions are. What were you thinking about?"

The opening of the elevator doors saved Gloria from having to answer that question. The ride down the four floors was quiet since there were others on the elevator. Gloria was glad for the reprieve.

The elevator doors opened again and they got off. Josh raced through the revolving exit doors ahead of her. She had to hurry her steps to catch him as he crossed the street to the car. Once they were in the car and buckled up, he asked, "Are you sure you want to look at the townhouse? Maybe it would be better if you went back to the hotel."

She knew he was upset. "Of course I want to see the townhouse. That's why I came up here, isn't it?"

"I'm beginning to wonder about that myself. So your first interview wasn't what you expected. Hell, I've been having disappointments like that for almost a year."

"And you've handled them so well," she replied, the sarcasm heavy in her voice. The nerve of Josh to complain about her attitude, given the way he had acted.

"What's it going to be? The hotel or the townhouse?"

She didn't want to visit this place that her husband would be living in without her, but she knew she had to go. "The townhouse, for God's sake. I'll be living there too. Rather, I'll be living there every other weekend."

They drove the remainder of the trip in silence. Josh decided to focus on his new job. He couldn't believe Gloria's attitude. Especially since their week had gone so well until now. Hell, it had gone better than well—it had been great, until she'd gone on that interview. He knew she was upset, but it wasn't the end of the world. It really wasn't. He was confident she'd find something. Soon.

Well, he wasn't going to let her ruin this opportunity for him and he wasn't going to let her ruin his good mood.

He was excited about this townhouse. It reminded him of the one he and Walter had shared when they started work in San Francisco. The one Gloria had helped pick out. He had been excited about showing her this place, wondering if she'd remember. Now he just wondered if they'd make it through the rest of the day without a fight.

When he turned onto Sycamore Street, he saw the owner's car parked on the street in front of the townhouse. He had intended to pull up behind the owner, but when the garage door began to go up, he pulled into the driveway and into the garage.

The owner greeted them when they got out of the car. Josh introduced Gloria and the owner led them through the garage door into the kitchen.

Though the tour was for her, Josh didn't think Gloria was interested at all. After they were done with the walk-through and were once again in the kitchen, the owner produced a contract, which Josh promptly signed. All the formalities completed, the owner left Josh and Gloria to enjoy their new home.

"It could be the same place," Gloria whispered.

"Did you say something?" Josh asked. He wondered what she wanted to bitch about now.

"I said this could be the same place. It's almost identical to the place you and Walter had in San Francisco. The exterior is different, but that's to be expected, East Coast, West Coast stuff, but the interior—it could be the same place."

She *had* remembered. Some of Josh's anger began to fade. "I noticed it right away."

"Is that why you decided to take it?"

Josh nodded, hoping that some of her anger was beginning to fade as well. "I knew immediately. It seemed like an omen of sorts. Maybe this will be a new start for us. Our love survived my six years in San Francisco with visits and telephone calls. Surely, it can take this commuter marriage for six months."

Gloria turned away from him to walk to the bay windows in the breakfast room. "That was actually a good time for us. Even though we were apart, I didn't feel separated. We had such a strong bond."

"Had? What about now?"

She turned around to face him. "I'd almost forgotten that we've spent most of our relationship apart. I always felt that you were with me."

"What about now?" Josh asked again. He wanted her to stop talking in the past tense.

"I don't know. For the past few months, I've felt apart from you a lot of the time even though we were sharing the same house and the same bed; that is, until you moved out of our bedroom."

She was right. He, too, had felt more distant from her in the last months than he ever had during the separation before their marriage. Maybe the difference was being married versus only being engaged. Maybe their expectations were different now. "I felt closer to you when we were on Bermuda than I have in a long while. I thought you felt it too."

She smiled and the tension between them lessened. "I did, Josh. And it made me so happy. It's just that the interview yesterday was a real letdown for me. I don't want to be separated from you."

He went to her and pulled her into his arms, soothing them both with his touch. "I don't want to be separated from you either. But our love has survived a separation before and it will again. Finding this townhouse was a sign. Do you like it?"

She pulled away from him and walked around the room. The contemporary furniture was even to her liking. "You knew I would. My tastes haven't changed much since then."

"You're right, I did think you'd like it. Since it's furnished, there's not much decorating to be done, but we have free rein in my office. How about we decorate it before you leave?"

"I'm ahead of you there, Mr. Martin—I packed the items from your old office. I figured you'd want to use them."

Josh walked over to her and pulled her into his arms again. "You think you're smart, huh?"

"Very smart," she said, "and don't you ever forget it."

Josh watched the seven men file out of the conference room. Their reactions had been predictable. A couple welcomed him as their new boss, three others were ambivalent, and two of them resented him. "Why didn't you prepare me?"

"I wanted to see how you'd handle it," Carla answered from her seat across from him. "They let me see their . . . ah . . . displeasure . . . when I told them we were going outside to fill the position. You handled it well."

"I know how they feel and in their positions I'd feel the same way. They're good men. As long as they do their work, we'll get along fine."

"Good. Now that you've met your team, it's time to meet the corporate people. I'm hosting a dinner party for them Thursday night. You and Gloria are the guests of honor."

"Thank you, we'll be there," Josh said, though he wondered if Gloria would be able to make it on such short notice.

"Don't thank me so quickly. I get something out of this too. Though the brass let me run this facility as I see fit, I like to give them the opportunity to commend my decisions."

"Well, I won't argue with you there. The more I learn about this job, the more I like it. I don't think I could have asked for a better match with my skills and interests. And," he added, "I know you couldn't have found a better candidate."

Carla stood and Josh did the same. "I'm glad to hear it. Now, I'd better get back to my office so you can get on with your day. My secretary will get the details of the party to Debbie."

Josh remained standing after Carla had left the room. He wasn't just blowing smoke when he'd told her how much he liked this job. It was a better fit for him than the job at General Electronics had been. He shook his head at the thought that it took getting fired and being out of work eight grueling months to get to this point. Maybe one day he'd be able to say that it was worth it. Not today, but maybe one day.

He picked up the phone and dialed Gloria's office. Her secretary answered. When she told him Gloria was in a meeting, he asked, "What's her calendar look like for Thursday and Friday?"

"A department meeting Thursday afternoon and a division meeting Friday morning."

Not exactly good news, he thought. Josh thanked her and hung up. Gloria's meetings complicated things. Should he tell her about the party and let her make the decision or should he not mention it?

"Mr. Martin, your wife is on the line," Debbie said after she poked her head into the conference room. "I can transfer the call in here if you like."

"That won't be necessary. I'm on my way back to the office."

Josh followed her to his office. He picked up the phone and pressed the blinking button. "That was a quick meeting."

"Not quick enough. You were hanging up when I walked through the door. Was there something special you wanted to talk about or were you just missing me?"

Josh smiled. Her flirting caused him to remember the last night they had spent together. It had been less than a week, but he missed her. "Both. Carla's hosting a dinner party for us. A really big event. All the corporate guys are coming.''

"That's great. This means a new dress."

Josh paused before speaking. "Thursday night."

Josh felt her thinking. "Not this Thursday?"

"Yes, this Thursday. Do you think you'll be able to come?"

Again, she was thinking. "There are a couple of things on my schedule. It's going to be hard to move them around, but let me see what I can do."

She would try. That was good enough for now. "Thanks, Gloria. I know this isn't much notice."

"I should know something in a couple of hours. I'll talk to you then."

Gloria stared at the handset she had just placed on the phone. Why hadn't she told Josh she couldn't make it? She had two important meetings this week—Thursday afternoon and Friday morning. How was she going to get into Raleigh for a Thursday night dinner party? It was obvious she couldn't make the meetings and the party. The most sensible thing to do was to call Josh and tell him about the meetings. He'd understand. She picked up the handset and dialed three numbers before hanging up.

This is a very important dinner party for Josh, she thought. At his level these parties were as important as board meetings. She knew it and she knew he knew she knew it. Unfortunately, her meetings were just as important to her career. How could she explain her absence to attend a dinner with her husband? She hadn't been in her new job long enough to give a reason like that.

Maybe the party could be rescheduled. This was pretty late notice anyway, she reasoned. His company would understand problems with the date better than hers would, since her meetings had been scheduled for over a month and Josh's had only been scheduled today. Yes, Gloria thought, that's the reasonable thing to do. She'd call Josh and see if he could get the party rescheduled. Next week would be perfect.

She picked up the phone to tell Josh her suggestion. This time he was in a meeting. She hung up and breathed a telling sigh. She was actually nervous about his response. She didn't want him to think she didn't want to come, especially after the way she had acted after her interview the last time they were together.

Now was too soon in their commuter marriage to make these types of decisions, she thought. She wondered if she and Josh would ever get a break. They seemed to move from one crisis to another. Just when it seemed they were getting it together, something else happened. It wasn't fair.

Gloria laughed at herself. Fair? What's fair got to do with it?

A knock at her door interrupted her thoughts. "How's the VP today?" Foster Dixon asked. "You have a few minutes for a friend?"

"Sure. Come on in." She welcomed the interruption.

Foster swaggered into the room. There was no other way she could think to describe the way he walked. The man obviously had no problem with self-confidence. Although sometimes his self-assuredness rankled. Today was one of those days. "What are you doing down here today? More gossip or is this actually official business?"

Laughing, he took a seat across from her desk. She had known he wouldn't be offended. The man didn't get insulted easily. "I wouldn't call it gossip exactly," he said.

"Okay, then, let's call it news. Have you heard any more news on my career? Am I up for another promotion so soon?"

"Ambitious, aren't we? That's consistent with the other news that I've heard."

Gloria strummed her fingers on her desk, impatient for Foster to get his news out. "Come on, spill it. I can see you're dying to tell me."

"Well, the word on the street is you and Josh are separated."

Gloria's fingers stopped strumming the desk. She knew the gossip mill was notorious, but she'd never expected this. "Where did you hear this?"

"Doesn't matter. Is it true?"

"Of course it's not true. You saw Josh and me at Portia's party. I'm surprised you didn't nip that rumor in the bud yourself. You're slipping, Foster."

Foster shrugged. "That was then, this is now. So you're telling me Josh hasn't moved to North Carolina?"

Gloria knew she shouldn't be surprised that the details were out, but she was. She and Josh had decided to keep their commuter marriage quiet for a while. Well, it seemed the while was over. "Josh is in North Carolina, but we're not separated."

Foster's frown showed his disbelief. "Unless I'm mistaken you're still here in Georgia."

"Don't be smart, Foster, it doesn't become you. Josh was hired by Carolina Microelectronics. He's working there, but we're still very much married, very much together. It's called a commuter marriage."

Foster lifted a finger to his chin and began to move his head up and down as if he were pondering some deep philosophical problem. "A commuter marriage? That Josh is a strange guy. If you were mine, you can bet I wouldn't be in North Carolina without you."

"Well, now, that's a moot point since I'm not yours."

"Not for lack of trying on my part."

Every conversation they had ended this way. "Foster . . ."

Foster must have sensed his time was running out so he stood up to leave. "Let me know if you get lonely in that big house all by yourself."

She raised a questioning brow at him. "The door, Foster." He gave her a puppy dog smile, and God help her, she returned it. "Leave. Now."

When he opened the door, Portia walked in. "Fancy seeing you here, Foster."

"Don't make anything out of it, Mommy. I'm leaving."

Portia watched him leave and closed the door behind him. "Josh hasn't been gone a month and Foster is already making a move on you."

"He's not making a move on me. He's flirting like he always does. You know Foster."

Portia took the seat Foster had vacated. "That's the problem. I do know Foster."

Gloria knew of only one way to keep Portia's determined mind off Foster Dixon and his intentions. "How's my godchild doing today?"

Gloria knew her ploy had worked when Portia placed her hand over her stomach and adopted a look that could only be described as "glassy-eyed." "Of course, it's too early for me to feel any movement yet, but I do think I'm getting bigger. What do you think?"

Gloria held back the grin that threatened to spread

across her face. Portia's stomach was as flat as it had always been. "I think I can see a little thickening around your waist."

Portia nodded her head in agreement. "I thought it was too early to start with the maternity wear, but I may need to. I don't want to look like I'm bursting out of my clothes."

Gloria picked up a pencil and began striking through some words on the pad in front of her. She didn't know what she was striking through, but she knew if she looked Portia in the face, she would laugh and Portia would be hurt. In that moment, Gloria realized that she had finally adjusted to Portia's pregnancy. She no longer envied her friend's good fortune. She was happy for Portia and that happiness was in no way colored by the problems she and Josh were having. "Well, I wouldn't say you're bursting at the seams yet. You have a few more weeks at least."

Portia looked skeptical. "If you're sure?"

Gloria did look at her then and she had to laugh. "I'm sure, Portia. I'll be the first one to tell you when your clothes start getting too tight."

Chapter 11

Josh packed his briefcase and prepared to go home. He thought about calling Gloria, but decided to wait. She'd said she would call him. If he didn't hear from her by ten, he'd call her.

He picked up the briefcase and headed for the door. The ringing phone stopped him.

"I'm glad I caught you," Gloria began. "I wasn't able to reschedule my meetings. Is there any chance the date for the party can be changed? They didn't give us much notice."

Josh placed his briefcase on the desk and sat down. He pinched his nose in frustration as he thought of a response. "There was nothing you could do?"

Josh could tell from the silence that she didn't appreciate the question.

"You didn't give me much notice," she said. "There wasn't a lot I could do. What do you want from me?"

I want you to be my wife. "Forget I said anything. At

least you got back to me today. I'll talk to Carla about rescheduling."

"Ask her if she can give a couple of dates. Or at least, if she can give more notice than before."

Yes, I wouldn't want to inconvenience you. Josh caught the words before he said them. Instead he said, "I'll see what I can do. Well, I'd better get out of here. Maybe I can catch Carla before she leaves for the day."

"Does everybody there work late hours? It's after six. I called you at home, and when you didn't answer, I decided to try you at work."

Josh knew his working late hours was nothing new. He had always done so. Why was she making a point of it now? "Well, I don't know about everybody else, but since I'm the new kid on the block, I'm out to do a good job. Now, I do need to hang up. I'll talk to you later tonight."

He stared at the phone after he hung up. He hadn't really expected her to make the party so he didn't know why her call had upset him so. He had a good job now and he was determined to do well at it. Things were looking up. Why then did this tension still exist between him and Gloria?

Josh picked up the briefcase and left for Carla's office. He wasn't surprised to see her seated at her desk with the door open.

"Do you have a few minutes?" he asked from the doorway.

Carla looked up from the papers she was reading to smile at him. "Sure, come on in. What can I do for you?"

Josh took the seat in front of her desk. "It's about the party Thursday. We have a problem with the date."

"That's not a problem. It was a bit much to expect you to be available on such short notice. We'll plan something else. This time with your schedule in mind."

Josh relaxed. Until she had spoken, he hadn't realized how tense he was. Thinking about it, he knew he had overreacted. He'd have to apologize to Gloria. "What will you do about Thursday?"

"Don't worry about it. You can meet everyone during the day. The party can wait."

That settled, Josh didn't have anything more to say. "I'd better go so you can finish up. I know you don't want to be here much later."

Carla smiled again, as if she knew something that Josh didn't. "I like the hard work and the long hours," she said. "Don't look so surprised. I bet you do, too."

Josh thought about it. She was right. When the work was good, the hours flew by for him. He was a goal-oriented guy and new projects with new problems always invigorated him. "I figure if you're going to work at a job forty hours a week, for forty or fifty years, you should enjoy it."

"That's my motto, too. You'll find that hard work is rewarded here at Carolina Microelectronics. We take the eager beavers and we work them hard. And we reward them well. Very well."

That was the sales pitch that had sold Josh on the company. He was the eager beaver. He was hungry. That period of unemployment had been a blow to his ego. This was his chance to get back what he had lost.

"You have what we look for, Josh. You're smart. That's a given. But you also have an edge. You want it. You want it all. I could tell during the interview.

You strike me as a man who knows what he wants and who's willing to do what it takes to get it."

There was something ominous about the way she spoke. Was she really complimenting him or was she issuing a challenge? She had read him well and that was all right, but he sensed there was something more in her words and that something made him uncomfortable.

"You're a pretty good judge of people," he said, trying to be neutral. "But I'd better get out of here or you won't finish your work."

Josh stood up to leave the room. The look in Carla's eyes told him she knew he was uncomfortable with what she had said, but that it didn't matter to her. Josh walked out of the office without another word.

Once he was in the hallway, he wondered again at her words. Was there a hidden message in there for him? He had known Carla was a single-minded woman, but that hadn't bothered him. In fact, it had drawn him to her. He liked her determination. He was impressed by what she had accomplished at Carolina Electronics. Hell, he even envied her a little, though he'd never admit it to anyone.

Get a hold of yourself, he thought. You're getting paranoid. Stop looking for problems where there are none.

Gloria couldn't sleep. Though it was late and she wanted to get out of bed, she didn't want to risk waking Josh. He had been tired when he had gotten in last night and she knew he needed his sleep. Besides, she was still somewhat miffed about his reaction when she couldn't make the party and she assumed he was still upset with her. She hadn't men-

tioned it last night and neither had he. Part of the
reason was the lateness of his arrival and the other
was simple avoidance. At least, that's what it was for
her. She didn't know about Josh. Although he had
held her close all night, he hadn't made a move to
get any more intimate. She wondered if that was a
sign he was still upset.

Gloria thought about the plans they had today with
Marilyn and Elliot. She was glad to be seeing the
couple again. Though she had first formed a relationship with Marilyn, she was finding that Elliot was a
good guy himself. Since she had referred him to one
of her co-workers about a loan, she had talked with
him regularly about the financing of his business.

Elliot was such a simple guy, unlike Josh in so many
ways. Elliot just wanted his dream. The money didn't
seem to matter that much to him. And Gloria knew
there would be money and lots of it. Elliot's idea
for fuel efficiency was a winner. He had gotten the
financing at her bank with little trouble.

She smiled when she thought about Elliot's
response when she'd told him he had gotten the loan.
He had picked her up, swirled her around, and given
her a big kiss. He had been embarrassed about the
kiss and had apologized profusely. She had only
laughed at him. Too happy for him to think much
about it then. It was then that he had suggested that
the two couples celebrate when Josh came home for
the weekend. So she and Josh were spending the day
with Marilyn and Elliot.

She heard Josh stir next to her. Unsure of what
his mood would be, she held herself still so that he
wouldn't know she was awake. When she felt him
leave the bed, she let out a deep sigh. When she
heard the shower go on, she got out of bed, grabbed

some clothes from her closet, and went to the bathroom down the hall to shower.

She wasn't in the shower long. She was surprised to see Josh leaning against the vanity with his arms crossed when she stepped out. She quickly pulled the towel around herself. "Good morning," she said, feeling stupid for trying to hide her nakedness from Josh.

"Is it?"

Did Josh want to argue this morning? she wondered. She hoped not, because she didn't. "Yes, it is a good morning. Seems like a great day to take the boat out."

"I wasn't referring to the weather."

She gave a sheepish smile. He did want to argue. "Okay, Josh, what were you referring to, if not the weather?"

Josh turned around so that she could see his face in the mirror. Her first thought was that they were an attractive couple. His dark brown complexion complemented the light-brownness of hers. Her soft features, his strong ones. Yes, they were an attractive couple. "I'm sorry I was so tired when I got in last night, but I've been busting my tail at work. Are you still angry with me about the party?"

Her anger left when she saw the sincerity and concern in his eyes. "Not anymore."

"I'll say it again. I'm sorry I overreacted. Now, how's your work going?"

She relaxed at his apology. "Pretty exciting right now. I'm working on the financing for two developments—the Turner Hill Mall and the strip shopping center on Cascade."

"How did you pull that deal together? I thought the Turner Hill Mall was dead."

Gloria shook her head as she applied her foundation. "Almost. The South DeKalb Chamber never gave up on it and the financing finally came through. The mall will be a boon for that whole area."

Gloria saw pride and interest in Josh's eyes. "A boon for you, too. That's great, Gloria. What's this about Cascade?"

She was happy to talk with Josh about her work again. It had been a long while since she felt comfortable doing so. "That's my special project. A few of the businessmen in the Cascade area came to me with an idea. They want to open a strip shopping center that houses only small businesses—no chains. They see the population exploding in the area and they want to make sure that some of the money stays in the community. What better way than to have local businesses serve the local community?"

"Sounds like a good idea, but can they pull it off?"

"It's going to take some time and we've still got a lot of planning to do, but I think I can line up the financing."

"Your bank is being very generous these days."

Gloria took that as a compliment. In her new position, she had found a new sense of purpose and satisfaction. She'd never considered herself a community activist, but she found herself assuming that role in her projects. And she liked it. And she wanted to do more of it. She wanted to direct the bank along the lines of more community development, more support of local businesses. There was money to be made financing chains relocating to the Atlanta area, but she knew there was an untapped market in financing local businesses. "Hey, we're just in it to make money."

"The bank might be, but it's more than that with you. I'm proud of you. You're doing a great job."

Gloria could tell from his expression, if not his words, that his thoughts were elsewhere. She wondered if he was beginning to see why she didn't want to pull up stakes and leave Atlanta so quickly. She was doing things here. Things that mattered to her and the community. She hoped Josh could see that, too.

"I'm glad you were able to help Elliot," he said.

Gloria placed the cap back on the eyeliner, done with her eyes. "I can't take credit for that. All I did was point him in the right direction. That business plan you helped him pull together was the real winner. The loan officer had nothing to question."

"Are you getting modest on me? I know you put in a good word for him and that word removed any doubts the loan officer may have had. I think Elliot knows that too. That's why they've invited us out to the lake today. I didn't even know they had a boat."

Gloria was pleased with Josh's praise, but she was also embarrassed. "They don't. They've borrowed a friend's boat. Elliot knows how much time we used to spend on the water and he wanted to do something special for us."

"So, you and Elliot have been spending a lot of time together?"

The question was innocent enough, but Gloria paused in the application of her lipstick to check Josh's expression. There didn't seem to be anything in the look he was giving her. "He's called me a few times. He looks at me as sort of an advisor."

"Has he asked you to be his partner yet?"

Gloria laughed at that. "In fact, he has. He was joking, of course. It was right after he got the loan. How did you know?"

Josh shrugged his shoulders. "It was just a guess. He asked me about it before I left for Raleigh."

"Elliot asked you to be his partner? You never told me that."

Josh turned around and leaned back against the vanity. She could no longer see his face in the mirror. "There was nothing to tell. The position in Raleigh is a lot more stable than a partnership with Elliot."

She turned to look at Josh's profile, her makeup all done. "I guess you're right, but I think Elliot is going to make a lot of money. He and Marilyn deserve it too."

Josh fingered the towel that Gloria had wrapped about her. "You're right about that. And so do we."

Gloria's attention focused on Josh's fingers. She wondered if he was going to unknot the towel. "So do we what?"

"Deserve good things," he said.

Before Gloria could comment, the phone rang. Josh's finger stopped moving on the towel and his eyes met hers. She stepped back and the towel fell to the floor.

"They'll call back," she said.

Josh and Marilyn sat around the table on the upper deck. Marilyn talked while Josh listened, or rather, tried to listen. His attention was constantly being drawn away to the sound of Gloria's laughter. She and Elliot were "manning the ship," as they called it.

"You haven't heard a word I've said, have you?" Marilyn asked. Her question brought his gaze to her face.

"I'm sorry, Marilyn. What were you saying?"

"Don't be sorry. It's endearing to watch you watch her with so much love in your eyes. You two probably wanted to spend some time alone today. Elliot and I should be sorry for interrupting your time together."

Josh hadn't realized his thoughts were so obvious. He did want to be alone with Gloria and he was jealous that she was spending her time laughing with Elliot instead of laughing with him. It wasn't that he didn't trust them or even that he suspected them, but he wanted all of Gloria's attention. Their time together was precious to him since they had so little of it. "You're our friends. We appreciated the offer."

"But it would have been more romantic if we'd just offered you the boat?"

Josh laughed. "I think we'd better end this whole line of conversation."

She laughed too. "How's the new job?" she asked.

Josh told her about the job and his new boss.

"I'm glad you like it there," she said when he'd finished. "How are you handling the commute?"

Josh glanced over at Elliot and Gloria again. "It's hard. I want her with me."

"That's only natural. Just keep telling yourself it's only for a few months."

He wished. From what Gloria had said about her job this morning, Josh knew she really didn't want to move. And he admitted to himself, he didn't blame her. "Yeah. Just a few months."

"You don't sound too sure about that. Do you want to talk about it?"

Josh realized Marilyn was concerned and that she wanted to be helpful but he didn't feel comfortable discussing his marriage with her. "Thanks for the offer. I may take you up on it one day."

Marilyn reached out and placed her hand across his. "We're here for you and Gloria if you need us. Anytime."

Josh nodded, then stood up abruptly. "I'll see if I can give Gloria and Elliot a hand." When he reached Elliot and Gloria, he asked, "What's so funny?"

Elliot looked at Josh and then back at Gloria. He and Gloria fell into laughter once more. "You had to be there," Elliot offered. When Elliot finally stopped laughing, he asked Josh, "Enjoying the trip so far?"

"Sure, but I don't think I was much company for Marilyn, though. You'd better go see about her."

Elliot again looked from Josh to Gloria and back again. "I can take a hint. I'm outta here."

Gloria was still smiling as she watched Elliot walk over to his wife.

"You and Elliot seemed to be having a lot of fun," Josh said.

Gloria nodded and began tying back the sails. "He can be a funny guy at times."

"I bet."

Gloria stopped what she was doing to look at Josh. She smiled before she said, "I don't believe it, you're jealous."

"I'm not jealous."

"Yes, you are. Don't deny it. You're jealous of Elliot. Why?"

Josh looked away. "I want you all to myself. You should be laughing with me, not with him."

She loped an arm around his waist and kissed him. "And I'd rather spend my time with you, but they invited us out and we have to be sociable."

"You're right, but all I can think about is this morning and the way we made love. I want to make love to you again."

Gloria felt the lower part of her body grow warm. "I want that too. Just think how much better it's going to be tonight when we finally get home. Anticipation is a great aphrodisiac."

Josh grunted and pulled her closer to him. "If I live that long."

Gloria felt his erection and she laughed. "You'll live."

He grunted again. "You're going to have to stand here awhile. If we walk back over to Elliot and Marilyn now, they're going to know what's on my mind."

Chapter 12

Damn, Gloria thought, we've got to do something about this gear shift. She wanted to get closer to Josh, but the gear shift prevented her from moving as close as she liked. Determined to get some action started in the car, she leaned across the gear shift and placed her arms around his shoulders.

"You'd better watch yourself, Gloria," Josh warned.

She ignored him and put her tongue in his ear. When he moaned, she asked, "Something wrong, Josh?"

"Stop it, Gloria, I'm trying to drive. You don't want us to have an accident, do you?"

Gloria moved her attention from his ear and began to place hot kisses down his strong jaw. "Stop what?" she asked with a tinge of innocence.

"You know what you're doing," he said. His hands gripped the steering wheel and his eyes focused on the road.

She moved her hand to rest on his chest and continued her kisses. "You don't like it?"

He cut his eyes in her direction. "You know I like it. That's the problem. I like it too much."

Her hand slipped from his chest to rest on his thighs.

"Gloria," Josh warned. He dropped one hand from the steering wheel and placed it atop hers.

She inched her fingers up his thigh, ignoring his feeble attempt to stop her movements. "This isn't affecting you, is it, Josh? It's not like you're about to run off the road or anything."

He cut his eyes in her direction again and the passion she saw in them almost made her forget the game she was playing. Josh wasn't playing, and as soon as they got home, she would pay for her actions. She shivered at the thought.

When Josh returned his attention to the road, Gloria's fingers resumed their motions. Evidently, Josh had decided to stop fighting her because he moved his hand back to the steering wheel.

"You're going to get it when we get home," he said. "Yes, you're going to get it."

When she looked down at the bulge in his pants, she knew he was right. She was going to get it when she got home. The thought made her warm all over.

She kissed him again on his jaw while her fingers made their way to the bulge in his pants. When she grabbed him there, the car swerved.

"Dammit, Gloria, you're going to get it."

She laughed.

When Josh pulled the Saab into the driveway, he was literally bursting at the seams. Gloria had settled back in her seat, looking as innocent as a Sunday School teacher. She was going to pay for what she had done to him and pay big.

He watched as she unbuckled her seatbelt. When

she moved to raise the latch to open the door, he asked her, "Where are you going?"

When she looked at him, he groaned and pulled her to him, gear shift be damned. No way was she getting away from him with a look like that in her eyes. She was just as affected by her sexual antics as he was.

He held her with one hand and lifted the steering wheel to its highest position with the other, all the while sliding his seat as far back as it would go. That done, he managed to position her so that she sat on his lap. Awkward positioning, but comfort was not his prime consideration now.

"You know you're going to have to pay up now, don't you, Gloria?" he asked.

She adjusted herself on his lap, trying to get closer to him. With her hands positioned on either of his shoulders, she asked, "How much do I have to pay?"

When he reached under her blouse, she sighed. Her arms automatically lifted as he pulled her blouse over her head to expose her lace bra. "A lot," he answered as he unsnapped her bra and slipped the straps down her arms. He inhaled her scent as he threw the bra into the back seat with her blouse.

"God, you have beautiful breasts," he said, his mouth greedily attacking first one breast, then the other.

He heard the rumbling sounds from the back of her throat and he knew she was getting her payback. With much self-control he pulled his mouth away from her breasts. "What? Nothing to say? Cat got your tongue?" Before she could answer, he captured her mouth for a ravaging kiss. He couldn't get close enough to her.

He ended the kiss and pushed her away from him.

We've got your authors!

If you seek out the latest historical romances by today's bestselling authors, our new reader's service, KENSINGTON CHOICE, is the club for you.

KENSINGTON CHOICE is the only club where you can find authors like Janelle Taylor, Shannon Drake, Rosanne Bittner, Sylvie Sommerfield, Penelope Neri and Phoebe Conn all in one place...

...and the only service that will deliver their romances direct to your home as soon as they are published—even before they reach the bookstores.

KENSINGTON CHOICE is also the only service that will give you a substantial guaranteed discount off the publisher's prices on every one of those romances.

That's right: Every month, the Editors at Zebra and Pinnacle select four of the newest novels by our bestselling authors and rush them straight to you, usually *before they reach the bookstores.* The publisher's prices for these romances range from $4.99 to $5.99—but they are always yours for the guaranteed low price of just $4.20!

That means you'll always save over 20% off the publisher's prices on every shipment you get from KENSINGTON CHOICE!

All books are sent on a 10-day free examination basis, and there is no minimum number of books to buy. (A postage and handling charge of $1.50 is added to each shipment.)

As your introduction to the convenience and value of this new service, we invite you to accept

4 BOOKS FREE

The 4 books, worth up to $23.96, are our welcoming gift. You pay only $1 to help cover postage and handling.

To start your subscription to KENSINGTON CHOICE and receive your introductory package of 4 FREE romances, detach and mail the card at right today.

We have 4 FREE BOOKS for you
as your introduction to
KENSINGTON CHOICE
To get your FREE BOOKS, worth
up to $23.96, mail the card below.

FREE BOOK CERTIFICATE

As my introduction to your new KENSINGTON CHOICE reader's service, please send me 4 FREE historical romances (worth up to $23.96), billing me just $1 to help cover postage and handling. As a KENSINGTON CHOICE subscriber, I will then receive 4 brand-new romances to preview each month for 10 days FREE. I can return any books I decide not to keep and owe nothing. The publisher's prices for the KENSINGTON CHOICE romances range from $4.99 to $5.99, but as a subscriber I will be entitled to get them for just $4.20 per book or $16.80 for all four titles. There is no minimum number of books to buy, and I can cancel my subscription at any time. A $1.50 postage and handling charge is added to each shipment.

Name _____

Address _____ Apt. _____

City _____ State _____ Zip _____

Telephone ( ) _____

Signature _____ KC0895

(If under 18, parent or guardian must sign)

Subscription subject to acceptance. Terms and prices subject to change.

"Let's go inside," he whispered, done with his game and ready to get down to business.

"Why do we have to go inside?" she asked. "I don't want to move until you give me what you promised."

"But we'll be more comfortable inside," Josh offered. When she rose up from him and, with the skill of a contortionist, removed her shorts and panties, he knew the tables had turned.

"Gloria," he warned.

She looked down at him, her eyes glazed with a sensuous mist. "Don't you want this?" She didn't wait for his answer. She unzipped his shorts, lifted him out of his shorts, and directed him into her entrance.

It had been past midnight when they had finally come into the house. Their time in the car had been exciting. And the night in bed had been even better. It was as if their sex life had taken on a new life. It had an urgency that Gloria once thought they had lost.

She felt Josh stir behind her and she snuggled closer to him. "Good morning," she said without turning around to look at him.

He pushed his arousal against her buttocks. "Very good morning."

She pushed her hips more tightly against him. "Don't you ever get tired?"

"Not of you," he said, placing a kiss on the base of her neck.

She turned around to face him. "You always say the right thing. Do you know that?"

He kissed her lips. "And you always do the right thing. I enjoyed our drive home."

She placed a hand on his chest, moving her fingers

through the light film of fur that covered it. "I told you."

"Told me what?"

She placed a kiss on his chest. "So you've forgotten."

"Forgotten what?"

She continued with light, feather kisses across his chest. "Shame on you, Josh. You did forget."

He placed a hand on either side of her head and lifted her face to his. "What are you talking about?"

She smiled. "The challenge that you made when we were on Bermuda. So, how does this weekend stack up against the one we just had in Raleigh?"

He laughed. "You mean you planned that garage escapade?"

"Did you enjoy it?"

He pulled her to him. His Gloria was turning wanton on him. Maybe this commuter marriage would work after all. "Maybe I should show you how much," was his answer.

Gloria walked through the house reliving the day she and Josh had shared after they'd finally gotten out of bed.

They'd had brunch with Dexter and Portia and had spent the early part of the afternoon with them. Josh had been in a rush to leave afterward and now he was gone. She missed him already. It was an ache that she guessed she would have to get used to.

The ringing telephone cut short her musing. It was Elliot looking for Josh. "You just missed him. He left no more than ten minutes ago."

"It's just as well. I promised Marilyn that I wouldn't bother you guys today, but I wanted to get Josh's opinion on something before he left."

"You can always call him in Raleigh. You have his number, right?"

"Yes, I've got it. Maybe I will give him a call. I don't suppose you'd want to look over my idea, would you?"

Gloria smiled at his manner. "Why not? I don't have any plans for the rest of the day anyway. Why don't you two come over and plan to stay for dinner."

"Sounds good, but it's just me. Marilyn went to visit a friend's mother in Columbus. She won't be back until later tonight."

"Well, why don't you come over?" she asked.

"I have a better idea. Why don't we go out? This is something we can discuss over dinner." When Gloria hesitated, he added, "I owe you, Gloria. You've done so much for us already. Let me do something for you."

She responded to the pleading in his voice. "Okay. As long as it's nothing fancy."

"You choose the place. How about I pick you up in about an hour and a half—say, six o'clock?"

"You don't have to pick me up. I can meet you there."

"I don't want you driving home by yourself after dark," he explained. "Even if we meet there, I'll have to follow you home so you may as well let me pick you up."

"Okay, I'll see you around six."

After Gloria hung up, she realized she was glad to be getting out of the house and away from her thoughts. She wondered what Josh would make of her dinner with Elliot. Elliot without Marilyn. She had been flattered by his jealousy on the boat yesterday. Though there was nothing, would never be anything, between her and Elliot, it was good to know Josh thought she was attractive enough to worry about. She shook her head, tossing those thoughts aside, and wandered into the bedroom to find something to wear.

Elliot picked her up promptly at six and they went to the Olive Garden for dinner. She listened to his idea and gave her opinion. They went back and forth on some issues before reaching a compromise. They were both feeling good about the evening when they left the restaurant.

On the drive home he asked about her work and she told him about the Cascade project.

"Seems like it's keeping you busy," Elliot observed.

Gloria nodded. "It is, but it's worth it. It means a lot to the small businesses in the area. It's important for the people in that area to keep their money in the community as long as possible."

Elliot pulled into her driveway then. She was about to invite him in for coffee, but he spoke first.

"It was good of you to help me out," he said. "I really appreciate it. You and Josh have both helped me tremendously. I don't know how I'll ever repay you. One of you should reconsider and become my partner. You deserve to get something out of this business."

Gloria wanted to reach over and touch his cheek, in a friendly gesture, of course. "This is your dream. We're just glad to be a part of it. We've enjoyed watching you embrace your success."

Was Elliot blushing? she wondered. He was a fair-skinned man, so the faint, reddish tint of his cheeks could be a blush.

"It's not success yet," he said, "but it's close. So close I can taste it."

"This is something you deserve. You took your unemployment, which could have been an ending, and made it a beginning. I'm impressed."

Yes, he was blushing, Gloria said to herself.

"I couldn't have done it without Marilyn," he continued. "She supported me, and I mean more than financially, when I really needed it. I'll never be able to repay her for that."

He sounded so forlorn as he spoke that she wanted to reassure him. "She doesn't want to be repaid. She did it because she loves you. It's her dream, too. I envy you both."

They were silent for a while. "You and Josh seem to be adjusting well to your commuter marriage."

She nodded. "It's hard but we love each other and we're determined to see this through."

"I know this is none of my business, but I don't think this commuter marriage is such a good idea. Married people should be together."

It was so simple for Elliot. Too bad it wasn't that simple for her and Josh. "Ours is a special case. We don't want to be apart, but there was no other way."

"We all make choices. You and Josh had a choice. You chose to be apart rather than to be together. That I don't understand. I would never choose to be apart from Marilyn."

Gloria felt her defenses rise. "It's complicated, Elliot. Josh has to follow his dream just like you had to follow yours. I'm supporting him in that, but I have dreams too. Should I have given up my dreams to follow him? Should he have given up his to stay with me?"

"I'm not saying you should have followed him, but I figured one of you needed to give in. You both made choices," Elliot continued, shaking his head, "but I can't see myself having made those same choices."

Her anger was immediate. "So, Mr. High and Mighty, you've judged Josh and me and found us lacking, is that it?"

Elliot reached for her hand. "No, that's not it at all. I care about you and Josh and I want you to be happy."

Gloria snatched her hand away and flung open the car door. She wasn't going to sit here and listen to Elliot's judgments. The things he had said had hit too close to home. At one time, she would have followed Josh anywhere. Why had she put her career before their marriage this time? She knew the answer, but she didn't like it and she knew Elliot wouldn't approve of it. Well, who the hell was Elliot to judge her anyway? She hopped out of the car. "Good night, Elliot," she said with obvious sarcasm. "I had a great time."

She heard Elliot say something but the words didn't register in her brain. She stormed to the front door, unlocked it, and let herself in. Once inside, she began to pace. Elliot and his opinions. Who asked him anyway? That's the problem with friends. They always gave too much advice. This kind of stuff she expected from Portia, not from Elliot. What did Elliot know about her marriage anyway? He couldn't even plan his own business without her help.

The more Gloria thought about his comments, the angrier she became. She wondered how many other people were judging her, looking for her marriage to fall apart. Well, other people didn't know about her and Josh. Their marriage was as strong as ever. This commuter arrangement was only temporary.

One good thing had come out of this, though. Josh would no longer have reason to be jealous of Elliot because Gloria was never going to see him again. That meant she wouldn't see Marilyn either, but she figured that was best. Marilyn probably shared Elliot's feelings anyway.

Chapter 13

Josh needed to leave early to meet Gloria's flight. Early was probably the wrong word. He wasn't leaving early; he just wasn't staying as late as usual. He had planned a romantic weekend that he knew Gloria would like. He could see it now. He'd whisk her into the townhouse for a candlelit dinner. Then, after dinner, he'd take her to the bedroom, where he had strewn red roses across the bed. The perfect beginning to the perfect weekend.

And they needed this weekend. In the last few months, their times together had been hit and miss, at best. If not her schedule, then his, had prevented them from getting together as planned. They hadn't been together, without the interference of work, since the weekend of their boat trip with Marilyn and Elliot. And that seemed so long ago, which was why Josh had planned such a special time this weekend.

And that's why Josh was so impatient with today's meeting. As soon as this meeting ended, his perfect weekend could begin. Would Carla never finish? he wondered. These Friday afternoon meetings were the only thing he didn't like about his job. Who scheduled Friday afternoon meetings anyway? And these meetings always lasted until six. That wouldn't be a problem if he and Gloria weren't commuting. But it was hell when he had to make an eight-hour drive to Atlanta or a run to the airport to pick up Gloria.

Finally, Carla was wrapping it up. He'd be out of the building in fifteen minutes. Twenty at the most. A quick stop in his office and then he'd be gone.

He saw the message propped on his desk as soon as he walked into his office. Don't let this be some major problem, he thought. He walked to the desk and picked up the note. From Gloria. Don't go to the airport, it read. Call her.

Damn, he thought. What was going on? He knew, but he didn't want to know. He flopped down in his chair and punched in her number on the telephone key pad. She picked up on the first ring. "Why are you still in Atlanta?" he asked.

"I'm sorry. I can't make it this weekend. The Cascade businessmen want a meeting tomorrow morning. We've run into a snag with the financing. It's an emergency, Josh. Please understand."

Josh didn't say anything. He thought about the townhouse. The dinner. The bed. His plans. Their weekend. All gone. And she wanted him to understand.

"Say something, Josh."

"I'm disappointed you can't make it," he said. *That was calm. That was good.*

"I'll make it up to you. I promise."

Sure. She had no idea of the plans he'd made and she was talking about making it up to him. What could he say?

"I know you're upset and you have every right to

be," she went on, "but this couldn't be helped. The Cascade people could blow this whole deal if I don't handle it just right. Help me out here, Josh. Tell me you understand."

"It's not that I don't understand. It's that I don't believe it."

"I knew this would happen. I knew you wouldn't understand. I'm trying to make the best of our situation. What more do you want from me?"

I want to come first. Before work. Before clients. Before projects. "Let's just forget it, Gloria. You can't come. Don't worry about it. I'll drive down instead."

When she didn't respond, he asked, "You do want me to come home, don't you?"

"Of course, I want you to come home," she began. "It's just that I'll be so busy. I'd hate for you to make the trip and then I can't spend any time with you. You know how upset you were the last time you came home and I worked all weekend."

Josh couldn't believe what he was hearing. Gloria's work had never been this important in the past. "I wanted to see you, but if you're going to be busy, I'll stay here."

"I'll make it up to you, Josh," she said again. "I promise."

He had heard that before. "I know you will, Gloria," he said, but he didn't mean it. He didn't think she had any understanding of how important this weekend was to him. So, how could she make it up to him?

"Call me tonight?"

What else did he have to do? "Sure. Right now I'm going to head out of here. I'll talk to you later."

After they hung up, Josh sat at his desk and stared at the phone. Carla unexpectedly walked in. "Problems, Josh?" she asked.

He looked up and saw her walking into the office. She took a seat in front of his desk. "No problems."

"Couldn't tell it by looking at you. You look like you've lost your best friend."

For some reason that made him laugh. That was exactly the way he felt. Gloria was his best friend and he felt as if he was losing her and there was nothing he could do about it. "Gloria and I had plans for the evening and she has to work. So, I'm left to myself."

"I'm sorry it's taking her so long to find work here. I thought it would've been much easier."

"She's had some offers. It's just that her job in Atlanta is perfect. She hasn't found anything comparable. We're hoping she will and soon."

"So do I. By the way, I'm having dinner with Tom Kennedy and his wife tonight. You're welcome to join us if you like. No business. Just dinner. Tom's a good person to know. We're meeting at Dominic's around seven-thirty. You can just show up if you don't find anything else to do."

Josh's first inclination had been to turn down Carla's invitation, but at seven o'clock he was at Dominic's, looking for her and Tom. He saw Carla first. She was seated at the bar and she had changed clothes. He was surprised he even recognized her. That slinky red dress was a lot different from what she usually wore to work and her hair was down, not pulled back in its normal bun.

He walked over to her. "I see I'm not as early as I thought."

She turned on her stool and he saw that the dress didn't even come mid-thigh. When Carla went casual, she went casual. "No, handsome, you're right on time," she said.

He couldn't form a response. Was Carla coming on to him? He looked around. Where were Tom and his wife? He didn't know what to do. Damn, this was awkward. "Are you all right, Carla?" He knew that was a dumb question, but he couldn't think of anything else to say.

When she laughed, he knew he had said the wrong thing. "What's so funny?"

"You," she said. "Hi, I'm Darlene, Carla's sister. Carla's twin sister. I'm meeting her here tonight before her dinner."

Josh knew he visibly relaxed and then he was more embarrassed. She had stopped laughing, but she was still smiling like the cat who had swallowed the canary. "You knew I thought you were Carla, didn't you?"

She nodded. "People mix us up all the time, even though we have totally different personalities, not to mention"—she looked down at her dress—"different tastes in clothes. Didn't it throw you a little to see Carla dressed like this? Unless my sister has changed drastically in the last day, she'd never wear an outfit like this."

Josh had to agree with her. But since she looked exactly like Carla, he had assumed that Carla had varying tastes in clothes. "You enjoy doing this, don't you?"

She smiled that smile again. This time it was contagious. "Carla's friends and co-workers are usually such stuffed shirts. It's fun to see their reaction. You must be new since most Carolina Micro people know me and they're used to me. How long have you been here?"

"Almost four months," Josh answered.

She extended her hand. "Welcome to Raleigh. I hope you're here to stay."

He took her hand. "Thanks. I hope I'm here for a while myself."

"Married?" she asked.

He was taken aback at the question, but he answered it by showing her the ring on his finger. "Almost two years."

"Talk about bad timing."

Josh knew she was flirting with him, but it was a harmless flirtation. "I'll take that as a compliment."

"It was. You know, it figures."

"What figures?"

"All the good ones are taken."

He laughed outright at that. "How do you know I'm a good one?"

"Don't tell me I'm wrong. A man who looks like you can't be bad. Well, you could be, but it would be a good bad."

He laughed again. She was charming. And sexual. Very sexual. "You're outrageous."

"I'll take that as a compliment. Have a drink with me while we wait for Carla."

Josh took the bar stool next to hers and ordered white wine. He didn't have to say much because Darlene kept up a steady stream of conversation. She told him all the twin tricks she and Carla had played over the years. The stories gave him another picture of Carla. One that was much different from the Carla he knew from work. He filed that information away to think about at a later time. Now, he just wanted to listen to Darlene.

"Where's your wife?" Darlene asked. No topic was taboo for her. "I can't believe she let you out alone at night. I wouldn't if I were her."

Josh really didn't want to talk about Gloria with Darlene. It made him feel guilty. He and Darlene were engaged in harmless flirting, but he knew Gloria wouldn't approve. "She's working."

"She needs better hours. There are some women out here who consider a man without a date on a

Friday night as available whether he's married or not."

"Are you one of those women?" He knew as soon as he asked that he shouldn't have.

She turned to look at him. "I haven't been in the past, but there's something about you that makes me think I need to reconsider my position."

After she said that, she turned back around and sipped her drink. All his words about harmless flirtation went out the window. Her last statement had been said in all seriousness. He knew he should get up and leave right now. He was about to do that when she started in with another Carla-Darlene story. He couldn't leave in the middle of her story, could he? That's what he told himself while he sat there and listened to her soothing voice as she told her funny stories.

Gloria told herself over and over that this meeting was important. That this was part of her job. A part she liked, even.

"Mr. Thompson, we're going to work it out. They can't take the land. You have the deed."

The gray-headed Mr. Thompson shook his head. "I've seen it happen before, Mrs. Martin. You know how those big companies are. They can do anything."

Gloria smiled. She knew Mr. Thompson knew she was right, but he needed someone to hold his hand. He was getting pretty close to having his dream of owning his own store in the neighborhood where he grew up and he was getting antsy. Understandable.

"They can't do anything and you know it. You're just worried about the meeting tomorrow. Everything is going to be fine."

"She's right, Grady," Mrs. Thompson chimed in.

"You're just getting jittery. Now calm down or Mrs. Martin is going to regret she agreed to give us the money."

Grady Thompson took his wife's hand in his. "We're putting up all the money we have in the world. My wife's security, the money we could leave for the kids and grandkids. Maybe we're too old to open a restaurant. Maybe it won't work and we'll lose all our money."

Mrs. Thompson shook her head. She was a petite woman, at least a hundred pounds lighter and six inches shorter than her bear of a husband, but Gloria knew Mrs. Thompson was her husband's anchor.

"Enough of that, Grady. You're exaggerating and you know it. Now we need to get out of here so Mrs. Martin can go home. Her husband will be upset with us as it is. It's almost ten o'clock."

Mr. Thompson grudgingly stood up. Gloria knew he could have talked for the rest of the night, but Mrs. Thompson was right. She did need to get home. She'd hated to cancel her trip to Raleigh this weekend, but it couldn't be helped. She had to meet with the Cascade investors tomorrow. In addition to being the one to pull the financials together, she had become a source of support and strength for the merchants. The support role was a new one for her, but she enjoyed it.

After she had led the Thompsons out of her office, her first thought was to call Josh. She picked up the phone to dial his number, but she changed her mind and put it back down. She knew Josh would still be angry that she hadn't made the weekend and she couldn't blame him. But she couldn't help it either. She was in the middle of this project and she had to see it through. And tomorrow was another full day of meetings. She knew her schedule was playing havoc with their weekend plans, but there was nothing she could do about it until the projects were wrapped up.

She sighed a long sigh and promised herself that she would make this weekend up to Josh. She didn't know when, but she would. With that thought in mind she packed her briefcase and left the office.

By the time Gloria arrived home, she had thought of a way to salvage some of this weekend with Josh. If she couldn't be with him in the flesh, the telephone would have to do and she was sure she could make it as interesting as any of those 900 numbers. It'd be something different too.

First, she took a long, hot bath and massaged her skin with the perfumed lotion that Josh liked so well. She pulled a light, blue negligee from her closet and put it on. She felt sexy just thinking about what she had planned. She knew Josh was going to love it. She turned back the covers on the bed and climbed in.

She was about to pick up the phone when she realized she had forgotten the wine. She got out of bed and went to the kitchen for the wine. She couldn't have a seduction scene, even a telephone seduction scene, without wine, she reasoned.

Once she was settled back in bed, she picked up the phone and dialed Josh's number. "Hiya, handsome," she said when the phone was answered.

"This is Josh," was the response she got. "Leave a message at the tone."

Her disappointment was palpable. Where was he? she wondered. She hung up the phone without leaving a message.

She called every fifteen minutes until she fell asleep. The last time she looked at the clock it was one twenty-five.

* * *

When Josh woke up Saturday morning, he didn't remember much of the dinner with Carla and Tom and his wife, but he did remember Darlene. He was thinking about her when the phone rang. It was Gloria.

"I tried to call you last night," she said. "But you weren't home. What did you do?"

"I had dinner with some people from the office."

"I'm disappointed that I didn't get to talk with you, but I'm glad you weren't alone. I'm sorry again about the trip."

"Let's not keep bringing that up. What time is your meeting this morning?"

"I'm on my way out of the door now. I just wanted to hear your voice. I love you, Josh."

"I love you, too, Gloria." Josh hung up. He did love Gloria, but he had flirted big time with Darlene. And it had been fun. He wasn't doing anything or thinking about doing anything, but he had enjoyed her company a lot.

That was part of his problem, Josh thought. He hadn't made any friends in the time he had been in Raleigh. He was working a lot of hours so he didn't usually miss it, but this weekend he didn't want to be alone. He didn't want to miss Gloria because missing her made him angry with her. So, he reasoned, the best thing he could do for his marriage was to keep from missing her. Armed with that rationale, he now had to find something to do today. Darlene had mentioned a Greek festival on the Chapel Hill campus. He could pull out his fraternity T-shirt and trek over there. What better way to meet people?

Josh went upstairs and dressed in his fraternity T-shirt and jeans. He got his map, and after finding and circling the campus, he headed for his car. As he drove to the campus, he told himself over and over that he was going only to meet people, make a few friends. His trip had nothing to do with Darlene's comment that she'd be there all day. Besides, with the number of people that usually went to a Greek festival, the odds of him running into Darlene were slim to none. No, he wasn't looking for Darlene. He wanted to meet some of his fraternity brothers.

He continued to tell himself this until he pulled into the University parking lot. As luck would have it, Darlene pulled up in the space next to him. He looked over at her and smiled.

Chapter 14

"What are you doing here on Saturday?"

Gloria looked up from the contracts on her desk and saw Foster Dixon leaning against her office doorway. "This is my office, my building. What are you doing here? Slumming?"

Foster pushed away from the doorjamb and moved to the chair in front of her desk. "I had to go by the library. What's your excuse?"

"Cascade. I met with the principals today."

Foster leaned forward in his chair. "How's that going?"

Gloria wondered at his tone. She knew there had been talk about the project. Some of the other vice-presidents didn't think it was worth the effort she was expending. "What have you heard?"

He leaned back. "Don't go paranoid on me. I haven't heard anything." He paused. "Much."

"What does that mean?"

"There's been some talk. They say you're going

out on a limb for no reason. That you could have picked a safer project."

"And you? What do you think?"

He waved a hand in her direction. "Come on, Gloria. This project is peanuts. If you close the deal, who'll care? If you don't close it, it'll be a mark against you. I thought you were smarter than that."

"I'm disappointed in you, Foster. When the black community comes together to do something for itself, there is always a bunch of nay-sayers. It surprises me that you're one of them. I can't believe you don't see the merit in this project."

Foster stood and leaned over her desk. "I'll tell you what I see. I see a Florence Nightingale trying to save the world."

Gloria leaned toward Foster until they were almost nose to nose. "I'll tell you what I see. I see a black man who's forgotten what it means to be black."

Foster moved back, stung. Gloria had hit her mark. "Is that what you really think? You think that I don't care."

She didn't really think that. She hadn't really thought about it. "What am I supposed to think when you say you don't see the importance of this project?"

Foster pinched his nose. "My problem is not with the project. It's with your timing. Do you have any idea how hard it will be to get another project like Cascade if you fail with this one?"

She had thought about it, but not much. One of her investors had pulled out, but she knew she would find the money. She had to. "I won't fail."

"Whether you fail or not has nothing to do with you, Gloria. That's what I'm trying to tell you. This matter is engulfed in politics. You know, there are other investors interested in that area. Investors with a lot more money. Some people around here are hoping that you don't pull it off. Those other investors will mean more revenue for the bank. A lot more."

She knew he was right. Some people were waiting for her to fail. "Are you one of those people?"

Foster lifted both arms in the air. "How can you even ask that?"

"Just checking. Things are getting hairy around here. I wish Portia were around. I could always count on her support." This wasn't the first time she had thought about her friend. The workplace wasn't the same without her.

"I don't want you to blow this out of proportion. Not everybody is against you. There are those who are pulling for you, those who are wondering why the bank hasn't taken on more of these projects."

She raised a brow in his direction. "Huh?"

"No 'huh.' There are those who are very impressed with what you're doing. I admit, they're the minority, but you do have some people pulling for you. Louise, for one."

She was glad her boss was on her side, but her boss wasn't a friend. Portia was a friend. She could express her insecurities to a friend. She couldn't do that with her boss. "That's good to know."

They were silent for a moment, then Foster asked, "How is Portia?"

Gloria didn't know how she was. They hadn't spoken since Portia left on maternity leave. "She's fine."

"She sure surprised me, leaving like that. I thought she would have stayed around until the baby came."

Gloria had been surprised herself when Portia had told her she was leaving early. She talked about wanting to decorate the nursery, get ready for the baby. Portia had even chosen an extended leave instead of the three months she had originally talked about.

Gloria shook her head. It was as if she and Portia had changed lives. Portia had been the one concerned about leaving her job. Gloria had wanted to stay home with the baby. Things surely had changed over the last year.

Foster snapped his finger in her face. "Earth to Gloria?"

She looked up at him. "Sorry, Foster, what were you saying?"

He repeated what he had said, but Gloria tuned him out again as soon as he began talking. Her thoughts were still on Portia. She missed her friend and she regretted the distance she had put between them. A part of her blamed Elliot and his commentary. Seeing Portia made her feel guilty. Guilty because Portia's priorities seemed to be in the right place, while hers were questionable.

Foster literally ran into Portia the following Monday morning. "Hey, you'd better watch where you're going, little mother."

"Oh, hi, Foster. I'm sorry. My mind was somewhere else. What brings you downtown today?"

"I should be asking you that. I'm meeting with Eleanor. What are you doing here?"

"I just thought I'd drop by and say hi since I was downtown."

"Shopping?"

Portia grinned. "I have to have everything ready for my kid when she gets here, don't I?"

Foster laughed. "You know, I never would have thought you'd take mothering so seriously, but you're having a ball, aren't you?"

Portia placed her hand on her protruding belly. "I never thought it either, Foster. But it seems I've just fallen into it. I thought being home would drive me crazy, but I'm really enjoying it."

"Well, it shows. Maybe you ought to give some of that spirit to your girl Gloria."

"What do you mean by that?"

He shrugged his shoulders. "She seems to be strung a mite too tight. Things not going well with her and Josh and this commuter marriage?"

Portia thought Foster was probably right, but she wasn't going to gossip about her best friend. Even though she hadn't seen much of that best friend lately. She knew her pregnancy made Gloria uncomfortable, but she wasn't sure if jealousy or something else was the cause of that discomfort. "That's just wishful thinking on your part. You'd love it if things weren't going well with Josh and Gloria. You'd try to move right on in, wouldn't you?"

Foster had the decency to be honest. "I've never hidden my feelings for Gloria. If Josh messes this up, I'll be more than ready to step in. But right now I'm worried about her. She's too wrapped up in these projects."

"Gloria's always taken her job seriously. What's wrong with that?"

Foster shook his head. "Maybe I'm wrong, but I think you should talk with her. Unless I'm reading her wrong, she could use a friend right now."

That was all Portia needed. She would see Gloria today and they would discuss whatever it was that was causing the strain in their friendship. She missed her friend and she hoped Gloria missed her too. "I'll stop by her office on my way out. Thanks, Foster. Maybe you aren't the lecher that I've made you out to be."

Foster laughed. Before he walked away, he said,

"Don't be too sure about that. There's more than one way to go about a task."

Portia watched him walk away with an almost smile on her face. Gloria had better be careful, she thought.

"Have you been avoiding me?"

Gloria looked up and saw Portia's head poked in her office doorway. She didn't answer immediately because Portia was partially correct. "Don't be silly. Come on in."

As Portia walked into the office, Gloria felt a familiar pang of jealousy. Portia looked as if she were about to deliver any minute now. Gloria hadn't realized the strength of her feelings about Portia's pregnancy. It still pained her to see her friend. She and Josh didn't need a baby now. She knew that. They needed to get their work situations settled before even considering a family. Then, why did looking at Portia's stomach make her feel so empty inside?

Portia eased down in the chair and put her hands on her stomach. "You didn't answer my question. Have I done something to offend you?"

Gloria felt guilty about the way she had treated Portia. "It's nothing you've done. It's me."

"It's okay if you don't want to talk about it," Portia said.

Gloria smiled. Portia was not being herself this Monday morning. It was very much unlike her not to want to talk about anything. She wondered if pregnancy had mellowed her some. A part of her hoped not. "No, I do want to talk about it. Do you have some time?" At Portia's nod, Gloria told her about the conversation with Elliot that had been gnawing at her.

"Does what he said bother you because you think he's right?"

"I'm not willing to say yet that I think he's right, but he has a point. Why would I choose this job over following Josh? Does that mean I don't value my marriage as much as I value my job? What kind of wife am I?"

"Hold on a minute here," Portia said. "First of all, you didn't choose your job over Josh. You compromised with him. He needed to take the job in Raleigh and you gave him a way to do so. That sounds like a good wife to me."

Gloria wondered how she could have forgotten how supportive Portia was. She has done herself and Portia a great disservice by distancing herself. She needed her friend now more than ever. "But did we do the right thing? Could we have done something else? If we were more in love, would we have done something else?"

"There's no right or wrong. You made the best decision you could at the time. Has it been working?"

Gloria shook her head slowly. "Not really. Our work schedules are so busy that our plans for swapping weekends aren't working out with any regularity. It's like we have two separate lives." The Cascade project was consuming more of her time than she had planned. Time that she and Josh had planned to spend together.

"Damn. That's not good. What's it like when you are together?"

Gloria remembered her last visit to Raleigh. *Cordial* was the first word to come to mind. They hadn't argued. It was as though they were determined to have a good weekend. If not arguing meant a good weekend, then they had achieved their goal, but using any other measure the weekend had been a failure. They had made love, but that, too, was cordial.

"So what are you going to do about it?"

"Do? What can I do?"

"Come on now. If this were a problem with venture capital, you'd already have your game plan in hand. This is no different. You've got to get to work, girl-friend. That is, if you want to save your marriage. But if you don't, then—"

"Of course I want to save my marriage. Why would you even say something like that?"

Portia slid out of her chair and raised herself up. "I'm calling 'em like I see 'em. You're sitting around pouting about something somebody said about your marriage instead of trying to fix what's wrong with it. Doesn't sound like the right use of your energies to me, but then, what do I know?" When she reached the door, she turned and said, "Join Dexter and me for dinner sometime. We miss you."

Gloria stared at the door after Portia had waddled out. What had started out as an encouraging conversation had quickly turned defensive. Well, Portia could have given her some advice. Portia always gave advice. Hell, Elliot giving advice and Portia not giving advice. Was she in the Twilight Zone or what?

She wasn't in the Twilight Zone, but she knew she was at a critical point in her life and in her marriage. When she had married Josh, everything was so clear. They would get married, get established, have a fam-ily. Josh's job loss caused the plan to get off track. Now that Josh was employed again they were back on track. Or they should have been. With the raise Josh had gotten in his new job, they had already restored the savings they had depleted so money was not an issue. They were on track for Gloria to get pregnant and quit work. Therein was the problem. Did she still want to get pregnant? If she did, did she want to quit work?

She knew how her mother would have handled a situation like this. Her mother would have had the kids and continued the career. That was her mom. She had done it all. Or she had tried. She kept everything orderly, all right, but she was not the wife and mother that Gloria wanted to pattern her life after. No way. Not that women couldn't do both. It was just that her mother hadn't done it well. Gloria always felt that her mother valued her career above her family. She had vowed not to repeat that mistake.

That's why Elliot's comments had hurt so much. They made her realize how much she had changed. It discouraged her to think that she had lived so long with such unrealistic thoughts. How many families today lived on one salary? What made her think she and Josh could? No, when Josh had lost his job, she had realized how fortunate they were that she was working. It made her shiver to think how they would have fared if they'd had a couple of kids and she hadn't been working. She was glad to have gotten the reality check.

And, she admitted, it wasn't only the money. It was the work. She loved it. In her new position, she could do things that made a difference in people's lives, in the community. Didn't she have a responsibility to do that? If she left the bank, would her replacement be as sensitive to the concerns of the African-American community as she was? She didn't think so. No, if she gave up her job, it would be a loss for her and for those members of the African-American community that she could help.

This didn't mean that she no longer wanted kids; she did. But she knew she wouldn't stop working when she had them. No, she would do both. Besides, she had come to realize how much she enjoyed her work. And like her mother, she felt that her work was important. She thought that Josh knew now how important her work was to her, but she didn't know if Josh had concluded that she didn't want to quit her job even to have children.

Children? How could she think about children now? It took two people to make a baby, and with the small amount of time she and Josh spent together, it would be a miracle if she got pregnant. Especially since she was still taking the pill.

Chapter 15

Josh did a double take on the date on his desk calendar. It couldn't be, he thought. It couldn't be. But it was. His anniversary was coming up in two weeks. He couldn't believe he had let it slip up on him like this.

He got out of his chair and walked over to the windows, his hands in his pockets. What was happening to him and Gloria? They were growing apart. That's what was happening. They were too busy. Too busy for each other. But not too busy for Darlene, a small voice said.

Josh pushed the thought away. Things with Darlene hadn't changed. They were friends. Nothing more. He was still in love with Gloria. They just weren't making time for each other as they should. Too many things were more important than their time together.

He walked back to his desk and looked again at his calendar. He had a meeting the Friday of his anniversary weekend, but he was going to cancel it. He and Gloria would have this time together regardless.

He picked up the phone and dialed her number. "I'm asking you for a date. The weekend of the tenth. You have to go. No excuses allowed. What do you say?"

"I say, yes," she whispered. She had realized the date herself only yesterday. It had pained her to think that Josh had forgotten. Thank God he had remembered. "I almost forgot."

"Sweetheart, we have to do something about this."

She knew he was right. Four months into this commuter marriage and they both had to acknowledge that it wasn't working as they had planned. Gloria knew that much of the blame lay at her feet. Her work was consuming more of her time than she had planned, but what could she do? Now that she was in this Cascade project, she had to see it through. "What are we going to do, Josh?"

She heard him sigh and she knew she had given the wrong answer. "Let's just enjoy our anniversary. We'll talk about everything else after our trip."

Gloria didn't argue. She wasn't all that anxious to discuss their commuter marriage anyway since she still didn't have any answers. "Where are we going?" she asked, changing the subject.

She heard the smile in his voice. "I'm not telling you."

"Tell me. You know I'm going to find out anyway."

Josh laughed then. It wasn't a real laugh, but it was close. "That's one thing I don't have to worry about. There's no way for you to search through the closet here in Raleigh before the trip."

Gloria was leaving for the airport when the phone rang. She was tempted to ignore it, but she thought it might be Josh. "Yes," she said.

"Gloria, it's Dexter. We're at the hospital. Portia's in labor."

Gloria dropped her bag. "How is she, Dexter?"

"The baby's early, but the doctors say they're both fine." The words rushed out of Dexter's mouth. "I've been with her, but they made me leave the room while they do some tests." He put his hand to his head. "You don't think anything is wrong, do you?"

Gloria withheld a smile. Dexter was nervous and it was so endearing. He probably needed her support more than Portia did. "How about I come down and sit with you?"

"Would you, Gloria? I'd really appreciate it. I'm a wreck right now."

She smiled. "Sure, Dexter, I'll be there in twenty minutes. Sit tight. Everything's going to be okay."

Gloria hung up the phone and took a deep breath before making her next call. "Portia's in labor," she said when Josh answered the phone.

"Are you at the hospital?"

"No, I'm still home. I was on my way to the airport when Dexter called. I told him I'd be there in about twenty minutes. I'm sorry, Josh."

"Don't be sorry. I'll take a flight down tonight and meet you at the airport. We don't want to miss the birth of our first godchild. We have the rest of the weekend to celebrate our anniversary."

Gloria let out the breath that she had been holding. She didn't know what she would have done with Josh's anger. "You're not mad?" It was more an observation than a question.

"I'm disappointed, but I'm not mad. I want to be there for Dexter and Portia. I should be able to get to the hospital in the next few hours. Why don't you go on over there? Tell Dexter I'll be there as soon as I can."

"I love you, Josh."

"I love you too."

Portia delivered the baby an hour before Josh's cab dropped him off at the hospital. He found Gloria standing in front of the nursery glass staring at the baby. He watched her, wondering, all the while knowing, what her thoughts were. He walked over and stood behind her, placing his hand on her shoulders. "Which one is it?" he asked.

Gloria pointed to the third bassinet from the left. It was pink.

"A girl," Josh said, his voice full of awe. "She's gorgeous. Have they named her yet?"

Gloria nodded. "Paige," she said, her voice muffled by what he expected had been tears. "They named her Paige."

Josh pulled Gloria back against him. "How is Portia?"

"She's fine."

"And how are you?" he asked, turning her around so that he could see her. He was right. She had been crying. He wiped her tears. "Happy tears, I hope."

She nodded again. "You should have seen them," she said, her voice stronger now. "I don't know who was more excited, Portia or Dexter."

"Where's the happy father?" Josh looked around the empty corridor.

"He's with Portia. He's spending the night with her. Do you want to visit with them?"

"No, we can come back in the morning. I'm sure they want to be alone tonight."

"I think you're right."

"Are you ready to go home?" he asked. When she nodded yes, he took her hand and led her out of the hospital.

They were quiet for most of the ride home. Josh

watched Gloria even as he drove. Her hands rested protectively across her stomach. He didn't have to guess where her thoughts were.

"Do you think we'll be able to reschedule our trip?" he asked.

"I don't know, Josh," she answered absently. "My schedule is pretty busy and will be until this Cascade thing is settled."

"I don't remember your working this much before. Is it my overactive imagination or are you really working more?"

"It's not you. This project is taking a lot out of me."

"Does it have to?"

She didn't like the question because she didn't know how to answer it in a way that would make him understand. "Right now, it does, but it should be over soon." She went on to tell him about the snafu that had come up in the Cascade project.

"Do you think you're going to be able to pull it off?" he asked.

"Yes." Her answer was immediate. "This project is too important for me to let it fail."

Josh heard the surety and passion in her yes answer and it saddened him. Where would they be if she had that same passion for their relationship?

Josh was already in bed when Gloria finished in the bathroom. His gaze caught hers as soon as she walked through the door and he never let it go. She slipped the straps of her gown down her arms as she walked toward him. By the time she reached the bed, the gown and her underwear were on the floor. She stood before him naked.

Josh responded to his wife's nakedness by reaching

out his hand to her. When she took it, he squeezed
it tight and pulled her to him. Her eyes widened
when she saw that he was also naked. His heartbeat
increased.

When her silky skin touched his, he felt her heat.
Or was it his? Maybe it was theirs. It really didn't
matter. What mattered was that this was their anniversary and they were together. They had made it
through two years of marriage. But would they make
it through a third? an unbidden voice pushed through
his mind. He shook his head slightly to force the
thought away. But it was too late. The damage had
already been done.

Gloria saw the flash of uncertainty pass across Josh's
face and she wondered what had caused it. She
touched her hand to his face and pulled him closer
to her. "I love you," she said. "I've always loved you."

But will you keep loving me? he asked silently. Will
we always be together? He couldn't bring himself to
ask the question aloud. He did the easier thing. He
kissed her. No, he ravaged her mouth. It was as if
this kiss had to bind him to her. He pushed deeper
into her mouth, crushing her body to his. When she
moaned, he wondered if he was hurting her. A part
of him knew he should ease up, but he couldn't. If
he eased up, he would lose her.

Gloria felt Josh's desperation and matched it with
her own. She knew what he was feeling because she
felt it too. They were in trouble.

Josh lay awake listening to the rapid beat of his
heart, stroking his hand down Gloria's back as she
lay contented on his chest. It would take him a while
to get over this last bout of sex. He'd had orgasms
before, but not like this. He had come and come and

come. Maybe she'd get pregnant, he thought, then our problems would solve themselves.

Gloria lifted her head from his chest. A grin covered her face. "Have you been taking Superman shots or something?" she teased

Josh couldn't help but grin. His masculine ego received the well-deserved stroke. "Do you think we made a baby?" he asked.

He would have sworn the light in her eyes dimmed. "Maybe" was all she said.

He squeezed her to him. "I hope so."

Gloria lay her head back down on his chest and chided herself for not telling him the truth. But, she reasoned, she hadn't really lied. There was a chance she could be pregnant. Come on, Gloria, her conscience poked, how can you be pregnant if you're still taking birth control pills?

Gloria wanted to push her conscience away, but she couldn't. She should have told him. She should have told him a while ago. She'd gotten back on the pill the weekend Josh had gone to San Francisco. It seemed such a reasonable move then. Now, it seemed like betrayal. A lie. How would Josh respond when he found out? She didn't know and she wouldn't find out today because she wasn't going to tell him.

Chapter 16

"You do this well," Darlene said when Josh handed her the next stack of T-shirts.

"You think I missed my calling—I should've been a T-shirt vendor rather than a corporate engineer?"

She shrugged her shoulders. "That's not what I meant. It's just that you seem so comfortable here. Sometimes you corporate honcho types have problems doing the small tasks. You're more comfortable giving orders."

"There's a time for everything and today's a day for fun. Being the boss can be a burden. I'm sure you know that from your sister."

Darlene shook her head. "Carla's not like that. She lives and breathes her work. Wherever she is, whatever she's doing, she's the plant manager. Look at her now."

Josh looked to where Carla was directing the sack race. Darlene was right. To look at Carla, you'd think she was planning a new clean room, not organizing a group of ten-year-olds for a sack race. "Your sister is intensive."

"About everything. To a fault."

Josh broke down the box that had held the T-shirts and folded it. "Do I detect a bit of hostility? I thought you and Carla got along well."

"We do. It's just that I find her intensity tiring. She was like this even as a child. I don't see how she keeps it up."

"So you went in the opposite direction?"

She punched him in the shoulders playfully. "I didn't know you were an armchair psychologist."

She hadn't answered his question, but he was willing to let it ride. "Are you planning to get into any of the games today?"

She looked at him as if he he'd ask her to fly to the moon. "Two guesses."

Josh laughed. He had known from her outfit that she wasn't going to participate. The shorts might allow it, but the braless T-shirt wouldn't. "Do you usually come to these company gatherings?"

"Every now and then. This is my first one in about four years."

"Why this year?"

"I think you know the answer to that."

Was she saying she had come because of him? he wondered. "I don't think I do."

"I came to see that invisible wife of yours. Why isn't she here today?"

Gloria. Josh hadn't thought about her today. They had decided last weekend that she wouldn't come to this event since it was being held during the week. Unlike the other times when their schedules hadn't allowed them to share events, neither of them seemed upset or disappointed by this. After the failed honeymoon trip and Portia's new baby, they needed the time apart. That was good and bad. Good, because they were supporting each other and trying to work through this separation as best they could. Bad, because maybe they didn't expect much of each other these days.

"So, where is she?" Darlene asked again.

"Working."

"And she couldn't get away?"

Darlene had to know about their commuter marriage. Surely Carla had told her. "She had to work today and tomorrow. It would have been too much for her to come up today and get back to Atlanta tomorrow."

"What's she doing in Atlanta?"

"Come on, Darlene. You know that Gloria still lives in Atlanta."

She shook her head. "I knew no such thing."

He sighed as he realized Carla hadn't told her.

"Gloria and I have a commuter marriage. She's looking for work here and I'm looking for work in Atlanta."

"Is it working? I mean, are you enjoying this?"

"I'd be lying if I said it wasn't hard, but we're getting used to it."

She looked skeptical. "I don't know if I believe that."

"Why shouldn't you?"

"Because of us."

Josh froze in the middle of stacking the T-shirts. "What us?" he asked, but he knew what she was talking about. Since that Greek festival at Chapel Hill, he and Darlene had found themselves in the same company six or seven times. They always suggested that it was coincidence, but they both knew it wasn't. They enjoyed being together.

"If you don't want to talk about it now, we won't," she said, "but soon you're going to have to decide."

Josh didn't want to think about that. He knew what she was talking about. So far they could honestly say that they had a platonic relationship. The most they were guilty of was flirting, but they both knew that with only a small step from him, the relationship would move to something more. Did he want that?

Josh knew that what he did or didn't do with Darlene was directly related to the state of his marriage. He knew things weren't good between him and Gloria now and he knew a relationship with Darlene would only make matters worse. He still loved his wife and he wanted his marriage to work, but sometimes he wondered if there was any hope of that happening. He had racked his brain and had concluded there was nothing he could do to make things better. If he quit this job and moved back to Atlanta, their situation wouldn't be any better. They'd be under the stress of his unemployment. Now, they were under the stress of their separation. They couldn't win for losing, he thought.

"Have I scared you away?" Darlene asked.

He brought his attention back to her. He could walk away from Darlene now if he wanted to. But he didn't want to. "Me, scared away? Never."

She smiled at his words and they were back on the merry-go-round.

Two weeks later, Josh went to a fraternity gathering where Darlene just happened to be present. He got home a little after midnight. The evening had been an eye-opening one. The sexual attraction between him and Darlene had always been there. Now, it was getting out of hand. He wanted her. And he knew she wanted him. It would only take a word from him and she'd be in his bed. They both knew it. He suspected Darlene was counting down the days until he broke. If things continued to progress as they were, he knew his days were limited. Now was time for drastic action.

Josh picked up the phone and punched the number to his home in Atlanta. "Hello," Gloria answered in a voice full of sleep.

"I'm coming home in the morning. I need a few days off."

"What?"

He knew she was half asleep but he had to do this now. "I'm driving home in the morning. I'll be there in time to meet you for lunch. Can you do that?"

"Lunch? Yes, I think so."

She was still groggy and he hoped she'd remember their conversation tomorrow. "I'll come straight to your office."

"Okay. I need to go back to sleep now."

Before he hung up, he added, "I love you." He heard the click of her hanging up so soon after his words were spoken that he doubted she had heard them.

He had taken the first step. He was going home to fight for his marriage, his wife. The way he saw things, he and Gloria needed to end this separation. Their six months were up. Since they had always planned for Gloria to quit work when they started a family, he would suggest to her that they start their family now. Why shouldn't they? They were back on track with their original plan now that he was employed, so they could pick up where they had left off. It's a reasonable plan, he thought. He knew she was tied to her job and he was willing to give her enough time to settle her two biggest projects. After that, he wanted her with him. He wanted them together.

As Josh got ready for bed, his thoughts turned to the possible objections Gloria could have to his proposal.

What if she didn't want to have a baby now? He disregarded that one as a low probability. He knew she would love to have a little girl like Paige. No, that shouldn't be an objection.

What if she didn't want to leave her job? That was an easy one. He'd suggest that she take a leave of absence instead of quitting.

What if she didn't want to move to Raleigh? That wasn't an option. The whole point was for them to be together. If he was going to be the working spouse, she would have to go where he was.

What if she didn't want to sell the house? He knew that could present a problem. That house represented many of their dreams. They could buy a house in Raleigh. Somehow he'd have to convince her to sell the house in Atlanta. Holding on to it was not a rational option.

Josh got into bed and finally faced the question that was forever in the back of his mind. What if she said their marriage wasn't worth the changes he was asking of her? That would be a killer. He had no answer for that. She had to still love him. She had to. But what if she didn't? Josh fell asleep without an answer.

Neither Gloria nor her secretary was present when Josh arrived at her office, so he waited. He was pretty anxious, though he tried to hide it. He had gone over every possible scenario in his mind during the trip down. They were going to work this out. They had to.

He sat in Gloria's chair with the back of the chair facing the door. He heard her voice and was about to turn around and greet her when he heard a male voice. For some reason, he didn't turn around.

He heard them move to the conference table. "About the Cascade financing," Gloria said. "What do you think of the numbers?"

Josh heard the shuffling of paper.

"Seems like a good deal for the borrowers. Couldn't the bank have gotten a higher interest rate?" The male voice belonged to Foster Dixon.

"I take that to mean it's a good deal."

"Let's not get into that again. When are you going to learn that this bank is not a charitable organization? We're here to make bucks. Big bucks."

Josh heard Gloria's laughter and could imagine Dixon's leering smile. The man was forever in Gloria's face.

"This is a good deal for the bank and you know it," she said. "A higher interest rate would be criminal since this is a community project."

"What else do you have for me?"

"That was it. I just needed some feedback on this package before I submitted it. It's going to fly. I know it."

Now get up and go, Dixon, Josh thought. You've done your duty.

"How about lunch?" Foster asked Gloria.

"Not today. I'm having lunch with Josh. As a matter of fact, I'm expecting him any minute now."

Dixon laughed and Josh wondered what was funny. He didn't have to wait long to find out.

"Come off it, Gloria. Josh might be Superman but not even he can go out to Atlanta for lunch, or are you telling me that he's moved back to town?"

The bastard, Josh thought. Trying to make a move on my wife. Josh felt like turning his chair around and telling that Dixon bastard exactly what he thought.

"No, he hasn't moved back to town, but he's going to be in town for a few days. Of course, you're invited to have lunch with us."

"Right," Foster said, his words dripping with sarcasm. "Like I want to have lunch with you and Josh. No, the invitation was for you only."

"I don't know why you keep pursuing this. You know I'm committed to Josh."

Good girl, Josh thought. Tell him.

"I was beginning to believe that until this ridiculous commuter marriage. No man in his right mind would leave you like that."

Josh heard more paper shuffling, then Gloria said, "I'm not getting into this with you again. Thanks for reviewing the file."

Her words sounded pretty final so Josh assumed she was signaling Dixon to leave. He was right.

"Okay, Gloria. I'll back off for now, but when you get tired of waiting for that guy to come to his senses, I'll be waiting."

"Then you'd better be prepared for a long wait," was Gloria's response.

"I've always felt that anything worth having was worth waiting for. And you're definitely worth the wait."

This guy was reaching back to lines from the seventies, Josh thought.

Josh heard Gloria's office door close and assumed that Foster was gone. He was about to turn around in his chair when Gloria caught the back of it and turned the chair around. She gasped when she saw him. "You scared me. Why didn't you say something to let me know you were here?"

"I started to, but when I heard Dixon's voice I decided not to intrude on the meeting. How is Dixon these days?"

"Foster?" Gloria was relieved their banter hadn't gone further. "Foster is still Foster."

"So, he's been giving you the rush while I've been away?"

"Like I said, Foster is still Foster. He's harmless. You heard our conversation."

"He didn't sound so harmless to me. The guy pledged to wait until you got tired of me."

Gloria leaned over and kissed Josh on the nose. "You're jealous and it's cute, but not necessary. You heard me tell Foster that he was in for a long wait."

Josh got up from Gloria's chair so she could sit at her desk. "Has he always been that bad?"

"How about the Crab House for lunch?" she asked, effectively changing the subject. "I have a craving for seafood."

"Craving?" Josh wondered if Gloria had been thinking about babies as much as he had.

"How about it?"

"Fine. Wherever you want to go. Can we leave now?"

"Sure. Let me check my messages first."

They decided to walk to the Crab House since it was only a few blocks from Gloria's office. They both had the special Chef's Seafood Salad. In a quiet booth in the back, they discussed their work.

"Congratulations on the financing for the Cascade

project." At the question in her gaze, he added, "I overheard you and Foster talking about it."

"Thanks. It was touch and go for a while, but now it's all done but the final paperwork. I'd guess two months tops."

"That's good. How's the Turner Hill project going?" If it were wrapping up, now would be the perfect time to bring up his ideas.

"Most of the work on that is done too. At least the part that I'll be involved in."

So far. So good. "So any other heavy hitters on your plate?"

She shook her head because she was chewing. "I'll be talking to Louise about that in the next few weeks. I've got my eye on a shopping center in South Fulton. How are things at Carolina Micro?"

If they were going to make a move, they'd have to make it before she got the South Fulton project, Josh thought. There was no doubt in his mind that she would get it. "We're as busy as ever. I'm overseeing an expansion that includes a new clean room. When it's up and running, the required direct and indirect support will increase my staff by seventy-five people."

"That's great," she said, but she was uneasy. Josh was building an empire, a life, in Raleigh. "How's Carla?"

"She's still the same. A little rough around the edges but she knows her job and she does it well."

"Good. And I'm glad that you've started to make friends outside of work. Your fraternity affiliation really panned out, didn't it?"

Josh's thoughts went immediately to Darlene. "Yeah, it did. The guys have kept me from being too lonely."

She winked at him. "I don't know if I like the sound

of that. I hope it doesn't mean that you don't miss me."

Josh laughed because Gloria was being coy. "No, it just means that I'm not miserable with loneliness. I miss you a lot."

"And I miss you. This separation has been a lot harder than I expected."

She'd given him the perfect opening. "Yeah. I've been thinking a lot about that. I think I have a solution for us."

"Have you found a job here?" she asked in a high-pitched tone.

"No, that's not it. I thought that since neither one of us was having success in that area, we needed to explore something different."

"Don't keep me in suspense. What's your idea?"

"I've been thinking that we should start our family. We were at that point when General Electronics caved in. Now that we're back on our feet, it's the perfect time."

The silence was loud. He could hear her thinking. She didn't like the idea. It was taking her too long to answer. "What do you think?" he asked.

"I'm surprised, Josh. I didn't expect this as your solution. How can we think about having a baby when we don't even live together?"

Josh thanked God that he had gone through the scenarios. "That's what's so good about it. We had planned for you to stop work when we started a family. So, you can move to Raleigh and we'll be together."

"You've thought this out, haven't you?"

He nodded. "What do you think of the idea?"

Gloria looked at her watch. "I think we don't have enough time to get into this now. I have to get back for a meeting. Let's table this discussion until I get home tonight."

Josh nodded his agreement and signaled for the check. He knew it was going to take some energy to get Gloria to agree with this idea. But he knew he could do it. He had to. Too much was at stake.

Gloria could barely concentrate on the meeting. Her thoughts were on Josh and their lunch conversation. So, he thought the solution to their problems was for her to get pregnant and move to Raleigh. Exactly what she had feared.

There was actually nothing wrong with Josh's proposal. It would have been perfect if she were the same person that she had been when they married, if she'd had the same goals. But she wasn't and she didn't. How was she going to make him understand that?

She thought he had seen how important her work was to her, but she must have been wrong. If he had understood that, he would never have proposed this solution. Well, she thought, Josh had one thing going for his idea if nothing else—timing. If she were to leave, now, with her major projects drawing to a close, was the perfect time.

"I'd like to see you in my office." It was Louise. Gloria knew the meeting was over because everyone was leaving. She hoped Louise hadn't noticed how distracted she was.

When she was seated in Louise's office, Louise said, "It's time to choose. Which one do you want—South Fulton or Alpharetta?"

Her answer was automatic. "South Fulton."

Louise pushed the folder that had been lying in front of her over to Gloria. "Somehow I thought that would be your choice."

South Fulton was written on the cover in big, bold,

red letters. Gloria opened the folder and scanned the first page. "I thought this was going to be a shopping center. This says medical complex."

Louise nodded with a knowing smile. "And look at the numbers."

"God! This is five times the amount that was needed for the shopping center."

"You're right and it's yours. It goes without saying that you're lucky to get this. Not that you aren't deserving, but pull this off and you're minutes away from your next promotion."

Gloria thought it ironic that this would happen on the same day as Josh's plan to change their lives. How could she even consider leaving now? A medical center in South Fulton. A project that would mean so much to that community. A project that would take at least a year to pull together. At least.

"I knew you'd be excited," Louise was saying. "The folks upstairs were impressed with the way you handled Cascade. The publicity it generated for the bank was invaluable. They were anxious for you to get this one. Aren't you going to say something?"

All Gloria could think about was the discussion that she and Josh were having tonight. She needed more time. She needed Josh to understand that.

"Gloria," Louise said, "I've never known you to be speechless. Say something."

"You know I love community projects. This hospital is just the type of project I wanted next. I need to look over the file, but I'm excited about it."

"Good. Take the time you need. We need to get a game plan together within the next month. I'll leave it to you to do that. Let's get together the middle of next month to see how you've sized it up. How's that?"

"Great, Louise."

Gloria left the office with conflicting feelings. A part of her couldn't wait to tear into the file. Another part of her was afraid to even open it. If she opened it, she knew there was no chance in hell she'd go along with Josh's proposal.

Chapter 17

Josh was listening to Gloria, but he couldn't believe what he was hearing. "We agreed on six months and it's been six months. You have to move to Raleigh," he said.

Gloria stood and began clearing the dishes from the table. He followed her into the kitchen.

"Aren't you going to respond?" he asked.

Gloria put the dishes in the sink and began rinsing them. "You aren't listening to me, Josh."

He grabbed her hand and turned her around. "Will you please stop with the damn dishes? This is an important conversation we're having."

Gloria removed her hand from his, pulled out one of the dinette chairs, and took a seat. "Okay, you have my full attention. Now tell me again that I should quit my job."

Josh put his hands on the back of the chair facing hers, but he remained standing. "Don't make me out to be the heavy here, Gloria. Our plan has always been for you to quit work when we start a family. Well, it's time to start a family."

"Says who? Don't you think we should make that decision together?"

Josh flopped down in the chair. "I thought we had already decided," he said softly. "It seems you've changed your mind."

"It's timing, Josh. I'm not ready to have a baby." She knew she was hurting him, but she had to tell him how she felt.

"I could see how you responded to Portia's pregnancy. You can't tell me that you don't want a baby."

He was right. She did want a baby. Just not right now. They both needed to find work in the same city first. "What if you're out of work again, Josh? What then?"

That was it. She had gone for the jugular. What could he say? "That won't happen."

"You promise?"

Josh stood up and presented his back to her while he went through the motions of getting a glass of water. She had him there. He couldn't promise. "We didn't go broke this last time, did we? Anyway, I'm more prepared now than I was last time. I don't have all my eggs in the Carolina basket."

"I'm scared, Josh. Scared. It was difficult when it was just the two of us. Think what it would have been like with a couple of kids. You have to admit that my working helped."

"You're right, it did. But that was then and this is now. We can't live our lives based on what bad things might happen."

"Neither can we afford to be naive about this. From a financial perspective, I need to keep working."

Josh pulled out his chair and sat again. "Look, Gloria, I don't have a problem with your working. If

you want to go back to work after you have the baby,
I'll support that decision. It won't be my preference,
but I promise I'll support your decision. But that still
doesn't address our present problems. This commuter marriage is not working. We're growing apart.''

She knew he was right. She just wasn't ready to
accept his alternative. ''We'll just have to do better
with our schedules . . .''

Josh jumped up out of his chair. ''Come on, Gloria.
Wake up and smell the coffee. It's not going to work.
You don't want another job, so you're never going
to find something you want in Raleigh.''

He was right. ''What about you? I don't see you
interviewing here in Atlanta.''

Josh shook his head back and forth. If she couldn't
see what was happening to them, there was nothing
he could do. ''I looked for nearly eight months before
I went to Raleigh. I've told you once and I'll tell you
again. There's nothing here for me.''

''There's nothing in Raleigh for me.''

''What about me, Gloria, don't I count for something?''

''I could ask you the same question. Why do I have
to give up my job?''

Josh was beat and he knew it, but he had to give
it one more chance. ''How about we compromise?
You take a leave of absence. We see how it works in
Raleigh. We think some more about a baby. This way
you won't have to give up anything.'' Even as Josh
said this, he knew it was risky. They were continuing
to postpone a decision that they had to make. He
would force it now, but he wasn't sure he'd get the
answer he wanted. ''So, what do you say?''

''I don't know, Josh. I'll have to think about it.
Taking a leave of absence is better than quitting outright.''

Josh hadn't gotten what he wanted. He had wanted her to put their marriage before her career. He had wanted her to believe in his ability to take care of her and their children. But she hadn't. He couldn't fault her reasoning, but where did reasoning leave them? She was in Atlanta. He was in Raleigh. Darlene was in Raleigh. And he needed a wife.

"Let me know when you decide what you're going to do, Gloria," Josh said as he got in his car for the drive back to Raleigh on Sunday morning. She said something, but he didn't bother listening. He started the car and pulled out of the driveway.

The tension between him and Gloria had intensified since their discussion Friday night. The more he thought about the situation, the angrier he became. Gloria was selfish. He wasn't asking her to quit her job, just to take a leave of absence. She'd think about it, she said. Well, he hoped she made the right decision. For both of them.

The message light on his answering machine was flashing when he walked into the house. His first thought was that Gloria had come to her senses. He rushed to the machine and pressed the Play button.

"Call me," the voice said. "I'm in the book."

It was Darlene. Josh pressed Rewind and then Play again. He did this three times.

He knew what he was doing when he went for the phone book. This was the first time Darlene had sought him out, called his house. He could have told himself that he had to return the call because it had something to do with work. Maybe Carla had an emergency. But he knew that wasn't it. No, Darlene had called because she had gotten tired of waiting for him to make a move. She was forcing his hand and he knew it. Hell, he'd half expected it. That was why so much had been riding on his trip to Atlanta.

He found Darlene's number and jotted it down on the pad next to the phone. Was this the moment of truth? What would he say if he called? What would she say?

He picked up the phone and dialed six of the seven digits written on the pad before hanging up. He couldn't do it. He couldn't coldheartedly betray his marriage vows. And he knew that's what he'd be doing with that phone call.

Josh finally saw Darlene Friday night in the bar at Dominic's. She was wearing the red dress she had worn the first night he had seen her. It was an understatement to say that she looked good.

He watched her take a seat near the end of the bar. Before she was fully seated, some guy was making a move on her. She smiled at him, but obviously she turned him down because he soon walked away.

She saw Josh when she turned to watch the man walk away. Without a second thought, she walked over to his table.

She looked around before taking a seat. "You've been avoiding me, Josh Martin. And now you're out drinking alone. Could there be a connection between the two?"

"How do you know I'm alone?" he asked. "Gloria could be here with me."

Darlene smiled and took a sip of her drink. "I don't think so, Josh. Something tells me you're very much alone."

Josh belted down his gin and tonic and signaled

the waiter for another. This was his fourth, maybe fifth, drink of the evening. "Darlene, the psychic."

"Don't be mean," she said, though she didn't appear insulted by his comment. "I may be the only friend you have right now. Why didn't you call?"

Josh drank from the fresh glass the waiter had brought him. "I think you know the answer to that. I'm a married man, Darlene."

"You could have fooled me. I never see any wife around."

Josh grimaced. "I'm not interested, Darlene. I'm perfectly happy in my marriage."

"Right. That's why you're out drinking yourself silly. What happened? Did the little woman let you down again?"

Josh knew Darlene had no idea how close to the truth she had gotten. Gloria had called this afternoon saying she couldn't make her visit to Raleigh this weekend. He wasn't surprised as much as he was hurt. He had hoped Gloria would have come to a decision about moving to Raleigh, but it seemed that all of her energy was directed toward her work. She probably hadn't even thought about them, their marriage. He reconsidered that thought. Maybe there was nothing to think about. Maybe her decision was already made and she just couldn't bring herself to tell him. That conclusion had led to his first drink and then his second and then his third . . .

"Afraid to answer the question, Josh?"

Josh put his glass down and looked at Darlene. At this moment, he hated her. At this moment, he wanted her more than he ever had. He took the last drop from his glass. "I'm leaving."

He swayed when he stood up and Darlene got up to help him. "How many drinks have you had tonight?"

Josh thought it was only five. Maybe it had been more. "A few."

"More than a few, I'd think. You're not driving home."

Josh pulled a few bills from his wallet and threw them on the table. "Like hell I'm not."

Darlene followed him to the parking lot, where he fumbled with his car keys. He tried to open the door, but he couldn't find the slot. "I need a little help here."

Darlene took the keys from him and dropped them in her purse. "You do need help. And I'm going to give it to you by driving you home. My car is over here."

Josh was in no mood to argue so he followed her to her car. He felt light-headed and his vision was fuzzy. The movement of the car out of the parking lot didn't help matters any. By the time they reached his townhouse, he knew he was going to have a terrible hangover in the morning.

Darlene helped him to the door, fished through his keys, and let them both in. He made it as far as the couch before he fell, more than sat, down.

"Thanks for driving me home," he said.

When she didn't respond, Josh looked around but he didn't see her. "Darlene," he called out. He thought about getting up to look for her, but his light-headedness made him remain seated.

When she finally came into view, he asked, "Where were you? Didn't you hear me calling you?"

"I heard you. I was just checking out the place. Nice bachelor pad you have here. Ready for bed?"

Josh knew it was another invitation. "Yes, but you're going home."

Darlene smiled and leaned over to take his arm,

pulling him up from the sofa. "I don't think you're going to be able to navigate those steps without my help, so be nice."

Josh didn't say anything, but he allowed her to help him up the steps to his bedroom. Once there, he sat on the edge of the bed and kicked off his shoes. He unbuttoned his shirt after a few false starts and flung it on the floor in front of him. He removed his belt, but he had trouble with his pants. He was able to pull them down past his hips, but Darlene had to grab both legs and pull them off. He opened his mouth to say something, but suddenly he was so very sleepy.

Darlene pushed him back on the bed. "Just go to sleep. I can let myself out."

She lifted his legs and placed them on the bed. He was asleep before he could thank her.

Darlene looked at his sleeping body, clad in only his undershorts. She had known from their first meeting that Josh would bring nothing but heartbreak her way. And she had been right. She looked at him now and she knew she was in love with him. As crazy as it sounded, she was in love with Josh Martin. Married Josh Martin.

She sat on the bed next to him and wondered how she could have allowed this to happen. A married man. A married man in love with his wife. She knew Josh loved Gloria. That she had never doubted. What she had doubted and what had given her hope for a relationship with Josh, was that she wasn't so sure that Gloria was in love with him. She knew that if Josh were her husband, she wouldn't be content to be separated from him the way Gloria was. No, Gloria didn't love Josh and she didn't deserve him. Josh deserved a woman who would love and support him the way he needed to be loved and supported. Darlene thought she was that woman.

She looked at her watch. It was after midnight and she was tired. The prospect of driving home didn't appeal to her. She looked again at the sleeping Josh and made her decision. She stripped down to her camisole and panties and climbed in next to him.

Gloria still didn't have an answer. She loved Josh and she wanted to be with him, but she was afraid to be without a job. She hadn't realized until lately how much of her self-esteem was wrapped up in her work. Could she make him understand that? Did she understand it?

The drive from Atlanta to Raleigh had given her some thinking time and she knew in her heart that she wanted to have that baby and be with Josh. She would tell him that when she surprised him with her visit.

Her thinking had started in earnest Friday night. After she had hung up from telling Josh that she wasn't going to make her trip, she had faced some truths about herself, him and their relationship. Josh was right that the commuter arrangement wasn't working. There were too many times, too many reasons, that she had let other things come first. So, even though she should be working this weekend, she wasn't going to. She was going to put Josh and their marriage first. Something she should have been doing since he moved away.

She pulled her car into the driveway and went to the door. She used her key because she wanted to surprise him. Once inside, she tiptoed up the stairs to his bedroom. Easing the door open, she walked slowly into the room. The blinds were closed, but the early morning light shone through the slits. Josh, dressed only in his undershorts, was asleep on the bed. Her heart filled with love for him. She moved to the bed, dropping her clothes among the ones he had discarded earlier.

When she sat on the bed next to him, she was naked. Instead of kissing him, she looked at him for a long while, thinking of the life they had shared so far and the bright future that lay before them.

As she leaned down to kiss him awake, a strip of white cloth caught her eye. She reached behind him and picked it up. She thought her eyes were playing tricks on her, but she was wrong. It was a half-slip. A woman's half-slip.

She held the slip in her hand, not wanting to face the reality of what it meant. She let her eyes wander to the clothes that were strewn across the floor. She wondered how she had missed them when she walked in. A dress. A bra. Shoes. None hers.

Her heart was breaking and there was nothing she could do to stop it. Should she wake Josh? What would he say if she did? What did she want him to say?

Oh, my God. Why hadn't it occurred to her before? The woman was still in the house. Gloria quickly put her clothes back on, gathered up the woman's clothes from the floor, and started through the house looking for her. She checked the bathroom first. No one there. Then she went downstairs. The light was on in the kitchen. She wondered why she hadn't noticed that when she first came in? She knew why. All her thoughts had been centered on seeing Josh. Nothing else had registered.

She walked toward the kitchen. As she got closer, she heard someone humming. Then she saw her. It was Carla, Josh's boss. Gloria couldn't believe it. Josh and his boss. She didn't know what she was going to say or do, but she had to face this woman who was sleeping with her husband.

Carla stood at the stove, half-naked and humming while she scrambled eggs. Bitch, Gloria thought. The nerve of this woman, standing in my kitchen, cooking my food.

"You and Josh have some extra work to catch up on last night, Carla?" Gloria asked.

Darlene turned around. She was shocked but she recovered quickly. "Who are you?"

Bold bitch, Gloria thought. "Surely you haven't forgotten me. I'm Josh's wife, Gloria. But then maybe it's to your advantage to forget about me. Makes it easier to carry on an affair with Josh, doesn't it?"

Darlene removed the fryer from the flames and cut off the gas. She turned to Gloria. Without bothering to correct Gloria on her identity, she said, "Josh and I are friends."

"Friends?" Gloria could have scratched the woman's eyes out then. "Right. Look, I'm not here to have a conversation with you. I want you the hell out of my house."

Darlene looked around the kitchen. "Your house? How much time have you spent here, Gloria?"

"Look, I want you out of this house now." Gloria walked over to Darlene and pushed her clothes into her hands. "Get your clothes on and get out."

Darlene laid the clothes on the counter and began to dress. "You don't want him, Gloria, and I do. Why don't you let him go?"

"Who are you to tell me what I want and don't want? Josh is my husband and I'm not letting him go. Not for you, not for anybody."

"Maybe you won't have to. Maybe Josh will make that decision for you."

Gloria reached out and slapped Darlene, then yelled, "Get out of this house now."

Darlene seemed unable to move. The slap had surprised her. Little Gloria had more spunk than she had given her credit for. "Why don't we ask Josh what he wants? He's upstairs, you know. Still asleep. He had a *long* night."

Gloria didn't miss the innuendo in Carla's words. She walked to the front door and held it open. "Get out."

"What's going on down there?"

Both women looked to the stairs. Josh stood there in his undershorts.

Chapter 18

Josh looked from Gloria to Darlene, then back to Gloria. "It's not what it looks likes."

"Get this woman out of my house, Josh."

Josh walked toward Gloria. "Don't come near me," she said. "Just get her out of here."

Josh looked to Darlene. "I think we need some time alone, Darlene. Thanks for bringing me home last night."

Darlene nodded at Josh, then looked over at Gloria. "My car is in the garage. She has to move her car from the driveway so I can get out."

Gloria slammed the front door and said to Josh, "You get her out of here." She then stomped up the stairs.

She first went to their bedroom, Josh's bedroom, but she couldn't stand it there, so she went into the other bedroom and sat on the bed. Agitated, she got up and began to pace the room. It all began to crash down on her. Josh had cheated on her! He had actually slept with somebody else. Not somebody else.

He'd slept with his boss. She couldn't believe it. What a fool she'd been.

She wondered how long it had been going on. She'd had an uneasy feeling about Carla since their first meeting. That understated beauty of hers. Well, it hadn't been understated today.

Gloria sat back down on the bed. Was Carla the reason Josh had agreed so readily to this commuter marriage arrangement? Had he planned to sleep with her from the beginning?

Before she could reason out an answer to that question, Josh walked into the bedroom. "It's not what it looked like, Gloria."

She looked up at him. How could she have been such a fool? "I find her clothes strewn across your bedroom floor—"

Josh held up his hand. "Hold on here. What are you saying?"

"Her clothes were strewn across your bedroom floor and she was standing half-naked in your kitchen. How does that look from your position, Josh? From mine, it's pretty obvious what went on."

Josh shook his head like an innocent. She was amazed that he could muster a look of surprise, no, shock, at her words.

"I don't know what you walked in on, but nothing happened between Darlene and me," he said. "I got a little drunk last night and she brought me home. I fell asleep and I thought she went home."

"Obviously, she didn't. And obviously, she slept here. With you. In your bed."

"I didn't sleep with her. I don't know what you found when you got here, but you have to believe me. I did not sleep with Darlene."

It registered that Josh called her Darlene. "Is Darlene some other woman you're seeing? That was Carla."

Josh walked toward her. "Carla? No, that wasn't Carla. That was Darlene."

Gloria held up a hand and Josh stopped in his tracks. "Stop the lies, Josh. I've met the woman before."

"I'm telling you that wasn't Carla. It was her sister, her twin sister, Darlene."

"Twin sister? You're sleeping with your boss's twin sister." She laughed an hysterical laugh. "You like living dangerously, don't you?"

"No, I'm not sleeping with her. And yes, she is Carla's sister."

It didn't matter who she was. Josh had broken their vows. He had brought another woman into their home and made love to her. "I can't believe you would do this to us, Josh. How could you after all we've shared?"

Josh looked at his wife standing away from him, tears, hurt, and anger in her eyes, and he knew this was the lowest point in his life. He never thought they'd come to this. He blamed himself. He had already told her that nothing happened with Darlene, but she didn't believe him. Maybe it was because he didn't say it with much conviction. The sad truth was he didn't remember. The last thing he remembered was Darlene helping him up the stairs.

He was ready to swear that nothing had happened between him and Darlene. How could it? He was drunk.

"I'm telling you that nothing happened. Darlene is my boss's sister, for God's sake."

Gloria laughed. If he hadn't been looking at her, he would have sworn it was a happy laugh. "Did you know that I was jealous of Carla when I first met her? Seems I was right to be so. It must have been easier for you to fall into the sack with the boss's sister rather than the boss.''

Josh went to her and grabbed her with both hands. ''I did not sleep with her. Why can't you believe me?''

She looked at his hands on her arms. ''Take your hands off me.'' When he didn't move, she added, ''Now. Take your hands off me now.''

Josh dropped his hands. He moved to put them in his pockets and realized that he wore only his undershorts. God, what a situation this was.

''She was practically naked when I found her in the kitchen this morning. Her clothes were strewn all around your bedroom. How do you explain that?''

Josh couldn't explain it. He couldn't remember. He cursed himself for drinking like that. There was really no excuse for it. God, he was just like his father. He hadn't hit Gloria like his dad hit his mother, but he had hurt her to the same degree, if not more. Right now he hated himself. ''I can't explain it. Just know that I'd never intentionally hurt you. Trust me.''

''You don't ask much, do you, Josh?''

''We can get past this, Gloria. It doesn't have to hurt us.''

She laughed that laugh again. ''Doesn't have to hurt? You must be joking. Do you know what your Darlene asked me?''

Josh had no idea what Darlene had said to her. He had rushed her out of the house so quickly that he hadn't had time to question her. ''What?''

Gloria met his gaze. The hurt he saw reflected there made him hurt. ''She asked me to let you go. Seems she knows a lot about our personal life. How did she get it? Pillow talk?''

"Dammit, Gloria. It's no secret that we don't have a traditional marriage. Most people here know that you still live in Atlanta."

"Don't even think about blaming me for what you did with Darlene."

"I'm not blaming you. I'm just saying that some people think our being apart means there are problems in our marriage."

"Right now, Darlene is the problem in our marriage. How long have you two been dating?"

"Dating? What the hell are you talking about?"

Gloria sat on the side of the bed again. "You said she brought you home. I assumed you had gone out together."

"Well, you assumed wrong. She saw me in a bar, and when she noticed I was a bit drunk, she offered to drive me home. End of story."

"Not according to Darlene. She didn't try to hide the fact that she wants you. Are you telling me that you didn't know she felt this way?"

Josh hated that question even though he had known it was coming. Yes, he knew Darlene's feelings, but he'd never encouraged them. But he hadn't done anything to discourage them either, and that was his mistake. "I knew."

"Did you discourage her interest?"

"Yes."

Gloria got up then and walked over to him. For the second time this morning, she slapped somebody. "I know you well enough to know when you're lying, Josh." She brushed past him and ran down the stairs.

Josh followed her.

"What did you do with my keys?" she asked.

"Where are you going?"

She found the keys on the kitchen counter. "I'm

going back to Atlanta. There's nothing here for me."
She walked past him to the front door. She opened
it and asked, "Where's my car?"

When he didn't answer, she asked again, "Where
the hell is my car?"

"It's in the garage. I moved it earlier."

She closed the door. "I see. You moved it when
your girlfriend moved hers out of the garage. To hell
with you, Josh Martin." Gloria stomped through the
kitchen and out the door to the garage.

Josh watched her leave and he could think of nothing else to say. The garage door went up and she
backed out. Without another look at him, she sped
off down the street.

Josh pressed the button on the garage door control
panel, causing the door to come down, and walked
back into the house, closing the door behind him.
He looked around the kitchen and saw that someone,
Darlene, had been preparing breakfast. He wondered
again what had happened between them. Had Darlene really spent the night in his bed? If she had, had
they had sex together?

He was angry with Darlene for what she had said
to Gloria. If she had told Gloria they were just friends
and explained what had happened the night before,
he and Gloria might have been able to work this out.
But no, Darlene had her own agenda.

He could only be a little angry with Darlene though,
because he knew he had led her on. He had allowed
her to think that there might be a chance for them.
There was only one person that he could be angry
with and that was himself. And maybe, Gloria.

If Gloria had listened to his plea last weekend, none
of this would have happened. He would have been
in Atlanta helping her pack instead of in some bar
getting drunk. Still, he knew that was no excuse.

The drinking had gotten him into trouble. If he hadn't been drunk, Darlene wouldn't have come home with him and set this horrible chain of events in motion. Yes, it was the drinking.

After she had turned off their street, Gloria realized she wouldn't be able to drive much farther. She was beginning to shake with nerves, and the tears falling from her eyes made it difficult for her to focus on the road. She headed for the main highway, where she hoped she could find a hotel.

Somehow she managed to register and get to her room. Once there, she stopped trying to keep herself together and let her emotions have free rein. It started with a wail, the sound of a wounded animal. She heard the sound and it startled her at first. Then she realized the sound had come from her.

Josh called Gloria in Atlanta every fifteen minutes after the time he thought it would have taken her to drive home. Either she wasn't home or she wasn't answering the phone. He prayed nothing had happened to her on the way. If something had happened, surely he would have been contacted. So, he assumed she wasn't answering his calls. He couldn't much blame her. He didn't know how he was going to fix this. He had checked the airlines and decided to take a Sunday afternoon flight into Atlanta. She needed some time. He'd give her some, but not much. They had to get this settled. Gloria needed time to adjust to her feelings, but too much time would allow her imagination to go overboard.

He had just dialed her for the fifth time Sunday morning when his doorbell rang. He wondered who was visiting at this hour. It wasn't like he had lots of guests.

He opened the door and was surprised to see Darlene standing there. "What do you want?" he asked.

Darlene pushed past him and came into the house. "Where's the missus?"

Josh stood at the door, not bothering to close it. Darlene would be leaving soon. "What did you tell her, anyway?"

Darlene sat on the couch. "You may as well close the door, Josh. I'm not going anywhere until we talk. And I know Gloria's not here."

Josh closed the door and walked over to her. He deliberately chose to sit in the chair opposite her and not on the couch next to her. "Okay, what do you want to talk about?"

"Us."

Josh shook his head. "I tried to tell you this yesterday, Darlene. There is no us. There can never be any us. I love my wife."

"But your marriage isn't working," she explained. "Can't you see that?"

Josh didn't like her attitude. It was one thing for him to think that his marriage wasn't working, but it was a whole other thing for someone else to sit in judgment. "You're way out of your league, Darlene. I'm not giving up on my marriage. Can't you get that through your head?"

"No, I can't. I thought you would know that about me by now. I don't give up easily when there's something I want."

Josh stood and walked over to sit next to her. "I know I've led you on, Darlene, and I'm sorry, but I'm not leaving my wife and that's final."

Darlene looked up into his eyes and smiled. Her look reminded him of a look he had seen once in

Carla's eyes. A look that made him wary. "I know you mean what you're saying, Josh. At least you mean it for now. But my guess is things are going to change. Your little Gloria is not very happy right now."

Josh knew there was no reasoning with Darlene. All he could do now was get her out of here so he could get to the airport. He stood and she stood, too.

"Okay, I'm leaving," she said. "You have my number." With that, she sauntered to the door and let herself out.

Josh stared at the door after her. At this moment he wished he'd never met her at Dominic's. After all that had happened, he was still attracted to her.

Gloria checked her answering machine, and as she had expected, all the messages were from Josh. He had no idea she was still in Raleigh. She debated stopping by the townhouse on the way home to give them one more chance at a reasonable discussion. She didn't make a conscious decision, but she found herself in front of the townhouse. She didn't stop, but she slowed her speed long enough to read the license plate of the car parked in the driveway. She didn't know why she was surprised—she had looked like a vanity plate kind of girl. Gloria sped away, the Darlene moniker firmly planted in her mind.

Josh was seated at the counter when Gloria walked through the kitchen door. She had known he was there because his car was parked in the garage. That had given her a few minutes to get herself together, to prepare what she was going to say to him. When she saw him, all that preparation went away. She was raw emotion.

"What are you doing here?" she asked.

He faced her, meeting her eyes. "I live here, remember?"

"Hmmph," was her response. She walked past him to the stairs, headed for their bedroom. When she walked through the bedroom door, the smell of betrayal met her. Even though she had found Josh and Darlene in the other house, somehow they had also invaded this bedroom, this bed. She backed out of the room, bumping into Josh in her rush.

He pulled her into his arms. "What's wrong?"

She jerked away from him. "I can't stay in that room. Not with you. Not without you." She moved on down the hall to one of the guest bedrooms, consciously not choosing the one Josh had slept in when he'd moved out of their bedroom.

He followed her down the hall and would have followed her into the bedroom, but she slammed the door in his face and locked it. He stood outside the door and twisted the knob. "Open the door, Gloria. We need to talk." When she didn't answer, he added, "Please open the door."

"There's nothing to talk about," came her voice from the other side of the door. She remembered Darlene's car in his driveway earlier this morning and wondered if he had made love to her before leaving Raleigh. Would the pain ever stop? She didn't even find peace in sleep. In her dreams she saw Josh making love to that woman.

"There's a lot to talk about. Our marriage. I love you, Gloria. I don't want to lose you."

Gloria sat on the bed, her head in her hands. She wanted to cry but she couldn't find the tears. They were all gone. She was one mass of shivering pain. "You should have thought about that before you went to bed with your girlfriend. Did you love me then? Were you thinking about our marriage then?"

"How many times do I have to tell you that I did not sleep with her?"

When would he stop lying to her? Even if he hadn't slept with Darlene last night, he would have in time. His look told her that. The boldness that Darlene exhibited with her was not just bravado. She had reason to believe she had a chance to take Josh away from Gloria. Gloria knew Josh had given her that hope. "What was she doing at the townhouse then? Is she the maid?"

Josh leaned against the door. "I told you. I was drunk. She drove me home. Can't you believe that? Gloria?"

"I drove by the townhouse this morning. Her car was parked in your driveway."

Josh fought for a response. There was no right answer. If he lied, she'd know. If he told the truth, he'd be in more trouble.

She lay back on the bed, eyes wide open, and stared at the ceiling. "Your lack of response answers the question. Now, will you please leave me alone?"

She wished she could erase the entire weekend from her memory. The scenes kept playing over and over in her mind. There was no way to escape them. She'd never forget the pain she'd felt when she'd seen the woman's clothes in their bedroom. Or when she'd found her half-naked in their kitchen. It was all such a nightmare. And then the humiliation of standing there arguing with that whore about her own husband. God, she couldn't believe she'd actually done that.

What was she going to do now? Everything was different. She and Josh weren't special anymore. They were just people. People who had somehow lost sight of each other. People who had a sham of a marriage. The tears began to flow then. She wasn't cried out after all.

Josh dragged himself back to their bedroom and sat on the bed they had shared. He lay back and remembered all the good times they had shared. In bed. And out. He squeezed his eyes shut and blocked out the other thoughts that fought with these happy ones. Images of Gloria's face when he'd walked in on her and Darlene Saturday morning. That was a look of hurt and anger that he'd never seen on her face before. And he was the cause of it.

If only he could undo this whole relationship with Darlene. He should never have encouraged her. It was all his fault. What was he going to do?

Chapter 19

Gloria was glad to go to work Monday morning even though she'd have to deal with Foster Dixon, who was shepherding the South Fulton deal. Finally, she could concentrate on something other than the problems in her marriage. Josh had gone back to Raleigh, thank God. She couldn't deal with him right now.

As if he heard her thinking about him, Foster walked into her office. "Ready?"

"Of course," she said. She got up from her desk and walked over to the conference table. "Let's get started."

Gloria was surprised at how well she and Foster worked together. For all of Foster's machismo, he was a team player, soliciting her ideas and considering her opinions. Not once did he make a personal overture.

"How about lunch?" he asked when they were finished.

Feeling good about their accomplishments, she said, "Sure. I could use a break."

They ended up at Mick's on Peachtree. Mick's brought thoughts of Josh, which she quickly shoved aside.

She ordered the pasta instead of her usual grilled chicken salad. Again, she wanted to keep thoughts of Josh at bay. Unfortunately, Foster ordered the salad.

"What's the matter?" he asked.

Surprised and embarrassed that her emotions were so close to the surface, Gloria shook her head. "Everything's fine."

"Good," Foster said. "I don't want you having second thoughts about lunch with me. I couldn't believe my good fortune when you decided to come without your chaperon."

Gloria laughed softly at his reference to Portia. "I usually need a chaperon with you. You can be bad sometimes."

Foster took a drink from the Coke the waiter had delivered to the table. "What was different about today? I really didn't expect you to come."

Gloria didn't want to talk about her reasons. She had told herself that she had come because Foster had behaved so well at the meeting, but she knew there was more to it than that. And that reason concerned Josh. "Maybe I just felt adventurous today," she said with a coy smile.

Foster nearly choked on his drink, though his recovery was admirable. "If I didn't know you better, I'd swear you were flirting with me."

She smiled, but said nothing.

"Well, well, well. Has Josh been a bad boy?"

That was the wrong thing to say. It hit too close to the truth. She never would have agreed to this lunch if things weren't strained between her and Josh. "Discussions about Josh are off-limits."

"Okay, pretty lady. I don't want to talk about him, anyway."

Gloria smiled again. This was what she needed. To feel desirable and attractive. Josh's betrayal had made her question her desirability and attractiveness. It was clear now why she had decided to lunch with Foster. She wanted him to confirm those things that Josh had caused her to question.

When they got back to Gloria's office, Foster asked, "How about dinner one night this week?"

She hesitated before answering. Did she really want to do this? "I don't know."

"I don't bite," he said with a grin.

"I'm not too sure about that."

"I'll make it easy for you. We can make it a working dinner. A brainstorming session of financing alternatives for South Fulton."

What's the harm in a little dinner? she asked herself, ignoring her conscience. "Okay, how about Thursday? That'll give us both time to think more about South Fulton."

Josh endured Monday morning. His thoughts were with Gloria, so concentration on work was impossible. Amazing, he thought, how the actions of one night could so drastically affect his life. Everything that he held dear was in jeopardy. Gloria and his marriage. They were what was important. How had he lost sight of that?

He had done nothing but think since Saturday. He wondered how things had gotten so far out of hand. How did he end up leaving Gloria in Atlanta in the first place? Married people are supposed to be together. Job or no job, they should've been able to work it out in Atlanta. Why hadn't they been able to do that?

That was the million-dollar question. Their marriage had been rocky ever since he'd lost the General Electronics' job. He had thought this new job would help put those problems behind them. Looking back on it now, he realized how naive they both had been. If they couldn't work out their problems together, they sure as hell couldn't work them out apart. Maybe that was what Elliot had tried to tell him. But he hadn't listened. And look where it got him. He should have taken Elliot's counsel more seriously. After all, he and Marilyn had made it through the rough patch in their marriage. Hindsight, he thought, was always twenty-twenty. Maybe he should have taken Elliot up on his partnership offer.

Josh knew he had to do something. Before Saturday's incident, he had hoped Gloria would move to Raleigh. Now, that was out of the question. She wasn't going to move and he didn't blame her. What woman in her right mind would give up her job and move away from a home she loved to follow a man she couldn't trust to be faithful to their marriage vows? Not Gloria.

He knew, too, that he and Gloria couldn't work out their problems apart. So, he had to move back to Atlanta. He picked up the phone and called Elliot. "Are you still looking for a partner?" he asked.

"You can't do it," Carla said.

"Watch me," Josh responded. He was surprised at Carla's attitude.

"You have a contract with Carolina Electronics and

I'm holding you to it. If you leave, I'll have you in court so fast, your head will spin."

He had seen that look on Carla's face before, the hard-driving, do-anything-to-get-the-job-done look that made him uneasy. "That doesn't make sense. Why would you go to all that trouble? Let me out of the contract and we can forget the bonus compensation that I've earned. I have to move back to Atlanta. Now."

Carla got up from her seat, walked around, and sat on the edge of the desk to face him. "And I need you here. Maybe we can work out some kind of compromise. I can give you a month's leave, six weeks tops."

He caught her gaze and held it. "That's not good enough. I need to move." Too much is at stake, he added to himself.

Carla went back to her chair and sat down. "Well, I won't let you out of the contract and you won't accept my compromise. Unless you can come up with another alternative, I'd say you're stuck."

At that moment, he wanted to wipe that silly smirk off her face. "I understand your position, Carla, and I know I'm asking a lot, but there's no way I can fulfill the terms of that contract."

She picked up a pencil and began writing on the ledger in front of her. Without looking up, she said, "I suggest you get back to work."

Josh stared at her for a few long seconds before leaving her office. He strode back to his office, slamming the door behind him. There was no way he was going to allow this job to cause him to lose his marriage. There was more than one way to skin a cat and to get out of a contract.

The phone rang and Josh picked it up. His "hello" sounding more like "What do you want?"

"It's Elliot. I got your message. Are you serious about coming into business with me?"

"I'm willing to talk about it. That is, if you're still interested."

"Hell, yes, I'm still interested. When will you be in town again?"

"This weekend." He'd have plenty of time to talk with Elliot since he had a feeling Gloria wouldn't be doing too much talking. At least, not to him.

"That's great. We'll talk then. I'm excited about this, Josh. I could sure use your help."

"From the little I've heard from Gloria, it seems you're on your way. I'd understand if I'd waited too late to take you up on your offer."

"No way. I'm not letting you out that easily. I need you, all right."

They said their goodbyes and Josh hung up. He wondered again why he hadn't considered Elliot's offer seriously when he had first made it. If he had, he wouldn't be having these problems in his marriage now. Well, it was too late to go down that road again. He had made what seemed like the right choice a few months ago. Only in the glaring light of hindsight was it so obvious that the choice was wrong.

Foster postponed his dinner meeting with Gloria until Friday night. She was surprised that she had such a good time with him. They talked business, but he also provided that confirmation of her womanliness that she so needed. And he provided it in such a way that she could still feel that she had been faithful to her marriage vows.

When he got back to her house, he invited himself

in for coffee. Against her better judgment, she allowed him in.

Foster followed her into the kitchen to help with the coffee. When she reached up to pull the coffee canister from one of higher shelves in the cabinet, Foster came up behind her.

"I'll get that." He came so close that his chest touched her back, then he reached up and got the canister. When he placed it on the counter in front of her, he rested both of his hands facedown on the counter on either side of her. She stood trapped in the middle of his arms.

She didn't know what to say or what to do. It had been such a nice evening that she didn't want to put a pall on it. So, picking up the coffee canister, she turned within his arms and smiled up at him, the canister the only thing separating them, "Thanks. Now, can let me out of this cage?"

Foster smiled back at her, but he didn't move. "You are the most beautiful woman I've ever known," he said. "I've thought that from the first day we met."

God, she needed to hear those words. Needed to know that someone other than Josh found her attractive. But she knew this situation could easily get out of hand. The flirting was okay, but she wasn't ready for anything more. A picture of Darlene flashed through her mind. Maybe she was. "Foster . . ."

"Don't, Gloria. For this one night, let me tell you how I feel. For a few minutes, let's pretend you aren't married. Hell, Josh doesn't even exist." When she would have interrupted, he added, "Just a few minutes. If you want me to go away after I've had my say, I will. But if you want me to stay, I'll do that too."

She looked up at him and saw the sincerity and love in his eyes. She wondered how she could have missed the depth of his feelings for her. All this time she had thought he was just flirting, but the look in his eyes told another story. Foster Dixon was in love with her.

He saw the recognition in her eyes. "You never knew?"

She shook her head. It was as if she was in some sort of trance. Maybe she never saw it because she only looked for love in Josh's eyes. "I'm so sorry, Foster."

He removed the canister from her hands and put a finger to her lips. "Don't say anything more. Let me have this time with you. Okay?"

She didn't say anything more. She just stood there thinking about this man who loved her. She knew then that there was more to Foster Dixon than she had ever imagined. It caused something inside her to open up and she knew that this was a moment that she wanted too. Not a lifetime, because she still loved Josh. But a moment. A moment to get herself back after that awful run-in with Josh and Darlene. A moment to show this wonderful man that she appreciated what he was doing for her.

Josh found them like that. Foster's body hid Gloria from his sight, but he heard Foster's words and he didn't see Gloria try to get away. Anger rose up in Josh like a fountain, and before he knew it, he had stormed over and pulled Foster away from Gloria. He turned Foster around and punched him in the jaw.

Foster, too surprised to block the blow, was knocked off balance. Gloria stood with her mouth open, looking from Foster to Josh and back again. Finally she said, "Josh, I didn't know you were coming in tonight." She could have kicked herself as soon as the words were out of her mouth.

Josh glanced at Foster. "That I believe. Was I interrupting something?"

Gloria decided this was a conversation they needed to have alone. She looked at Foster, who was rubbing his jaw. "Are you all right?" she asked. When he nodded, she said, "Let me walk you to the door. Josh and I need to talk. Alone."

Foster nodded at Gloria, but his look sent daggers at Josh and he didn't move to follow Gloria out of the room.

"Foster, please don't make this situation more difficult than it already is."

Foster brushed past Josh and followed Gloria out of the kitchen. At the front door, he asked, "Are you sure you're going to be okay?"

Gloria nodded. "He's not going to hit me, if that's what you mean. More than that, I can't answer."

"I'm sorry if I've caused you any problems, but I had to tell you how I felt. It's been eating me up for years. Maybe now I can get over you. That is, unless you decide you do feel something for me."

"Oh, Foster, I'm in no position to feel anything for you. Regardless of what happens with Josh and me, you should go on with your life. There's some lucky woman out there just waiting to make you happy. Don't waste your love on me." She reached up and kissed him on the cheek. "Thanks for dinner and everything else. You'll never know how much the evening meant to me, how much I needed what you gave me. I'm just sorry I couldn't give you more."

Foster stared at her for a few seconds as if willing her to love him back. Then he nodded and headed for his car.

Gloria eased the door shut and leaned her head

against it. Josh's voice caused her to turn around. "What did you say?" she asked.

"You heard me. I asked how long you've been seeing him."

Gloria saw the hurt in Josh's face and a part of her was glad that she was able to hurt him. Another part of her wanted to hold him in her arms and let him know that no other man had taken his place. Instead, she brushed past him and went back to the kitchen.

Josh followed her. "Are you going to answer my question?"

Gloria put the coffee canister back in the cabinet. She no longer wanted coffee. All she wanted was to go to bed. Alone. "I'm going to bed, Josh. I'm not going to stand here and be interrogated by you."

Josh watched her leave the kitchen as if nothing had happened, as if he hadn't seen her standing in Foster Dixon's arms. That bastard. Josh wished he'd given him more than that one punch. He couldn't believe it. The guy was in his home, making time with his wife.

Josh pulled out a dinette chair and sat down. It was too much. First, him and Darlene. Now, Gloria and Foster. What was happening to his marriage? His life? Would he ever get back what he had? At this point, he really didn't know. All he knew was that, right now, he hurt as he had never hurt before. And the worse part of it was that he had brought it all on himself.

He put his head in his hands and cried.

Chapter 20

Josh looked for Gloria after he got up the next morning, but she wasn't in the house. She may have eluded him this morning, but she couldn't avoid him forever. He'd see to it. It was probably good that she wasn't in now since he was scheduled to meet with Elliot this morning.

An hour later, he was in Elliot's garage. "So, you've decided to join me in this venture. I'm glad, but something tells me it's not just the great opportunity that I've put before you that led you to this decision."

Josh knew Elliot deserved an explanation. If they were going to be partners, they needed to be honest with each other. "You're right. It's not just the opportunity. I think I should have seen that earlier." When Elliot didn't respond, he continued, "I also should have listened to your advice on this commuter marriage. It's not working."

Elliot took two chairs from a table, offered one to Josh, and took a seat himself. "I'm really sorry about that, Josh. Marilyn and I both hoped you and Gloria would pull it off."

"Well, we couldn't. And now I need to get back to Atlanta to save my marriage."

"Is it that bad?"

Josh nodded. "It's worse than you think. Gloria thinks there's another woman."

"And why would she think that?"

Josh looked at his hands because he didn't want to see the look on Elliot's face. "Because there was."

"Josh! I don't believe it. Not you. You didn't cheat on Gloria."

He looked up at Elliot. The shock and disbelief that he saw didn't surprise him. "No, I didn't, but I came close. And she found out. I have to move back to save my marriage."

In a way, Elliot felt relief at Josh's words. Maybe now he could let go of the guilt over what he had said to Gloria that night. "I'm sorry it took these circumstances to bring you back, but I'm glad to know that I'll have you on my team. I need you, Josh."

"That's good, because I need you too. There's something else you should know."

"What's that?"

"Carolina Electronics is making noise about not letting me out of my contract. I think it's a scare tactic, but I thought you should know."

"Can they really do that?"

Josh nodded. "I signed the contract so I'm legally bound, but I don't see why they'd want a disgruntled executive. I've offered to forgo all bonus compensation. That should be enough to satisfy them."

"Could they make you stay?"

"Technically, but it'd take a court battle and I don't think they're up for that."

"If they are, would they win?"

"Unfortunately. I'm trying not to think about that. I just want you to know that all our discussions are based on the assumption that I can get out of the contract. Is that okay with you?"

Elliot nodded. "Of course, I'd like it better if everything were settled, but I can dangle for a while."

"I should know within the next month. How's that?"

"Hey, I want you with me and I'll take you any way I can get you."

"Good then. Now that we've gotten all that out of the way, let's talk shop. Where do things stand?"

Josh spent the rest of the morning going over Elliot's plans for his first production run. By lunchtime, he was excited about their prospects. He knew they would make a lot of money if they did everything right.

"Do you want to stay for lunch?" Elliot asked. "Marilyn would love your company."

"Not today, maybe some other time. Has Gloria talked to Marilyn about our problems?"

Elliot shook as head. "If she has, Marilyn hasn't told me. Actually, we haven't seen much of Gloria lately."

"Maybe it's been too difficult for her, knowing that you two made it through your rough time and we didn't."

Elliot nodded, but he knew the real reason Gloria hadn't been around. It was him. He had overstepped his boundaries. He knew he had to come clean with Josh about it. "That's not all of it."

Josh looked up at Elliot. "What more is there?"

"I told Gloria how I felt about your commuter marriage arrangement."

"And she didn't take it too well," Josh finished for him. "What exactly did you say?"

"I don't remember exactly, but I know she took my comments to mean that I thought you and she had misplaced priorities."

Josh nodded. "Well, you were right."

"But that doesn't help me with Gloria. We haven't spoken since then."

Josh clapped Elliot on the back. "Don't worry about it. You told Gloria the truth and she wasn't ready to handle it. I wasn't ready then either, but I am now."

"Do you think you and Gloria will work things out?"

Josh only knew what he wanted. "I know we will," he said and added a silent prayer that he was right.

"Maybe he's telling the truth," Portia said, her gaze on the napping Paige in the stroller in front of their bench. "Maybe nothing happened."

Gloria lifted a brow in Portia's direction. "You've got to be kidding. Josh was lying to save his ass."

Portia took her eyes off her baby and looked at Gloria. "Maybe not. Josh is an attractive man and women today will do anything to get an attractive man. Maybe it happened the way he said. She brought him home and he fell asleep. Everything else could have been her doing."

Portia had no idea how much Gloria wished she could believe that. Unfortunately, she didn't have the luxury of wishful thinking. "It was more than that. You didn't see her and you didn't hear what she said. Something was going on between them. Even if he didn't sleep with her that night, they were involved."

"I still can't believe it. Not Josh."

"I guess you don't want Dexter to be like him, now, do you?"

Portia looked away from Gloria and toward the mime who was performing in the park. "Maybe the rub-off worked the wrong way and Josh is being like Dexter."

"What do you mean by that?"

"Dexter has . . . ah . . . strayed in the past."

Gloria touched Portia's arm and Portia looked at her with tears in her eyes. "Portia? When? Why didn't you tell me?"

"It was the second year we were married. I think it only happened once. And I didn't tell you because it was too painful and our friendship was too new."

"Oh, I'm so sorry, Portia. I can't imagine going through something like this alone. I knew I had to talk to you. If I had known it would be painful for you, I—"

Portia patted Gloria's arm. "That's all right. I'm just glad I can be here for you."

"How did you deal with it, Portia? You and Dexter seem to have recovered very well. I would never have guessed."

"It was very difficult. The most difficult thing I've ever done. My whole world crashed when I found out."

Gloria understood those feelings because they were hers exactly. How did you get past them? she wondered. "How did you find out?"

"She called me. Can you believe the nerve of that bitch? She said that she was sleeping with my man, and if I didn't believe it, I could find his car at her house at a certain time."

"Oh, no, Portia. What did you do?"

"I hung up on her, but I couldn't forget the call. Though I told myself over and over that I would trust Dexter, I checked it out. Dexter said he was going to a basketball game with a few friends. An hour or so after he left, I drove by her house. His car was parked out front."

"God, Portia. You didn't go in, did you?"

"No. I couldn't go in. I didn't want to see them. Sometimes I think that's why we could get past it. If I had seen them together, I don't think I would have been able to erase the picture from my mind."

The picture of Darlene in the kitchen of the Raleigh townhouse flashed in Gloria's mind. "That's the way I feel. Even though I didn't see them in bed together, I saw her standing in his kitchen in her panties and camisole. She was cooking breakfast like she lived there. I can't get it out of my mind."

"You're going to have to find a way to deal with it or you and Josh don't stand a chance."

"I know that. I just don't know how to do it. What did you do after you saw Dexter's car?"

"Somehow I drove myself back home. I don't know how, because I cried all the way. I still couldn't believe it. I told myself over and over that there was some other reason that he was there, but deep down, I knew there was no other reason."

"Did you confront Dexter about it?"

She nodded. "When I got home, I sat on the living room couch and waited for him. I sat there for almost three hours waiting for him. You can imagine the thoughts that went through my mind. Those were the longest three hours of my life. Anyway, Dexter knew something was up as soon as he walked through the door."

Seeing her friend's distress, Gloria became concerned that this conversation was too much for her. "Portia, you don't have to do this. I'm sorry I brought it up. Let's talk about something else."

"That's all right, Gloria." she said. "I want to talk

about it." Then she continued as if she was reciting facts about a project at work. "First, I told him about the call. I remember very clearly what he did next. He sat next to me and he took my hand. He looked into my eyes and told me that he loved me. At that moment, I hated him. How could he say that he loved me, when he had just been with another woman? I didn't say anything, I just got up and went to bed. In the guest room."

"And that was it?"

Portia shook her head. "Not by a long shot. That was just the beginning. The next day Dexter told me that he had ended it with her and he begged my forgiveness. But I had to put him through hell first. Betrayal like that does something to your insides. Your self-esteem goes straight to hell. I felt like I had to get back what he had taken. I thought I had to find that in another man's arms."

Gloria had thought the same thing and had tried it with Foster. "Did you?"

"I tried, but I couldn't do it."

"Because you still loved Dexter?" Gloria asked.

Portia shook her head. "I couldn't do it because I still loved myself. If I had done it, I may never have gotten my self-esteem back. No, what I did, or didn't do, I did for myself. Not for Dexter."

"Is that when you decided to forgive him?"

"I think so, but we still weren't out of the woods. Even though I had forgiven him, I still didn't trust him. The trust he had to earn. And only time brought that about."

Time. One thing Josh and Gloria didn't have with their current living arrangements. "To look at you two now, you'd never know it."

Portia smiled a smile that lit up her whole face. "I'm not saying that we aren't happy, but there are scars. The wounds heal, but the scars remain. We're not the same people that we were then. Our marriage isn't the same. Something like that changes you. You have to change to get past it."

"Did you ever think about walking away from the marriage?"

"I did walk away in my mind. That's how I endured the initial pain. In my mind, our marriage was over."

"But it wasn't."

"No, it wasn't. Dexter kept it together. He wouldn't allow me to throw it away. And now I'm glad he didn't. Are you thinking about walking away?"

"Not really. I don't know. I just know that every time I see Josh's face, I remember all I saw that morning. Therefore, I don't want to see him. The memories are too painful. I just want to forget."

Portia touched her friend's hand. "That's normal, Gloria. You have to take care of yourself. You aren't responsible for Josh's feelings right now. You have to do whatever it takes to make it through the day."

"So much for our perfect marriage and relationship, huh?" It seemed so long ago that she had thought she and Josh had a perfect marriage and relationship.

"Not necessarily. You and Josh can still have a marriage if that's what you want. There's no reason you can't."

"I don't see how, Portia. I can't even think about making love with Josh again. It turns my stomach to even think about that."

"That's normal, too. You're human, Gloria, and you're having a human reaction to an awful situation. Take your time. You and Josh have plenty of time to make a decision about your marriage. I still believe that Josh loves you."

She wanted to believe that too. "How could he do it if he loves me?"

"Who knows what was going on in his mind? But I do know that you two have to acknowledge what happened before you can move on. If Josh did it, he needs to fess up. If he didn't, he needs to make you believe him."

Gloria didn't think she'd ever believe Josh wasn't guilty of something, but there was no need to go through that again with Portia. "I guess we'll start on this tonight. I left home this morning before he got up. I just couldn't bear to see him, but I know I can't avoid him forever. We'll talk tonight and he'll leave tomorrow. Then, I'll have some peace. But not until he's out of my house and out of my sight."

Josh was there when she walked through the door. She made for the stairs to avoid talking to him, but he called to her. Knowing she couldn't continue to avoid him, she walked into the living room where he was seated on the couch.

"I missed you this morning," he said.

She was in no mood for chitchat. "What do you want, Josh? I don't have all day."

He patted the couch next to him. "Sit down, Gloria. We need to talk."

She looked at the couch, then took a seat in the chair opposite him. "What do you want to talk about?"

He began quickly, "For the record, I didn't sleep with Darlene." When she would have interrupted, he said, "Listen, I know what it looked like, but I didn't sleep with her. I was drinking and she brought me home from the bar. Evidently, after I had fallen asleep she pulled off her clothes and got into bed with me. I swear I didn't touch her."

"And I suppose you have some land in Florida that you want to sell me?"

He ignored her question because he understood her pain. "The most I'm guilty of is flirting with her."

"Come off it, Josh."

"And leading her on. But I didn't do it because I loved her. I did it because I missed you."

Gloria stood then. "Right. You flirted with her because you missed me. I'm not going to let you make this my fault, Josh. It was your fault, not mine."

"What about what I saw between you and Foster Dixon. I could accuse you of sleeping with him."

"You could."

"That's all you're going to say? You're not going to deny it?"

"You'd like that, wouldn't you? If I slept with Foster, that would somehow absolve you of what you've done. Well, I didn't sleep with him. I went to dinner with him."

"And that's all?"

"No, that's not all. I learned something last night. I learned that even if you don't love me, Foster does. I don't know how, since God knows I've never encouraged him, but he does. I never thought I'd need to hear those words from another man, but I needed to hear them that night."

Each word she spoke pierced his heart. He felt her pain and he felt his own. It was almost unbearable. "Did they make a difference?"

"I don't know, Josh, I just don't know." With that, she ran up the stairs and to the bedroom she was now using.

Josh knew things looked pretty bleak for them now. Gloria still didn't believe he hadn't slept with Darlene.

And he couldn't much blame her. It was a flimsy story. Now this complication with Foster Dixon and his declaration of love. Well, Foster was in for a fight if he thought Josh would give Gloria up. No, Josh had just begun to fight.

Josh prepared breakfast for both of them Sunday morning. He wanted one more chance to talk with her. When she didn't come down, he took a tray upstairs. He was relieved when she granted him entry into her room after his knock.

"What are you doing?" she asked.

"Serving you breakfast in bed."

"Well, it seems guilt brings out the best in some people." She looked at the food on the tray. French toast with maple syrup, scrambled eggs, bacon, hash browns, and orange juice. "And all my favorites, too. Why, Josh, you've outdone yourself."

Josh would have smiled, but her voice was laced with sarcasm. He ignored it. He had to if they were going to save their marriage. "I hope you enjoy it."

She grunted, but she picked up a fork and stabbed it into the French toast. She cut off a square and popped it into her mouth.

He pulled a chair up to the bed. "I'm moving back to Atlanta."

"Whatever for," was her flip response.

He kept telling himself that she was hurt, so he tried to ignore her attitude. "I'm quitting Carolina and going into business with Elliot. What do you think about that?"

Elliot, boy, had he called it right, Gloria thought. If only she had listened to him instead of getting angry. "Why would you want to go into business with Elliot? I thought you were the big corporate mogul."

At least he had gotten her interest. "Some things are more important than work."

"Like what?"

"Like us. Our marriage."

"It's a little too late for that, wouldn't you say?"

"I don't think it's too late. I love you, Gloria. I always have and I always will. I know you don't believe me about Darlene, but it's the truth. I swear it. And someday you'll believe me."

His words touched her but she couldn't let him continue. She wasn't ready yet to soften toward him. "Nice speech. Do you want me to clap?"

"No, I want a chance to prove myself to you. That's all I ask. Will you do that?"

Chapter 21

How could he even ask me that? she thought. "I can't make any promises right now, Josh, and I'd advise you not to make any hasty decisions."

"What are you telling me?" Josh choked out the question.

She pushed the breakfast tray away from her. "I need time and I don't know how much time. All I know is that what I saw that morning hurt worse than anything I've ever felt. That pain is still with me. I have to learn how to handle it before I can begin to think about what's next for us."

Josh didn't like what he was hearing. He needed her to give him some hope. "We've shared too much to let this end what we have." When she didn't respond, he asked the question that he most feared the answer. "You do still love me, don't you, Gloria?"

She looked at him, knowing the tears in his eyes were matched by tears in her own. "Right now, all I feel is pain. I can't feel anything else."

Josh got up and took the tray from the bed. He

had to get out of the room while he still had his emotions under control. When he reached the door, he turned back to her. "I'm not giving up on us. I'll give you the time you need, but I'm not giving up on us." With that, he opened the door and left the room.

Gloria lay back down on the bed and closed her eyes, not bothering to wipe at the tears that seeped through her eyelids. She knew Josh was hurting, but there was nothing she could do to ease his pain. He'd have to deal with it alone because she needed all the energy she had to keep herself from falling apart.

Josh's mind was made up. He was leaving Carolina Electronics and Carla would have to deal with it. He walked into her office Monday morning to tell her that.

She glanced up when he walked into the office, then went back to what she was writing without saying a word.

"Carla, I need to talk with you."

When she finally looked up at him, her smile and her relaxed manner took him off guard. He wondered what she was up to. "And what did you want to talk about?" she asked.

"Our discussion last week. I'm sure we can work out something."

She put down her pencil. "I don't know what more I can say. You have a contract. I've offered you time off. That's all I can do."

"You could let me out of the contract."

She smiled as if she knew something that he didn't. "That wouldn't be fair to you, Josh. You wouldn't want a reputation for reneging on your word, would you?"

He knew it was a threat. "Let's just say I'm willing to take the risk."

She shrugged her shoulders. "It's your career, but I think you'll find it fairly difficult to get another position if you break this contract."

Josh shook his head, not believing this conversation. "Why are you making this so difficult when you can hire somebody else?"

Carla picked up her pencil and twirled it between her fingers. "I have plans, Josh, and those plans include you. When I interviewed you for this job, I was also looking for someone who could one day take my place as Plant Manager. It just so happens that the time is coming sooner than I thought."

"Why would you be looking to replace yourself? That doesn't make sense."

She put the pencil down again and leaned forward. "Because when I leave this office, I'm going to an office at Corporate Headquarters, an office with Corporate Vice-President on the door. The corporate boys like you. They like the idea of your taking over here once I'm gone. You're not going to screw this up for me. And you shouldn't screw it up for yourself. You want this as much as I do. I know it. I saw it in you the first day we met. That's why I hired you."

Josh leaned forward. God help him, he was interested. He was still convinced that this was the best job he'd ever had, and even more so now with this new opportunity. He couldn't afford to be too hasty. "What kind of time are we talking about for these . . . ah . . . changes to take place?"

"A couple, three years, if things work out like I think they'll work out."

Josh sat back. Before he had walked through her office door, he had thought that he couldn't get good luck if they were selling it on the street. And now this.

Well, maybe it wasn't good luck after all. It was an opportunity that he had to turn down regardless of how good it was, because it wasn't worth giving up his marriage.

"If you give me the option of taking a six-week leave," he said, "I'll have to take it, but I must tell you again that it's very unlikely I'll be back. Given that, I'll understand if you withdraw the offer."

Carla stood, a satisfied smile on her face. "Let's have this talk again in about six weeks." He stood when she walked around her desk to escort him to the door. "Now, get things lined up in your office and be sure to let me know when you're leaving."

When Josh got back to his office, Darlene was seated at his desk. Oh, hell, he thought, here we go again.

"What are you doing here?" he asked.

She didn't bother getting up. She just looked up at him. "I'm having lunch with my sister so I stopped in to say hi."

Given the low cut of the dress she wore, he seriously doubted lunch with Carla was all Darlene had in mind. "Well, you've said it. Shouldn't you be getting to your sister's office?"

When she stood, he knew she had more on her mind than lunch with Carla. The dress fell across the top of her thighs. He acknowledged again that she was one fine woman. "There's no need to be mean, Josh," she purred. "I thought we were friends."

Josh walked past her to his chair. He picked up a

pencil and pretended to write. "Our friendship ended the night you got in my bed."

She sat on the desk and leaned toward him. When he looked up, he saw what she wanted him to see. "You know that's where you wanted me. I dare you to deny it."

He pushed back his chair so she wouldn't be so close. He may have thought it, but it was only a fantasy. He knew that now. And he had known it that night. "I admit we may have gotten our signals crossed earlier and I may have led you on, but I'm telling you now that I love my wife and I'm not giving up on my marriage. You need to find yourself somebody who's interested. It's not me."

She slid off the desk and walked to the door, undaunted by his comment. "I'll see you around, Josh. You take care now."

Josh shook his head. Women. The three in his life were driving him crazy. Carla, Darlene, and Gloria. Well, he needed to get two of them out of his life and he was starting with Darlene.

"Your mind's not on the work, Josh. Do you want to talk about it?"

Josh looked at Elliot, who was seated at the desk across from him. Elliot had brought a new desk into the garage for Josh. It was a bit crowded, but they knew it was only days before they found suitable office space. "I'm losing her, Elliot," he said. He threw down the papers that he was reading. "I'm losing her and there's nothing I can do."

"I don't know what to say. What's going on with you two?"

"She hasn't spoken to me since I got in Sunday.

It's Tuesday and she's still either too busy or too tired. We don't eat dinner together. Nothing. I could have stayed in North Carolina.''

"You knew she was going to need some time. Just be patient.''

"That's what I keep telling myself, but it's hard. I didn't do anything, and I'm getting tired of being treated like an adulterer.''

Elliot only smiled. "It's been two days. Give it some time.''

"But it seems like forever.'' They were both silent for a while. Josh hated his inability to exert any pressure in this situation, but all he could do was be there when she decided to forgive him. "Enough of that. Let's get back to work. We should visit the site on Stone Mountain Industrial. I think it suits our purposes.''

"You can't keep running from me,'' Josh said. It was Friday and things between him and Gloria weren't getting any better. "We have to talk. We've been living like strangers.''

Gloria was seated on the bed in the guest bedroom that had become her haven. "I'm not ready. I need more time.''

"And I've been trying to give you time, but think about me. Do you think it's easy for me to live in this house with you and not see you, not talk to you, not be with you?''

She didn't want to hear this. It still made her nauseous even to think of sex with Josh. She was nauseous a lot lately. "I told you not to make any rash decisions. You should have stayed in Raleigh.''

"Is that what you really want?''

"I want you to leave me alone."

Josh walked over to her and pulled her up from the bed. The tears in her eyes ripped at his heart. "Don't you know that I love you? I'd never do anything to hurt you. You do know it, I can see it in your eyes."

God help her, he was right. She was still in love with him. And that was why she couldn't be around him, talk with him, be with him. She pulled away, not trusting herself not to respond to the need she saw in his eyes. "This is hard for you? Well, it's also hard for me. And I can't take it anymore."

"What do you mean by that?"

She stormed out of the room and went to the master bedroom they had shared before, with him trailing behind her. "It means I can't take it anymore," she said, standing in her walk-in closet.

"What are you doing?" he asked.

She threw a suitcase on the bed, opened it, and began throwing in clothes from the closet and the chest. "Packing."

Josh watched her, not believing what he was seeing. "Packing? Where are you going?"

"I'm getting out of here. It's hard for you. It's hard for me. I'll make it easier for both of us."

Josh grabbed her arm as she pulled another garment from the middle drawer of the chest. "What are you talking about? You're not going anywhere. This is our home."

She jerked her arm away. "Watch me."

Josh watched as she flung garment after garment into the suitcase. When she tried to close it, it was too full. She grunted and pulled out another suitcase. She moved clothes from one bag to the other until she was able to close them both. Without a word, she pulled both bags from the bed and stumbled to the door under their weight.

Josh followed her out of the room. For some stupid reason, he wanted to help her with those bags. When she got to the top of the stairs, she dropped them beside her to take a rest.

"You can't just leave like this. Where would you go?"

She shook her head, breathless. "I don't know where I'm going. I just know I have to get out of here."

"You're not even going to give us a chance to work this out?"

"Work what out, Josh? Face facts. It wasn't just your . . . ah . . . encounter with Darlene. We've been having problems for a long time. Maybe they wouldn't have surfaced if you hadn't lost your job, but since that happened, we haven't really been a couple. Not really."

Josh rejected the truth he heard in those words. "All couples have problems. If they really love each other, they work them out."

She picked up her bags again. "Don't you see, Josh? That's it. Maybe we don't really love each other. Maybe we never have." She made her way down the stairs, stopping a few times to catch her breath. When she reached the bottom, she put the bags down again, walked to the living room table, and picked up her purse. Picking up the bags again, she stumbled out the front door.

Josh was left staring at the door as she closed it behind her. It was as if he were held in place by some invisible force. When he heard her car start, he was riveted out of his pose and out the door. He reached the sidewalk just as she pulled out into the street.

"Gloria," he called, but it was too late. She was gone and it felt as if she had taken a part of him with her.

As Gloria drove down the street, she remembered the last time she had left the house in anger. The night of their first fight. This time was different though. This time she didn't know if she'd ever be back.

She felt the tears build up in her eyes, but she was determined not to cry. She had cried enough. Now it was time for action. She had to find a way to pick up the pieces of her life. Then, maybe she could pick up the pieces of her marriage. Maybe.

When she stopped driving, she was in front of Portia's house. She wasn't sure of the welcome she'd get or what she'd do afterward, but she needed to talk to her friend.

"Gloria," Portia said when she opened the front door and saw her friend standing there. "God, I'm glad to see you. Josh called an hour or so ago and we've been worried since. Come on in."

Portia stepped back and Gloria followed her into the den. When they were seated, Portia asked, "What happened?"

Gloria wiped her hands down the side of her face. "What hasn't happened? I left home. I left Josh."

"Oh, Gloria. I'm sorry it came to this. Are you sure you couldn't work it out?"

Gloria shook her head. "Not now. I need to be on my own for a while. To think about what I want."

"I take it Josh didn't understand that need."

Gloria turned up her nose. "We argued. I left. Not exactly an amicable parting."

Dexter rushed into the room and kissed Gloria on the cheek. "I saw your car outside. God, am I glad to see you. What's up with you and Josh?"

Gloria looked askance at Portia. "I haven't told him," Portia said. "That's your decision."

Dexter looked from one woman to the other. "What are you talking about?"

Gloria nodded, then Portia got up and kissed Dexter on his forehead. "I'll get us some coffee. Have a seat and keep Gloria company until I get back."

Dexter watched his wife leave the room, wondering what was going on. He looked back at Gloria. "What's up with you and Josh?" he asked again. "When he called here, he sounded out of control."

Gloria told him how she had left the house.

"But why, Gloria? You and Josh have a good marriage. Why can't you work this out?"

Portia walked back into the room before Gloria could answer. She handed them both a cup of coffee, settled herself on the arm of Dexter's chair, and reached for his hand. "Gloria found Josh in a compromising situation with another woman."

Dexter squeezed his wife's hand and then asked Gloria, "Are you sure?"

Gloria jumped up from the couch. "How can you ask me that? I saw her."

Portia stood up and pulled her friend into her arms. "Don't get upset, Gloria. Dexter didn't mean anything by that. He wanted to understand. We love you and Josh."

Dexter joined in their embrace. "That's right, Gloria. I can't believe Josh would do something like that. He loves you too much."

Gloria pulled out of their embrace. "What does love have to do with it?"

Dexter had a bewildered look on his face and he turned to his wife for direction.

"She knows about us," Portia said softly.

"Oh," was Dexter's only response. He walked back to his chair and sat down. Portia joined him. "You probably don't want to hear anything I have to say now, Gloria, but know that I never stopped loving Portia through the whole thing. I just thank God she was able to believe in me again. I hope that you'll give Josh the same consideration."

Gloria stared at her friends seated there in the same chair, offering comfort to each other. She knew it was difficult for them to discuss this, and she was touched that they cared enough about her and Josh to sacrifice their own feelings. "I love you both for what you're trying to do, but I'm not ready to do anything yet. I think I'd better leave."

"Leave? Where are you going?" Portia asked.

Anywhere but home. "I don't know yet. I'll find a hotel room until I can rent a place."

"You'll do no such thing," Dexter said. "You'll stay here with us. You and Josh may not be able to live together right now, but that doesn't mean we're no longer your friends."

"I couldn't do that. I wouldn't want to impose. Not with the baby . . ."

"That's why we need you here," Portia said. "You need to spend more time with your goddaughter. It'll be good for you both. And, God knows, I can use the company around here."

Gloria smiled and felt relief at their offer. She would feel better around friends. "But I won't be good company. I don't want to put a damper on your lives."

"We're going to worry more if you go someplace else, so you have to stay here."

"I'm still not sure . . ."

Dexter stood up. "Well, I am. Are your things in the car?" At her nod, he ordered, "Give me the keys."

Gloria reached for her purse on the couch and gave him the keys. "Are you sure?"

"Yes," they both said and then they laughed.

"Thanks a lot, you two," Gloria said. "I hope you don't live to regret this."

Chapter 22

"I'm sorry I'm late, Portia," Josh said. He pulled out a chair and sat down. "Why don't we go ahead and order? You must be hungry."

"Actually, I'm not."

Josh sobered. "Neither am I. How is she?"

"About as well as can be expected. She's working out her troubles. Between work and Paige, she keeps herself pretty busy. So busy she doesn't think about her problems."

"Damn," Josh said, his frustration mounting. "She needs to think about the problem and the solution. What am I going to do, Portia? I love her and I know I'm losing her."

Portia's heart contracted at the anguish she knew Josh felt. "I wish there was something I could say, but there isn't. You have to wait her out."

"I can't accept that."

"You don't have a choice."

"And that's what's killing me. My life is in her

hands and I have no influence on her decision. Or when she's going to make it. This is impossible."

"It's impossible for her, too, Josh. Her world has been turned upside down. She needs time."

"She told you?"

Portia nodded.

"It's not true, you know. I didn't sleep with Darlene. Sure, I thought about it a couple of times. But each time I thought about it, I was angry with Gloria. It was never because of anything I felt for Darlene. It was always about what I felt for Gloria. Do you believe me?"

Portia nodded. "But unfortunately, I don't count."

"You do count. It's such a sick story that I'm glad somebody believes it. It gives me hope that one day Gloria will believe it too."

Portia didn't want to dash Josh's hopes, but she wanted him to be clear. "It's more than that, Josh."

He waited a few seconds before responding. "I know, but I've been telling myself that this was the major thing. Am I right?"

"In a way. But the only reason she can believe you were unfaithful is because of the way you two handled the unemployment thing. That made her think she didn't know you as well as she thought. That's why she can believe the worst about you."

Portia wasn't telling him anything he didn't already know. "Problems really compound, don't they?"

Portia nodded. "You can't run away from them. You have to solve them or you're right, they compound."

"And now I've got problems at work," he said aloud, though he was really talking to himself. "When it rains, it pours."

"Oh, Josh, I'd forgotten about that. How long are you going to be away from work?"

He gave a wry smile. "I'm working here."

"What? You're back in Atlanta for good."

So Gloria hadn't thought his move back important enough to tell Portia. "Unless I end up in court."

"That you have to explain."

Josh explained his partnership with Elliot and the lawsuit Carla had threatened.

"A lawsuit? Does Gloria know this?"

He shook his head. "We haven't talked long enough for me to tell her."

Portia covered his hand with her own. "I know you're hurting and right now you think you and Gloria may never get back together, but there is hope. Yours wouldn't be the first marriage to survive infidelity. Or supposed infidelity."

Josh was disappointed at the platitude. "Been reading Dear Abby?"

"Not quite. I lived it."

"You and Dexter?" Though he said the words, he didn't believe them.

She nodded. "Maybe you should talk to him."

"How are you this morning?" Portia asked when Gloria joined her for breakfast. Portia had been up for a while feeding Paige, then putting her back to bed. She was now on her second cup of coffee.

"Not so good," Gloria answered. "I feel awful."

"You've been having bad mornings ever since you've been here."

"I know. I must be worrying too much."

Portia drank from her milk glass. "Could be something else."

"Like what?"

"You could be pregnant."

Gloria touched her stomach. "Pregnant? That can't be."

"You should know better than me, but you're showing the symptoms of the early months of pregnancy. When was your last period?"

Gloria searched her memory for the date. "I don't remember. I've had so much on my mind the last few months."

"Well, you should see a doctor."

"I don't think I'm pregnant." She couldn't be pregnant now. Not now.

"Even if you aren't pregnant, you need to see a doctor. You shouldn't be sick like this every day. You need to find out what's wrong."

"I know I'm not pregnant, but I do need to find out what's wrong, so I'll make an appointment with the doctor."

Pregnant. She was pregnant. She and Josh were going to have a baby. He'd be so happy about this. She went to the phone to call him. She hung up before she dialed the first number.

She couldn't tell him. Not now. So many things had changed. She didn't even know if they still had a marriage. She couldn't complicate the situation with a baby, could she?

"What did the doctor say?" Portia asked as soon as Gloria walked through the door.

"You were right. I'm pregnant."

Portia ran to her and hugged her as best she could with a crying Paige in her arms. "I'm so happy for you. I know how much you've wanted a baby."

Portia's happiness almost made Gloria forget her

situation. Almost. She nuzzled the baby fat of Paige's neck, loving its softness. "Josh and I wanted a baby. Oh, Portia, what am I going to do?"

"Come over here and sit down. You're getting all worked up for nothing."

Gloria followed Portia to the couch. "This should be one of the happiest days of my life and I feel so lost. What am I going to do with a baby?"

Portia gave Paige a sucky kiss on the cheek that made the baby gurgle. "You're going to love him or her. That's what you're going to do."

"That's easy for you to say. You and Paige have Dexter. How can I have a baby when my marriage is in the toilet?"

"This baby may be the best thing to happen to you and Josh," Portia said, settling Paige on Gloria's lap.

Gloria rubbed the soft hair on the baby's head. "How's that? Do you think I should go back to him because I'm pregnant? I hope that's not your solution."

"That's not what I'm saying."

"Well, that's what it sounds like. How can you say it's the best thing to happen to Josh and me?"

"Perspective and speed, Gloria. This baby is what's important. If you can't forgive Josh and continue your marriage with him, you need to make that decision and begin to plan a life for this baby. But if you can forgive him and make a good life for you and the baby with him, you need to make that decision so that you and Josh can enjoy this time."

"So you think the right thing for the baby is for me to go back to Josh?"

Portia shook her head. "How can you think that's what I want. I'm the one with the parents who fought all the time. No, if you love Josh and can forgive him, then go back to him. But if you don't and can't, then make a clean break so you can focus on your baby. And you do have other options.''

"Like what?''

"Adoption and abortion.''

Gloria pulled Paige closer to her breast. "What? You can't be serious. Why would I want to carry the baby to term and then give it away? That makes no sense.''

"You didn't say anything about abortion.''

"God forgive me, it did cross my mind. But I could only have done that if I'd never told anyone about the pregnancy. As soon as I told you, abortion was no longer an option.''

"I'm relieved to hear it because I know how much you want this baby and I know you'll be a great mother. Besides, we could end up in-laws.''

"Wouldn't that be something? I'm glad our children will be around the same age. They'll have so much fun together and so will we.''

"You're right," Portia said. "It'll be a lot of fun.''

"If I get past the next few months. You're right about one thing though. I don't have a lot of time. I can't keep sitting around here not making a decision. I have my baby to think about now. I have to deal with Josh and my feelings for him.''

"Dexter is having dinner with Josh tomorrow night.''

"Whose idea was that?'' Gloria asked.

Portia removed the fussy Paige from Gloria's lap. The baby had responded to Gloria's mood change. "Mine. I had lunch with Josh the other day. He wants you back, Gloria, and he's lost without you. Plus, he has no idea what you're thinking right now. The man is scared. I thought talking to Dexter would help him. You're not angry, are you?''

"How can I be angry after all you and Dexter have

done for me? I'm just sorry that you have to bring up the ugly time in your marriage. Especially now with the baby and all. You two should be focusing only on happy times."

Portia kissed her baby on her eyes to dry her tears. "We can handle it. It's still painful for us. Dexter more than me, I think. But we look at what we have now and we're glad we worked through it. I would hate to have missed the time I've had with Dexter since then."

Gloria felt the loving feelings she had always had for Josh bubbling up in her, but she wasn't ready yet to deal with them. "What else did Josh say when you had lunch with him?"

"Did you know he had quit his job at Carolina Electronics and gone into business with Elliot?" Portia asked.

"He said something about that, but I can't imagine Josh giving up that job."

"He hasn't actually quit yet."

"I knew it." Josh did a lot of big talking, but Gloria knew he wouldn't give up that job easily.

"It's not like that. He offered his resignation, but it was turned down. They won't let him out of his contract. If he's not back in Raleigh in six weeks, they're taking him to court."

"Can they do that?" Gloria asked.

"According to Josh. He didn't think they would go that far, but his boss seems pretty determined to keep him."

Gloria shook her head. "I don't understand that at all. Why would they want to keep someone that doesn't want to be there?"

Portia repeated what Josh had told her about Carla's expected promotion and what it could mean to him.

"Josh should have stayed there. There was no need for him to move back so suddenly."

"To him there was a reason. You and your marriage."

Their marriage, Gloria repeated in her mind. What had happened to their marriage? "Sometimes I can't believe we're even in this situation. Not Josh and me."

"And sometimes I feel it's partly my fault," Portia said.

"How could you think that?"

"Well, the commuter marriage was my idea. If you hadn't gone that route, you wouldn't be in this situation."

"There's no reason for you to feel guilty. Our problems lay at our feet. The commuter marriage interval just brought to light problems that had been simmering on the back burner."

"You don't blame me, even a little?"

Gloria shook her head. "Not even a teeny bit. You've been a lifesaver for me from the time we found out about Josh's job loss. I know I acted ugly when I found out about your pregnancy and I'm so sorry about that. You're my best friend and I love you."

"I love you too. It hurt but I understood it. And now you're pregnant."

"And now I'm pregnant. Can you believe it? I'm going to have a baby." For the first time since she got home, Gloria grinned.

"I never knew," Josh said. He and Dexter were seated in Josh's living room, drinking beer.

"It's not the kind of thing we discuss over dinner," Dexter said. "That was an impossible time for us. I guess you know that now."

Josh nodded and took another swig of beer. "You can say that again. I've never felt so helpless, so lost in my entire life."

"That's the feeling, all right. And if you're like I was, it's worse because you know it's your fault. What can you do in a situation like that?"

"What did you do?"

"I ended it, confessed, and begged Portia's forgiveness."

"That was it? Portia went for it?"

"Yes, but only after she put me through hell. For a while, I had myself convinced she was deliberately torturing me. I knew she was in pain and I tried to allow for that, but I was in pain too. And I had no one to turn to. Who understands a man who's cheating on his wife?"

Josh laughed a hollow laugh. "Another man who's cheating on his wife. Thanks for coming over, man. I needed to talk to somebody."

"Hey, that's what friends are for. Portia and I want you and Gloria to work this out."

"Do you think we have a chance?" Josh held his breath while he waited for an answer.

"Where there's love, there's always a chance. Do you still love her?"

He nodded. "One thing this situation has made me understand is just how much I love her. I lost sight of that in all the things we've gone through in the last year or so. Just how precious she is to me and how my life is nothing without her. I can't lose her, Dexter. It would kill me."

"You're not going to lose her," Dexter said.

"What makes you so sure?"

"Because she still loves you."

Josh perked up. "How do you know? Did she tell you?"

"It's nothing she's said. But I know. She's hurt because she loves you so much."

"Maybe it's wishful thinking. She wouldn't have moved out if she still loved me. Am I being a fool here? Is it already over?"

"It's not over, but you're going to have to give her time."

Time. "It's been almost two months. How much time does she need?"

"Until she feels she can trust you again. It's not that she doesn't love you. She just doesn't trust you. She's wondering if you really love her."

"I do love her, but how can I show her if she won't even talk to me."

"It's hard, I know. I've been through it. But in a way, she's testing you. You'll have to prove your love over and over before she's confident enough to believe you. What happened affected her self-esteem, Josh. She has to get that back."

Josh was still amazed at how much that single event had changed his life. "I can't believe that one incident can wipe out almost ten years of love."

"It wasn't just an incident, Josh. She thinks you broke your vows. That's major."

"I know, I know," Josh said, resigned to wait. "Well, tell me how she's doing, what's she's saying, everything. I'm starving for her."

Chapter 23

Gloria had just put Paige down in her crib for the night when the doorbell rang. She took a final look at the baby, hoping she would stay asleep, before heading down the stairs to get the door.

"I'm coming," she yelled as she raced to the door. Whoever was at the door was leaning on the bell. She wondered who it could be. She looked through the peephole and saw Josh standing there. Her heartbeat raced. She was glad to see him, but she didn't want to see him. He leaned on the bell again.

She opened the door and stepped back. "What do you want?"

He smiled as if she'd asked a pleasant *How are you?* "It's good to see you too. May I come in?"

She wondered why he bothered asking, since he didn't wait for an answer. He strode into the house as if she had invited him over. She closed the door and followed him into the living room, where he took a seat on the couch. She didn't bother to sit. "What do you want?" she asked again.

He looked up at her, his smile still in place. "To see my wife."

His gaze made her uncomfortable. God, he was undressing her with his eyes. She shifted her weight from one foot to the other and ignored the urge to grab a pillow from the couch and cover herself. "Tonight's not a good time, Josh. I'm babysitting for Dexter and Portia."

"It seems there's never a good time. When—"

The sound of the crying baby interrupted him. "I've got to go check on her," Gloria said.

A few minutes later, she came back downstairs, holding Paige in her arms. Something stirred inside Josh when he saw her holding the baby. It brought images of her holding their baby.

He watched her walk around the room, cooing to the baby. "What's wrong with her?" he asked.

Gloria stopped walking and gave him an accusing glare. "You woke her when you rang the bell."

Josh stood up and walked over to them. "Come here, Paige. Let Uncle Josh get you back to sleep." To Gloria's surprise, the baby went willingly to Josh. She even stopped crying.

Josh smiled down at the baby. "You're a good baby, aren't you?"

"When did you get so good with babies?" Gloria asked. She knew she sounded antagonistic, but she didn't like the thoughts that were running through her mind now. Thoughts of her and Josh and a baby— the baby she was now carrying.

"I've always loved kids. You know that. We both have. That's why we wanted to start our family so soon." He lifted a brow in her direction. "Maybe you've forgotten that?"

He wasn't going to get to her that way, she thought. "I remember, Josh. Unfortunately, I also remember a lot of other things." There. She'd done it. She'd brought Darlene into the conversation.

It didn't seem to bother Josh. He went back to his seat on the couch and cuddled the baby in his arms. Paige's eyes were droopy and Gloria knew she would soon be asleep. "I wish we had one just like her," he said. He looked up at Gloria with love shining in his eyes. "You'd be a great mother. And I'd be a great father."

If only he knew how much she needed to hear that now. If only they didn't have these problems. "Right." The word was full of sarcasm.

"I have dreams of you pregnant, your middle swollen with my baby. I still want that, Gloria."

She didn't say anything, couldn't say anything. He had disarmed her with his words.

"Let's take her upstairs." The sound of Josh's voice broke the silence.

Josh got up and headed for the stairs and Gloria followed him as if in a daze. Once in the baby's room, he gently lay her in her crib. Gloria watched him observe the baby for a few minutes and she knew he had spoken the truth about wanting a baby. Now was the perfect time to tell him.

"Josh . . ." she began.

He put a finger to his lips to shush her and pointed to the door. She followed him out of the room. When she would have spoken, he shushed her again. "No more harsh words, Gloria. Not tonight. I know you're hurting and God knows I'll never forgive myself for what I've done to you. To us. But it has to stop somewhere. You have to decide if you want to continue in this marriage. I'm going to wait, but I won't wait forever. I love you too much for that."

She knew when he finished speaking that he was going to kiss her. She knew it and she could have stopped him. But she didn't. No, she wanted the kiss as much as he did. Even though she didn't know what she would do later, she knew that right now more than anything she wanted this man to pull her into his arms and kiss her.

Josh reached for her and pulled her to him. She went willingly, almost eagerly, into his arms. She peered up into his eyes and the love shone brightly for her to see. It was a familiar look on his face. A look she had missed for what seemed like forever. He slowly bent his head until his lips touched hers.

She told herself to let him do the work, let him kiss her. But her body betrayed her. This man was her husband, the father of the baby she carried. And tonight she needed him to hold her, to kiss her.

When his tongue slipped past her lips, her legs went weak. She tightened her hold on him to keep from falling. She heard Josh groan as he deepened the kiss even more and then she felt his hands at her breast. Somehow that touch broke the spell he had cast over her. She pulled away and moved to wipe her hand across her mouth, effectively removing his kiss. He stopped her. The pleading in his eyes caused her protest to die on her lips.

"Don't," he said. "We both needed that. There's no reason to pretend you didn't."

His stare kept her rooted in place. He lifted his hand and ran a finger down her cheek. "I do love you," he said. With that, he turned and ran down the stairs and out of the house.

"Josh was here last night," Gloria told Dexter the next morning over breakfast. Portia hadn't come down yet. "Did you tell him I would be here alone?"

Dexter pushed back from the table and yawned,

obviously still tired from his late night with Portia. "No, I didn't tell him. I may have mentioned that Portia and I were going out, but there was nothing contrived about it. I didn't set you up."

Gloria took another bite of her dry toast. That was all she could eat this early in the morning. "What did you two talk about then?"

"He's hurting, Gloria. He knows he screwed up and he wants the chance to prove his love to you. It's frustrating that you won't talk to him. That's probably why he came over."

"What should I do, Dexter?" she asked, not really expecting an answer.

"You mean about the baby?"

She nodded, not surprised Portia had told him about her pregnancy. "You didn't mention that to Josh, did you?"

"I wouldn't do that. That's your job. When are you going to do it?"

She remembered the picture Josh had made when he held Paige the night before. She had almost told him then. "When we settle things between us. I don't want the issues to get confused. I have to go back to him because I love him, not because of the baby."

"Do you love him?"

"Yes." She was sure of that. "But he hurt me and I have to find a way to get past that."

"He says he didn't sleep with her." At Gloria's glare, Dexter added, "He doesn't deny flirting with her, but he's adamant that he didn't sleep with her."

"And you believe him?"

He nodded. "What reason does he have to lie? In a way, it'd be easier if he had slept with her. Then, he could confess and beg you to forgive him."

Dexter was partially right. It did irritate her that Josh wouldn't confess what he had done. If he would admit it, she could work on forgiving him. Now, she had to deal with his lying on top of everything else. "How does he explain her clothes strewn around his bedroom and in his bed?"

"He doesn't. He still maintains that Darlene brought him home from the bar and put him to bed. Alone. The sound of arguing woke him up the next morning. He was surprised to find it was you and Darlene."

At least Josh was sticking to the same story, she thought. She had to give him credit for that.

"If you don't think you can forgive him," Dexter said, "you need to tell him. Soon. He's turning his life upside down now in hopes that you two will work it out."

"You're talking about his job with Elliot?"

"That and the fact that he broke his contract when he left Carolina. They've held off on filing the lawsuit, but he's convinced they're serious. If you aren't going to take him back, he's enduring a lot for nothing."

"You're blaming me for Josh's problems? How fresh. If he could make a decision to come back here now, why couldn't he have done it before all this trouble?"

"I don't know. You'll have to ask him that. You can't expect to work out your problems if you won't talk to him."

Dexter got up from the table just in time to greet his wife and baby. Portia pulled the high chair near the table and deposited Paige in it. She took Dexter's seat while he prepared Paige's breakfast. After placing the food on the baby's tray, he gave his wife a goodbye kiss and left the kitchen.

"Feeling nauseous again this morning?" Portia asked.

"It's getting better. Dexter was telling me about his visit with Josh."

"What did he say?"

She shrugged her shoulders. "Nothing new really. The lawsuit from Carolina Electronics. Josh may have been too hasty in leaving, especially since they were offering him a promotion."

Portia buttered a piece of toast and took a bite. "He's here because you're here. Would you consider going back to Raleigh with him?"

Two months ago that had been her plan. Amazing how quickly things changed. "Maybe once, but not now. Too much has happened."

"I guess he has no choice but to stay here then. And if he stays here, they're going to file suit against him. This has been a hell of a couple of years for Josh."

Gloria hadn't thought about it like that but Portia was right. Josh had suffered a great deal of disappointment in the last two years. And now he was having to give up a perfect job situation. She wished it didn't have to be so. "We both have. It hasn't been exactly easy for me either."

"At least Josh has this partnership with Elliot. Do you think they'll make a go of it?"

Gloria nodded, though she was uneasy about the partnership with Elliot. More precisely, she'd been uneasy about her relationship with Elliot since their argument. "There's no doubt. It'll be a couple of years before they see any real money, but the concept will work."

"You sound pretty sure of that."

"I am. The bank financed the venture. It wasn't considered that risky at all."

"Thank God for Elliot."

Gloria wondered about that. Elliot needed someone like Josh to help him. She knew Josh's input had gone into the winning business plan. Yes, he and Elliot would make a good team. If only . . .

"What are you thinking about?" Portia asked.

"Nothing."

"I don't believe you. Something's on your mind."

"It's Elliot."

"What about him?"

"We had a run-in a few months back."

"A run-in? You had a fight with Elliot? About what?"

Gloria shook her head. "It wasn't a fight. He said some things about my marriage that I didn't appreciate."

"Oh."

"Yes, oh. And guess what? He was right."

"Is that going to present a problem for you and him in the future?"

That was exactly her concern. If she and Josh worked out their problems, she didn't want her relationship with Elliot to cause problems for him and Josh. "I don't think so, but I'm not sure. I haven't seen him since then."

Portia wiped the baby's mouth. She turned her head from side to side in a manner which said she didn't understand Gloria. "As thorough as you are at work, it amazes me how you allow personal matters to linger. It's almost as if you think that if you run away from them or don't deal with them, they'll go away. But they don't. You do see that, don't you?"

It had been a week since Josh had seen Gloria, but it seemed like only yesterday. The kiss was still fresh in his mind and in his heart. It had given him the hope he needed to endure their separation. She was still attracted to him. He hoped that meant she still loved him.

If only his work situation showed some hope. Things were moving forward with Elliot and the business, but the threat of the Carolina lawsuit still hung over his head. His last conversation with Carla hadn't yielded a satisfactory resolution. She was still dangling the carrot of a promotion. It wasn't as attractive now as it had been when she had first mentioned it. No, that carrot had been dangled at General Electronics and the result had been his termination. Now was not the time to base any career or life decisions on what may or may not happen at a corporation. Josh had gone through a lot to learn that lesson, but learned it he had.

He was actually excited about the work with Elliot. He didn't understand why he hadn't taken him up on it when Elliot had first proposed the partnership. If he had, maybe his marriage wouldn't be in trouble.

This partnership was giving him a sense of control in his life that he hadn't felt in a long time. He and Elliot could make a go of it. The future was theirs to make. Right now, the money was practically nonexistent, but that was okay. He and Gloria had savings and those savings and her salary would tide them over until he began drawing a salary from the company.

His readiness to accept Gloria's help to make it through this period made him smile. She'd tried to tell him earlier that this was what marriage was all about. Two people working together toward a common goal. He wanted this partnership for both of them. He longed for the day he could share that with her.

The ringing doorbell interrupted his thoughts and he realized he didn't know what was happening in the game on the television. He flicked it off with the remote control and went to the door.

He opened the door to find Darlene standing there. "What are you doing here?" he asked.

She pushed past him and into the house without answering his question.

"Don't sit down, Darlene," he said. "You're not staying."

She made for the couch and took a seat as if she hadn't heard him. "I think I am. At least until I can give you a message from Carla."

Josh reluctantly closed the door and went over to sit in the chair across from her. "You don't expect me to believe that Carla sent you, do you? Surely, you can do better than that."

She threw her head back and laughed. "You do know me well, don't you? I wanted you to know that Carla isn't going to prosecute. She just hates to lose. That trait runs in our family."

"And what's that supposed to mean?" he asked.

"Loosen up, Josh," she said. "I'm apologizing for being a sore loser. I couldn't accept it when you chose your marriage. Even though I knew you were in love with your wife, I didn't think she was in love with you. That made you fair game."

"You make it sound like a hunting expedition. This is my life we're talking about here."

She sobered and he knew she was serious. "And mine too. It was a game between us, Josh. At first. We parried back and forth, we flirted. It hurt to know that I was just a diversion for you. I thought there could be something between us."

Josh felt like a heel. "I was wrong to do that. You're right, I never had any intention of breaking my marriage vows or starting something with you. I'm sorry I hurt you."

"I'm a big girl," she said, her playfulness back. "The way I figure it, we're even now."

"And how do you figure that?"

"I may have lost you, but you've lost your wife. I'd say you're hurt a lot worse than I am."

That hurt. It was true, but it hurt. "Is that why you came today, Darlene? To gloat? To be happy that my marriage is torn apart?"

She sobered again. "No, that's not the reason I'm here. I wanted to tell you that I did spend the night in your bed that night. After you fell asleep, I undressed and got into bed with you. I had plans of seducing you, but you were too out of it. When I woke the next morning and you were still asleep, I decided to prepare breakfast for us. That's where Gloria found me."

He rubbed his hand across his head in frustration. "God, Darlene, why couldn't you have told her that?"

"Tell your wife, or even you, for that matter, that I placed myself in your bed, uninvited, with plans to seduce you?" She said it as if that were the most ridiculous thing she'd ever heard. "I don't think so."

"Instead you made Gloria think something had happened between us."

"She thought I was Carla and I didn't bother correcting her. She assumed we had slept together and I didn't bother correcting her on that either."

"What did you hope to gain?"

"I don't know. A part of me hoped she would leave you and then you'd realize that you loved me. She did leave, but you still didn't want me."

Josh never knew that Darlene cared so much. "What made you come here today to tell me all of this?"

She shrugged in a noncommittal way. "Simple guilt. It's all gotten out hand. When Carla told me about your leaving and the [ ] something to do with the day [ ] run-in. It wasn't that hard to [ ] came clean with Carla. After [ ] relationship might come out i[ ] against the lawsuit.''

''Are you sure about that?''

''Very. Carla doesn't want the fa[ ] through the courts. Might get in the[ ]

He knew she was right about Car[ ]s were more important than anything. He had been like that at one time, but he'd learned that plans could become prisons. People were important. Love was important. Plans were, well, they were just plans. ''You didn't have to come here to tell me that. Carla could have called.''

''I know that, Josh, but I felt I owed you. If you want me to talk with your wife or something, I'll do that. I don't know if she'll believe me, but I'm willing to give it a try. What do you say?''

Chapter 24

Gloria was tired when she woke up Saturday morning. Thoughts of herself, Josh, and the baby had her tossing and turning for most of the night. Outside forces were taking away the leisure she had with which to deal with her situation. She had to make a decision. The sooner the better.

She knew what she wanted. She just wasn't sure it was the right thing to do. Shouldn't Josh have to suffer longer for his indiscretion? Would she be a fool to forgive him so quickly? Would he do it again if she did?

The rational part of her knew that her forgiveness would have no bearing on Josh's future fidelity. But her emotions continually told her that if she made him suffer enough, he'd never betray her again. She needed to do something to give herself that security.

But on this Saturday morning, she knew there were no guarantees. If she took Josh back, there was no surety that he wouldn't stray again. The only surety would be her trust and faith in him.

Could she allow herself to trust him again? She wanted to. God knows, she wanted to. But before she could give in to her desire, she and Josh had to come to an understanding about what had happened. Either he had to tell the truth or she had to believe his version of the events of that fateful Saturday.

With that in mind, Gloria got out of bed and dressed. Breakfast was out of the question since her stomach was still playing tricks on her. She grabbed a piece of dry toast and hit the streets.

Elliot and Marilyn were having breakfast when she arrived. She greeted Marilyn with a kiss on the cheek before asking to speak with Elliot alone.

"I need a man's view on this situation with me and Josh," she said to Marilyn. "Do you mind if I borrow Elliot?"

In answer, Marilyn gave her a compassionate hug, smiled at her husband, and left them seated in the kitchen.

"How are things going with you and Josh working together?" she asked.

"Great. Josh and I always got along well."

"No problems?" she asked. Now that she was here, she was getting cold feet.

He shook his head. "I'm sorry for what happened between us, Gloria. I didn't mean to sound so self-righteous."

"That's not why I'm here, Elliot. I owe you an apology. You were right about everything. Can you forgive me?"

A grin spread across Elliot's face and Gloria knew she was already forgiven. "Consider it done," he said.

"Good," she said. "You and Marilyn have been good friends to me and Josh, and I need to know that the friendships can continue."

"I don't think we'll have any problems." His eyes

smiled for the first time since the conversation had started. "I'm glad we had this talk."

She smiled. "I'm glad we talked, too. I'm learning the value of keeping the air clear at all times."

"Now that we have that settled, when are you and Josh getting back together?"

She rose from her seat and smiled again. "Soon, Elliot, real soon."

Gloria recognized the car as soon as she saw it parked in the driveway. Her driveway. Her first emotions were anger and hurt. Anger that Darlene would dare come to her home. And hurt that Josh would allow it. Her first inclination was to speed past the house without stopping. She didn't do that though. Running away wouldn't solve anything. If she went into the house now, she might get the answers she needed. Though not necessarily the ones she wanted.

She pulled her car into the driveway and got out, taking care not to slam the door. She walked slowly to the front door, afraid of what she might see when she walked in. She considered ringing the bell, but decided against it. She needed to walk in unannounced.

She turned the knob and the door opened. She heard voices coming from the living room as she closed the door and walked quietly into the foyer. She knew she should make her presence known. That was the honest thing to do. But she didn't do it. She stood in the foyer, hidden from their view, and listened to their conversation.

As the words flowed between them, she felt the tension in her fade away. She felt as if a weight had been lifted from her. Josh had been telling the truth after all. He hadn't slept with Darlene. Her relief was so powerful that her knees almost buckled and she had to lean against the wall to maintain her posture.

"If you want me to talk with your wife or something, I would do that," she overheard Darlene say. "I'd be willing to give it a try. What do you say?"

"I appreciate your offer," she heard him answer, "but that's not what Gloria and I need right now. You aren't the problem. The problem is us. It's taken me a while to see it, but I see it now. This is something that Gloria and I have to work out."

"If you're sure," she heard Darlene say.

Gloria turned and left the house as quietly as she had entered. She had heard enough. Enough to make her happy. But also enough to make her sad. Josh was right. His supposed infidelity was only a part of the problem. They couldn't get back together just because that was resolved. No, they needed to address the bigger issues that lay between them. She hoped they had the courage to do that. Deep down inside she knew they did.

Gloria wasn't surprised when Josh showed up at Dexter and Portia's later that night. She was half expecting him. After greetings and some cursory conversation, Dexter and Portia left them alone in the living room.

"When I lost the job at General Electronics," Josh began, "I felt like a failure. No, it was more than that, I felt like history was repeating itself. I thought I was going to be like my father. And do you know what, I became him."

Gloria knew something special was happening between them. Josh was going back to the beginning, telling her things that had bothered him. Things that she had sensed, but that he wouldn't share with her. Her heart overflowed with love for him.

"I never told you about him. At least, not in any detail. He lost his job the year I was eleven. I'll never forget it. At first, there was no change. We were such a happy family. So close. There was always laughter around the house. Dad was a big kidder and he kept Mom and me laughing.

"But then he began to drink and he and my mother began to argue. His jokes stopped being funny and the laughter and playfulness around our house ended. One night I saw him hit her. They didn't know I was watching them. I wanted to help my mom but I was afraid my dad would hurt me. So, I waited until he left the house before going to her."

Tears formed in Gloria's eyes as he told her about the little boy who had been forced to grow up much too soon. She heard guilt in his voice, and sought to ease it. "You were a child, Josh, there was nothing you could do. I'm sorry you had to go through it."

"My mom and I never discussed what happened," he continued, as if she hadn't spoken. "I think she knew I saw it, but she never talked about it. Anyway, my dad died for me that night and I promised myself I would protect my mother from that point on."

"Oh, Josh," she said. She wanted to comfort him, but she sensed he needed to do this alone.

"Life was never the same for us. Even though Dad had another job by the time I was thirteen, we were never able to recapture what we had. It was as if we had become a different family. I can't really explain it. When I look back on it now, I see that I blamed my father and his job loss for everything. If only my dad had been able to keep his job, none of those things would have happened. We could have stayed the happy family. Of course, I never said any of this, but I'm sure my dad knew. I'm sure he did."

"You don't have to do this, Josh," she said again. His pain was almost unbearable for her. "You don't have to relive it."

"Let me finish, Gloria," he said. "I need to finish. For us, if we're going to have a life together. Anyway, I made it through high school and I actually felt relief when I left for college. My parents were killed in a car accident at the beginning of my sophomore year. Dad had been drinking. That was one habit he hadn't gotten rid of when he got his new job." His voice broke then and he wiped at his eyes. He was silent for a few long seconds. "I've always felt that I could have somehow prevented the accident had I been there. I hadn't kept my promise to take care of my mom. It was my fault she was dead."

"Josh, that's not so. There was nothing you could do. It was an accident. You can't blame yourself for that."

"But for a long time I did. I stayed in school and dedicated myself to my studies. I never dated much before that but afterwards I stopped altogether. That's how I got the nickname *Iceman*. I didn't trust myself with women. Didn't trust myself to take care of them."

It was all making sense now. Somehow in his mind he had gotten his supposed responsibility with his mother mixed up with her. Somehow his not having a job meant he wasn't taking care of her.

"Then I met you." He looked over at her and smiled. "It was as if something inside me opened. You crawled inside me and all my defenses were gone. And the amazing thing was that I didn't fight it. I knew I loved you from that first day and I've never stopped."

The tears streamed down her face at his words. He did love her. How could she have doubted it?

"You remember how we used to talk about our future together. I loved making plans with you. And I loved seeing them come true. When I lost that job at General Electronics, something inside me broke. On the outside I tried to remain calm and optimistic. But inside I knew I was my father all over again. Fear crippled me and distorted my view of everything. My sole goal was not to become my father and here I was doing the same things he had done."

"No, Josh."

"My self-esteem, my manhood, my pride, all took a beating. Every job lead that didn't turn out, every interview that led nowhere. It was a constant battle to keep up a front of control. I was dying inside. And I began to feel that I was letting you down. Not living up to the life that I had promised you."

She remembered him saying something like that before. She had tried to reassure him, but obviously it hadn't been enough.

"I was really hurt the night I overheard your conversation with Marilyn and found out about your promotion. I knew then that things were getting away from me. That you were getting away from me. Then, when Portia announced her pregnancy, well, that was the last straw. I knew drastic measures were called for." He looked over at her again. "I knew you didn't want to move, but I had to go to San Francisco. I thought I was losing you and I couldn't lose you without a fight. I thought I needed a job, any job, to fight for you."

"Oh, Josh," Gloria cried.

"When the job in Raleigh came through, I had to take it. For me, for our marriage. At least, I told myself it was for our marriage. Now I know it was for me.

With that job, I got back my self-esteem, my pride, my manhood. I know it sounds crazy, but that's how I felt."

"It doesn't sound crazy at all. You were hurting. I'm sorry we couldn't have helped each other out better then." She had harbored some not so positive thoughts herself. Thoughts she would have to confess, but now was not the time.

"I looked at Raleigh as the answer to our problems. I wanted to pick up with our dreams and plans as if nothing had happened. When you wouldn't make the move, my insecurities kicked in again. I wondered if I had taken too long, if irreparable damage had already been done."

She could see how he would have thought that.

"Now I know that my leaving and your staying here were the worse things we could have done. That's why I've left Carolina Electronics and started the partnership with Elliot. It's not just for me this time. It's for us. I want you to be a part of this company with me. I won't have a real salary coming in for a while. I need to know that you'll support me in making a decision like this. We have savings to last us a while. We saw a big boost in our accounts in the last year—with your promotion and my new job. It shouldn't be a hardship for us. I don't expect your answer right now, but I need to know soon if you're with me on this, if this is the right thing for us."

She was ready to answer him now, but he wouldn't let her speak.

"Now, for the matter of Darlene. I didn't sleep with her. She deliberately let you assume the wrong thing that morning. I swear that's the truth. All I have as proof is my word and my love for you. You've got to decide whether that's enough. If it is, I promise you I'll never hurt you like that again. And if it isn't, well . . . I can't think about that because I don't think I can live without you.''

When he had finished speaking, he stood up and she knew he was going to leave without allowing her to respond to all that he had said. She followed him to the door, almost bumping into him when he turned around to look at her. He lifted a finger to her cheek. ''I love you so much it hurts. I hope you'll give me the chance to prove it to you.'' Then, he gave her a gentle kiss on the lips, turned, and left the house.

Gloria stood there for a few long minutes with a finger against the spot on her lips that he had kissed. The man that just left was the man she had married. The man she wanted to spend the rest of her life with. He wasn't perfect. No, he was a little too macho in his outlook to be perfect. But he was hers and she loved him.

Gloria sat in the familiar bedroom she had shared with Josh since they had bought the house. It hadn't taken her long to unpack since she hadn't taken that much with her. God, it was good to be home.

She had decided last night that she was coming home today. She would have told Josh then, but he hadn't given her the opportunity. It was probably better this way. She'd surprise him with dinner and then she'd tell him her side of the story.

Everything was all set for six o'clock. She looked at the clock on the night stand. Josh should be home any minute. She had told Marilyn of her plans and had gotten her promise to have Josh out of her house by five-thirty. Yes, any minute now her life would start again. She had so much to tell him.

* * *

Josh felt the difference the minute he entered the house. When Gloria greeted him at the door, he wasn't sure what to expect. She smiled and he took that as a positive sign.

"How was your day?" she asked as if she asked it every day.

"Fine. It was fine." What was she up to?

She kissed him softly on the lips. "Well, come on. Dinner's ready."

She led him to the dining room, where the table was set for an intimate dinner for two—champagne, candlelight, and all. He looked over at her, a question in his eyes. "What are we celebrating?"

She took a seat at the table and smiled. "My coming home, of course. Now, are you going to sit or not?"

He wanted to sweep her into his arms and tell her how happy he was, but he sensed that she had other plans. He took his seat across from her. "I can't think of any better reason for a celebration, Mrs. Martin."

She poured them both a glass of champagne and then lifted her glass for a toast. "To beginnings."

He tapped his glass to hers. "Beginnings." He took a swallow and found it wasn't champagne, but sparkling cider. Different, but good. Hell, water would have been good tonight. He had his wife back. And for good, he hoped.

They didn't talk much after that, but the silence wasn't a bad silence. No, it was a comfortable silence. A peaceful silence. Their love filled the space between them. It was heaven to bask in that love.

When they had finished their meal, Gloria suggested they have more cider in front of the fire. Josh ached to hold her in his arms. It had been so long.

He didn't want to wait. He knew this was her night, but he offered a suggestion. "What if we have our drinks upstairs?"

Gloria felt her loins tighten at his words. It had been so long since they had been together. She wanted it. She needed it. She had planned to talk first, to clear the air between them. But now what she had to say didn't seem that important. She would show him instead. "That sounds like a good idea."

Josh reached for her hand, its softness a balm to every hurt he had felt over the last two years. He wanted to be gentle with her tonight, to show her how much he cherished her, how much he loved her. But he didn't know if he had that kind of control.

Gloria allowed him to lead her up the stairs to their bedroom. His quick intake of breath, followed by the passionate gaze that he sent her way, told her that he appreciated what she had done. There were flowers everywhere. Flowers and candles. And the bed, with its satin sheets, was already turned down.

She dropped his hand and went into the bathroom to put on the negligee she had bought especially for this night. As she undressed she realized that she was nervous. It had been a long time. And she had gained weight. She wondered if he would notice. If he would be pleased.

When she walked out of the bathroom, Josh was already in bed. He hadn't bothered covering himself, so she could see how ready he was for her. It made her weak. And wet.

The look in his eyes told her that he liked the gown. He leaned up on an elbow and reached out his hand to her. She placed hers in it and he pulled her down to him. "God, you're so beautiful," he said. "You drive me crazy. You always have."

She smiled a soft, feminine smile. The smile of a woman secure in her man's feelings for her. "I guess that means you like the gown?"

He pulled the straps from her shoulders. "The gown has nothing to do with it. As a matter of fact, the gown is in the way." He pulled it down farther until her breasts were uncovered. Then he grazed his fingertips across them. She shivered in response, and he met her gaze. "You're more beautiful than I remember. It seems even your breasts are fuller."

It was one of the changes the baby was making in her body. They were slight changes and it only made her wetter to realize he had noticed them. She would have responded to his comment, but at that moment he chose to flick his tongue against one of her nipples and all thought of anything but that left her mind. Not wanting the other breast to be left out, he used his finger to tweak its nipple. She moaned aloud at the sensations his touch invoked.

It was taking all of Josh's control to go slowly. He wanted her so badly. The fact that she wanted him as badly didn't do anything to help his control. As he massaged her breasts, he felt her squirm against him. If she didn't stop, he was going to lose it. But he didn't want her to stop. What he wanted was that gown out of the way.

With his free hand and her help, they were able to pull the gown down her body until nothing separated them. He rubbed his hands down her back, her buttocks, her legs. He was still convinced that she was the softest woman alive. He forced himself to leave her breasts and then took her mouth in his. God, he could lose himself in her kiss. Her response was more than he had hoped.

The kiss only made Gloria want more. She was impatient for Josh to be inside her. She felt she would die if he didn't come inside her very soon. She pushed her hips against him to give him that hint and was frustrated that he didn't respond to it. She decided to take matters into her own hands.

She tried to pull away from his kiss so she could sit up, but he followed her, not ready yet to end the soul-searching, life-giving connection. In spite of that, she was able to position herself so that she could guide him into her entrance. When she felt him fill her completely, she knew she had finally come home.

Chapter 25

Fear snaked up Josh's body when he awoke alone in bed the next morning. Had it all been a dream? he wondered, shaking his head slowly. No, it hadn't been a dream. He could still smell her perfume, and her side of the bed was mussed. Where was she?

As if she heard him, she strode naked from the bathroom. "Looking for somebody?"

His relief was palpable. "Welcome home, Mrs. Martin," he said once she was back in bed and cuddled in his arms. "I've missed you."

"I've missed you too." She squeezed him to her. "We almost lost each other, Josh."

"I wouldn't have let you go. I love you too much. I would have found some way to keep us together. Even if it killed me." The words were strong and he meant them. She was everything to him.

"The things you said to me the other night at Portia's meant a lot. I had almost given up hope of your opening up to me. We've been so distant."

"That's in the past now," he said. They had made

mistakes. Both of them. But dwelling on those mistakes wouldn't help. "Thank you for believing in me."

Gloria knew he was talking about Darlene and she wondered if she should tell him what she had overheard. No, she wouldn't tell him. It would be the last thing she would keep from him. "I never stopped believing in you. I just got a little scared, a little confused."

She could tell from his silence that he was waiting for her to say more. "It wasn't just you who lost a job; we lost a job. I was hurt you didn't allow me to share your pain."

"I couldn't, Gloria. I didn't know how. And I was too scared. Too ashamed."

"I know that now, but I didn't then. All I knew was that you were keeping everything inside and not letting me in. I think it hurt more since before that we'd shared everything. Then, all of a sudden we were walking on egg shells around each other. When you stopped sharing, I thought I should do the same."

"Would it help to talk about it now?"

Gloria breathed deeply and snuggled deeper into Josh's arms. Now was her time of reckoning. She had to give an accounting of herself so they could put the past to rest. For good. "I got scared. Here we were the perfect Buppie couple, not a care in the world. Reality hit when you lost your job. We weren't any different from anybody else. Our dreams weren't guaranteed. Maybe they were even unrealistic."

"It was a wake-up call for both of us. You can bet we'll never be that naive again."

"Right, Josh. But neither can we go to the other extreme, which is what I started to do."

"What do you mean?"

"I started to focus on money and security too much.

I needed guarantees. Guarantees that couldn't be provided."

"You mean, I couldn't provide them."

The pain in his voice would have stopped her, but the soothing touch of his hand up and down her arm let her know it was okay to continue. "In a way, yes. In spite of all the college and my success at work, my only real goal in life was to be a wife and mother. I wanted to be the mother that I never had. My family would come first."

"There's nothing wrong with that."

"You're right, it's not. But when you lost your job, I became my mother. The importance of my work went up. And that was as it should be. The problem was the way I blew it out of proportion. I began to do the what-if's—what if you lost your job again and I wasn't working, what if we had kids. My work became my security."

"There's nothing wrong with that either."

"Not by itself. But then I began to question our dreams, our plans. Who was I to think I could be a full-time mom? Everybody else works, why shouldn't I? I even began to sympathize with Mom. Maybe her need for security drove her to work so much. Surprisingly, that was a comforting thought. Better than thinking she loved work more than she loved me."

"I never knew you felt that way."

She shrugged. "Neither of us ever talked much about our families. They weren't happy stories, Josh."

He knew she was right. They had tried to build a life and a future together without dealing with the past. It hadn't worked. Thank God they had the chance to try again.

"Anyway, the thing about my mom confused me," Gloria continued. "Things weren't clear-cut anymore. I didn't know what was right or what was wrong."

"It's not a matter of right and wrong."

"That's what I finally realized. It really wasn't about right and wrong. It was about choices. About risks. About love."

"I reached that conclusion too after that awful Saturday in Raleigh. There was no compelling reason for us to do that commuter marriage. It was a choice, and I know now, a bad choice."

"You're right, of course. It took me a little longer to realize it though." It hadn't really become clear for her until she learned she was pregnant.

"This may sound corny," Josh said, "but I think our marriage is stronger because of what we've gone through."

"It's not corny. I remember Portia telling me that a year or so ago. I see now that she was right. We've gone through a rough passage and we're still a team. That makes me think we can handle anything."

Josh felt the same way. Except for one question that continued to play on his mind. "Do we need to talk some more about the incident with Darlene?"

"That hurt. More than you can imagine. More than I thought I could bear. I knew we were having problems, but it never occurred to me that you might be having an affair."

"I wasn't."

"I know that now."

"How can you be sure?"

"Because I'm sure of you. You love me and there's no reason for you to lie."

"That simple?"

She couldn't continue with the lie. "I overheard you and Darlene the other day."

Josh's hand stopped its soothing rub down her arm. "When?"

"I came by the house to see you, to tell you that I still loved you and I wanted us to work it out. Darlene was there. I know I was wrong, but I sneaked into the house and listened to your conversation."

When he didn't say anything, she asked, "Are you upset with me?"

He shook his head and his hand began its rub again. "Not upset. Even though a part of me wanted you to believe me based on my word alone, I was worried that the question would always be in the back of your mind. But since you know for sure, I won't have to worry about that. I'm glad you know."

"It took a lot for her to come here."

He didn't want to talk about Darlene. "Hmm . . ."

"She did keep you from going to court."

"But she caused a lot of problems for us. Don't get me wrong. I know a lot of it was my fault. I should have discouraged her. I'm just glad that part of our life is over."

"Me, too. And since we're clearing the air, you've never made me answer for the incident with Foster Dixon that night."

"I had a pretty good idea what was happening. You were vulnerable and Foster was taking advantage. He's never hidden his attraction for you."

"You never wondered if something more was happening?"

"No. I hit him because I knew what his intentions were and I knew that the only reason you were susceptible to him was because of what I had done. I hit him because I couldn't hit myself."

"You're right. I only turned to him because I was

hurt. I never intended for anything to happen. Do you forgive me?"

"There's nothing to forgive. I love you and I'll never put you in a situation like that again."

They were quiet for a long time, enjoying the feel of being in each other's arms again. Josh broke the silence. "What do you think about my going into business with Elliot?"

"If it makes you happy. I want you to be happy."

"And I want you to be happy, but that doesn't answer the question."

"I just hate that you're giving up the job at Carolina. Dexter told me about the promotion possibilities. Are you sure you won't regret it someday? You know, feel like you missed out on something big."

He shook his head. "Like I told you before, I'm never going to be that naive about business again. There are no more guarantees at Carolina than there were at General. That opportunity didn't mean much to me."

"So you're really excited about this partnership with Elliot?"

"Very much so. We're going to do great things."

Gloria nodded. "You and Elliot do make a good team."

"Correction. You and I make a good team. We're in this together, or we're not in it all. Okay?"

"Okay."

"How do you feel about supporting us until the business starts to make money?"

"I'm glad you're willing to let me help, but you may have waited too late."

Josh felt a bubble of fear. "What do you mean by that?"

"Maybe I'm not interested in working much

longer. Maybe I want that family that you've promised me."

Josh was overcome with joy. "You want to start our family now? I thought you wanted to wait awhile."

"That was fear talking. I want to have your babies and I want to stay home and raise them."

"Are you sure this is what you want?"

"Positive."

"Maybe I shouldn't go into business now. I could always go back to Carolina."

"No, you can't. We've decided. You're going into business with Elliot. We have money, Josh. At least enough to keep us going through the business start-up. And I can still work and I want to keep working after the baby is born. Not full-time, but I want to work." She took a deep breath before continuing with her most important thoughts. "I'm good at my job, Josh, and I make a difference. This South Fulton project is going to mean accessible health care for that community, a predominantly black community. I'm the cause of the bank taking on projects like that and I want to see them take on more. I want to be a part of them doing more."

"You seem to have this all worked out. You must think you got pregnant last night. Was it that good?"

She decided not to tell him yet. She'd save that surprise for another time. "No, it was better than good."

Josh and Gloria sat on their private beach on the shores of Aruba. She sat between his legs while he rubbed the round mound that represented their baby. "I'm glad you wanted to come back here," he said. "I think we should do it every year."

"You think the kids would like it?"

"Kids?" he asked, his hands continuing their massaging motion across her belly. He hoped to feel a kick. Gloria had felt them, but he hadn't felt one yet. "Let's have this first one before we start talking about the next one."

Josh had been overjoyed to hear about her pregnancy. He saw the baby as evidence of their love and the cement that helped bring them back together after a rough time. "You do want more, don't you?"

"Only a dozen or so."

She placed her hand atop his on her stomach. "How would you feel about two this time?"

Josh's hands stopped their soothing movements. "What?"

"Twins. We're going to have twins."

"How? When?"

"The doctor told me a few weeks ago. I wanted to surprise you."

He hugged her to him, feeling that life couldn't get much better than it was right now. "Every dream we had is coming true," Josh said. "I love you, Mrs. Martin."

HISTORICAL ROMANCE FROM PINNACLE BOOKS

LOVE'S RAGING TIDE   (381, $4.50)
by Patricia Matthews

Melissa stood on the veranda and looked over the sweeping acres of Great Oaks that had been her family's home for two generations, and her eyes burned with anger and humiliation. Today her home would go beneath the auctioneer's hammer and be lost to her forever. Two men eagerly awaited the auction: Simon Crouse and Luke Devereaux. Both would try to have her, but they would have to contend with the anger and pride of girl turned woman . . .

CASTLE OF DREAMS   (334, $4.50)
by Flora M. Speer

Meredith would never forget the moment she first saw the baron of Afoncaer, with his armor glistening and blue eyes shining honest and true. Though she knew she should hate this Norman intruder, she could only admire the lean strength of his body, the golden hue of his face. And the innocent Welsh maiden realized that she had lost her heart to one she could only call enemy.

LOVE'S DARING DREAM   (372, $4.50)
by Patricia Matthews

Maggie's escape from the poverty of her family's bleak existence gives fire to her dream of happiness in the arms of a true, loving man. But the men she encounters on her tempestuous journey are men of wealth, greed, and lust. To survive in their world she must control her newly awakened desires, as her beautiful body threatens to betray her at every turn.

"There he is! There he is!"

Cody jumped up and down excitedly, pointing out the farmhouse window.

Her fatherless son, playing pretend again. Arianne went along with the game. "Quick! Don't let Santa see you're still awake!" She raised Cody's bedcovers and beckoned.

But Cody hesitated, his small brow furrowed. "Mommy, maybe we'd better go outside and get him."

Arianne obligingly looked where Cody pointed. As the wind gusted the blizzard aside for an instant, she saw a figure stagger like a drunken snowman, then fall facedown near their doorstep.

"Somebody's out there!" she exclaimed, clutching Cody close.

"I know," Cody said calmly. "It's—"

"Sweetheart, it's *not* Santa Claus. Trust me on this."

The man outside raised his head, then sank back into the obscuring whiteness.

"I know *that*," Cody insisted. "It's a daddy!"

Dear Reader,

Enjoy the bliss of this holiday season as six pairs of Silhouette Romance heroes and heroines discover the greatest miracle of all…true love.

Suzanne Carey warms our hearts once again with another **Fabulous Father:** *Father by Marriage*. Holly Yarborough thought her world was complete with a sweet stepdaughter until Jake McKenzie brightened their lives. But Jake was hiding something, and until Holly could convince him to trust in her love, her hope of a family with him would remain a dream.

The season comes alive in *The Merry Matchmakers* by Helen R. Myers. All Read Archer's children wanted for Christmas was a new mother. But Read didn't expect them to pick Marina Davidov, the woman who had broken his heart. Could Read give their love a second chance?

Moyra Tarling spins a tale of love renewed in *It Must Have Been the Mistletoe*. Long ago, Mitch Tyson turned Abby Roberts's world upside down. Now he was back—but could Abby risk a broken heart again and tell him the truth about her little boy?

Kate Thomas's latest work abounds with holiday cheer in *Jingle Bell Bride*. Sassy waitress Annie Patterson seemed the perfect stand-in for Matt Walker's sweet little girl. But Matt found his temporary wife's other charms even more beguiling!

And two fathers receive the greatest gift of all when they are reunited with the sons they never knew in Sally Carleen's *Cody's Christmas Wish* and *The Cowboy and the Christmas Tree* by DeAnna Talcott.

Happy Reading!

Anne Canadeo
Senior Editor

Please address questions and book requests to:
Silhouette Reader Service
U.S.: 3010 Walden Ave., P.O. Box 1325, Buffalo, NY 14269
Canadian: P.O. Box 609, Fort Erie, Ont. L2A 5X3

CODY'S
CHRISTMAS
WISH

Sally Carleen

Silhouette

ROMANCE™

Published by Silhouette Books

America's Publisher of Contemporary Romance

For my Aunt May
for patchwork quilts and Christmas
and for loving her sister's child as if I were her own.

 SILHOUETTE BOOKS

ISBN 0-373-19124-3

CODY'S CHRISTMAS WISH

Copyright © 1995 by Sally B. Steward

Printed in U.S.A.

Books by Sally Carleen

Silhouette Romance

An Improbable Wife #1101
Cody's Christmas Wish #1124

Silhouette Shadows

Shaded Leaves of Destiny #46

SALLY CARLEEN

For as long as she can remember, Sally planned to be a writer when she grew up. Finally one day, after more years than she cares to admit, she realized she was as grown up as she was likely to become, and began to write romance novels. In the years prior to her epiphany, Sally supported her writing habit by working as a legal secretary, a real estate agent, a legal assistant, a leasing agent, an executive secretary and various other occupations. She writes full-time now and looks upon her previous careers as research and/or torture. A native of McAlester, Oklahoma, and a naturalized citizen of Dallas, Texas, Sally now lives in Lee's Summit, Missouri, with her husband, Max, and their very large cat, Leo. Her interests, besides writing, are chocolate and Classic Coke.

Dear Santa Claus,

I have been a very good boy all year except for
when I made pancakes and the toaster burned up.
I want a red bicycle and a red truck and a daddy and
a baby brother. Mommy says she doesn't want anything,
but please bring her a new toaster.

Your friend,

Cody

If you can't bring me something because of the toaster,
I have an old yellow truck I can play with and my
Friend Pete lets me ride his bicycle but I really really want a
daddy and a baby brother.

Chapter One

"I heard sleigh bells! Did he come yet?" Halfway down the stairs, Cody stopped and peered through the rails, brown eyes round and shining like one of the ornaments on the big cedar tree in front of the living room window.

Arianne closed her book and raised a skeptical eyebrow. "Sleigh bells? Nice try, hotshot, but, as you can see, we don't have any new presents." She waved a hand toward the shimmering, twinkling tree with the colorful array of gifts beneath.

"I *did* hear sleigh bells," he insisted. "I'm not playing pretend." He scuttled down the stairs, his determination oddly incongruent with his blue flannel pajamas and small bare feet.

He made a close inspection of all the presents, then turned to face her. Pushing aside the lock of sandy hair that insistently strayed over his eyes, he scowled. "Maybe he didn't stop 'cause you're still up."

The tree lights blinked on and off, shading the child's small face in one color then another, making him look like a worried elf.

Arianne ducked her head and bit her lip to hide her smile. "You could be right," she conceded. "Maybe we should both go up to bed."

She really wasn't ready for bed. Even though the storm had brought darkness several hours ago, it was only nine o'clock. Besides, the scent of cedar from the tree and the crackling flames leaping in the fireplace made the living room snug and cozy. With the blizzard raging outside, it was probably the only really warm place in the drafty old house, especially since she'd turned off the gas heater in the corner when she'd sent Cody to bed.

She shivered at the thought of leaving her nest in the big, overstuffed chair. But somehow she had to get Cody to go to sleep—not an easy task with a five-year-old on Christmas Eve.

"There they go again!" He bounced to the side of the tree, sending a couple of bright balls trembling precariously, and peered around it through the dark window.

Arianne fancied she heard a faint jingle, herself. The boy's overactive imagination was getting to her. Or maybe they both actually did hear bells. It was possible. The howling winds that had brought in one of the worst freak snowstorms in Kansas's recorded history could conceivably bring in sounds from incredible distances. Two miles away, her closest neighbors, the Martins, had horses and probably harness bells. Though the harness bells would be stored in a barn, not out in this weather. Just a bizarre sound in the wind, that's all she'd heard, she decided.

"You may be right, Cody. Santa could be in a holding pattern over our house waiting for us both to go to sleep." She stood, shrugging out of the folds of her afghan and picking up her book. "Let's scoot," she urged, regretfully closing the glass doors of the fireplace insert. "Race ya."

She charged up the stairs behind Cody, marveling at how fast his short legs could move, especially considering he was giggling hysterically at the same time.

"I win, I win, I win," he gloated, jogging into his room and over to the window. "It's still snowing. Do you think Santa Claus'll get lost?"

"Not likely since you just heard his sleigh bells."

Cody turned back to her and rolled his eyes. "I mean *after* he leaves here."

"Of course. How silly of me. Well, don't worry. He has Rudolph." She crossed the room to straighten the pile of quilts on the little boy's bed. The intricate scrollwork of the iron frame was cold to her touch, but the covers still retained Cody's body heat. "Into bed with you now," she ordered.

"There he is! There he is!" He jumped up and down excitedly, pointing out the window.

Playing pretend again. The boy spent too much time alone.

"Quick!" she said, going along with the game. "Over here! Don't let him see you're still up!" She raised the covers and beckoned.

But Cody hesitated. "Mommy, he fell down." He faced her, small forehead furrowed. "Maybe we better go get him."

Puzzled at the twist her son's story had taken, Arianne went over to wrap her arms around him. She shivered as the wind whipped snow and sleet against the glass and brought a chill into the room through the cracks where the old window frames had settled many years ago.

"Brrr," she said, hugging Cody tighter. "Let's close the drapes and get you into bed before you freeze."

"Mommy! We have to go down and bring him in!" Cody insisted.

She looked obligingly to where he pointed. For a moment, she saw nothing but snow. But as the wind gusted the curtain of white aside for an instant, she saw a figure rise, stagger a couple of steps like a drunken snowman, then fall facedown.

"There's somebody out there!" she exclaimed, clutching Cody closer as if to protect him from the stranger below.

"I know," he said calmly. "It's—"

"Sweetheart, it's *not* Santa Claus. Trust me on this."

The snowman raised his head and pushed up a few inches, then sank back into the all-obscuring whiteness.

"I know that," Cody insisted. "It's—"

"Whoever it is, we can't let him freeze," she said, turning away from the window.

"Yeah! We can't let him freeze. We have to go get him."

She raced downstairs with Cody close on her heels and yanked her coat from the hall closet. Coming up behind her, Cody tugged down his jacket and started to put it on.

"No way," she said, pulling on her boots, gloves and ski mask. "You stay right here. I mean it." Then, at his distressed expression, she said, "Run up and get a quilt from the linen closet. Whoever's out there is going to need it."

"Yeah!" Cody charged off happily, one sleeve of his jacket on his arm, the other flapping behind.

She grabbed a flashlight, flung open the door and ducked her head as the wind slapped her in the face, slamming stinging snow and sleet into the facial openings of the mask. Determinedly, she pushed forward, moving the beam of light in a wide arc. The person she'd seen couldn't have been more than a dozen feet from the door, but it seemed to take forever to cover the distance. Although at five feet eight inches, she was by no means tiny, she felt like a rag doll fighting against the wind.

Finally, when she thought she must surely be lost, her light traced the form of a body partially covered with snow. She could tell little about him, only that he—or she—was lying facedown and was a large person—likely a man. Getting him back to the house would not be easy.

She pushed and tugged until she managed to roll him over. His snow-encrusted features told her he was male, and a groan told her he was still alive. Thank goodness for that! But if he had any chance of staying that way, she had to get him out of the cold immediately.

She slapped his face, trying to rouse him. "Get up!" she shouted, leaning close to his ear so the wind wouldn't blow her words away before he heard them.

His eyelids fluttered open, but his eyes appeared unfocused.

She pulled his arm over her shoulder and tugged. "You have to get up!"

Reluctantly, it seemed, he began to push himself upright, leaning on her for support.

"Come on!" she ordered as soon as he had one foot beneath him. He was like a deadweight; his lassitude frightened her. She knew the final stage in freezing to death was resignation and a desire to sleep.

As she half supported, half dragged him to the house, she had to constantly urge him onward, shouting and pulling, trying to get them both back to the light shining from the open door, promising a warm haven.

A particularly dense blast of snow and wind momentarily obliterated the light from the door, even the twinkling lights of the Christmas tree in the window, and when it cleared, Cody stood by her side.

"I'll hold his other arm," the boy shouted, standing in the snow that was hip-deep on him.

"No! Get back in the house! Please." Her voice softened on the last word. He was only trying to help, but she didn't need to be worrying about him on top of everything else.

Cody chose that moment for one of his rare bouts of rebellion. As though he hadn't heard her, he grabbed the man's left arm. Surprisingly, his minimal efforts seemed to help, and, with a rush of relief, Arianne saw that they had reached the front porch steps.

But getting the man up the steps took all their combined strength. With little help from the stranger, they practically dragged him inside and over to the fireplace, then pushed him to the floor, his back pressed against the stone hearth. Arianne opened the glass doors to allow the heat into the room.

"Cody, where's that quilt?" she asked, working off the man's coat. Already the snow on it was starting to melt, and soon the wool would be a cold, wet mass. Briefly, she wondered what kind of idiot would come out in a Kansas blizzard wearing only a wool coat, sleek leather gloves and no boots. His lightweight charcoal slacks and silvery cashmere sweater looked more appropriate for a party than a storm.

Cody rushed up with a patchwork quilt, and the two of them wrapped it around him. The man's eyes opened briefly, and his lips parted as if he was going to say something, but no sound came out. Nevertheless, Arianne felt encouraged.

Pulling off the stranger's gloves, she rubbed his cold hands briskly between her own.

A gust of wind blew the front door open and reached its icy fingers to her.

"Cody, close the door," she called over her shoulder. "The lock didn't catch."

The man shivered—another good sign. "I'll get you something hot to drink," she told him, rising—just in time to see Cody heading out the door.

With a lunge, she caught the tail of his jacket. "Where do you think you're going?"

"We have to go back!" he insisted, tugging at her coat.

"What on earth for?" She leaned against the door, forcing the blizzard back as she closed it.

A strange noise from across the room drew her attention. The man wrapped in the quilt was struggling to a sitting position and trying to talk through chattering teeth.

For the first time, Arianne noticed that he was actually a very attractive man. Thick, sandy hair fell across his forehead and gleamed with a red cast from the firelight. Strong facial features with a distinct Roman nose and square jaw made him appear to be in control despite his disheveled appearance and inability to speak coherently. She met his gaze and shivered.

His steely gray eyes seemed to have captured the cold and brought it inside.

Arianne realized she was pressing against the closed door, leaning away from the cold in the stranger's eyes. Cody, however, scurried over to him as fast as his clumsy snow boots would allow.

"We didn't bring in my baby brother!" He grabbed the man's quilt-wrapped arm, trying to pull him upright.

"Cody, stop that right now." The boy released the man's arm but didn't move away from him.

Arianne shook her head and spread her arms in a helpless gesture in response to the puzzled gaze that met hers over Cody's head. The boy's fantasy baby brother had been a frequent visitor in their house for the last several months, but this was the first time Cody had lost him in the snow.

"I'll make some coffee," she offered, shrugging out of her coat. "That should help you warm up."

He nodded. "Th-thanks."

But Cody continued his frantic efforts. "Tell Mommy we have to go get him. If we don't, he'll freeze," he pleaded, tears starting in his eyes. "Tell her, Daddy!"

The stranger jerked away, eyes wide, as though Cody had struck him. Arianne dashed over to wrap protective arms around her squirming son and pull him back.

The boy's timing was lousy. He'd never run this scenario with any of the scattered dates she'd had, the way normal kids did with their mothers' male friends. Oh, no. Her son had to wait until they found a strange man in the snow, a man who apparently didn't like children, then call him Daddy.

"He didn't mean any harm," she said, trying not to sound as defensive as she felt at the man's overreaction. "He plays games a lot. He's an only child."

The man wrapped the quilt closer around him, though his shivering had almost stopped, and regarded her with his strange, cold eyes. "Where is his father?" he asked.

Arianne hesitated. She knew nothing about this person. He could be a serial killer, a homicidal maniac—whatever, she didn't want him to know she and Cody were alone. But Cody saved her the trouble of making up a lie.

"My first daddy died. But you can get more. Pete—he's my best friend—he has three." He looked up at Arianne. "So I asked Santa for a daddy and a baby brother, and my brother's still outside. Please, let's go get him." He struggled to break free of her hold.

"No," the man said. "There's no baby brother in the snow, and Santa didn't bring me."

He spoke in an unhurried drawl she recognized immediately as Texan, though his tone was brusque. Arianne held Cody closer, trying to cushion him from cruel reality, but the child's faith was not so easily destroyed.

"If Santa didn't bring you, how'd you get here?"

A good question. Arianne wanted to hear the answer to that, herself.

"My car slid off the highway down by your mailbox. I couldn't get it out of the ditch, so I set off to find your house. But the storm—I couldn't see anything—except—" He looked around the room, his gaze settling on the Christmas tree. His statuelike features actually relaxed, and the corners of his mouth turned up slightly in a wondering half smile. "It was only the star on your tree. I thought for a while there, I was hallucinating, seeing a light twinkling in the middle of the storm like that, but I followed it, anyway...and ended up here." He cleared his throat. "You mentioned some coffee? I'd sure appreciate something hot."

"Oh, yes. Of course. Cody, come help me."

She herded the boy into the kitchen where she measured coffee into the filter. Cody reluctantly pulled off his coat and gloves.

She squatted to his level to help him. "Sweetheart, I promise there's no baby brother out in the snow. He'd be crying if he was, and we'd hear him." She held his small, soft cheeks between her hands, brushed his hair back and forced him to look into her eyes. "Okay? Do you believe me? You won't worry anymore?"

Cody lowered his eyes sadly and nodded.

She tilted his chin up with one curled finger. "Someday, maybe you'll have a baby brother. But the way that works is, I have to get married first, then we get the baby brother." It wasn't a real lie, not when she prefaced it with *maybe*. She might get married someday. And when she did, her husband might already have a son. Or they might adopt one. Anything was possible. Ten years ago, she'd have scoffed at the possibility of Cody.

Cody's expression brightened at her reassurance. "So marry my daddy right now, and Santa will still have time to bring my baby brother."

Arianne rolled her eyes heavenward and threw up her hands in a gesture of surrender. "How about I fix you a cup of hot chocolate?"

When she returned to the living room with Cody trailing her and a mug of coffee in her hand, the stranger was up and wandering around the room—stretching his legs or being nosy?

"It's only really warm in front of the fire." Arianne indicated the chair in which she'd previously been reading.

"Thanks." He accepted the mug and perched tentatively on the edge of the chair. If he was a serial killer, he was certainly a nervous one. He seemed as leery of her as she'd first been—though somehow wasn't now—of him.

Cody flopped onto the braided rug, sipped his hot chocolate and gazed up at the man, an act which seemed to increase the stranger's unease.

Arianne tossed another log onto the fire and poked the embers. "Well, Mr. . . . ?"

"Sloan," he supplied. "Ben Sloan." He watched her closely as he spoke his name, as if it might mean something to her.

She didn't recognize it, didn't make any association with anything she might have heard on the ten o'clock news, but she maintained her grip on the poker—just in case.

"Mr. Sloan. I'm Arianne Landis, and this is my son, Cody."

"Cody." He stared at the boy for a long moment as if in a trance, then seemed to recollect himself and turned his attention back to her. "It seems you saved my life. Thank you." His wide mouth stretched into a faint smile, but his eyes remained cautious.

"At the risk of sounding immodest, it seems we did. But the one you have to thank is Cody. He spotted you when you fell."

"Then . . . thank you, Cody." His voice was tentative. He lifted a hand as if to reach toward the boy, but changed direction halfway through the motion and shoved his hand into his pants pocket. Cody really did seem to make him uncomfortable, but she supposed some people just weren't accustomed to being around kids.

"So where were you going when you slid off the road?" she asked him.

He sipped his coffee, his gaze never leaving her face. "I was on my way to visit . . . a relative."

"Then we'd better call and let them know you're okay."

"That's not necessary. It was going to be a surprise visit."

"Cody, it's time for you to go to bed." She didn't like Ben Sloan's answers. She'd get the boy upstairs, then see what information she could pry out of the stranger.

"Mo-o-om," Cody protested even as he pushed sleepily to his feet.

She bent over to accept his embrace and kiss his velvety cheek. "Hit the stairs, hotshot."

He turned to the stranger and raised his arms. The man recoiled.

"He only wants to kiss you good-night," she snapped, losing her patience. Just because the man wasn't used to being around children didn't give him the right to hurt her son's feelings.

Ben looked at her, his expression unreadable, then leaned stiffly forward to permit the child's embrace.

Satisfied, Cody charged up the stairs, but paused on the landing. "Good night, Mommy. Good night, Daddy."

Ben watched the little boy as he disappeared down the hallway. His face was still warm from the touch of the tiny hands, the kiss of the soft lips. He clenched his teeth and reminded himself that he couldn't afford to let emotion cloud his thinking, distort the facts—whatever they might be.

"Mr. Sloan, if you don't mind, I'd like some answers."

He returned his attention to the woman, Julia Norton's "best friend and cousin, like a sister." In many ways, she reminded him of Julia. She even looked a little like Julia. They were both tall and fair with dark hair and eyes, though this woman's body was more willowy than seductively curvaceous as Julia's was, and Arianne moved with a boneless, unconscious grace rather than a very conscious sexuality. Where Julia's eyes were dark pools, Arianne's were flecked with green sparks, and her polished, walnut hair was long and straight—the way Julia's probably had been before the blond streaking and stylish scissoring.

But in spite of Arianne's disarming appearance, the innocence in her eyes and her seeming lack of recognition of him, she must be involved in the scam.

Otherwise, why had the kid called him Daddy?

Chapter Two

"Mr. Sloan?" She stood in front of him, arms akimbo, fear and determination equally evident in her stance and on her face. Fear because she didn't know who he was or because she did know?

He decided to change tactics. "Please call me Ben," he said, smiling his best "trust me" smile. "Since you've just saved my life, we ought to be on a first-name basis."

She moved to stand beside the fireplace tools, casually laying a hand on the poker. Clearly, she didn't like the good-old-boy routine. It was possible she really didn't know what was going on, he thought. Oddly, he wanted to believe that. She was making such a valiant stand, he wanted to admire her—but it was also possible that she was a damned good actress . . . like her cousin.

"About this relative you were going to visit—this is a small town. I probably know him."

"You probably do." *You just kissed him good-night.* If the boy really was his son. "And that's exactly why I don't want to talk about the ... uh ... situation. I'm not trying to be evasive, but ..." He shrugged. "I'm sorry. I can't tell you my relative's name. Anything else about my life you want to know, you got it." *Almost anything.* He lifted the heavy mug from where he'd been cradling it in his lap and drained the last drops of now-cold coffee.

"Fine. Who are you, where are you from and what were you doing traveling in the middle of a blizzard?" She maintained her contact with the handle of the poker.

Ben shifted uneasily, a little guiltily. She seemed genuinely fearful. If she really didn't know who he was, his mysterious actions would be enough to frighten any woman alone, but she wasn't backing down. She stood her ground looking fragile as crystal and tough as mesquite. He had to admit to a grudging respect. *If* she wasn't involved.

"I'm Ben Sloan," he said, "from Dallas."

"You say that like it ought to mean something to me. I'm sorry, but it doesn't. We're a little out of touch here with movie stars and football heroes and that sort of thing, so I'm afraid you're going to have to tell me a little more than your name and where you live."

She was damn good ... or damn honest. He had to give her the benefit of that last unlikely possibility. Julia was undoubtedly capable of lying. "I'm nobody famous. I own a computer company. Most of the time I work seven days a week. I live alone in a condominium in north Dallas. I work out when I can, eat high-fiber, low-fat foods, except when my passion for greasy hamburgers overtakes me.'' He shrugged. "What else can I tell you?''

"What you were doing driving in that blizzard.''

"I didn't know there was going to be a blizzard. The forecast was possible snow. Down home, that means a few flakes.''

"So you drove all the way from Dallas on Christmas Eve, taking a chance your relative would be here.''

"Not exactly,'' he said smoothly. "I flew into Denver. I thought if this thing with my relative didn't work out, I could do a little holiday skiing so the trip wouldn't be wasted. I rented a car, got hopelessly lost once I crossed the Colorado–Kansas border after I turned off Highway 36 onto those damn little roads that go nowhere and don't have any signs, and the snow caught me. I finally got back on the right road, then slid into the ditch when I was checking the name on your mailbox.'' Everything he said was the truth, he justified to himself. Just not all the truth. Nevertheless, it was deceit, and he hated that necessity, even considering the circumstances.

"And you followed the star on my Christmas tree right up to my front yard.'' She sounded a little skeptical.

He looked over at the star shining brightly atop the tree. Shivering, he recalled the intense cold invading his bones and the terrible feeling of being completely lost when he'd only gone a few feet from the car, even unable to determine which direction the car was. "I was completely disoriented.'' He tried to smile, but couldn't quite pull it off, not while he remembered the sheer terror of being lost in that snow. "We don't have storms like this in Dallas.''

"How could you have seen such a small light through that blizzard, all the way down to the road?"

"I don't know." Now that he had time to think about it rationally, it did seem strange. "But I did. I saw it, and I followed it. Thank God."

"And thank God Cody saw you."

"Yes," he agreed, realizing he owed his life to the people whose lives he'd come to disrupt.

He felt a twinge of guilt, but shoved it aside. He hadn't created this situation. Whatever the situation might be. One way or the other, somebody was lying, Julia or this woman or both of them.

"Would you like some more coffee?" she asked, interrupting his thoughts.

"Please," he answered, handing her his cup. "I don't think I'll be really warm again until the temperature gets over a hundred next summer. Our Texas summers would thaw the North Pole."

"I used to live in Dallas. I know about your summers, and however hard you may find it to believe right now, it gets just as hot here." She took his cup and walked across the room.

She had admitted she'd lived in Dallas... but admitted it easily and guilelessly. He still didn't know what to make of her.

His gaze followed her lithe figure as she disappeared into the kitchen. Although she resembled her cousin, he couldn't imagine Julia in faded jeans and an oversize sweatshirt. Both times he'd seen her, she'd worn clinging, high-fashion fabrics that molded to her body. Arianne was unsophisticated, wholesome, not sexy... yet she was. Somehow, Arianne managed to look incredibly provocative, rouse him in a way that could easily get out of control if he let it.

Which wasn't what he should be thinking about. His hormones had already caused him enough problems. Although, if the problem actually existed, it had been caused by timing and need more than by hormones.

Arianne returned with another mug of steaming coffee, and he reminded himself to look at her with skepticism, to keep his guard up, to remember that she must have coached the kid to call him *Daddy*.

"Thank you," he said, accepting the coffee gratefully, warming his hands on the outside, letting the steam warm his face and finally swallowing the warmth.

She crossed the room and stood for a moment with her back to him.

"Sheriff Bridges, it's Arianne Landis." She turned to face him defiantly, speaking into a black, old-fashioned telephone.

Damn! Was she going to have him thrown into jail for running into her ditch? Though he had no idea how the sheriff would be able to get here in the storm that still raged outside.

"Fine," she said. "How about you?... And Nora?... Good. Sheriff, I wanted to let you know that Cody and I took in a traveler whose car slid into the ditch in front of our house. His name's Ben Sloan, and he lives in Dallas.... Everything's fine. I just wanted you to know what's going on. Oh, and Sheriff, don't mention it to my grandparents. You know how they worry about Cody and me, anyway, and Gramps's heart isn't what it used to be.... Thanks a lot, Sheriff," she said, and placed the receiver in its cradle.

Registering him with the local law. A smart move for an innocent woman alone. Or for a woman pretending to be innocent.

"Whenever you're ready, I'll show you where you can sleep," she said. "But I have to warn you, we don't have central heating here—just lots of quilts."

"Sleep?" His mind spun crazily. For the barest moment, he wondered what she was suggesting, what the next move in this game would be.

"You can't go back out in that blizzard. I'm afraid you're stuck here for at least the night."

She was right, he realized with consternation. Beside him, the fire snapped and crackled. He was warm; the side of him nearest the fire was almost hot. The heat, the smells of the burning wood and the cedar tree, all wrapped around him cozily. Still, considering the reason he was here, he didn't want to be obligated to her, not even for a night's lodging.

But the windows were black with the wind slapping bursts of snow against them, rattling the panes and howling eerily. He shivered again at the very thought of being out in that nightmare.

And he couldn't have asked for a better opportunity to find out what was going on... to study the boy up close... to know for certain who was being dishonest.

"I know this is an inconvenience for you," he said, "especially on Christmas Eve. I insist on paying the same rates as I would at a hotel."

Her eyes—her whole face—darkened at that. "This isn't a hotel," she said curtly. "I'm offering hospitality, not selling it."

He retreated from her prickly attitude, lifting his hands in a gesture of surrender and his lips in what he hoped looked like an apologetic smile. "Whatever you say. I'm in no mood to go back out in that storm." He'd figure out a way to repay her later. Whether or not Cody was his son, whether or not Arianne was in on the scam, he wouldn't be indebted to her.

Half an hour later, wearing a pair of Arianne's grandfather's old pajamas, Ben slid between the cold sheets in the cold room at the end of the upstairs hallway and began to shiver all over again. Arianne hadn't been kidding about the lack of heat in the house. He'd been reluctant to pull off his clothes at all, had considered sleeping in them. Even with the rug on the hardwood floor, his bare feet had immediately turned to chunks of ice.

As he settled in bed, he thought he'd surely be crushed from the weight of all the covers. There must be half a dozen of them. If she wouldn't accept payment for his staying here, no matter how things turned out, he'd get Arianne and the boy electric blankets. That should even the debt, in either event.

Slowly, he began to warm, and he had to admit—albeit grudgingly—that there was something comforting about tucking his head under the mound of quilts and curling into his own body heat.

Sometime later, he awoke with a start, completely disoriented. He sat up in the dark room, listening for the noise that had awakened him and trying to remember where he was. The rush of frigid air that enveloped him the instant he threw aside the covers cleared his head immediately.

He was in Arianne Landis's house.

Faint noises sounded in the total silence and clarity of the cold air. Someone was up and about downstairs. Arianne? What would she be doing up in the middle of the night? He supposed he needed to find out, though he really wanted to slide under the covers and go back to sleep.

Instead, he tossed them off with a rapid thrust, bursting into the icy air as though plunging into a swimming pool for the first time in March. This air was as all-encompassing as the water...and many degrees colder.

Slipping on his socks and the faded navy blue robe Arianne had laid out for him, he tiptoed to the landing and peered over.

With a half-assembled bicycle in front of her, Arianne sat beside the Christmas tree, swearing quietly but sincerely, trying vainly to get the chain around the gears. In her white fuzzy robe, with the tree lights shining rainbows in her veil of dark hair, she looked like a frustrated Christmas angel.

As one of the stairs creaked beneath his weight, she looked up, startled. Smiling, she lifted a finger to her lips, raising her eyes toward a closed bedroom, presumably where Cody would still be sleeping. He nodded an acknowledgment.

He'd discovered the source of the noise that had awakened him; Arianne wasn't doing anything that concerned him. He could go back to bed. But instead of crossing the landing to the room where his sheets were probably already turning to ice, he found himself trying to be as quiet as possible while he went down the ancient stairs. They creaked and groaned with every step. Cody must be a heavy sleeper that he didn't wake up to all this noise.

The way he'd been a heavy sleeper at that age. His mother had sometimes dragged him out of bed and stuck him in a cold shower to get him awake for school.

Which didn't mean a thing. Sleeping so soundly was probably one of those kid things.

"Need some help?" he asked, sinking onto the floor beside Arianne.

She pushed her hair back from her face and sighed. "Gramps was supposed to help me do this, but he and Gramma—they live in town now—didn't dare come out in the storm." She handed him a wrinkled sheet of paper covered with microscopic print and strange diagrams.

He looked at it a moment without comprehension, then set it down. "I take apart and reassemble computers all the time, and last month I helped a friend put together an exercise bike. This shouldn't be too tough."

He selected a piece of metal and examined it. Obviously, it didn't belong, must have been put in the package by mistake. He laid it aside.

Ten minutes later, he was trying hard to refrain from giving vent to all the swearwords Arianne had missed.

He looked at her. She was sitting on the floor, robe draped around her, arms crossed under her breasts, the corners of her mouth turned up in an expression that was somewhere between a grin and a smirk.

"Where are those..." He ground his teeth and swallowed the descriptive word he wanted to use. "Instructions," he finished.

She spread the sheet on the floor in front of them without a word. They both leaned over the paper, her smooth cheek only inches from his, so close it was a blur in his peripheral vision. The side of his face next to hers began to feel warm, and he couldn't decide if the heat radiated from her or from inside his own body, generated from her closeness.

Her silky hair slid over her shoulder, a dark, shimmering cloud between them. He drew in a deep breath, trying to divert his attention, to regain control. Bad idea. Arianne smelled like Christmas—piquant, woodsy, bursting with promises to be fulfilled.

It was only the cedar tree, he pointed out to himself, combined with the scents of various spices she'd probably been cooking with during the day.

Nevertheless, he couldn't get the idea out of his head. She smelled like Christmas.

"I think," he said, reminding himself of why he was here, "you've got some of these parts on backward."

"Backward? Are you sure?" She studied her handiwork, consulted the instructions and uttered another exasperated oath.

Ben laughed at the incongruity of her angelic appearance, the serene setting and her worldly vocabulary. She raised her eyes to his, frustration obvious in their depths, then slowly she relaxed and her lips spread in a sparkling smile...

A familiar smile...Julia's smile. For a few seconds there, he'd forgotten. This was Julia's cousin, her best friend, her coconspirator.

"Well," he said, returning his attention to the bicycle, "I guess we'd better get busy."

The assembly wasn't easy, he discovered, even with the directions—the deranged directions. He could understand how she'd gotten it together wrong.

"Apparently, this isn't one of those men things," she observed as he tried to fit together two recalcitrant parts.

"No, but it gives me an idea for a new computer program—one that deciphers incoherent instructions."

"Right. And it'll come with a complete set of incoherent instructions."

He couldn't stop himself from smiling, couldn't deny that he was actually enjoying himself. God, how he hoped Julia had lied, not this woman. He didn't want to hate Arianne.

But if Cody was his son...

He slid on the last handlebar grip, then gave the imitation-leather seat a final pat.

If Cody was his son, he deserved at least a top-of-the-line ten-speed bicycle with a real leather seat. And Arianne—

She stood with him. "Thank you so much, Mr. Sloan—Ben." His name fell from her lips with just a trace of a Texas drawl, languorous and inviting... though he would have sworn she hadn't intended it to sound that way, was unaware of her sexuality. That is, he would have sworn it if he'd never met Julia.

"You're welcome," he said, his words coming out husky in spite of his own mental warning.

Her eyes widened and darkened as he stared at her, as though she could read his mind, see his doubts, his desires.

Abruptly, she whirled away, her curtain of hair swirling, a slow-motion copy of her movements. "I'll go get the rest of the gifts," she said.

"The rest?" An image of a mountain of jumbled parts and wrinkled instruction forms rose in his mind.

Already halfway across the room, she turned back with a grin. "Don't worry," she teased, "the rest came assembled."

"In that case, I'll come help."

She unlocked the storage closet beneath the stairs, and they emptied the contents.

Life in a small town was certainly different, Ben reflected as he and Arianne positioned the presents beneath the tree. Cody's gifts included a set of some sort of plastic blocks for constructing things, a sled, a bright red truck, a couple of small toys and several items of clothing—but no video games, no plastic monsters or mutants, no videocassettes—nothing he'd seen in shop windows or advertised on television.

"There," she said and stood back to survey the results. "How about a quick cup of cocoa before we hit the frozen beds again?"

"That would be great. Thanks." He should have refused. He should have gone straight up to bed. He shouldn't accept any more of her hospitality than he absolutely had to.

But, against his will, he seemed to be getting sucked into the depths of a Norman Rockwell painting. No, not against his will. He had to admit he was fascinated. Christmases had been pretty bleak when he was younger, a barren monument to their poverty and his mother's hatred of his father for deserting them. Since then, he'd worked at Christmastime or gone on a holiday trip.

He looked at the display of gifts, the gaudy tree and the star. Had he really followed the light from an ornament through the snow to safety? To Arianne's yard, his arrival witnessed only by Cody—the boy with his hair and Julia's eyes. It was almost as if he was meant to be here.

He pulled his gaze away from the tree, focusing on the snow still blowing against the dark windowpanes. He was being irrational and foolishly sentimental. Fate had nothing to do with this. He was here because Julia needed money to get to Hollywood.

As for the boy, his eyes were as much like Arianne's as they were like Julia's, and blond, unruly hair could have come from thousands of other men besides himself. The fact that the kid called him Daddy was just another piece of evidence that Julia and Arianne had cooked up this thing together. Maybe Arianne wasn't planning to go to Hollywood, but looking around this place, it was pretty obvious she needed money, too. Maybe they expected him to pay child support, or something.

He had to keep all that in mind, remember that Julia couldn't be trusted. He couldn't let himself get caught up in this charming little family Christmas and lose his objectivity.

"Here you go." The voice came from behind him, interrupting his thoughts.

He turned to see Arianne offering him a cup of hot chocolate.

"I added a little Kahlúa," she said. "Antifreeze."

"Thanks," he said quietly.

He took the cup from Julia's cousin and, as he sipped the steaming beverage, he studied her in wariness, confusion and inexplicable, unwelcome desire.

"Mommy! Come see what Santa Claus brought me!" Cody's excited chatter assaulted Arianne's ears at the same time the cold air assaulted her face. Already dressed in a sweatshirt and blue jeans, he stood beside her bed, holding the covers up, peering in at her with eyes that shone as brightly as the Christmas tree lights.

"Is it morning already?" she groaned.

"I'll go get Daddy!" Cody spun away before she could protest.

Oh, dear. She'd hoped he would have forgotten that *Daddy* business by this morning. Usually, he abandoned one game of make-believe for another with dizzying rapidity. Just her luck this would be the one that stuck.

She slipped into her robe and staggered sleepily to the window. Pulling back the heavy curtains, she peered out. Snow still swirled from cloud-hidden skies, but the storm seemed to have blown out some of its fury. Maybe by afternoon the weather would start to clear.

It was impossible to guess how much snow had fallen because the galelike winds had created huge drifts and low valleys. A mountain of white leaned against the side of the barn, reaching almost to the roof. The trees stretched barren, crooked, brown arms upward through the cold; if the wind continued to die down, they would soon have white blankets.

It would be a beautiful Christmas—though not quite the same with her grandparents stranded at their new house in town. The roads would be closed, and they'd never be able to make it out here today.

Which meant Ben wouldn't be able to leave. His car was probably nothing but another mound by now. Even if the sun broke through immediately, he wouldn't be able to get out. He was stuck here for Christmas.

That thought both intrigued and irritated her. He was an incredibly attractive man, and she didn't meet many of those. In fact, she didn't meet many single men of any description living in Silver Creek, Kansas. Thirteen miles from Silver Creek, actually. Maybe that was why she was so drawn to him, why she'd gotten all tingly just sitting beside him on the floor last night as they'd worked on Cody's bike. In spite of his unorthodox entry into her life—an entry she still wasn't quite sure about—he definitely made her very aware of the fact that he was a man and she was a woman.

Which didn't mean a thing, over the long haul. Her father had probably made her mother feel like that at one time, but in the end, it hadn't mattered. To her, all that mattered was Cody, a miracle she'd never even dared hope for. He was her priority. Their life together was good, perfect. A sudden burst of inexplicable erotic urges was nothing compared with that. As she thought of Cody, she realized a part of her resented Ben's intrusion into their Christmas, the perfect Christmas she wanted to give Cody.

She dropped the curtain in place, shutting out some of the cold, and turned around. Not a very charitable attitude for Christmas, she chastised herself.

With a twinge of guilt, she recalled that when she'd come back into the room with hot chocolate last night, Ben had been staring at the tree, his eyes filled with agonized longing. If he was planning to spend Christmas skiing in Colorado, that probably meant he didn't have any family. His aborted trip to see some relative here—likely a distant one—made it obvious how desperate he was to be with family for the holidays.

On the other hand, people who went skiing in Colorado for Christmas didn't need a family. She knew that from her own experience.

She scowled at her image in the dresser mirror across the room. The image scowled back. She was being absurd, obsessing about Ben's part in hers and Cody's Christmas. He was stuck here, so she needn't worry about whether she liked it or not. She only needed to be concerned about making Cody's Christmas the best ever.

She made a quick trip to the bathroom to brush her teeth and wash her face, then she slipped into the red knit jumpsuit she'd been saving for Christmas, ran a comb through her hair and dabbed on a smidgen of lipstick.

"Mommy! Hurry!" Cody stood at her door, bouncing up and down impatiently. Behind him, wearing the same pale gray sweater and dark gray slacks they'd found him in and looking just as out of place, Ben watched her with an unreadable expression on his face.

"I'm ready," she said, though she wasn't sure she was. "Let's go get those Christmas presents!"

Cody was off like a shot, his rapid footsteps sounding loud on the wooden stairs, then muffled as he raced across the living room rug.

"Come on," she urged Ben. "This is the best part."

She didn't hear his footsteps behind her on the stairs for several seconds. Did she care? Did she really want him to be a part of Cody's Christmas, anyway?

Midway down, she heard him following her, his steps slow and ponderous.

As she reached the foot of the stairs, Cody turned toward her, face shining like a floodlight, a huge grin stretching from ear to ear. His small hands gripped the handlebars of the bicycle. "Look! It's red! Just like I wanted!"

"That's great! What else did Santa bring you?"

Ben came up beside her then.

"Look, Daddy! Look what Santa Claus brought me!"

She cringed and felt Ben stiffen beside her. She quelled her resentment; naturally, she'd think any man would be thrilled to have her wonderful son call him Daddy. Realistically, she had to admit it would probably make most men a little uncomfortable.

Telling herself she had to be objective and not quite making it, she crossed the room to light the gas heater then rekindle the fire in the fireplace. That accomplished, she sat down on the floor near Cody, in the midst of the presents, available to inspect all his glorious finds.

"Mommy, see my new truck? See, Daddy?" Cody held the toy briefly for her inspection, then trotted over to Ben, holding it up to him. Ben's square jaw tensed, and he made no move to take the truck, offered no praise.

Okay, that did it. She'd have to have a talk with him. Granting him permission to feel a little uncomfortable was one thing, but she wouldn't have him upsetting her son while under her roof, not even if that son insisted on calling him Daddy.

"Is that a new sled?" she asked, diverting the child's attention.

As soon as Cody scampered over to inspect the sled, she stood and moved to stand beside Ben, and even in the midst of her righteous anger, she couldn't help noticing that he turned her blood to hot molasses. "Haven't been around many kids, have you?" she asked, trying to sound nonconfrontational, trying to sound less breathless than she felt.

"He keeps calling me Daddy."

"He's just playing pretend. He'll go on to something else soon. Next, you'll probably be a creature from outer space. Christmas is a time for fantasies."

He looked at her then, his eyes searching hers for answers to questions she could only guess at. He lifted his hand, and for a moment she thought he was going to touch her face, but at the last instant, he changed direction and raked his long fingers through his tousled hair, pushing it back from his forehead. The gesture seemed oddly familiar and endearing, almost as though she'd seen it before. But she couldn't quite place it.

"Christmas fantasies," he repeated and turned to look at Cody.

"Can we open the presents from Gramma and Gramps and Aunt Julia?" Cody asked, wrapping his arms around a gaily wrapped package.

"Yes, you greedy little boy," she answered, laughing, and he began ripping paper.

"Aunt Julia?" Ben asked, and something in his tone sent an odd chill trickling down her spine. Maybe she'd better put another log on the fire.

Chapter Three

"My cousin," Arianne explained, stirring the fire and adding another log. "The glamorous, talented part of the family. She's a model and an aspiring actress. She's from Dallas, too. Though by now she could be in Hollywood or maybe even Hong Kong. Julia's very unpredictable."

"I see," he said.

"She's also very generous." She picked up the package wrapped in bright red foil with an ostentatious gold bow that Julia had sent for her gift and tried to stop babbling nervously. She'd only imagined that Ben had responded to her mention of Julia's name. Dallas was a big city. There was no reason to think Ben's presence was in any way connected with Julia.

No reason except the fear she lived with on a daily basis.

"Look what Gramma and Gramps got me!" Cody

brandished a new bat in one hand and a ball in the other.

"Cool!" Arianne enthused. "You can go right out after breakfast and play with it."

"Mo-o-om!" Cody rolled his eyes in Ben's direction as though the two of them shared an impatience with her oddball humor. "Daddy and I can play after the snow melts."

Ben regarded Cody with a faraway look, but the boy didn't seem to notice. He swung the bat a few times, then lit into Julia's gift with the thrill of discovery only the very young could know.

"So," Ben said, turning a guarded look on her, "what did this paragon relative give you for Christmas?"

Arianne tensed at his sarcasm. *You're being paranoid again,* she reprimanded herself. She did sometimes tend to overemphasize Julia's good points so the bad wouldn't be quite so evident.

She sat on the hearth and eased off the lid with its gold specialty-shop lettering to expose a glittering red-sequined jacket. She held it up, laughing and shaking her head. "Julia means well. Can you see me wearing this to the next elementary school teachers' meeting?"

"You're an elementary school teacher?" Ben asked, his tone just short of incredulous.

"Yes, I am. I love children. Teaching them is a very rewarding career," she said, knowing she sounded defensive and a little pompous...but he'd had no reason to sound shocked.

"Wow! Look what Aunt Julia got me!" Cody struggled to hold up a box showing a video-game unit. Just the type of gift she didn't want him to have.

She grimaced, and Ben laughed. "She means well," he reminded her. Then, his expression shifting back to guarded, he said, "Doesn't she?"

A little confused at his odd reaction, Arianne folded the jacket into its box. "Yes, she does."

"Daddy, can you put this in the television?" Cody stood in front of Ben, holding the video game and looking up trustingly.

Ben appeared a little dazed, but he leaned down, reaching for the box Cody offered.

"I'll do it," Arianne said, crossing the room to take the game from Cody just as Ben grasped the other end. For a long moment, she stood beside him, so close she could smell traces of expensive cologne mingled with the minty toothpaste she'd left out for him to use, could see tiny laugh lines around his eyes, could feel the energy coming from him, merging with hers, surrounding the two of them . . .

"Let Daddy do it, Mommy. It took you three days to hook up the tape player. Remember?"

She cringed at Cody's continuing reference to Ben as his father. The boy's words sliced between Ben and her, separating them as cleanly as a blade.

She turned loose of the box, more to get away from Ben's gaze than to concede the matter. "Sweetheart," she said, kneeling to Cody's level, "Ben is our guest, not your father." Cody lifted his small, square chin defiantly, but she didn't give him time to protest. "It's bad enough he's trapped with strangers for Christmas, but he may not want to spend his time hooking up your video game."

"I don't mind," Ben said, and Cody's face lit up. He scampered away from her.

She turned to see him take Ben's hand. Ben looked down at him for a moment as if not quite sure what to do next. Cody tugged, and the two of them walked away from her across the room toward the television set.

"You can share my presents, Daddy," Cody said. "I guess nobody had time to get anything for you since you just got here. Next year, you'll have lots of things."

Arianne watched them with a strange tugging at her heart. Cody imitated Ben's masculine stride exactly. She'd never before realized how badly he wanted a father, so badly he'd take up with a stranger.

She'd thought she could provide him with all the love he needed, with Gramps as a male role model. Of course, he'd expressed a desire for a father when he'd discovered his friends had something he didn't. But he'd also asked for a baby brother, a motorcycle, a puppy, a video game, a horse...an average of one new thing a week.

She had to get Ben out of their house before Cody became too involved in this game he was playing, before he got hurt when the game was over and reality returned.

Ben's fingers seemed to have grown larger and become suddenly clumsy as he worked at hooking up the video game to Arianne's old television. Because of the age of the set, he had to make a couple of modifications, and that was simple, nothing like the complicated modifications he'd made to computers in his lifetime.

No, the clumsiness he was experiencing was directly related to Cody's tiny fingers trying to help, getting tangled with his. They were so small, so soft, so defenseless. He hadn't realized children's fingers were such perfect miniatures.

Actually, he'd never thought much about children, period. He was too busy to have time for a family. His divorce had proven that.

But then Julia had come up to him at that party a couple of weeks ago. At first he hadn't remembered her. He'd been pretty drunk the night they first met, drowning his sorrow over his divorce. Or his lack of sorrow, to be precise—his total lack of feeling over something that should have been monumental.

So he'd gone to a club and met Julia and had enough to drink that he'd believed he was having a good time— until morning.

Then Julia had come up to him six years later with her bizarre story that the night he barely remembered had resulted in a son and, for the "paltry" sum of ten thousand dollars, she'd tell him where that son was.

Much to his surprise, that had caught his attention. He didn't really believe her, certainly hoped it wasn't true...but the idea had eaten at him that he might have a child who would never know his father. If there was any chance she was telling the truth, he had to find out. He'd given her the money, and she'd told him the child was being raised by her cousin in a farmhouse in Kansas...with no father and a mother who lied to him about where his father was. The only difference in the way he'd been raised was the location; he'd been in Texas instead of Kansas.

"Wow!" Cody exclaimed when the first game booted up on the television screen. He picked up the control and began to explore the functions. With his left hand.

Ben lifted his own left hand and stared at it, opening and closing the fingers slowly, recalling how hard his mother had tried to make him use his right hand after his father disappeared...so he wouldn't be *just like your father*. What percentage of people were left-handed? What did that do to the odds that Cody was his son?

Or maybe kids used both hands at that age. Maybe this business of being right- or left-handed came later, like a guy's voice changing. Damn! He really didn't know squat about kids. What would he do if Cody really was his son?

"Show me how to do it," Cody entreated, handing the control to Ben.

He took a step backward. The room had become suffocating. All those open flames in the heater and the fireplace gobbling up the oxygen. "I...I don't know how."

"Instructions." Arianne was suddenly, miraculously, between them, unfolding another ominous-looking piece of paper. At least the print on this one was a little larger. She sank onto the sofa that looked as though it had seen better days and gazed at him. "I thought you said you had a computer company. Don't you play computer games?"

He shoved his hands into his pockets. Why was he letting this woman and this small child make him uncomfortable? "If I spent my time playing computer games, I wouldn't have a company for long." That was a slick move. Being rude and arrogant was sure to net him a lot of points.

"I understand," she said curtly and began to read the directions. Cody flopped down beside her.

Ben stood watching them, feeling inexplicably awkward, an outsider. He hadn't felt that way in years, not since he'd been the kid in school who didn't have the right clothes or the latest toy, the kid who didn't have a daddy, not even one who came to visit on weekends. He didn't like being reminded of that feeling.

Did Cody feel that way... left out and different? If this was his son, he had to do something.

The ringing of the telephone startled him. It was a loud, demanding ring, not the subdued burring he was accustomed to. Arianne stood and brushed past him, stirring the air around him, trailing the scents of cedar and cinnamon and cloves, surrounding him with this Christmas that didn't belong to him.

The phone rang again, and he felt a sudden burst of fear. What if that was Julia on the other end of the line? What if she was calling to see how their plan was going? Or what if she was calling to confess to Arianne about what she'd done and who he was? He didn't know which he feared the most.

Holding his breath, he watched as Arianne sank into a chair beside a small table and lifted the receiver of the old black telephone.

"Merry Christmas to you, too, Gramma," she said.

He was able to breathe again.

"Gramma, Gramma!" Cody darted across the room to join his mother. To join Arianne, Ben amended. Not that he could say for sure she wasn't his mother. He just didn't know, and every minute he spent here, he became more confused, not less.

She spoke a few more words over the phone, then handed the receiver to Cody, beaming down at him. She loved the boy. He didn't doubt that for a minute.

But his mother had loved him, which didn't mean she'd always done things in his best interest.

Arianne came back across the room and stood beside him. "My grandparents on the phone," she explained. "Cody's their only great-grandchild, and they spoil him rotten."

"What about your cousin? Julia doesn't have any children?"

"Julia's not their grandchild. They're my mom's parents. Julia's father and mine are brothers."

She'd skirted the issue, hadn't really answered him, hadn't denied that Julia had children.

On the other hand, maybe she'd answered the question the way an innocent person would. Maybe he was seeing suspicious elements where none existed. Maybe he should just ask her. He'd never liked being deceptive, and the longer he spent with her, the crummier he felt about it.

Arianne watched Ben's forehead crease, his eyes darken as he seemed to struggle with some deep problem. Her family relationships couldn't be that complicated . . . or that interesting to a stranger. Was she still being paranoid, or did he seem unusually concerned with Julia? She'd sound totally irrational if she asked if he knew Julia. So what if her cousin and Ben had lived in the same city until Julia left a week ago. The two of them and about a million other people.

"Mommy, Gramma wants to talk to you!" Cody shouted.

Arianne went over to take the phone from her son.

"Baby, what's this business of Santa Claus's leaving Cody's daddy in the snow?" Gramma sounded worried, and that was the last thing Arianne wanted.

Both her grandparents were in their seventies and didn't need stress.

"He's playing pretend again. A traveler got lost in the snowstorm, and we took him in and thawed him out. Now, of course, he's stuck here until the roads are cleared. But don't worry. He's a perfectly nice person."

"That's what people said about Ted Bundy."

Arianne laughed. "Oh, Gramma. You can relax. This guy..." She crossed the fingers of her hand not holding the phone—a childhood sign, king's-x against telling a lie. "He's not very big. Short and scrawny. I can handle him."

"Hmmph. Just the same, I'm going to call George Watson and see if he'll get his scraper out and clear your road first thing in the morning."

"You do that. Then you and Gramps can get out here, too, and we'll have a belated Christmas dinner. I'm going to have plenty of leftovers."

She hung up the phone and turned to see Ben watching her with his arms folded across his chest and a wide grin on his face. Slowly, he lowered his gaze to scan his own over-six foot, well-muscled body. He looked back up at her, his lips mouthing the words "short and scrawny," one eyebrow lifting quizzically.

"I think it's time for me to fix breakfast and get the ham on for dinner," she said.

"I'll help," he offered.

She glanced at Cody sitting on the floor in front of the television, playing with his new video game. He'd doubtless be thrilled if Ben stayed to play with him... but she wasn't sure she wanted that. The more attached he got to Ben, the more disappointed he was going to be when the roads were cleared and Ben was gone. Maybe she couldn't always protect him from the pain of loss, but right now, she'd do her best.

"Thanks," she said to Ben. "I'm a little short-handed without Gramma."

"Short," he repeated.

She smiled. "She's afraid you're Ted Bundy's protégé. Come on. We're just going to have oatmeal for breakfast, but you can peel the potatoes for dinner."

"With a knife? What would Gramma say?"

"Guess you'll have to use a potato peeler. I don't think many people are killed with potato peelers."

The joking, the sharing of a secret, all seemed to create another link between them. She turned away, and he followed her into the kitchen, his presence behind her almost like a touch. Even if he chose to peel those potatoes with a meat cleaver, she reflected shakily, concern for her physical safety wasn't anywhere close to the top of her list of worries.

Arianne had always loved the kitchen in her grandparents' house—her house now. It was the same size as the living room, with plenty of cabinets, a large window over the sink, an outside door just past the cabinets and a bay window at the opposite end with ample room for the breakfast table.

But today, as Ben worked beside her helping to clean up the breakfast dishes and prepare dinner, the room seemed to have shrunk. Every time she moved, she brushed against him.

"Okay," he said, "potatoes peeled and chopped. What next?"

Go sit down and relax, she ought to say. *I can handle it.* She could. She should. She was perspiring even though, with all the windows and all the drafts, this room never got really hot in the winter. She should send Ben away. But she didn't want him to spend any more time with Cody than she could help.

She took the pan of potatoes from him, her fingers touching his on the handle as they made the transfer, sending tingles across her hands, down her arms, all through her. She leaned over the sink to turn on the water. Her shoulder touched his chest and electricity danced from his body to hers. She held the pan under the faucet, and neither of them moved to break the contact. Did he stay where he was because he didn't notice . . . or because he did?

However much she flinched from admitting it, Cody wasn't the only reason she didn't want Ben to leave the kitchen. Her mind was fuzzy, her skin sensitive to every sensation, her heart beating faster than it should . . . and she didn't want any of it to stop.

She was insane. She knew that. It would stop when he left. But right now . . .

Water sloshed over the edge of the pan of potatoes, into the sink.

"Damn!" She turned off the faucet, tipped out some of the water and whirled toward the gas range.

Still she didn't send him away. Instead, she showed him how to knead the dough for the dinner rolls. "Beat it. Torture it. Pretend it's . . . pretend it's your ex-wife." She didn't know why she said it, only that she wanted to know something about this man, wanted some piece of his past, some clue to who he was.

He grinned wryly. "I have nothing but sympathy for my ex-wife."

"Why?" she asked quietly, though she suspected she already knew the answer. He'd admitted he worked

seven days a week, that he didn't take time for play—
except on Christmas when he went skiing by himself.

His enigmatic gaze scanned her face, and for a moment she thought he wouldn't reply, would deem the
question too personal... though she couldn't imagine
feeling more personal with anyone than she felt in this
kitchen with this man.

"Because I was a bigamist. I was married to my
work, even in those days."

"You ignored her."

"I guess I did. And back then, I didn't make enough
money to make my absence worthwhile. I don't hate
her. I probably don't really feel sorry for her. To be
perfectly honest, I don't remember feeling much of
anything except annoyance when she complained that
I didn't spend any time with her."

His words seemed almost to be a warning... an un-
necessary warning. She knew all about men like him.
Her father, Julia's father, all their friends... she had
plenty of examples of the futility of becoming involved with their kind.

But his eyes drew her to him even as his words
pushed her away. The gray color was molten steel now,
liquid and fiery.

He lifted a hand and touched her cheek lightly with
his fingertips. His fingers were on fire. Her skin where
he touched her was on fire. Her lips tingled as though
he'd kissed her, and, against her will, she felt them part
slightly, anticipating, wanting, fearing.

She ordered herself to turn away, to get away, but she
was as powerless to follow that good advice as she had
been to tell him she didn't need any more help in the
kitchen.

Instead, Ben was the one who stopped, who removed his hand and himself. "Okay," he said.

Thud. He punched the bread dough viciously. "So I pretend this is the face of that nasty kid in the second grade who bloodied my nose. Right?" *Thud.*

Shaken...shaking...Arianne went to check on the ham. Her face was still hot, but for a different reason now. Was she as desperate for male companionship as Cody? So lonely, she'd want a complete stranger to kiss her?

No. She was alone by choice. Because Cody was her life, a blessing that wouldn't be repeated.

Or, she asked herself bluntly, was it because none of the men she'd met had made her feel the way Ben did? Suddenly, she had a better comprehension of why her mother tolerated her father's behavior. Was this the way he made her feel?

She opened the oven door and the heat rushed out at her, the temperature about the same as hers.

Chapter Four

The morning passed in a haze. She had to concentrate to remember how to make gravy or to add butter and salt to the green beans.

A little after two in the afternoon, she set the last dish of food on the big wooden table in the dining room and stood back to survey it. Even with the extra leaf in the table, there was barely enough room for everything. On the tablecloth, which had once been white, so Gramma said, but had been a soft ivory as long as Arianne could remember, Gramma's best china and silver gleamed. The ice tea in the tall old glasses shone like liquid jewels.

"It's beautiful, but you've got enough food for the entire town," Ben said, coming up behind her. Even though he didn't touch her, she could feel him there, would have known he was there even if he hadn't spoken. She could feel the outline of his body as surely as if she were running her hands over it.

"It's tradition," she blurted out, pulling her thoughts from their tantalizing, dead-end paths.

"You do this every year?"

She moved to the side of the table and adjusted the position of the bowl of corn. It didn't need adjusting. But she'd needed to move. "Yes, we do this every year. That's what makes it a tradition. We used to have lots of relatives, but the last few years it's just been Gramma and Gramps and Cody and me. This year, it's Cody and me..."

"And the stranger in the snow," he finished for her.

"Well, stranger, I hope you have a hearty appetite. Cody! Go wash up. Dinner's ready."

"Arianne..."

She didn't want to look at him, but didn't see how she could avoid it.

"Yes?"

He stood with his hands shoved deep into his pockets. "This is really nice of you. Sharing your Christmas with somebody you don't even know."

He was saying the right words, expressing the right sentiment, but something about the way he said it tweaked at the pit of her stomach. "As you can see, we have plenty to share," she replied ... and waited. She couldn't have said for what, but definitely for something.

He compressed his lips and cleared his throat. "Arianne, I need to talk to you."

Just then, Cody burst into the room, waving his small hands, sending drops of water flying. "It's almost quit snowing. We can go out and play with my sled after dinner." Even though he held his hands up for Arianne to inspect, the direction of his gaze left no doubt as to the person he expected to go out and play with him.

"They're clean," she approved, "but have you ever wondered why I keep those towels in the bathroom?"

Ignoring her, he darted to the side of the table and slid into his chair. "Sit here, Daddy." Cody leaned over and patted one end of the table.

Arianne sat down at the other end, draped her napkin across her lap and looked up to see Ben still standing, gazing at her. Did he need her permission, too? "Please," she said, indicating the opposite place setting.

Slowly, tenuously, he made his way around and took a seat facing her. Even though he was five feet away, she felt again that sense of touching, a connection between them. For an instant, the rightness, the completion of sitting at a table opposite Ben swept over her.

She gave herself a mental shake. The table was complete with just Cody and her.

She folded her hands. "Cody, would you ask the blessing?"

"God-is-great-God-is-good-and-we-thank-him-for-our-food-Amen. Mommy makes the best smashed potatoes in the whole world. Can I have gravy on everything?"

Ben was feeling guilty about abusing Arianne's hospitality—he hadn't intended to eat very much dinner—as if the less food he consumed, the less deceitful he was. But everything was so good, he soon found himself groaning in dismay that he couldn't hold any more.

As he leaned back in his chair, clutching his stomach, he saw from the corner of his eye that Cody was doing the same thing. With the same hand.

His son. The words echoed through his brain.

He had to tell Arianne the truth about why he was here. And when he told her, she'd probably kick him right out in the snow. But he couldn't go on eating her food, sleeping in her guest room...and wanting to hold her in his arms, kiss her until they both forgot about the world outside this little house, all the while knowing he was deceiving her.

"Ready for pie?" Arianne asked, rising from her chair.

"Yeah!" Cody cheered.

"Pie? When did you make pie?"

She smiled, gathering up the dirty plates. "All week. I have pecan and pumpkin and coconut and mincemeat. Real mincemeat made with pork, not just fruit and spices. And a chocolate cake."

"I want chocolate cake!" Cody declared, his eyes shining in anticipation. "No, wait. What are you gonna get, Daddy?"

Nothing. I can't eat another bite. "Maybe just a little piece of pecan. I've always been partial to pecan pie."

"Me, too, Mommy. I've always been par'l to pecan pie."

It should have been annoying, the way the boy parroted his words, his actions. But somehow it wasn't. Actually, it gave him a kind of warm feeling somewhere inside.

His son?

Arianne returned with three pieces of pecan pie on clean plates. Ben ate every crumb, his mouth exulting even while his stomach protested.

"That was delicious," he said. "Everything. What did you do to that ham? I've never tasted anything like it."

"Mr. Kemp gave it to us when he butchered hogs," Cody supplied. "He gave us ham and bacon and some other stuff, and we gave him green beans and tomatoes and pickles and some other stuff."

"You grow green beans and tomatoes out here?" Before the snow had completely overtaken him, he'd marveled at the desolation of the land.

"We had a garden," Cody said, "but it went away when it got cold."

"We irrigate. Everybody around here has wells. We also have a branch of the Beaver River running through our land, and on the rare occasions it has any water, we use that, too," Arianne explained. "The people who named the town Silver Creek had great imagination and poor eyesight. Muddy Creek would be more like it. Anyway, when I was little, Gramma and Gramps had a big farm. Now we just have a small garden for our own use."

"And Mr. Kemp's."

"Neighbors in the country trade food instead of bullets."

He clutched his chest in mock pain. "Ouch!"

She laughed ... almost a giggle ... and Cody joined her.

"I didn't mean to sound so self-righteous," she said. "Did you grow up in Dallas?"

He nodded. "It wasn't quite so big in those days. Northwest Highway was part of what we called Loop

12, a loop around the outskirts of the city instead of smack in the middle of things like it is now. But we never had a garden, and we never had food like this."

Cody nodded knowingly. "Pete's mommy makes awful smashed potatoes. They come out of a box."

"Pete's mommy and daddy are divorced, and she works hard all day," Arianne protested.

"Did your mommy work all day and make smashed potatoes out of a box?" Cody asked.

Ben nodded. "Yeah, she did. And pies out of a can. But your mommy works hard all day, too, and she's a good cook."

"She doesn't have dates and go places at night like Pete's mommy does. She always stays at home with me," Cody explained, and unwittingly bolstered Ben's growing certainty that Arianne couldn't possibly be involved in whatever Julia was trying to pull. His first impression of her had been right. She was totally unsophisticated . . . naive.

Arianne laughed, her head tilted to the side and slightly back, eyes crinkling and turning up at the corners, lips parted to reveal even, white teeth. He had to remind his hormones that he preferred sophisticated, worldly women; they were the only kind who could tolerate his life-style.

"You have no secrets around a five-year-old," she said. "Okay, hotshot, now that we've established that your mom has no social life, why don't you grab a few dirty dishes and help me clear the table."

Cody scooted his chair back and picked up his plate. "Daddy can help, too. He's bigger than me. He can carry more stuff."

"Cody!"

Ben smiled. "Sounds logical to me. I'll take the biggest bowls." He picked up the ham in one hand and the mashed potatoes in the other.

Sooner than he would have believed possible, considering the massive quantities of food and dishes, the table was clear, the dishes stacked on the counter and the leftover food in the refrigerator.

Arianne turned on the faucet, squeezed in some soap and bubbles began to rise from the sink. Ben would never have thought a woman washing dishes would be sexy, but Arianne was. She leaned against the sink, the soft fabric of her red jumpsuit caressing her rounded bottom. Her slim fingers shone with the soapy water as she lifted her hand, took a plate and plunged it beneath the bubbles.

When he got back to Dallas, he'd surely be able to remember that he wasn't attracted to naive, unsophisticated women. But right now, in this isolated rustic setting where this house seemed like the world and nothing existed outside, he was having a hard time remembering. He was having a hard time keeping his hands off her.

"It's 'bout quit snowing, Mommy," Cody said, reminding him the boy was still in the room with them. "Can we play on my sled?"

"We'll see. I'll tell you what." Then she turned her gaze from the window back to him, and he blinked rapidly in an effort to hide the direction his thoughts had taken. "As soon as I get these dishes done, we should be able to make our way to your car and get you a change of clothes. I suspect you're stuck here for at least one more night."

Stuck. One more night. Christmas was almost over and tomorrow was another workday. He'd planned to catch an early flight the next morning. He had things he needed to take care of. The thought of missing a day of work held a slight edge of panic.

But not half the panic raised by the other side of the coin. He'd be spending another night under the same roof as Arianne.

But even while he cursed the snow that kept him here, his heartbeat accelerated and his mind filled with a picture of her looking up at him when he'd touched her soft cheek, of her lips as they'd parted—waiting, asking to be kissed.

"I'll dry the dishes," he offered, trying to distract himself.

"That's not necessary. Why don't you call your family and wish them a merry Christmas while I'm doing this?"

"I really don't have any family. My mother died ten years ago."

"Oh. I'm sorry. Your father then."

Was she prying or being considerate? "My father and I aren't very close." She stood with her arms submerged to the elbows in soapy water, her eyes searching his. She was definitely prying... and, as a woman alone, trapped with a stranger, she had every right to. "He has another family. My parents got divorced when I was a baby, and I didn't see him again until I was an adult. It was a little late to establish a relationship."

"I see. How about the relative you were coming here to visit?"

He looked down at the small white tiles of the counter, at the polished marble design gray-and-white vinyl on the floor...anywhere but at her. He had to tell her the truth. He couldn't do this any longer.

"Cody, go see if you can find one of Gramps's old coats and a pair of boots that Ben can wear in the snow," she said.

She must have sensed something was wrong, he decided. She'd sent the boy out of the room deliberately. It was showdown time.

The telephone rang, and intense relief spread over him. A few more minutes to figure out the best way to say it. As if there could be any good way.

"Mommy," Cody called from the living room. "It's Aunt Julia."

Chapter Five

Arianne wasn't sure whether Julia's timing was great or terrible. Ben had been about to tell her something, she thought. And certainly her curiosity about him was overwhelming. But, irrationally, she wasn't sure she was ready to hear what he had to say.

She took the receiver from Cody. "Did you thank Aunt Julia for her gift?"

"Thank you, Aunt Julia!" he shouted.

Arianne lifted the receiver to her ear. "He loves it, Julia," she said into the mouthpiece. "He's been playing with it all day. And the jacket you sent me is so...festive."

Julia's laugh tinkled across the wires. "I know you, Annie. You think it's too gaudy. Well, you need to be a little more gaudy. Wear it. It'll look super with those gold pants I sent you for your birthday."

"The next formal party I attend, I'll be sure to wear

them both. Are you going to a lot of parties? What do you think of Hollywood?''

''It's wonderful! And the weather's so warm! I went to this absolutely incredible party last night in this unbelievably posh mansion, and we all went swimming at midnight! One of the guests was a director. I'm meeting all the right people. I've almost for sure got this part in a new vampire movie, as a vampire! Is that a kick or what?''

''That's wonderful, Julia. I'm really happy for you.'' Julia was flighty, and that was okay. Arianne understood why her cousin acted the way she did, why she dashed wildly from one flower to another . . . why she had been desperate to get to Hollywood in time for the holidays.

Arianne knew what it felt like to be a burden, to feel in the way of her parents' good times. If not for the accident that had landed her on her grandparents' farm when she was twelve, she might be out there with Julia, searching.

''Well, enough about me,'' Julia bubbled. ''Are you and Cody having a good Christmas? Are your grandparents there?''

''They haven't made it out yet. I know you'll find this hard to believe as you stand there in your bikini, but we're having a nightmare snowstorm here. The roads are closed. No way in or out.''

''You know, I did hear something about that on the news. Bad, huh? I guess you've got enough food and everything. I know you and your Gramma were always canning and freezing and that kind of thing.''

''We're fine. We just had a disgustingly abundant dinner. The three of us barely made a dent.''

''Three? The three of you? Who else is there?''

Arianne gave a brief imitation of a laugh. Something in the tone of Julia's voice sent a chill down her spine. "Don't sound so worried." *Naturally, Julia would be worried at the thought of Cody and her stranded with a stranger.* Except she hadn't said he was a stranger. Maybe she hadn't been completely off base when she'd thought Ben had shown an unusual interest in anything to do with Julia.

"Annie, who else is there?" Julia demanded.

Something was wrong. Arianne had no specific reason to think that, but fear fluttered its bat wings inside her chest.

"Actually, it's kind of a funny story," she said, trying to convince herself it was. "Last night, Cody and I found a man buried in the snow, so we brought him in and thawed him out and Cody asked Santa for a daddy for Christmas, and he thinks this is his Christmas present. It's been a very interesting Christmas." She was babbling. For no reason. Did she think Julia was going to tell her the man was a serial killer? Julia didn't even know who the man was.

"What's this guy's name?"

"Don't sound so ominous. He seems to be a perfectly nice man. He helped me put Cody's bicycle together, and he hooked up the video game you sent. He's much more mechanical than I am. Of course, most people are." Why couldn't she stop babbling? She had an eerie premonition, a feeling that she didn't want to hear what Julia had to say.

"This nice guy's name wouldn't be Ben Sloan, would it?"

Arianne made a noise she intended to be a laugh, but it came out as a hiccup. "Since when did you turn psychic?"

Julia sighed heavily...dramatically. "Oh, dear. I'm afraid we may have a teensy, weensy little problem here."

The bat wings inside Arianne's chest threatened to suffocate her. "What do you mean?"

"Well, you know how much I wanted to get out here before the holidays, and you know how nasty Daddy's been about sending money since he married his latest bimbo."

"Julia, stop making excuses and tell me what you're talking about."

Julia sighed again, more heavily, more dramatically. "I needed the money really bad. You're probably the only person in the world who'd understand, but I just couldn't face all that Christmas garbage."

Arianne gritted her teeth to keep from screaming. "Stop whining and tell me what you've done."

"Ben gave me money for telling him where you and Cody live."

"Why would he pay to know where we live?" Surely homicidal maniacs didn't pay for addresses of new victims. And surely even Julia wouldn't sell them out to a homicidal maniac.

"Well, you remember our little situation and how we assumed Lewis Davidson was Cody's father?"

"Assumed?"

"What else was I to think? There was only one other possibility, and it was such a remote one."

Arianne looked around to see if someone had opened the front door, if there were some explanation for the cold wind that suddenly engulfed her. "What possibility?"

"Oh, one night, Lewis broke a date to go to some dinner with his wife, and I went to this party and met

Ben. He's a real hunk, as you've probably noticed. Anyway, he'd just found out that day his divorce was final, and we kind of got together and drowned our sorrows.''

The cold wind sucked Arianne's breath away. Julia couldn't be suggesting . . . no, the idea was too awful, too terrifying. She couldn't even frame the thought in her mind. "Did you . . . ?''

"I don't remember all the details, but, yeah, I'd say we did.''

"So you're not sure?'' *Please say you're not sure.*

"Okay, I'm sure. I remember that much. But when I found out about Cody being on the way, well, Ben was struggling to start his own company then. He wouldn't have been able to pay the bills for me to have Cody. Maybe you wouldn't have got to keep him if not for Lewis. And the odds were certainly in Lewis's favor that he was the father.''

"Julia, you're not making any sense.'' She heard her cousin's words, knew what each one meant, but they weren't coming together to form a meaningful idea.

"Yes, I am. I saw Ben again a couple of weeks ago at a party, and it was really obvious. I mean, he looks exactly like Cody. But I swear I never dreamed he'd go to your house. I mean, what does a bachelor, a workaholic from what I hear, want with a kid? Probably he just wanted to see what Cody looks like.''

The room spun out of control around her. Julia couldn't mean it. This man who'd entered their lives so suddenly couldn't be Cody's father.

Yet Cody had insisted on calling him *Daddy.* Had he known, with the eerie, almost supernatural knowledge of the young and innocent?

"Annie, are you there?''

Arianne had to try twice before her voice worked. "Yes."

"You're all upset. I can tell. Damn! Why'd he have to come to your place and bother you? Look, it'll be fine. If the snowstorm hadn't trapped him there, he'd have taken one quick glance to satisfy his curiosity and then run like a scared rabbit straight out of town."

She had to control herself. Both Cody and Ben were probably listening. She bit her lower lip to stop the trembling. "I hope you're right," she said.

"Of course I'm right. You and I both know that kind of man wants his hormonal accidents to stay in the background, out of the way of his good times."

It was the first comforting thing Julia had said, the only reason Arianne didn't reach through the phone wires and throttle her.

After she hung up, Arianne stood for a few minutes with her hand on the receiver, trying to catch her breath, trying to comprehend what had just happened . . . and what she should do next.

She was having a hard time accepting that Cody might be Ben's son, that this man who'd come in with the blizzard, who'd shared Christmas dinner with her, had helped her put Cody's bicycle together...this man who Cody called *Daddy* might have fathered her son. Julia had sounded so positive, but there was really no way to be sure except through a blood test. She wouldn't—couldn't—believe it until that time.

And she prayed that time would never come. Surely Julia was right. Probably Ben only wanted to see Cody out of curiosity. Probably he'd have been long gone if he hadn't been trapped by the storm. Probably he just wanted to look and be gone, leaving no strings dangling behind. Otherwise, surely he would have confronted her, brought everything out in the open and accused her of stealing Cody.

But all those *probablys* represented a chance she couldn't afford to take. Cody was her life, and she was his. No matter that she hadn't given birth to Cody. He was her child. She'd never let him be raised the way she'd been raised, and Ben's life-style was distressingly similar to her father's ... to Julia's father's.

She'd left Ben in the kitchen when she came in to answer the phone. He'd probably overheard everything she'd said. Not that it mattered. There was only one course of action she could take.

Slowly, she turned, walked on numb feet to the kitchen. He stood at the counter exactly where he'd been when she'd gone to take Julia's call. Frozen in place. Listening.

The suds in her dishwater had vanished, leaving it dingy and cold-looking.

"We need to talk," she said quietly.

"Here, Daddy!" Cody rushed in carrying old boots, gloves and a coat left there by her grandfather. "You got to dress warm to go out in the snow." He repeated to Ben her familiar advice as he offered the clothing to him.

The look on Ben's face—fear, uncertainty and a possessive longing—confirmed her deepest terrors. He wouldn't stop with an inspection of her son. He wouldn't stop until he had a place in Cody's life. He could take Cody away from her. She had no legal right to him. The very best she could hope for was that he'd be willing to share Cody with her ... and even so, their lives would be totally disrupted.

This was the moment she'd dreaded, the moment she'd prepared for that night over five years ago when Cody was born.

Cody was happy, and she'd see to it that he stayed that way.

"Cody, why don't you go in the living room and play while... while Ben and I finish up in here." For a moment, she hadn't known what to call him. She'd almost said *your father,* then started to change it to *Mr. Sloan.* But that wouldn't do, either. She had to appear completely normal, sound undisturbed. She didn't dare let this man know how distressed she was. How desperate.

"Then we'll go play in the snow?"

"I promise. Run along, now. Ben, if you'll excuse me for a minute, I'll be right back and we can...finish this."

Ben sank into a wooden kitchen chair at the scarred drop-leaf table as he watched Arianne leave the room, her slender back straight...too straight. Where was she going? To get a gun and shoot him? He tried unsuccessfully to give a mental laugh at his own bad joke.

Realistically, where could she be going? She couldn't be planning to snatch the kid and run away into the snow.

From what he'd overheard, Julia had obviously told her who he was. And it had just as obviously been news to her. This whole thing had been Julia's idea and Julia's only. Knowing Arianne had no part in it buoyed his spirits immeasurably. He still didn't know if Cody was really his son or not, but at least he didn't have to distrust Arianne.

She, however, had every reason to be upset with him. If only he'd told her the truth before that blasted phone call came.

As he'd waited for her to get off the phone, he'd prepared a defense of his actions. He didn't want her to be angry at him. He wanted her to look at him again with dark eyes full of desire, to part her lips again and wait for him to kiss her...even though he knew he couldn't let himself do it.

But she hadn't been angry. She'd been reserved, cool, unknowable. Surely she didn't think he'd try to take Cody away from her? Not since he'd met her and seen her devotion to the boy. He'd never be able to give anyone such total devotion, not when he spent twelve hours or more every day at work.

Actually, he wasn't sure what he'd do if Cody was his son.

He'd do something, though. Whatever it took to ensure that his son had everything he needed, that he himself was a part of Cody's life, that Cody knew the truth. He'd figure out what to do when...and if...the time came.

As for Arianne—surely this attraction would pass. He'd deal with that later, too.

If Cody wasn't his son, there would be nothing to deal with. He'd be gone tomorrow and never see her again.

Somehow, the thought failed to comfort him.

She returned to the kitchen clutching a manila envelope and a brown leather purse. Only her white knuckles and a barely discernible tightness in her jaw muscles betrayed her tension.

"I'm afraid my cousin has done something unforgivable," she said, sliding into a chair opposite him and laying the envelope on the table between them.

From the living room came the electronic noises of Cody's video game, interspersed with his little-boy whoops.

The wooden seat of the old chair became hard and uncomfortable as he waited for her to continue.

"She confessed to me on the phone," Arianne went on. "I know what she told you. About Cody. What she said isn't true. You've been conned. I really am Cody's mother, and his father really is dead, killed in a car accident. A drunken driver."

He stared at her, hearing what he'd expected to hear, what he'd wanted to hear. That she was innocent, that Cody wasn't his. He wouldn't need to make any changes in his life-style, try to work a child into his schedule . . . he and Arianne wouldn't have any disagreements about visitation or custody. They could be friends. Or at least not enemies.

So why didn't her pronouncement make him happy?

She opened her purse and took out a checkbook. "I'll give you a check for the money you gave Julia, and by tomorrow you should be able to get back to Dallas."

"The money? Where would you get ten thousand dollars?" It wasn't what he'd meant to say, but it was the only coherent thought he had at the moment.

She smiled without parting her lips. It was the coldest smile he'd ever seen. "I'm a very frugal person."

He shook his head. "I don't want your money."

"You can't have my son." She opened the manila envelope and slapped a square of paper onto the tabletop. "I am Cody's mother," she repeated.

Slowly he lowered his gaze to the paper, to the birth certificate for Cody Lee Landis, born to Arianne Landis and Samuel Landis.

"I apologize for Julia's behavior," Arianne said. "She's not a bad person, just an amoral person. Her parents are quite wealthy. They taught her to enjoy money without teaching her to respect it."

"If she has money, then why did she concoct such a wild story to get mine?"

Arianne's smile was brittle. "My uncle is on his fourth or fifth—I can't keep up—trophy wife. With all that alimony and all that child support, he has to cut back where he can. Naturally, his oldest daughter would be one of the first luxuries to go."

Ben smoothed the birth certificate with one finger. "I'm sorry," he mumbled, not completely clear what he was sorry for.

"There's no reason for you to apologize. On behalf of my cousin, I should be the one to do that." She ducked her head, her pen moving over a check.

He reached across the table and laid his hand on hers, stopping the motion. Her fingers beneath his were cold. "Don't," he said. "Don't write me a check and don't apologize."

She regarded him calmly, stoically, and he realized one of the things that bothered him. He would have preferred that she be angry, that she be hurt, that she feel some emotion, anything other than this cold aloofness.

He took his hand from hers, and she finished writing the check, then proffered it to him. He tore it into confetti while she watched with no change in expression.

He ran his fingers distractedly through his hair, pushing it back from his forehead, and he thought her eyes widened, her pupils dilated. But he couldn't be sure, nor could he see any reason that his simple gesture would frighten her.

She dropped her gaze to the table, picked up the birth certificate and slid it back into the envelope, splaying her fingers across it, pressing it to the tabletop.

"In any event, I regret that my cousin disrupted your Christmas, and you ended up snowbound with total strangers." Her words were measured—not exactly insincere, but distinctly hollow.

He shook his head. "I don't regret spending Christmas with you."

At that moment, Cody charged into the room and ran over to grab Ben's thigh with both hands. "Daddy, come on! It's going to get dark pretty soon and we can't play outside."

"Cody, stop it!" Arianne snapped. Cody's head jerked in her direction, his eyes wide. Obviously he wasn't accustomed to having his mother speak to him in that tone of voice.

She blushed and drew a shaky hand across her forehead. "Cody, you've played pretend long enough. This gentleman has a name. From now on, until he leaves tomorrow, I think you should call him Mr. Sloan."

Ben flinched. That sounded a little harsh. He was about to suggest *Uncle Ben* as a compromise, when

Cody thrust out his chin defiantly. "Can't." He turned and scampered from the room.

To his surprise, Arianne didn't seem angry at her son's refusal. She watched him leave with apprehension and fear written all over her face, but not anger. And she had every right to be angry—at him, at Julia, at the snowstorm.

"It's okay," he assured her. "I'll soon be out of your lives, and he'll find something else to pretend."

"That's why it's not okay. No child should have to live with thinking his father doesn't want him. Even if he's wrong about who his father is."

Ben nodded. "That's one thing we agree on."

She picked up the envelope and held it against her breasts with both arms crossed tightly over it. "Yes," she said, her words coming out in a monotone. "You said your father left when you were a baby and you didn't see him again."

"Until my mother died. She refused to let him see me, but she lied to me and told me he never tried. I guess that's why I was so upset when Julia told me I had a son. I don't want any child of mine to go without anything, including a father."

"I'm sure your intentions are good, but earlier you admitted you were a lousy husband. What makes you think you could be a good father?"

"Because..." He hadn't really thought about it in those terms. "Because being a parent is something that comes naturally. You should know that. And because I have a lot more to offer now than I did when I was married. My company is doing fine. I could give my kid the best of everything."

She studied him silently for a minute, the intensity of her gaze making him uncomfortable.

"I guess the point is moot since you don't have a son," she finally said.

"Yeah," he agreed. "I guess it is." So why did he have this queasy feeling of unfinished business?

She raised her head, fixing a guileless gaze on him that gave him some ideas of his own.

"I think he's still in a foul mood. You don't want a fussy son, same trouble now."

"No, ma'am," he said fervently. "No," she said as she gave him a glance.

Chapter Six

Arianne slid her chair back from the table and stood. "Cody's right. Nightfall will come early. We'd better go to your car if we're going. See if those clothes will fit you while Cody and I get bundled up."

Heart pounding madly, guilt and fear battling for ascendancy, she climbed the stairs, carrying her purse and Cody's birth certificate. She'd heard that people surprised themselves with their calmness under stress. She couldn't have been under any more stress if someone had held a gun to her head; she was amazed that she'd managed to handle the situation as well as she had.

She'd done what she had to do, and part of that was to ignore the guilt. Cody's happiness was all that mattered, she repeated to herself. *If* Ben was his father— and that remained to be proven—she suspected that Ben would never let him go, even though he didn't have a clue about what it meant to be a parent. Love created a parent, not just passing on a set of genes. Julia was certainly no mother.

Ben didn't love Cody. He'd be the same kind of father that hers had been—that Julia's, Cody's grandfather, had been. He'd give his child everything—everything that money could buy, then shove him into a corner and ignore him.

He'd probably keep her on as a nanny, she thought wryly.

She wouldn't let that happen. Checking Julia into the hospital under the name *Arianne Landis*—her own first name and her grandmother's maiden name—was the smartest thing she'd ever done. When Lewis Davidson, Julia's married lover, had refused to sign adoption papers because that would be admitting the child was his, Arianne Norton had assumed the name Arianne Landis. She had insisted on the deception . . . just in case.

And *just in case* was here.

Right now, her sole Christmas wish was that the roads would be plowed tomorrow, and she could get Ben out of here before he had any reason to doubt that she'd given birth to Cody.

She came back downstairs dressed in wool slacks and sweater to find Ben in the foyer helping Cody button up his coat. On the last step she paused, her heart squeezing painfully at the sight. She could see how Julia was so positive about the relationship between man and child. The resemblance was almost eerie. How could Ben fail to notice?

She glanced out the window at the snow, glaring at it, willing it to melt.

Ben and Cody were laughing and clowning around...looking every inch the happy father and son. With the belief that Cody wasn't his son, Ben seemed to have lost his tenseness. Which only proved she'd done the right thing. He didn't want to be a father.

"Okay, guys," she said, making a determined effort to sound cheerful, "let's prepare to brave the elements."

"I gotta get my sled!" Cody ran back into the living room while Arianne slipped into her coat and boots. From the closet shelf, she took down gloves and ski masks for herself and Cody, then added an extra one for Ben.

"Better put this on," she said, meeting his eyes for the first time since she'd come downstairs. She almost sagged with relief when she saw no suspicion, no doubt, no accusations. He believed her.

"I have plenty of warm ski clothes in the car," he protested. "If we go in a straight line this time, it shouldn't be far. Right?" He grinned, making light of his near-fatal arrival.

"Take the mask. You can get frostbite in less time than it'll take to get to your car. This isn't Texas or the ski slopes of Colorado. The weather gets down and dirty here."

"Yes, ma'am." He pulled the mask on. "This is yours, isn't it?" His voice was no longer teasing. Instead, it held a husky undertone.

"Wear it. Ski masks are gender neutral."

"It smells like you."

She could barely see his eyes through the holes, but she could see enough. They, like his voice, were smoky with desire.

"I'll get you a clean one." In dismay, she heard her own words come out sounding throaty. In spite of knowing why he'd come there, what his life was like and that he'd be gone tomorrow, she was still drawn to him, still ached to touch him, to feel his lips on hers. Her body seemed to have detached itself from her brain.

"Let's go!" She whirled to see Cody dragging his sled, beaming happily.

She stooped to put on his gloves and ski mask, to hide from the look in Ben's eyes, from her own need.

"Hurry, hurry!" Cody bounced from one foot to the other. When Arianne finally freed him, he dashed for the door. "Come on, Da . . ." He stopped and looked back at her guiltily, then up at Ben. "Come on. I'll show you how to build a snow cave."

If that was his compromise, to use no name at all, she could accept that. Just so long as he didn't call him *Daddy*.

She followed close behind as he and Ben plodded out the door into the arctic air. As soon as they stepped off the porch, Cody dropped his sled and flopped backward, almost disappearing into the snow.

"Cody!" Ben lunged toward him, but Arianne grabbed his arm.

"Snow angel," she explained as Cody moved his arms and legs up and down, forming arcs. He clambered up, eyes shining expectantly.

"Best angel you've ever done," Arianne enthused.

"Cool," Ben approved, looking it over. "That's *all right*. It really does kind of look like an angel."

Cody bounced onward, kicking up small flurries of powdery snow. "Mommy, can we build a snowman?"

"Not today. It's too cold. The snow won't stick together. Maybe tomorrow."

"Tomorrow, tomorrow, tomorrow," Cody half
grumbled, half sang as he made his way through the
snow, stepping as high as his short legs would allow.

"Sounds like good lyrics for a song," Ben said.

He had not only lost his tension, he seemed absolutely delirious since learning that Cody wasn't his son.
Though she knew that was for the best, a part of her
resented it. How could anybody be glad not to have
Cody as part of his life?

Cody stopped and tried to form some of the snow
into a ball.

Arianne shook her head and laughed softly. "He
never takes anybody's word for anything. He always
has to find out for himself."

"Good for him," Ben said. "Keep trying, Cody!"

"Come help me. You got big hands. You can smash
it harder."

Ben looked at her, shrugged as if in embarrassment,
then went over to where Cody stood. He scooped up a
handful of snow, squeezed his hands together, then
separated them to reveal loose snow.

"I think your mom's right this time."

Cody bent down again, burying his arms up to the
elbows, then came up swiftly, giggling and throwing
snow all over Ben. For a moment, Ben stood frozen in
place as if stunned. Then he dipped up a double handful of snow and trickled it over Cody's head.

"All right, boys," Arianne interrupted, stepping
between them. "It's much too cold to get into a snow
fight." But it was the feeling of being excluded from
Cody's fun that bothered her more than fear of the

cold...as though being excluded now could mean she'd be excluded from the rest of his life.

Accepting the doctor's pronouncement that she'd probably never be able to have children had been devastating, a devastation she still lived with every day. But those children she'd never conceive had been faceless; Cody had a face, a smile, a voice, a niche in her heart. Losing him would mean losing a part of herself. The best part.

"Aw, Mom."

"Don't give me any lip, hotshot. Move it along." She swatted his well-padded rear.

Though she couldn't see Ben's face beneath the ski mask, she imagined he was looking at her curiously, questioning her behavior. But she knew that was only her guilt and paranoia talking. She hadn't done anything out of the ordinary.

As they walked into deeper snow, Cody was having a hard time making headway. Ben reached down and scooped him up, settling him on his shoulders.

He was definitely a lot more relaxed around Cody than he'd been before.

Ahead of them a mailbox cleared the snow by only a few inches. Beside it stood a vaguely car-shaped white mound.

Ben stopped in his tracks and whistled. Cody imitated him. Arianne's heart clenched.

"The other side's probably a little cleaner," she said, going around to the lee side as if that were her only concern. "It would have been sheltered from the wind."

"Amazing," he murmured, setting Cody down and coming up behind her. "You can tell it's a car over here but not on the other side."

Ben opened the trunk and took out one suitcase, a ski jacket and boots. "Your grandfather's feet were smaller than mine," he explained.

She nodded, suddenly anxious to get away from the car with its set of skis in the back seat. This was Christmas, a time for home and family, not ski trips. Suddenly, she wanted to be in her house with her son, warm and safe.

"We need to start back. I think it's getting colder."

The phone was ringing when they got back to the house. Arianne yanked off her ski mask and gloves and grabbed the receiver.

"Merry Christmas, baby," her mother's voice trilled.

"Thanks, Mom. Same to you."

"Thank you, sweetheart. Actually, it was Christmas here yesterday. I'm getting ready to go out and lie on the sunny beaches of Australia and turn my skin to leather."

"Oh, well, that sounds like fun." It was like talking to a stranger. Worse, really. She never knew what to say. She didn't want to ask how her father was; her mother probably had no idea, and asking would only remind her.

"Did you and Cody get the check I sent for Christmas presents?"

"Yes, we did. Thank you. It was very generous."

"Darling, you know everything I have is yours."

"I know, Mom."

"Oh, someone's at the door. I'd better run. The beach is waiting."

Arianne hung up the phone and took a deep breath, filling her lungs with fresh air, air from the house where she lived with her son, air filled with love that could drive out the emptiness she always felt after talking with her mother. Cody would never experience such emptiness. Whatever it took, she'd see to that.

Arianne came downstairs after tucking Cody into bed.

"He's a great kid." Ben sat on the hearth, one foot on the floor, the other on the stone surface with his sweater-clad arm draped across his knee. His eyes followed every move she made, and she felt warm everywhere his gaze touched her, as though he were caressing her.

"Yes," Arianne agreed. "Cody's pretty special." She sank into her chair, automatically reaching for her book, then halting midway. That would be rude. Not that she could concentrate on reading right now, anyway.

All day, even after their confrontation, she had been tantalizingly aware of Ben's presence. Now they were alone in front of a roaring fire, neither of them able to leave even if they wanted to. A romantic setting straight out of one of the novels she loved to read. With one exception. They were real people, not characters in a book. Their actions had consequences.

She cleared her throat. "Would you like to watch television?"

He continued to gaze at her for so long without answering her, she wasn't sure he'd heard her, wasn't completely certain she'd spoken. Finally, he shook his head slowly. "Not unless you do."

"No." She swallowed. Maybe she should plead exhaustion and go to bed even though it was only nine o'clock.

But she couldn't do that. She didn't seem capable of anything except sitting glued to her chair, gazing back at Ben. The backdrop of flames created a flickering luminosity around him, while shadows softened his strong features. The crackling, popping noises the fire made as it consumed the logs seemed to come from the electricity flowing between the two of them.

"The fire's nice," he said as if reading her thoughts. She had to remind herself he was talking about the blaze behind him, not the one between them. "It smells good, sounds good, feels good."

She nodded jerkily, making a determined mental effort to clamp down on her runaway fantasies that attached a double meaning to his words. "That's what it's for. The gas heaters warm your body, but the fireplace warms your soul."

He smiled lazily, seductively. "That's nice, too."

She could feel herself blushing and hoped the lights were low enough he wouldn't notice. "It's not original. Gramma used to say that when Gramps complained about the price of wood. We don't grow a lot of our own in these parts."

"I noticed. How long have you lived here? You mentioned that you used to live in Dallas."

"I lived in Dallas until I was twelve years old, lived here until I was eighteen, then I went to college in Denton and taught school in Dallas for a year, and back to Silver Creek for good."

"You must have missed big D. You went back."

"I went back to go to school with Julia. We were best friends from the time we were in diapers until I moved here. I know you don't have a very good image of Julia, but she's really a lonely, insecure person. She needed me to be with her in college."

He raised one eyebrow skeptically, then seemed to reconsider and nodded. "Yeah, I guess I can see that. But only because you pointed it out."

"It could just as easily have been me," she said quietly. "I had an accident water skiing when I was twelve, and my parents sent me up here to recover."

"And you stayed until you were eighteen? That must have been some accident."

She laughed. "No, it didn't take me six years to heal. My bones mended fast. I recovered completely except..." She bit her tongue. She'd been about to say, *Except my chances of having children are virtually nil.* That wouldn't be a wise thing to say if she wanted him to believe she'd given birth to Cody.

"Except...?" He paused.

She lifted her hands in a careless gesture. "Except I didn't want to go back to Dallas. I stayed because I love it here. The best thing that could have happened. Well, gosh, I'm really tired. It's been a busy day. I think I'll call it a night. You stay up as long as you like."

He rose at the same time she did, standing only inches away, so close she could feel his breath warm on her cheek... so close she fancied she could hear his heart beating.

It was really only hers doing double time; she knew that.

Just then, he placed his hands on the sides of her face. His fingers were big and capable and tender.

"Arianne?" he whispered, making a question of her name.

She knew she had only to make a halfhearted protest and he'd walk away from her, go upstairs, leave tomorrow...and she'd never know how his lips felt on hers.

She raised her hands, spread her fingers across his chest and lifted her face to him.

Slowly, she let the wonder, the ecstasy, wash over her as his mouth touched hers, gently, tentatively, exploring every sensitive nerve, then moving with more certainty, more possessiveness, and it seemed their lips had known each other forever, had kissed this way a thousand times.

She responded to him, her own lips taking and giving, opening to invite him to more of her. His hands threaded through her hair, and she pressed her body closer to his, her arms wrapping around his broad back, feeling the muscles beneath her fingers, every contact point creating another exploding sensation. He was solid against her, filling her arms, her mind, her soul, making her aware of every inch of her body even while she felt weightless, as though she might float to the ceiling at any minute.

And then he drew back...slowly, reluctantly, it seemed.

She wanted to pull him to her again. She wanted the exquisite feelings he roused in her never to stop. This must be the way people felt when they talked about being high on drugs.

"I think," he whispered, drawing one finger across her bottom lip, "I'd better go upstairs."

"Yes," she agreed. "You'd better." *Before I become addicted.*

As if pulling against a magnet, she turned away from him and concentrated on banking the fire. "Good night," she said. "I'll call first thing in the morning about getting the roads cleared."

She'd needed to say that, to remind herself that he was leaving tomorrow, that this one kiss was all she'd ever have of this particular drug. A potentially lethal drug.

"That's good," he said, his voice sounding disembodied as it came from somewhere behind her.

Arianne closed the fireplace doors, but she didn't turn around until she heard Ben's footsteps going up the stairs. Only when she heard his door close did she follow him up.

As she passed Cody's door, she opened it to check on him. And found him standing at the window. He turned around as she came in, a startled, guilty look on his small face.

"What are you doing?" she asked.

He thrust out his jaw stubbornly. "Asking Santa for another snowstorm."

"Another snowstorm? Why? Don't you think we have enough snow already?"

"So Da... So *he* won't have to go away tomorrow like you said he would."

She sighed, crossed the room and lifted the boy. "Ben has to leave. He has a job and friends and a home he has to get back to."

"He has us now."

She laid him on the bed and tucked him in. "Ben is leaving tomorrow as soon as the roads are clear. The forecast is for clear and warming." She brushed back the lock of hair that fell over his forehead...just the way Ben's did. "Sweetheart, Christmas is over. Santa Claus can't grant any more wishes until next year."

"Christmas isn't over 'til midnight."

"You're talking technicalities, hotshot, Trust me, it's all over." All of it. The fear of discovery, the feel of his lips on hers that drugged her mind and body...all of it. Finished.

Chapter Seven

Arianne awoke with a start and snatched up her bedside clock. Seven-thirty. Damn! She'd overslept.

She'd lain awake for a long time last night, the events of the day replaying over and over in her head... especially the way she'd felt when Ben had kissed her. It was a good thing he would soon be gone, or she could end up like her mother—charmed by a man capable only of giving material gifts... and delectable kisses.

She should have set the alarm clock. Oversleeping with a five-year-old boy in the house wasn't a good idea. The last time she'd done that, he'd poured pancake mix and milk into the toaster. After the appliance blew up, he'd explained that, on television, waffles came out of the toaster.

On her way to the bathroom, she noticed that Ben's door was open and the bed made. He was downstairs with Cody. So the toaster was probably safe...but she wasn't so sure about Cody's future. The more time Ben spent with him, the more attached Cody would become to him, and the more likely Ben was to discover her deception. She showered and dressed hurriedly.

As she came down the stairs, Ben and Cody looked up. Both of them wore blue jeans and flannel shirts as they sat on the floor with Cody's new set of plastic blocks spread out between them. For a moment, she was struck by the harmony of the scene before her. They looked as if they could be father and son... together... a family.

But this was an instant out of reality. This wasn't the way Ben normally lived. If he were at home, he'd already have left for work...if he'd come home the night before. Ben wasn't a "family" person. He'd admitted that.

"Good morning," Ben said, smiling, his warm gaze stroking over her peach-colored sweater and faded blue jeans.

She felt the heat rise to her face, but the truth was, after an argument with herself, she'd worn the clothes on purpose, knowing both garments flattered her. She'd wanted Ben to look at her just that way. After all, she was safe. He'd be gone in a few hours.

"Mommy, Mommy!" Cody ran to grab her around the waist, his face wreathed in a smile. "Santa Claus came last night!"

"Night before last," she corrected. "Is that coffee I smell? How long have you two been up?"

Ben grinned ruefully, rising from the floor. "Yes, it's coffee, we've been up about an hour and I'm afraid *last* night Santa Claus came back to bring Cody one more present."

"Come see!" Cody tugged on her hand, pointing to the window. Huge white flakes drifted down silently, slowly and inexorably.

She blinked, not quite believing her eyes, then walked over to stand in front of the window.

"Santa Claus brought more sno-o-ow," Cody sang happily.

And Ben can't leave today.

Her mind raced with thoughts of what this meant.

More chances for him to discover the truth about Cody.

More chances for her to be near him, to touch him, to kiss him.

More chances for Cody and her both to become attached to him...

"It's beautiful," Ben said, coming up beside her. His shoulder barely touched hers, but she felt wrapped in an embrace. "When I was a little boy, I had one of those snowstorm globes with a tiny house and a tree inside. That's what it feels like now, like I'm inside that house."

She nodded. "Safe and warm." But her world wasn't safe as long as Ben was here. "You may be stuck here for another day unless it stops soon." *Another night.* No, her world was definitely not safe.

Another day. The words echoed in Ben's mind, and he felt a sudden surge of panic. Christmas Day had been one thing, a holiday, sort of a dream, actually. But Christmas was over. He needed to get out of here. He needed to be back in his office where he belonged, where he understood what was going on, where he could negotiate a deal and know the outcome, see the profit margin in black and white. He didn't belong here... in this house, with these people.

Cody wasn't his son.

And Arianne...well, Arianne was a delectable temptation and something of an enigma. What had she been about to tell him last night? *Except...* She'd hesitated then had finished with some lame stuff about not wanting to leave here. But he didn't think that had been her original thought.

While he might not know what she'd been going to say, he did know that she wasn't the kind of woman he could fit into his life, someone he could spend the night with when he could spare the time, someone he could pick up from time to time as his schedule allowed, someone who'd understand his schedule. She was the kind of woman who'd want a commitment, a man who came home for dinner every evening, who remembered her birthday...and she was the kind of woman who deserved a man like that.

Ben turned from the window and the fairy-tale scene outside, from the warmth of her shoulder next to his.

"I'd better start breakfast," Arianne said, moving farther away, increasing the distance between them.

"We already had breakfast, Mommy."

"You did?" She looked at Ben and lifted a quizzical eyebrow.

"Yeah, we had chocolate cake," Cody said, beaming up at him.

"With a glass of milk," Ben added hastily.

Arianne folded her arms beneath her breasts, stretching the fabric of the sweater over their soft curves. If she was trying to look stern, she wasn't doing a very good job of it. "A glass of milk," she repeated.

Cody wrapped both small arms around one of Ben's legs. "Chocolate milk," he said proudly.

Ben flinched and grinned wryly. "Cody, we need to talk about how you shouldn't always tell everything you know."

For an instant, Arianne looked stricken, an odd reaction to his joking comment and, he couldn't help thinking, further proof that she was hiding something.

"That's right," she agreed softly. "You shouldn't." So what was she not telling him?

She smiled and shrugged, turning away to go into the kitchen. "Well, at least you didn't blow up the toaster."

"Blow up the toaster?" Ben repeated. "Why would you think we'd do that?"

Cody took his hand. "I don't tell everything I know."

Ben felt the small, warm fingers wrapping around his, heard the noise of Arianne in the kitchen rattling dishes, smelled the cedar tree, the spices from Arianne's Christmas cooking, the wood they'd burned the night before and a lingering, elusive scent he noticed every time he got close to Arianne.

Panic overwhelmed him again. "Okay if I use your phone to check in with my office?" he called. *Check in with the real world, reestablish contact, before I get so lost in this snowstorm-globe world, I can never find my way back.*

Arianne leaned through the doorway of the kitchen. "Sure. Help yourself. Is your office open the day after Christmas?"

"Of course. It's Tuesday. Just another weekday."

"Of course. I suppose we teachers are spoiled by having the whole week off between Christmas and New Year's."

Arianne retreated into the kitchen and spooned sugar over her cold cereal, involuntarily listening as Ben talked to his office. In an authoritative voice, he discussed sales figures and meetings and contracts, and she felt as though she were Cody's age again, listening to her father.

With a start, she realized she'd spooned half a bowl of sugar over her cereal. And maybe that wasn't such a bad idea. She was going to need all the help she could find to get through this day. A sugar high was as good a beginning as anything else.

After finishing her cereal—minus most of the sugar—and cleaning up her dishes along with the ones Cody and Ben had left, Arianne went into the living room. Ben sat on the sofa, apparently absorbed in a stack of papers while Cody played at his feet.

The room felt chilly.

"Hey, hotshot, want to come with me to the shed room and bring in some more wood for a fire?"

Ben looked up and Cody scrambled to his feet. "Come on," he urged Ben. "You're bigger. You can carry more."

"Cody! Leave Ben alone. He's working."

He laid down his papers and rose from the sofa. Yes, Arianne thought, swallowing hard, he was definitely bigger. Big and virile and, in those blue jeans, deliciously tantalizing.

"I think I can spare some time to bring in wood," he said. "Where and what is the shed room?"

"It's back there." Cody indicated the far side of the living room. "It's where we keep the freezer and the snow shovel and stuff that doesn't belong in the house and where we go to pull off our shoes when it's muddy outside. Don't you have one?"

"No, I don't. You see, I live in a condo. An apartment."

"Boy, I bet you track in a lot of mud." Cody turned and set off toward the rear of the house.

Ben looked at Arianne helplessly. She shrugged, suppressing a smile. "Get a shed room. Your housekeeper will thank you."

Cody yanked open the door at the end of the living room, went into the darkness and began jumping up and down.

"What's he doing?" Ben asked.

Arianne stepped into the room and pulled the chain, turning on the bare light bulb dangling overhead. "Trying to do that. A couple more years to go, I'm afraid."

Cody grabbed a stick of wood and dashed out.

"It's cold in here," Ben observed.

Arianne knelt to pick up a couple of pieces of wood from the dwindling pile. "Not much point in heating it."

Ben crouched beside her and took the wood from her. "Let me. I'm bigger. Remember?"

That was for sure. He seemed to fill the room...and it definitely didn't feel cold anymore as his shoulder brushed hers, as heat seemed to flow from his entire body. She could no longer feel the weight of the firewood in her arms, but she could feel every millimeter of flesh where his fingers touched hers as he reached to relieve her of her burden.

Suddenly, she realized his hands were no longer moving. They had stilled, entwined with—bonded to—hers, and she no longer felt the roughness or the weight of the wood. She could feel only Ben's flesh touching hers. She could hear herself—or him—breathing, saw their mingled breaths coming together in puffs of white.

Afraid of what she'd see, knowing what she'd see, she raised her eyes to his, to the gaze that had seemed so cold the first time she'd seen him and now gleamed as charcoal filled with banked fires. The desire that flowed between them was almost palpable.

"More!" Cody burst into the room with a shout.

Arianne gasped, dropping the wood and almost losing her balance. Ben grabbed her shoulders, steadying her with a firm grip. "You okay?"

She nodded, rising rapidly, needing to escape the touch she didn't want to escape. The falling wood had left a splinter in one finger, and she focused her entire attention on that.

"What's the matter, Mommy?"

"Nothing. Just a little splinter."

And Ben was there again, pressing against her though he stood inches away, making her body tingle, taking her hand in his. "Let me see." Gently, he removed the offending object.

"Kiss it," Cody demanded. "Kisses make the pain go 'way."

Arianne didn't doubt that for a minute. If Ben kissed her finger, she was positive she wouldn't feel any pain. Plenty of other things, but definitely not pain.

"It's fine. It doesn't hurt." *Pull your hand away from his,* she ordered herself, but her brain had short-circuited. She was paralyzed. She stood motionless, her gaze riveted to the sight of her hand cradled in one of his, while one broad finger stroked the spot where the splinter had been.

Why hadn't Santa Claus dropped off an elderly man with no hair and buckteeth?

"Come on," Cody urged impatiently, and the spell was broken. She couldn't have told who stepped back first, but a tiny part of her hoped it had been her, that he'd been at least as reluctant as she to break the contact.

"You're running low here," Ben mumbled as he stooped to retrieve the wood they'd dropped.

"We have plenty more in the barn. This is enough for today." And by tomorrow he'd be gone.

And Cody would be safe.

And she'd never again know that soaring heart-pounding sensation he evoked in her.

The day passed...slowly...rapidly...Arianne couldn't decide which. Time had lost its consistency as she wished Ben away yet dreaded his leaving.

Gramma called, concerned that she and Cody were still stranded with Ben. Arianne wanted to tell her everything, to share her fears with the woman who'd helped her through so many childhood fears. Gramma knew about Cody, and she'd understand. Only recently, Gramma had confessed how often she'd worried that Arianne's parents would try to reclaim her after she and Gramps had come to love her so much that losing her would have devastated them.

But Arianne couldn't tell her grandmother. For one thing, she couldn't talk without Ben's hearing her. Though the main reason was that she didn't want Gramma to worry, to go through the same pain and fear of loss she herself was going through. So she reassured her that everything was fine.

Arianne played games with Cody to entertain him, and Ben, between calls to his office and doing paperwork, joined them.

It was during one of the board games that she first noticed Ben was left-handed...just as Cody was. No one in her family was left-handed. But for all she knew, Lewis Davidson might be. It proved nothing. Still, it made her more nervous.

And the snow came down...sometimes light, sometimes heavy, each dancing flake making it more and more certain that Ben wouldn't be leaving the next day.

They had an early dinner of leftovers, and Ben and Cody helped her with the dishes.

"Whaddaya wanta do now?" Cody asked as Arianne was wiping off the countertop.

She turned to answer Cody, but he was looking up at Ben.

Ben cast a glance in the direction of the telephone, the object that had been attached to his ear much of the day, then looked down at his watch. It was probably frustrating for him, she thought sarcastically, to have to stop working at a normal hour just because everyone else at the office had gone home, leaving no one to answer the phone.

He shifted his attention back to Cody's expectant little face. "I don't know. What do you think? Maybe watch a little television?"

"Okay! Come on." Cody charged from the room and Ben looked at Arianne.

"Is that all right?" he asked uncertainly.

"Sure. I know you're probably bored out of your mind playing games with a five-year-old."

"No," he said. "I'm not bored." His gaze held hers for a moment more before he turned away and left the room to follow Cody.

Arianne stood staring after him. If he wasn't bored, it was probably because he'd been on the phone to his office much of the day. As long as men like him were immersed in work, they would never be bored.

But his gaze, his voice, had been hot and hungry, suggesting that he was thinking of other things with which to entertain himself.

She scrubbed the enamel surface of the stove.

She wasn't going to be one of those other things.

A few minutes later, she entered the living room to see Ben on the sofa with Cody curled beside him.

"Now the team in the red has the ball, and they're going for a first down. Do you know what a first down is?"

"Nope."

Oh, Lord, they were watching football.

She picked up a book and sat down in her favorite chair. But tonight she had a hard time concentrating. The sounds of the game didn't bother her; what bothered her was the sound of Cody and Ben discussing the game, of Ben explaining and Cody questioning, of the two of them cheering and booing.

She felt sure, in spite of Ben's explanations, that Cody didn't understand what was going on, but he was obviously enthralled with the idea of watching the game with Ben, of mimicking Ben's actions. Though Cody had stopped calling Ben *Daddy,* she could tell he hadn't relinquished his game of pretend.

Momentary anger stirred against Ben. He was leading Cody on, letting him sample the delights of having a father, then he'd yank it all away when he left.

But that wasn't fair. Cody was hard to ignore... and hard to resist. Her son was adorable. How could even someone like Ben not be drawn to him?

3 WAYS TO PLAY *see inside*

1

for big CASH prizes and FREE GIFTS!
First play your "Win-A-Fortune" game tickets
to qualify for up to
<u>ONE MILLION DOLLARS IN LIFETIME INCOME</u>
– that's $33,333.33 each year for 30 years!

WIN A CASH F⊕RTUNE

GAME TIX NO. **1a**

Game Ticket values vary. Scratch GOLD from Big Money Wheel to determine the potential cash value of prize you will receive if the sweepstakes number assigned to this ticket is a prize winning number.

DO NOT SEPARATE—KEEP ALL GAMES INTACT

WIN A CASH F⊕RTUNE

GAME TIX NO. **1b**

Game Ticket values vary. Scratch GOLD from Big Money Wheel to determine the potential cash value of prize you will receive if the sweepstakes number assigned to this ticket is a prize winning number.

DO NOT SEPARATE—KEEP ALL GAMES INTACT

WIN A CASH F⊕RTUNE

GAME TIX NO. **1c**

Game Ticket values vary. Scratch GOLD from Big Money Wheel to determine the potential cash value of prize you will receive if the sweepstakes number assigned to this ticket is a prize winning number.

DO NOT SEPARATE—KEEP ALL GAMES INTACT

WIN A CASH F⊕RTUNE

GAME TIX NO. **1d**

Game Ticket values vary. Scratch GOLD from Big Money Wheel to determine the potential cash value of prize you will receive if the sweepstakes number assigned to this ticket is a prize winning number.

DO NOT SEPARATE—KEEP ALL GAMES INTACT

WIN A CASH F⊕RTUNE

GAME TIX NO. **1e**

Game Ticket values vary. Scratch GOLD from Big Money Wheel to determine the potential cash value of prize you will receive if the sweepstakes number assigned to this ticket is a prize winning number.

DO NOT SEPARATE—KEEP ALL GAMES INTACT

FOLD ALONG DOTTED LINE AND DETACH CAREFULLY

With a coin, carefully scratch off the three gold boxes. Then check the chart below to learn how many FREE BOOKS will be yours!

7	7	7	**WORTH FOUR FREE BOOKS!**
🔔	🔔	BAR	**WORTH THREE FREE BOOKS!**
🍒	🍒	BAR	**WORTH TWO FREE BOOKS!**
BAR	BAR	BAR	**WORTH ONE FREE BOOK!**

You'll receive brand-new Silhouette Romance™ novels. When you scratch off the gold boxes and return this card in the reply envelope provided, we'll send you the books you qualify for <u>absolutely</u> free.

And if he was Ben's son...a possibility she still refused to concede...was there a natural biological bonding?

No.

Cody had never shown any such feelings for Julia. He was just playing a game of make-believe, pretending to have a father like his friends. It was unfortunate that this latest snowfall had placed them in a position where he could go on pretending.

If Ben was his father, he was not and never would be any more of a parent than Julia.

It took more than an accident of genetics to make a parent. She knew *that* only too well.

Chapter Eight

Ben wasn't particularly interested in the football game. The Cowboys weren't playing, and he had a lot of things on his mind. He would have liked to make one more phone call to see how things were progressing at the office. If he was at home, he'd still be down there, making sure things went right. But he wasn't at home.

And it was kind of neat watching the game with Cody. Maybe because the kid hung on his every word and looked up at him with those big, trusting eyes. Who wouldn't like that kind of adoration?

Cody was bright, too. He only had to explain things once, and the boy caught on.

"Look!" Ben shouted, directing Cody's attention to one of the players on the screen. "He's going for a touchdown! Come on!"

"Come on!" Cody echoed.

Just then, the screen went black, dwindled to a tiny spot of light and winked out, along with the other lights in the room.

"Did he make a touchdown?" Cody asked, his small voice loud in the sudden silence.

"Don't panic," Arianne said. "We've got candles and kerosene lamps."

As Ben's eyes adjusted to the pale light from the fire, he saw her take from the mantel a lamp he'd assumed was only decorative. He heard a scratching sound and saw the flare of a match. She touched the flame to the lamp, slid the globe back on, and a soft glow filtered into the room, spreading a surreal haze over her face and hair.

"What happened?" Ben asked, needing to hear the sound of his own voice. "Did we trip a breaker?"

"Maybe," Arianne said. "I'll go check, but probably the weight of the snow downed a power line."

"Don't worry," Cody assured him. "Gramps got us a gen'ator so our food won't melt."

"A portable generator," Arianne explained. "But I don't think we need to worry about our food melting tonight."

Ben would have to agree with that. The *shed room* where they kept the firewood and the freezer was little more than a closed-in porch. The food wouldn't thaw in there even if they took it out of the freezer.

"Where's your breaker box? I'll check for you," he offered.

"In the basement. I'll go. You'd never find it." She set the lamp on the mantel and headed toward the kitchen.

Ben leaped to his feet and started after her. "I'll come with you."

Living in a city where homes were built on pier-and-beam or concrete-slab foundations, he didn't know a lot about basements, but he suspected this wouldn't be one of those cozy ones with indoor/outdoor carpeting and a pool table. Arianne didn't need to be going alone into a dark, damp haven for spiders, snakes, scorpions, rats...who knew what might lurk in such a place?

"Me, too." Cody slid off the sofa.

Arianne looked back from the kitchen doorway. "Both of you stay here by the fire. I won't be gone five minutes."

Ben turned to Cody and hooked a thumb in the direction of the sofa.

Cody heaved a dramatic sigh and climbed back up.

"Lead on," Ben said.

"This isn't the first time I've gone into my own basement, and I can guarantee you it won't be the last," she protested.

"Humor me. We don't see many basements in Dallas."

"There's not much to see." She crossed the kitchen, took a flashlight from a drawer and opened a door on one side of the room.

The wooden stairs seemed fairly stable; the walls, comprised of large stones cemented together, were lined with jars of canned fruit and vegetables and old furniture and boxes were stacked everywhere. He didn't see anything crawling or scuttling across the floor. In fact, what little he could see of the cracked concrete floor was immaculate, like the rest of her house.

Still, the place had a dank, musty odor and the moving flashlight beam sent eerie shadows darting into gloomy corners. Not somewhere he pictured a woman coming alone.

Arianne shone her flashlight on a breaker box. "The problem's not here." She trained the beam on a small generator. "If the power is still off tomorrow, we'll get some gasoline from the barn and hook this thing up."

Ben eyed the equipment dubiously. "Have you used this before?"

"No," she admitted. "But I've got the instructions upstairs."

"Mmm. Like the bicycle."

She laughed, the sound mellow and musical and out of place in the dreary basement...in the distressing situation.

"Not quite the same thing," she said. "All we have to do is hook it up, add gasoline and start it. Trust me. We'll manage."

She headed back upstairs, and he followed. "So, if you haven't used the generator, do I assume this is the first time the electricity's gone out?"

"Oh, heavens, no. Just the first time since Gramps got the generator. The last time, we lost half the food in the freezer. When he and Gramma lived here, they didn't have a freezer. Gramma canned everything, and still does, as you saw in the basement. I rarely have the time. So, we have a freezer and a generator."

And live about fifty years behind the rest of the world.

Not that it was any of his business.

The warmth of the living room was seductive as they reentered.

And that was archaic, too, having only one room comfortable.

Arianne stopped halfway across the room, switched off the flashlight and laid a gentle restraining hand on his arm. "The perpetual-motion machine has given it up," she said softly, indicating Cody stretched out on the sofa.

"He's asleep?"

She nodded. "He's had a long day."

"That's amazing. We were only gone for a few minutes."

She raised her eyes to his, and he could feel the intensity of her gaze even in the dim light. "Haven't been around many kids, have you?"

"None. Why? Is that a kid thing, dropping off to sleep like that?"

"Yes, that's a kid thing." She handed him the flashlight and crossed the room to bend over Cody. As he watched, she lifted the boy. Cody mumbled something, wrapped small arms around her neck and rested his head on her shoulder, but kept on sleeping.

"Let me," he said, stepping forward. "He must be heavy."

"I can handle it. We do this often." She took a couple of steps, then stopped. "You can turn down his bed if you like," she said, her words sounding somehow reluctant.

"Okay, sure." He strode ahead of her up the stairs and into Cody's room.

The boy's bed had the same heavy mound of covers as the one he'd been sleeping in. Of course, the room was icy. He turned back the quilts. As soon as Arianne laid Cody down, the child snuggled sleepily into the pillow.

"He's still wearing his clothes," Ben observed.

"I know. This is the fun part, undressing and dressing a sleeping kid without waking him up."

She took a pair of pajamas from a dresser drawer and, amazingly, accomplished the task, then tucked

Cody in, covering him to his chin, and planted a kiss on his cheek. She stood looking down at him for a minute, then turned and abruptly walked out of the room.

Ben followed, stealing one last glance at the sleeping child even though he could barely see Cody's face in the darkness. Something tugged in the vicinity of his heart. The kid was so small, so defenseless. His body barely made a mound under the pile of quilts. Ben felt strangely unwilling to leave him in the cold, dark room.

They went back downstairs, and Ben sank onto the sofa beside Arianne.

"Don't you ever miss living in the city?" he asked.

She shook her head, the firelight shimmering in her hair. "Absolutely not. What's to miss?"

"You're living like . . . like a pioneer woman. Only one room of your house is warm. Your electricity goes out. You have to go into a dark, musty basement with who knows what creatures hiding in the corners. If nothing else, surely you miss central heating and air-conditioning. You said it gets as hot here in the summer as it does in Dallas."

"We don't have your conveniences," she admitted, "but we don't have your problems, either."

"Yeah, yeah, I know, high crime rates, pollution, traffic jams versus comfort, convenience, restaurants, theaters. Do your parents still live there? Do you ever visit them?"

"My parents still live there, sort of, but I never visit them. They travel a lot. Mom's in Australia right now, and Dad's supposed to join her as soon as he gets his latest business deal closed."

She sat primly on the edge of the sofa, hands folded in her lap, gazing into the crackling flames, looking like a brave but forlorn fourteen-year-old.

"Well," he said, feeling his way around the apparently ticklish subject, "that doesn't sound so bad. So your dad had to be gone a few days. They'll still have some time together, right?"

She looked at him then, her eyes becoming cold and distant...accusing. "Business always comes first with him. His girlfriends are second, golf third and skiing fourth. Family comes last. No, it's highly unlikely they'll have any time together. I'm not sure they've been in the same room together half a dozen times this year."

"Oh." He stood, walked over to the fireplace and poked at the burning logs. She obviously didn't think much of her parents' marriage, but he had no reason to assume her cold stare had anything to do with him personally. Except he could see some parallels. His attitude toward business had wrecked his one attempt at family life, and she knew that. "So why doesn't your mother divorce your father?" he asked.

"She's addicted to the money." She delivered the indictment casually, but he suspected she didn't really feel casual about it. "And after watching how much money his brother—Julia's father—lost through his marriages and divorces, Dad will never leave Mother. So he has his business and his affairs and Mom has her trips and new clothes."

"And you have Cody."

A shadow crossed her face...maybe from the flickering light of the lamp. But he had that niggling feeling again that she was hiding something. He gave himself a mental shake and tried to dismiss the feeling. Arianne wasn't like Julia or his mother. She wasn't deceitful. She was an open, honest, caring person.

"I have Cody," she replied, "and Gramma and Gramps and a real home. Leaving me here after my accident was the kindest thing my parents ever did for me."

He didn't miss the fact that she said her parents had left her here, whereas before, she'd indicated she'd chosen to remain, but he didn't mention it. He did, however, understand a little better her attachment to this old house, to this life-style. "How did your accident happen?" he asked, pretending not to notice the admission he felt might embarrass her.

"I was trying to water-ski. I was never very good at it. One day when I was twelve and had grown a foot almost overnight and my legs hadn't yet figured out how to function with those extra inches, one ski went up, one went down and I broke a leg and my pelvis. Since my parents were busy people, they sent me here to recuperate. I've been here ever since. Except for college and that year I spent teaching in Dallas, of course."

"And Cody's birth."

She took a throw pillow from the end of the sofa and picked at lint he couldn't see. There it was again, that sensation that things weren't quite right. "Cody was two months old when we moved back here."

"Oh? Did his father move back with you?" He knew the answer to that even as he asked. This was her home. There was no trace that a husband had ever lived here.

She kept picking at the pillow, didn't look up, and in the twilight of the room, he sensed rather than saw her tension. "No. We were alone by then."

Something was definitely wrong. He couldn't bring himself to believe she was lying, but neither could he quite believe she was telling the truth. Perhaps she'd never been married to Cody's father. That would explain her unease. That would also explain why she had no pictures of him sitting around.

However, there was no longer any stigma attached to single mothers, and he couldn't imagine that would bother someone as independent and strong-minded as Arianne, anyway. There must be more to the story.

"What was Cody's father like? Do you have a picture of him?"

She stood abruptly, her gaze meeting his, her knuckles white as she clutched the throw pillow to her breasts. "Cody's father was consumed by his work. That was all that mattered to him. He was no more ready to be a father than mine was." She tossed the pillow to the sofa. "Would you like a cup of hot chocolate before we go to bed?"

He stared at her pinched features, trying to read her mind. He was sure of it now; she had secrets. It would seem her marriage or relationship or whatever it was hadn't been a pleasant one. Well, that was none of his business.

"Thanks," he said, accepting her sudden change of subject. "That would be great."

Arianne took the lamp from the mantel, trying to keep her hand from shaking, trying to keep Ben from noticing. Why was he asking her so many questions about Cody, about Cody's father?

She'd told him more than she'd intended about herself, but it had all seemed so natural at the time. She supposed it was impossible not to feel a connection to someone you'd been in such proximity with...someone whose touch started normally quiet parts of her body singing.

But then he'd begun asking about Cody and Cody's father.

She hurried into the kitchen. As she poured milk into a saucepan, her hand shook so badly that she sloshed some of it onto the counter. Grabbing a dish towel, she wiped off the pan, set it on the stove and mopped furiously at the spill.

"I didn't mean to be nosy."

She jumped, gasping loudly at the sound of Ben's voice behind her.

Gently, he clasped both hands on the sides of her shoulders. "I didn't mean to scare you, either," he said, his breath warm on her neck.

And those mutinous parts of her body were off singing and dancing again. Her brain knew she had to avoid Ben like the plague...but her body had no sense. The cold, clear air in the kitchen surrounded her, entering her lungs with every breath, and somehow intensified the effect Ben had on her. He was the direct opposite. Heat from his hands, from his nearness, warmed her. His scent drifted to her in distinct waves.

"You didn't scare me," she said, standing stiffly in his almost-embrace. Then she laughed at her own absurdity. "You did startle me. A little."

It was silly to be talking to someone behind you. She should turn and face him. But then he might drop his hands from her shoulders. Or he might pull her to him. She didn't know which she feared . . . or desired . . . the most. She stood still, waiting, savoring . . .

Then he took one hand away.

Lifted her hair off her neck.

And pressed his lips to a spot just below her hairline, a spot she'd never before realized was packed with nerve endings that shot tingling, lilting sensations to the farthest parts of her body.

"Arianne," he whispered, his lips moving against her skin as he spoke, as he traveled to the side of her throat. "You're irresistible."

The cold in the kitchen had completely disappeared. All she could feel was Ben.

As if of its own volition, her head tilted to one side to allow him better access, and a small moan escaped her lips.

"Ben, don't. We can't." She spoke the words she knew she must; they had no meaning at the moment, but it was the best she could do. If he didn't listen, if he didn't stop—

"Okay," he said softly, moving away from her, allowing the cold to return, to enfold her and pull her back to the reality of the drafty, cavernous kitchen, to the reality of the life that suddenly seemed remote... though she wasn't sure from what.

She shivered as she watched Ben's back disappearing through the doorway, into the semidarkness. She hadn't felt such an emptiness since the Christmas gathering when she was seventeen and she'd held her hand over her very pregnant relative's stomach to feel the baby kick—and had realized with a start what it meant that she'd never carry a child in her damaged womb.

But then Cody had come along, and she hadn't felt empty again...until now. So it wasn't an emptiness of the womb after all; it was an emptiness of the heart.

She'd go in and check on Cody before she went to bed, let the sight of him fill her to the brim with love, as it always did.

But for the first time, she wasn't sure it would be enough.

Chapter Nine

Ben got up the next morning, showered and dressed without opening the curtains to look out. If it was still snowing, that meant he'd be trapped here for another day, unable to get back to his work, his home, his life. If it wasn't snowing, he'd soon be leaving. He'd never again see Arianne or Cody, the son he'd almost had for a little while, the boy who, as Julia claimed, looked amazingly like him.

Neither option had much appeal.

He glanced at the curtains, then decided to make the bed first, postpone knowing for a few more minutes. He straightened the brightly patterned quilts, smoothing each one as he pulled it up.

Of course, he could always come back to visit Arianne. Business occasionally took him to Denver, and he could probably arrange for it to happen more often. Maybe she and Cody could even come to Dallas sometime. After all, she'd said her parents still lived there. He could take her to the Mansion restaurant, eat Tex-Mex food at Cozymel's, go sailing on White Rock Lake in the summer. The two of them could take Cody to Six Flags amusement park.

But there was no point in even thinking about it. As he told himself before, Arianne wasn't the type of woman who could fit into his schedule, and he'd already discovered he couldn't change. In fairness to everyone, he needed to find a woman as driven and career-centered as he.

A relationship with Arianne would be as disastrous as the one he'd had with his ex.

More disastrous, he amended, because Arianne was more of a home- and family-oriented person than his ex had been. More disastrous because—

He fluffed the heavy, down-filled pillows and plopped them into place on the bed, then stared unseeingly at the multicolored quilt on top.

Because Arianne was a sensitive, caring person, vulnerable to hurt. He didn't want to hurt her.

And because she got under his skin in a way his ex never had, in a way *no one* ever had. Because he could get really involved with her. She wasn't the only one who could get hurt in this deal.

Not to mention the boy who, even though he'd stopped calling him *Daddy* with his words, still called him that with his eyes. Popping in and out of Cody's life wouldn't be fair, either.

For everybody's sake, he hoped the snow had stopped and the road would be plowed soon.

He jerked open the curtains.

The sky was a light gray, but nothing fell from it.

He might be able to leave today. If the thought didn't make him happy, he refused to let it make him unhappy.

Anyway, he still couldn't rid himself of the feeling that Arianne had a hidden agenda. He knew that suspicion was irrational and unfair, that he was being obsessive about deceit. She had no obligation to tell anyone, much less him, all the details of her life. He'd come here, if not under false pretenses, at least with lots of omissions from his story. Still . . . unfair or not, there was something . . .

From the bathroom he heard the sound of the shower. Arianne was up.

If that image didn't light a Fourth of July sparkler inside his chest, maybe he'd be able to get a little more excited about the prospect of leaving.

He hurried downstairs to start the coffee. If the electricity was back on.

Okay, he admitted to himself, he hurried to avoid meeting her in the hallway in a robe, with her face wet and shiny and a bed only a few feet away.

Cody, dark eyes dancing, lock of hair hanging over his forehead, ran to meet him before he cleared the last step. "Want some more chocolate cake? I can get it. I know how."

Ben wanted to lean down and embrace him, touch that childish exuberance and boundless hope. But he didn't. That wouldn't be a good idea, encouraging the boy's attachment. "If we wait a few minutes, your mom will be down, and maybe she'll make oatmeal."

"Yech. I don't want any old oatmeal. Want to play with my new space attack game?"

Ben smiled at the eager face. "Let me put some coffee on first. Okay?"

Cody skipped across the room. "Can't. The 'lectricity's still gone. Can I have some coffee, too?"

"Oh, that's really what you need, hotshot."

Ben turned at the sound of Arianne's voice behind him.

"A little caffeine to give you some energy," she continued, speaking to Cody, her smiling gaze flicking over Ben only briefly as she passed him. "When you start drinking coffee, I'll have to start drinking alcohol."

She crossed the room and stooped to light the gas heater, her faded blue jeans stretching taut across her rounded bottom, her silky hair sliding forward on each side of her face. The spot on her neck where he'd pressed his lips last night was bared to his gaze. A feeling of intimacy swept over him, as though he were seeing her completely nude.

"Are we gonna eat oatmeal for breakfast again?" Cody asked.

She blew out her match, went to him and pushed the hair off his forehead. "We could have sausage and eggs. Does that sound better?"

"And pancakes!"

"Okay. And pancakes. But first I need to get the gasoline from the barn and start up the generator so Ben and I can have coffee."

"Can I go, too? It's not snowing anymore."

"No, you can't go, too. That snow's almost as tall as you are. You stay here with Ben."

"Okay!" He charged across the room. "We'll make pancakes for you."

"No!" Arianne protested.

Ben caught Cody in the child's forward lunge. "Whoa, kiddo! Are you sure you haven't been into the chocolate cake *and* the coffee this morning?"

Arianne shook her head and laughed. "Just keep him out of the pancake mix until I get back." She opened the hall closet door and yanked her coat off a hanger.

"You stay here, Arianne" he said, turning Cody loose and going over to the closet. "I'll go get the gasoline and some more firewood." He reached inside the closet and found his own coat.

"I'll go," she insisted. "I know where it is."

He took her coat from her. "I think I can find the barn." He'd never doubted Arianne was independent, but her determination seemed a little out of character. She'd been glad enough to have his help putting Cody's bicycle together, but now she acted as though his assistance would compromise her in some manner.

Arianne turned away from Ben's probing gaze. She had to stop worrying about his every move. Carrying a can of gasoline and some firewood from the barn wasn't going to give him a right to her life...or Cody's.

"It's hard to miss," she told him. "After you step off the porch, turn right. The small building in front is the garage, and the barn's the big one behind it. I'll get breakfast started, and as soon as we're through eating, I'll check around about getting the road plowed."

Did that make her sound eager to get rid of him?

Probably not. She was obsessing about her behavior again. He was every bit as anxious to be gone as she was for him to go. Just because some rebellious, irrational, heretofore unnoticed part of her wanted him to stay didn't mean he had those same illogical feelings.

She went into the kitchen, put some sausage into an iron skillet to fry, set a griddle over another burner to heat and took down the pancake mix. From the window, she could see Ben trekking across the snow, his strides long, high and determined.

She heard a scraping noise, and Cody appeared beside her, dragging a chair. He climbed onto it and looked out the window. "Is he gonna leave today?"

"Probably. If not today, definitely tomorrow."

Ben disappeared into the barn, then emerged with a can of gasoline in his left hand. He wasn't wearing his ski mask, and she could see that errant lock of hair tilting over his forehead, just as Cody's always did.

He's Cody's father.

"Are you sure?" Cody asked.

"What?" Had she spoken aloud?

"Are you sure he's gonna leave?"

"I'm sure. Go open the door for him."

There's no proof he's Cody's father, she told that tiny, troublesome voice in her head. If she knew for certain that he was, she'd have to tell him. She'd have to expose Cody to a life-style...a father...that no child should have to endure.

And if that wasn't enough, she had to worry about her own exposure. How could she possibly be so attracted to him, yearn to be with him, when she recognized not only his potential to disrupt her life, the sadness he'd bring to Cody, but also the sadness he could bring to anyone who cared about him?

More and more she was beginning to understand her mother. And fear her own emotions.

Arianne had breakfast cooked, and Ben was still in the basement, working on the generator. Though she'd given him the kerosene lamp, he'd also requested the flashlight, and Cody had eagerly volunteered to hold it for him. Occasionally, an ominous sound rose from below, but the electricity was still off. Obviously, it hadn't been the simple matter he'd anticipated.

She set three plates on the kitchen table, then went to the basement door and opened it. "Breakfast's ready, you guys."

"In a minute." Ben sounded as if he was speaking through clenched teeth.

In a minute. She'd heard those words from her father often enough to know what they meant.

"Scrambled eggs, sausages and pancakes are really awful when they get cold," she called down. "Why don't you come eat now and finish that later."

"Yeah, we can finish later," Cody said. "I'm hungry."

"Okay, kiddo. Let's do it."

The two of them appeared at the top of the steps sporting grease spots and dirty streaks on their faces and clothes.

"How on earth did you get dirty holding the flashlight?" Arianne demanded of her son.

"I helped," he said proudly.

"I can see that. You helped take up some of the grime after Ben got his share. Go wash your face and hands before we eat."

He charged upstairs and Ben grinned. "Guess I'd better do the same. Pretty bad, huh?"

She smiled at him and resisted the urge to wipe at a black streak under one eye. "Pretty bad. What's the problem? Gramps said this would be so simple, even I could do it."

"It should be, but something's wrong. I think I can fix it. It's just going to take a little while."

She sighed involuntarily. It seemed as though something was always going wrong. Much as she loved this place, she couldn't deny that it was old and falling apart. "Don't worry about it. The power will be back on today or tomorrow."

"You can't go that long with no electricity."

"Sure we can. We just can't read at night."

"What about the food in your refrigerator?"

"We'll put in pans of snow. It'll be like the old iceboxes."

"What about coffee? Maybe you're able to get along without every other convenience, but what about that electric coffeemaker?"

She shrugged and started into the kitchen. "Oh, we're tough out here in the country. We just put a coffee bean between our cheek and gum, and we're set." She turned back to look at him, then couldn't contain her laughter at his openmouthed astonishment.

"I'm kidding," she assured him. "I dragged out Gramma's old percolator and made us a brew that'll have us bouncing off the walls the way Cody does."

He blinked, then grinned wickedly, coming toward her. "I knew I smelled coffee."

"But you thought it was just my breath after chewing on those beans." She started backing away.

He caught her, holding her with one arm while he drew a dirty finger across her cheek.

"Cut that out!" Laughing, she tried to free herself from his grasp.

"Okay." He rubbed his grimy face against her other cheek.

And suddenly the laughter fell away. His freshly shaved skin was smooth as it slid along hers, more slowly now, in a journey that she knew would end when his lips reached hers. His arm wrapped around her and pressed her close to him. She ceased her efforts to get away from him. Instead, she leaned into him, into the desire that swept over her.

"I'm clean!"

She sprang away from Ben to see Cody standing in the doorway with shiny wet hands and face.

"Your turn!" He scrambled into a chair at the table. "You're dirty, too, Mommy. You got to wash up, too."

"So I do," she mumbled, going to the kitchen sink to wash her hands, to splash cold water on her burning face.

Her first thought was to wonder how married couples ever had a second child, and her next thought was relief that Cody had appeared, that he was always there. She sent up a silent prayer that Ben would be able to leave today. Her brain applauded the prayer, but her heart refused any part of it.

Ben helped her with the breakfast dishes, then promptly checked in with his office. Arianne took Cody and went to the basement, ostensibly to check out what he'd been doing to the generator.

She didn't want to hear him talking, in his role as the quintessential businessman. The contrast was so great to the teasing side of him she'd seen as he'd smeared grime on her face... then almost kissed her. She knew that side only existed in this situation, in this moment. Today or tomorrow, he'd return to his real life, his real self.

She knew that, but she didn't really want to face it head-on.

"Mommy, I think you better wait for *him* to do this," Cody suggested as she stood in the pale light from the lamp, staring unseeingly at the baffling piece of machinery.

"Don't worry, sweetheart. I have no intention of making matters worse by messing with this thing."

"I'm glad to hear that," Ben said, coming down the steps. "Otherwise, we might have the electricity coming in instead of going out."

She hid a smile at his oblique reference to her putting Cody's bicycle together backward. "I may not be very mechanically inclined, but I think even I can pronounce this thing dead. Let's go upstairs where it's warm." She laid a hand on the back of Cody's neck.

"I'm not cold," her son protested. "I got a coat if I get cold."

"It's warmer down here than it is in my bedroom." Ben walked over and shone the flashlight beam onto the generator.

"We're below ground. The temperature's more constant. You're welcome to sleep down here if you'd like," she teased.

He looked around and gave a mock shudder... or maybe it was a real one. "No, thanks. We've got the right idea in Texas. We build from ground level up. No basements." He squatted beside the generator and picked up a screwdriver. Cody rushed over to take the flashlight from him.

"Thanks, kiddo. Shine it right in there. That's good."

"Really, Ben," Arianne protested, "you don't need to waste time on that thing. We'll be all right until the power is restored. People managed to get along just fine for thousands of years without electricity."

"Yeah, I know," he said, looking up at her, his eyes full of shadows in the dim light. "And people still get along without it when they can't pay their utility bills, but that doesn't make it acceptable."

His tone had gone so dark, and he seemed so determined to get the electricity back on, she had to wonder if perhaps his mother hadn't been able to pay the utility bill a few times after his father had deserted them.

That would go a long way toward explaining his obsession with work, too. Explaining but not excusing.

"Carry on, then," she said. "I think I'll go make some phone calls and find out the prognosis for getting the roads cleared."

"We'll fix it, Mommy," Cody assured her as she started up the stairs. "What's that thing there?"

She turned back, but he was talking to Ben. She didn't hear Ben's answer. It didn't matter. What mattered was Cody's total absorption with him.

From the first time she'd held Cody in her arms— only hours after his birth—she'd vowed to give him everything he'd ever need. It had never bothered her to say no to the new toys he saw on television, the motorcycle, the video game—before Julia's intervention— and the horse. He didn't need those things. If he had needed them, she'd have given them to him. She had plenty of money saved from her parents' guilt gifts.

She hadn't even been concerned when he'd asked for a daddy and a baby brother for Christmas. He had her. He didn't need anyone else.

But the way he'd taken to Ben indicated otherwise. Maybe he did need a father. And she couldn't give him that.

She thought of Julia's story, of the uncanny resemblance between Ben and Cody, and amended her statement.

She couldn't give him *the kind* of father he needed.

She went to the living room to call her grandparents and assure them everything was all right.

Her second big lie in as many days.

Arianne was sitting beside the window reading a book when a strange voice spoke.

She gasped, dropping the book and shooting to her feet, her heart pounding in fright.

The television. They hadn't turned it off after they lost the electricity.

Which meant—

Footsteps pounded up the basement stairs along with the sounds of laughter and shrieks.

"We did it, Mommy! It works!"

Cody and Ben burst into the living room, both beaming proudly.

Cody ran to her, and she leaned over to give him a big hug. "You're wonderful," she assured him, then looked up at Ben where he stood just inside the doorway, flushed and smiling. "Both of you."

"I don't know how long it'll be good for," Ben said. "I didn't have the right parts. I had to improvise. But right now—" he grinned and spread his hands "—right now, she's working."

He looked so proud of what he'd achieved, so open and eager to please. Arianne swallowed hard, forcibly reminding herself who he was, why he was here and what he'd soon be returning to.

"I have more good news," she said. "I talked to Gramps, and he said they're starting to clear the highways today. As soon as they get the main road open, George Watson will plow ours, and you can—" She hesitated, feeling Cody's body tense in her arms even though she hadn't completed the sentence.

"How about some lunch for your starving mechanics?" Ben asked, changing the subject, apparently aware of the effect her almost-pronouncement had on Cody. "After we wash up, of course." Ben crossed the room toward her. "Come on, valued assistant," he said to Cody. "I'll show you how to use a towel." He took Cody's hand, and the two left the room.

Ben couldn't help noticing that Cody had lost some of his bounce as he trudged up the stairs beside him. The boy didn't say anything until they'd both washed their hands and faces and were sharing a towel in the bathroom.

"Mommy didn't really mean you have to go." Cody kept his gaze glued to the towel as he rubbed it over his hands repeatedly.

Ben squatted beside him and tilted the boy's face up with one finger until he could see his eyes...deep brown without the green flecks in his mother's.

Deep brown like Julia's.

No, he had to give up that fantasy. Arianne might not be telling him the truth about something in her past, but birth certificates didn't lie. Even if Arianne hadn't been married to Cody's father, she was his mother, which meant there was no chance he himself was Cody's father... a fact he didn't find as comforting as it ought to be.

"I do have to go," he said. "I have a job and a home in Dallas."

"Do you have another little boy?"

"No, I don't."

"Are you married to somebody?"

"No, not anymore."

"Then why can't you stay with us? Don't you like us?"

"Of course I like you. I like you a lot." *Far too much to even think of doing anything stupid.* "But I have a home in Dallas, and you have a home here, and Dallas is a long way from here."

"You could move here. We have lots of room."

Ben rocked back on his heels, sighed and ran a hand through his hair. "Someday, your mommy will meet somebody from around here, and you'll both like him a lot, and he'll move in with you and be your daddy."

The thought of Arianne sleeping with another man sent an arrow straight through his heart... but that was only because he'd been and still was in such close quarters with her, he told himself. After he'd been gone a while, he'd forget the way her soft body felt, the way her eyes looked when they were glowing with desire, the way her lips tasted, the way her hair trickled through his fingers like strands of warm, silky night air.

Cody stomped one small foot and stuck out his lower lip. "That's not a real daddy. Santa Claus brought you. You're my real daddy."

Ben took a deep breath. He had to set Cody straight. He had to come out and say it, *I'm not your daddy.*

But the words stuck somewhere between his mind and his mouth.

"Come on, kiddo," he heard himself saying instead. "Let's go eat lunch."

Chapter Ten

Arianne made molasses taffy that evening after dinner. It was one of Cody's favorite things, and he obviously needed some cheering up. He'd been unusually subdued all afternoon in spite of Ben's offers to play video games with him.

She suspected Cody's mood had something to do with the fact that the sun had begun sending intermittent pale streaks through the clouds just before it set, and twice they'd overheard Ben assure someone in his office that he'd be returning tomorrow evening or the day after, depending on the flight schedule out of Denver.

Actually, Cody mirrored the way she felt. Ever since she'd put into words that soon Ben could...would...be leaving their lives forever, ever since she'd heard him put it into words, the afternoon had begun to feel like goodbye.

And in spite of the fact that she knew she and Cody would both be better off when Ben was gone, the prospect made her sad. She supposed that was normal; the three of them had been thrust together so closely for the last few days, she'd come to think of Ben as part of the family.

And that was all just so much rationalization, she admitted to herself. What she felt for Ben wasn't at all familial.

Resolving to get a grip on her runaway feelings, Arianne set three bowls of taffy and three saucers with butter on the kitchen table.

"Okay," she instructed as she spread out buttered waxed paper. "First we all grease our hands, then, Cody, you show Ben how to do it."

Cody obliged, gradually cheering up as he stretched the warm, sticky confection, folded it back on itself and stretched again, giving serious, detailed instructions as he went. "You do it like this 'til it gets nearly white."

"Nearly white?" Ben looked at Arianne skeptically.

"Nearly white," she repeated, taking up a glob of her own. "Then what do we do, Cody?"

"Then we twist it and put it on the waxed paper to get hard and then we eat it!" He snapped his teeth together and giggled.

Ben picked up a glob of taffy, looked at it dubiously and stretched it—so thin the strands fell into his lap.

Cody and Arianne both laughed.

"Didn't your mommy ever make 'lasses taffy for you?" Cody asked.

"No, she didn't. But I can learn this. Just give me a minute." He worked at it intently—the way he did everything. "Hey! You're right. This stuff is getting pale!'' He looked at Arianne. "This is neat. Where did you learn this? No, don't tell me. Your grandmother. Right?''

"Right.'' An inordinate amount of pleasure washed over her at his fascination with making the simple candy.

"Your grandparents must be really special people. I wish I could—'' He stopped midsentence, compressed his lips and returned his attention to the taffy. "I think this is about ready to twist. What do you think, Cody?''

Wished he could what? Meet her grandparents? Whatever he'd been about to say, he'd certainly cut it short. Of course he wouldn't want to meet her grandparents. He'd have absolutely nothing in common with them. No more than he had with her.

When all the candy had been duly pulled, twisted and laid aside to cool—a process which wouldn't take long in the drafty kitchen—Cody slid out of his chair and yawned.

"Can I turn on the Christmas-tree lights?'' he asked.

"You can plug in the lights, yes.''

"And then can we watch television?''

"If you'll go upstairs and put on your pajamas first.''

"Okay.'' He disappeared from the room at almost his normal speed.

And she was left alone with Ben.

She stretched her lips into a smile and tried to think of something upbeat to say. But her mind was blank. It would take more than a taffy pull to restore her holiday spirits.

It would take time, that was all, she told herself firmly. When Ben was out of their lives for a few weeks, she wouldn't be able to remember what he looked like.

Oh, yeah? that tiny voice inside her head sneered.

"That was fun," Ben said. "I really want to thank you for sharing your home and your Christmas with me."

More of the sounds of goodbye.

She shrugged as though the whole thing were inconsequential. "If you hadn't been here to fix that blasted generator, Cody wouldn't be able to watch television tonight."

He grinned, looking pleased with himself. "Actually, that was kind of fun, too. In the early days of my company, I did a lot of hands-on work with computers. I still pride myself on being able to keep up with my employees. Of course, your generator was a lot tougher to figure out."

Cody burst into the room, still wearing his blue jeans. "Come look! It's daytime outside!"

They followed him into the living room, over to the window. The sky had cleared, and the nearly full moon shone brightly, its silver glow reflecting off the pearly blanket of white.

"You're right," Ben said. "It's lighter than it's been all day."

"Can we go outside, Mommy? Please?"

"It's awfully cold and late."

"What's a few minutes?" Ben added his voice to Cody's plea.

She looked at Ben as he stood beside her at the window, his half-smiling face bathed in the soft moonlight. It was impossible to say *no* to a walk with him through the magical world just outside that window.

A *final* walk, she reminded herself.

Somehow, that didn't seem to matter. Tonight, right now, that was all that mattered. She'd have plenty of time to deal with tomorrow when it got here.

"You'll have to get bundled up really well," she said, returning her attention to Cody. "And we can't stay out long. It's too cold."

"*Okay!*" He ran to the closet and began tugging on the sleeve of his coat. "Do I have to wear my ski mask? I can't see good with it on."

"I guess not, but that means we have to come back really soon." She'd never be able to wear a ski mask again without thinking of what Ben had said when he'd put on hers... that it smelled like her.

A few minutes later, the three of them stepped onto the porch.

"Wow!" Cody exclaimed.

"Yeah. Wow," Ben echoed more softly.

All around them as far as they could see, the gleaming snow covered the earth and frosted the tree branches. Cold crisp air touched her face and filled her lungs with the clean scent of white. The deep, reverent silence of an empty church filled the air.

"Come on," Cody urged, bounding off the porch and starting down the path left by Ben's earlier trips to the barn.

"It seems a shame to disturb such perfection," Ben murmured, his voice full of wonder.

"Mmm," Arianne agreed. "You almost sound like you've never seen snow before. You may not get this much in Dallas, but I'm sure you do up on the ski slopes in Colorado."

He looked at her. "No, I've never seen anything like this before." His voice was hushed, his gaze intense, and for a dazzling, unreal moment, she thought he was talking about her.

But he meant the snow, of course.

She forced herself to laugh. "I guess the mountains and trees would get in the way. We don't have much out here to obstruct the view. Just miles and miles of snow."

"And moonlight." He took her arm, and in the thick, padded clothing they wore, he wasn't even close to touching her. But it seemed as if he were, as if his hand and her arm were inside the same jacket, together, warm from the cold. "Come on," he said, echoing Cody's words as he guided her off the porch.

And suddenly they were in a different world, a world of magic where only the three of them lived, where Cody laughed and frolicked in the snow and Ben walked beside her, holding her arm . . . a world where they were, at least temporarily . . . a family.

"I can walk in your steps," Cody announced, positioning his feet where Ben had left tracks earlier.

Ben watched the boy tottering from one of his footprints to another. Some of the prints were coming and some were going, but Cody walked indiscriminately in whichever he could reach with his short stride.

Somehow, moving through the strange night, bathed in the eerie silver glow, he could almost believe Cody was his son, that the boy would literally be walking in his footsteps one day . . . that he and Arianne would tuck him in together every night, as they'd done last night . . . that he and Arianne would sleep together in her grandmother's bed with no secrets between them, sharing the warmth of their bodies so there was no need for the mound of quilts.

He slid his hand from her arm to her waist and pulled her closer to him. She leaned her head on his shoulder, and, even in the bulky clothes they wore, her willowy slimness molded to him.

Just ahead of them, Cody reached the barn door, the end of the trail he himself had packed down earlier during his repeated trips back and forth. Cody whirled and fell backward into the untouched snow beside the path.

Ben exchanged a smile with Arianne. Her fair skin glowed luminescent in the moonlight.

"I remember. Snow angel," he said, describing Cody's floundering actions.

She looked at the boy, now covered with snow, as he struggled up. "Yes," she said. "He is."

Cody charged up to her and lifted his arms. "I'm tired, Mommy. Carry me."

"No way, hotshot. You're too big."

He turned to Ben, again raising his small arms. Ben felt himself reaching for the child, when Arianne's voice intruded.

"Don't ask Ben to carry you. You're covered in snow. Come on. I'll race you back."

Cody giggled and charged forward, his progress slowed and hindered by the irregularly packed snow. Ben couldn't seem to dislodge his fantasy that Cody really was his son. His heart ached with longing and with loss for the child he'd had for a short time, until he'd discovered Julia's duplicity. His heart ached for the child who'd walk in his footsteps for tonight only.

He reached down and lifted Cody to his shoulders. "A little snow never hurt anybody, did it, kiddo?"

Arianne looked at him, her eyes bottomless and un-fathomable in the moonlight, then she turned away abruptly and started back toward the house. He followed, Cody's slight weight a strangely welcome burden.

"Look." Arianne stopped and pointed toward the house.

In the window, the lights of her Christmas tree twinkled, bright colors contrasting gaily with the white wonderland surrounding them. And on top, the star, a beacon to guide them home, the beacon that had guided him to her.

"I still can't get over how I could see that star in such a terrible blizzard. If it wasn't for your Christmas tree, I'd be lying under that snow—" He looked around, trying to determine exactly where he could have fallen.

"Right over there." She pointed to an area as smooth and undisturbed as the rest of the landscape.

He shivered and tightened his hold on Cody, on life.

When they were in the house once more, Ben stomped the remaining snow from his boots onto the entry hall rug, then set Cody on the floor. Cody yawned and rubbed his eyes with a gloved hand.

The boy was already half-asleep. No wonder he'd been so quiet on the trip back. Ben tugged off his own gloves and prepared to help Cody out of his gear, but Arianne beat him to it. Probably a good thing, too, he thought. He didn't know the first thing about undressing a kid.

But he was a little disappointed.

"We have here one little boy who'll be out like a light the minute his head hits the pillow," Arianne said, pulling off Cody's boots, then leading him upstairs.

And Ben found his heart beating faster at the thought of Cody's being in his room, sound asleep. He and Arianne would be alone together, in front of the fire....

And he wasn't going to do a damn thing about it. This was no casual romantic encounter between two consenting adults out for a good time and no hassles. This was a woman to whom he owed his very life, a woman he cared about, a woman who had her own world with no place in it for someone like him ... and he had no place in his world for someone like her.

If he was so certain of all that, why did he have to keep reminding himself over and over? What was that old quote? "Methinks thou doth protest too much," or something like that.

He pulled off his coat and went to warm himself in front of the fire.

He'd wait until Arianne came back down so he could express his gratitude for all she'd done for him, so he could offer one more time to compensate her for her trouble, and so he could say good-night. Then he'd go immediately to bed ... and sleep with no covers if necessary to cool his desire to hold her, his need to make love to her.

One more night, and he'd be gone, away from temptation.

Arianne walked slowly down the stairs, excitedly, frighteningly aware that Ben was waiting, that this was the last night he'd be waiting.

"Well," she said as she came off the last step and rounded into the living room, "the little man has given it up. He was asleep before I had him covered."

Seated on the sofa, Ben turned and looked at her. "He's had a big day."

She nodded. "Every day's big when you're that age." Totally inane conversation. And that was all right. That was best.

She crossed the room to her favorite chair, debating if she should turn on the overhead light. The room was dim with only the fire and the Christmas-tree lights. But flooding the room with a hundred watts of voltage would be admitting she was nervous, would be announcing the fact that she saw the soft lighting as more than just an absence of illumination.

She sat down in her chair.

"Would you like some hot chocolate?" she offered.

"No, thanks. I'm pretty tired myself. Think I'll make an early night of it."

"Good idea. You'll have a long drive to Denver tomorrow."

"Yes. And then the flight to Dallas."

The dry, stilted conversation tore jagged holes in Arianne's heart. She and Ben were talking like strangers. In spite of the reason he'd come here, in spite of the way she'd had to deceive him, they'd shared a closeness beginning the night he'd helped her put together Cody's bicycle. Now they were a million miles apart. She could accept and deal with the fact that he was leaving, but somehow this emotional separation cut deeply and painfully.

"I guess you'll be glad to get back to—" What was he going back to? No family. A condo for a home. With no shed room, she recalled, almost smiling at the memory. But the corners of her mouth never made it upward. Cody. If Ben had no family to go back to, could she deny him the chance to find out if he had a son?

He didn't have a son. If she told him the truth, he'd insist on DNA testing. Cody would be confused. While they waited for the results, would Ben assume the role of father even more than he'd been doing? Where would that leave Cody when the tests came back negative?

Where would that leave Cody if the tests came back positive? She shivered at the possibility she didn't dare consider.

"I guess you'll be glad to get back to Dallas where it's not quite so cold," she finished lamely. "And to your company."

He smiled then. "Yeah. I know it's crazy, but I worry about my business when I'm not there. And I miss it, almost like it was a person."

"Yes, your business," she said, latching on to this reminder of why he wouldn't be a good father, why it was justifiable to keep the facts of Cody's birth from him. "Your business means a lot to you, doesn't it?"

He nodded, his features oddly softened by the flickering firelight. "We didn't have much when I was growing up. My mother worked hard, but she didn't have what we now call marketable skills. We never went hungry, but we never had any extras, either." His gaze darted around her house, and she wondered if he was comparing it to his childhood home.

"When I was a kid," he continued, "and somebody asked me what I wanted to be when I grew up, I always said, *rich*. So I started my own company as a means to an end, but somewhere along the way, the means became the end. It's not such a bad life, being totally immersed in what you do for a living."

"I'd have to agree with that. I love teaching. I always wanted a house full of children. If I can't have that, at least I can have a classroom full."

He stared at her intently for a moment. "You're young," he said, his voice low, scarcely more than a husky whisper. "And very beautiful. You'll find someone to give you all those children."

Lovely words of comfort, but they weren't for her. "No, I—" She stopped, gulping down the rest of her sentence. What had she been about to say? *I can't have children?* Yes, that was exactly what she'd almost said. She didn't want to deceive him any longer. The burden was getting too heavy. "After the accident," she blurted out, suddenly unable to stop herself, "after the water-skiing accident, the doctor said I'd have trouble getting pregnant, that he didn't think I'd ever be able to."

"But you did, and you can again. Doctors aren't always right. Did you have any problems when Cody was born?"

Cody. The mention of his name brought her back to sanity. Confessing might relieve her conscience, but it would put Cody in limbo, in emotional danger.

She leaped to her feet. "I think I'll go make some hot tea. I have this wonderful herbal blend that's really relaxing."

She darted into the kitchen, with trembling hands held the teakettle under the faucet, then set it on the stove and stood staring at it blindly. Ben did strange things to her, made her lose control of her thoughts and actions... of her common sense.

"None for me."

She gasped and whirled at the sound of his voice behind her.

He grimaced. "Sorry. Guess I did it again. I really don't mean to sneak up on you and scare ten years off your life."

With both hands behind her, she braced herself against the stove. "You don't. I mean, it's just that I'm not used to having anybody else in the house. Except Cody, of course." She was babbling again. He had that effect on her, too.

He nodded. "Well, so, I guess I'll go on up to bed."

He made no move to go. His eyes searched hers, flicked over her face, and settled on her lips, warming them, teasing them.

Then somehow she was in his arms, kissing him with her lips and her heart and her soul as if there were no tomorrow... and there wasn't. Not for them.

"Turn off the stove," he whispered.

She did, and let him lead her into the living room, onto the sofa. Again his lips found hers, his arms held her close to him, and her heart soared. Vitality and life flowed from him to her and her to him, a continuing circle, complete only when they touched.

Her lips parted and his tongue traced just inside, touching nerves she'd never known she possessed...just as he touched emotions in her she'd never known. His mouth was wet and slick and tasted of molasses taffy and desire.

Her hands caressed his broad back, her fingers stymied by the thick knit of his sweater, the barrier that kept her flesh from his.

And then his hands slid under her sweater to stroke her bare skin, building a heat in her to match that of the blazing logs.

He drew back from her... a few inches, but it might as well have been miles. Trailing beneath the faint fragrance of his cologne, his male scent came to her as a piece of him, making him forever a part of her. Shadows and light danced across his face as the flames leaped in the fireplace . . . and in her.

"Arianne," he whispered, his breathing as hard and fast as her own, "I'm leaving tomorrow. I—"

She placed one finger on his lips to cut short his protest. "I know. Tomorrow the snowstorm globe breaks, and we spill into the real world." She replaced her finger with her mouth. This was now. Tomorrow hadn't arrived yet.

He moaned . . . or she did . . . as he leaned back on the sofa, pulling her with him, atop him. Her legs lay on his, her pelvis against his hardness, her breasts on his chest . . . and still it wasn't close enough. She needed all of him.

His hands fumbled at her back, and she felt her bra loosen, then his fingers sliding along her ribs, stroking the sensitive flesh. She raised herself slightly, drawing away from his kiss, offering her breasts to more of his touch, aching for more. He pushed her sweater up, exposing her to his sight, to his hands.

"You're unbelievably gorgeous," he whispered. "I want you so much." He drew his tongue slowly over one nipple, then hesitated. "I—I know you don't go out much. I don't have . . . anything with me. Are you protected?"

She had to try hard to focus her whirling mind, to make sense of what he was asking. She didn't want to think, she only wanted to continue this glorious feeling. Ben was worried she'd become pregnant; if only his worry were valid. "It's okay," she reassured him. "I told you what the doctor said."

"But you had Cody."

She froze, blazing desire suddenly replaced by chilling fear.

"I'm sorry, I didn't bring anything," he said, obviously mistaking the reason for her distress. "I didn't think..." He kissed her forehead softly. "We could—"

Frantically straightening her clothes, she struggled off the sofa, away from him. "I can't." She stumbled across the room and up the stairs, her feet seeming to move in slow motion as in a bad dream when a monster chased close behind.

In her room she closed the door and leaned against it, heart thudding painfully. What had she almost done? If she'd made love with Ben, would he have been able to tell she'd never given birth, never even been intimate with a man before? How could she have come so close to putting Cody in jeopardy?

It seemed an eternity before she finally heard Ben's footsteps ascending the stairs, pausing in front of her door, then going to his room. Only then did she dare come out, go down to turn off the gas heater, bank the fire, unplug the Christmas tree lights, be sure the house was secure.

But the fire was out and the Christmas tree was only a shadowy silhouette in front of the window. Ben had shut it all down. The house, big and empty and remote, was dark and rapidly becoming cold.

Chapter Eleven

When Ben came downstairs the next morning, the sun was shining brightly through every window, each beam magnified in intensity as it bounced off the glaring surface of the snow. There was no doubt that he'd be able to leave today.

He smelled coffee brewing and bacon frying and heard the sounds of dishes rattling in the kitchen while Cody jabbered happily. For a single instant, a sensation of belonging, of being part of a family, washed over him. But that feeling was immediately replaced by one of being left out, excluded, once again the child who didn't fit in.

That was ridiculous. Of course he was excluded from Cody and Arianne's relationship. He was a stranger who'd intruded into their lives for a short time. Now that time was almost over. They'd go back to their normal routines, and he'd go back to his.

In a way, he was glad Arianne had called a halt to their lovemaking last night. She was going to be hard enough to forget about already. If they'd made love, it would only have strengthened that inexplicable tie between them, made it even tougher for him to walk away. And he couldn't have stopped on his own. He wanted her so badly, all reason and logic and self-control had deserted him.

He walked into the sunny kitchen. Arianne stood at the stove turning pieces of bacon in a black iron skillet, and he had to fight with every ounce of willpower to keep from going over to her, wrapping his arms around her, lifting her hair and kissing the back of her neck.

"Good morning," he said, holding his hands stiffly at his sides.

"Hi!" Cody greeted, looking up from the array of toy cars and trucks on the kitchen table. "The sun's shining. We can go out and play in the snow now."

"After breakfast," Arianne said without turning around. Her back, he thought, had stiffened with the knowledge that he was in the room. "Good morning, Ben."

He went over to stand beside her, not quite touching her, not daring to touch her. "About last night," he said softly.

"It's all right," she said, but he could tell it really wasn't.

"I want it to be all right."

She looked at him then and made an attempt at an embarrassed smile. Her eyes were haunted, the brown almost completely overpowering the green flecks. "It is. It will be. Scrambled eggs okay?" She raised her voice to normal volume on the last sentence.

He wasn't sure he believed her reassurances, but he didn't know anything he could do about it right then. "Scrambled sounds great. Do I smell biscuits? We're going to have to run around in the snow for hours to work off all these calories."

"You can ride on my sled," Cody offered.

Ben went over to the table and sat down beside him. "Where are you going to ride that sled? I haven't noticed any hills around here."

"The kids take turns pulling one another," Arianne explained. "Today, I imagine you and I will be doing all the pulling."

"I see. Now I understand the big breakfast." In spite of a major attempt to quell the feeling, the picture of himself pulling Cody around on the sled was warm and appealing.

For the first time since he'd been here, Arianne left the dirty dishes in the sink. She seemed almost as eager as Cody to get out into the gleaming white world. Ben found himself looking forward to it, to enjoying what was left of the isolated, magical world inside the snowstorm globe.

Cody darted out first, and when Ben and Arianne stepped onto the porch, a small snowball landed with a plop, falling apart at Ben's feet. Giggling loudly, Cody leaned down to get more snow.

"Oh, so that's the game?" Ben responded, leaping off the porch to find his own ammunition. But before he could retaliate, a larger, better packed snowball splatted against his shoulder. He looked up in surprise to see Arianne laughing. Cody took advantage of her distraction to run up and throw his latest effort from a foot away, hitting her squarely in the chest.

Before long, they were all three covered with snow.

"Cody, you look like a snowman," Ben said. "You could stand real still, and we could attach a carrot to your nose, and nobody could tell you were a real boy until you thawed in the spring."

Cody giggled. "No way, man."

"No way, man? Where did you learn that?"

"Television. Let's make a real snowman. We can put Gramps's hat on him."

"Good idea," Arianne approved, shaking the white frosting from her dark hair. "If we keep this up, we'll all turn into snowmen and be frozen solid until spring."

"Can we make a whole family?" Cody asked. "Mommy and Daddy and a little snowboy!"

"We'll see," Arianne hedged. "Let's take them one at a time."

"First, the daddy!"

"Okay," she agreed. "You make a little ball for the head, Ben can make a big one for the bottom and I'll make a medium-size one for the middle."

Before long, they had assembled a reasonable facsimile of a lopsided snow creature.

"He's tilted," Ben noted, leaning sideways in a mimicking gesture.

"He's got a broke leg," Cody explained, imitating Ben's pose.

Arianne stood next to Ben, tipping her head to the side. "I'd say he's vertically challenged."

"I'll go get Gramps's hat," Cody volunteered, running toward the house.

"And some raisins for eyes," Arianne called after him.

"And a cherry for a nose! Okay?"

"Okay."

Cody disappeared into the house, slamming the door behind him.

"This guy really does have a problem," Arianne said, studying the result of their joint efforts. She packed more snow on one side of the snowman's middle section and smoothed it carefully.

Ben's gaze was drawn to her middle section, to her well-covered breasts. A surge of desire shot through him as he remembered what they'd looked like the night before, naked, gleaming in the firelight, her raspberry nipples erect.

"Can I make the middle one when we get to the snow mommy?" The teasing words were out of his mouth before he realized he was bringing up an awkward situation, reminding her of something she obviously wanted to forget.

She blushed, but smiled and stepped closer to him . . . and rubbed snow all over his face.

"Oh, so that's the way it's gonna be!" He leaned over to pick up a handful of snow, and she took advantage of his off balance position to topple him.

Laughing, she fell on top of him. "Eat snow," she demanded. "You have to eat snow or I'll never let you up."

"Is that right?" With a single heave, he reversed their positions, holding her arms out to the sides, crouching above her. The green sparks in her brown eyes twinkled in the bright light. Her cheeks were rosy from the cold. Her hair spread over the snow in a dark, burnished fan. Her body beneath his wriggled enticingly, and he could all too easily imagine them making love.

Either she read his mind or the same thought came to her. She ceased her struggles, and the expression on her face changed from gaiety to sensuality.

"We got you now, Mommy!" Cody rushed up and flung himself to the ground beside them, dropping a worn, shapeless felt hat and grabbing his mother's arm. Raisins and cherries and a few unidentified objects spilled from the hat. "You're our prisoner, and you can never escape!"

"You could be right," she said softly. Her words were addressed to Cody, but her eyes never left his.

"Whaddaya wanna do with her? Bury her?" Cody asked enthusiastically.

No, that wasn't even close to what he wanted to do with her. "That could be a little drastic, kiddo. Who'll cook lunch if we bury her? Why don't we just make her eat snow?"

"Yeah! You gotta eat snow. Lotsa snow! Hey, what's that noise?" Cody leaped to his feet. "Look! It's the plow."

Ben had become so lost in Arianne's eyes that he hadn't heard the rumbling, groaning sound. Knowledge swept over her face, sobering her features and replacing the wanting in her gaze with emptiness. Or maybe it was his own feeling of loss he saw reflected there.

He released her and rose, looking in the direction of the noise. A plow attached to the front of a pickup truck moved slowly down the road, shoving the snow to the side, clearing a path. Arianne stood up, slowly brushing the snow from her clothing. Neither of them spoke as the vehicle approached. A dark blue car followed the truck.

"Gramma and Gramps," Arianne said quietly.

In a few short minutes, the pickup had passed their house, leaving the automobile parked on the road near the white mound that was his rental car. An older couple climbed out and came toward them.

"Gramma! Gramps!" Cody ran to embrace the couple. "See our snowman? He's challenged. I'm gonna put your hat on him!"

Arianne introduced him to her grandparents, Samuel and Margaret Lawton. They both looked him up and down assessingly, and Ben remembered the story Arianne had told them about his being short and scrawny.

You see? She is deceitful, a tiny voice whispered somewhere on the outskirts of his mind.

A white lie, he defended. That didn't necessarily validate the uneasy feeling he still couldn't dismiss that she wasn't being totally honest with him.

"That your car?" her grandfather asked, indicating the mound.

He nodded.

"I'll help you brush off the snow," the older man volunteered.

Ben nodded again, recalling Arianne's comment that her grandparents were concerned he might be Ted Bundy's protégé. They were probably eager for him to be on his way. That was doubtless why they'd followed the snowplow so closely. Their concern touched him. Arianne was lucky to have them.

But it reminded him that he had no place here; it was time to go.

And he wasn't ready.

"Me, too," Cody said. "I'll help, too."

Samuel Lawton produced a couple of brushes, giving one to Ben, and a short while later, the car emerged from the snow. Somehow, that sight put the period to his sojourn here. When he'd emerged from that vehicle and entered the blizzard a few days ago, everything had changed. Now the silvery metal glared starkly, a symbol pulling him back.

With what seemed like dizzying speed, the task was over, and everyone headed in, every step closer to the house taking him farther away from Arianne and Cody. They went inside the house that had suddenly lost its familiarity and become a strange place, a place he didn't belong.

"We've been so worried about you and Cody, sweetheart," Mrs. Lawton said, pulling off her coat and scarf.

She was a striking woman, tall, like Arianne, her silver hair still streaked with brown, dark eyes lively and skin softly crinkled by smile lines. Arianne would look like her when she grew old. For a fleeting moment, he wished he could be around to see each silver hair, each smile line make its appearance, to hear Cody's children call him *Gramps* and run to throw their arms around him.

From somewhere far away he heard a telephone ringing.

"It's your office," Arianne called.

Reality check. The sun was out, the roads clear and his office was calling. Time to turn loose of this fantasy world. The snowstorm globe had broken and dumped him out.

He walked over to the telephone and picked up the receiver, amazed and puzzled that this was the first time today he'd thought about his company.

He reassured the vice president that everything was fine even though it was nearly noon and he hadn't phoned in. "I'll be in tomorrow," he promised, then replaced the receiver and went upstairs to pack.

Within ten minutes, he had his bag packed and sitting in the hallway. No evidence remained in the bedroom to prove he'd ever been there. Would the same be true in Arianne's life? A year from now—next Christmas—would she remember anything more than the fact that she'd shared her holiday with a stranger?

He regarded the bare room silently—the iron bed frame painted shiny white, the handmade quilt, the scarred dresser topped with a crocheted doily, the glass-based lamp with an aged-ivory shade...quaint and old and not his style. Still—the trappings of a home.

He forced himself to pick up his bag, put one foot in front of the other, and make his way down the hall. The open door to Arianne's bedroom stopped him. He peered in. The room was very similar to the one he'd stayed in—a little more furniture of the same type, a book on the nightstand, a ballerina music box on the dresser. Similar to the other room, but not the same. Arianne slept here. Her invisible essence drew him inside.

He looked around intently, needing to memorize every detail, to have as much of Arianne as possible to take with him. A year from now he'd remember every detail of this Christmas, every word they'd said, the satin feel of her skin, the silk of her hair, the texture of her lips against his...and all the scents of Christmas would now be the scents of Arianne. He took a deep breath as if he could inhale some of her essence.

This wasn't accomplishing a thing. He needed to get on with things. One last look around.

It was only in that last glance that he noticed the top quilt on her bed had writing all over it. No, he corrected himself, the writing was embroidery. Square blocks of alternating blue and white, each with a name on it, surrounded a large white heart in the middle with more writing. Samuel Lawton and Margaret—

Then suddenly, Cody was in the room. He flopped onto the bed in front of him. "Are you gonna leave?" he asked, his mouth downturned, his eyes full of sadness.

"I have to," Ben said.

Cody picked at the quilt top. "When are you coming back?"

Tell him the truth, Ben ordered himself. Get it over with fast, a clean cut. "I don't know," he said, chickening out, telling a white lie himself. He couldn't stand to see the child's pain. He had to think of some way to distract him. "That's a neat quilt. How did they get all those names on there?"

Cody shrugged. "Everybody signed and then they sewed over it," he said without enthusiasm. "It's called a friendship quilt."

"Is that your Gramma and Gramps in the middle?"

"Uh-huh." He scooted over so he could trace the date, June 4, 1943, with one finger. "That's when they got married. I wasn't born yet. When are you gonna come back and marry Mommy and find my baby brother?"

If only it were that simple. He sat on the bed beside the boy and lifted him onto his lap, cuddling him close, inhaling his little-boy scent, drinking in the feeling of the small body. *If only it were that simple.*

"Cody?" Arianne stopped short in the doorway of her room, hand to her throat, her heart suddenly racing. Ben sat on her bed holding Cody in his lap, his bag on the floor beside them. Had he discovered her secret? Was he planning to take her son with him? What could she do to stop him?

She was being irrational. She knew that. Still, she had to force herself to stand unmoving, her knuckles white as she clutched the door frame, to restrain herself from dashing across the room and snatching Cody away from Ben.

Ben looked at her curiously. "He's okay. Aren't you, kiddo?" Cody slid from his lap, and Ben let the boy go, made no effort to restrain him.

Even though she knew she was overreacting, Arianne crossed the room, knelt and drew Cody into her arms. He buried his head against her neck.

"I don't want Daddy to go away," Cody said in a tiny voice. She didn't reprimand him for calling Ben *Daddy.*

"I know," was all she could say. *I don't want him to go, either.*

Ben crouched beside them. "Cody, sometimes adults have to do things they may not really want to do, like when your mommy goes to work and she'd rather stay home with you." He gazed at her over Cody's head, and she wanted to believe he was talking to her, that he really didn't want to leave them even though they both knew he had to.

"Sweetheart, let's go downstairs with Ben and tell him goodbye."

Cody shook his head, refusing to look up.

"It's okay," Ben said, standing. "Don't make him do that. Stay here with him." He rubbed his hands on the legs of his blue jeans and shifted from one foot to the other. "Arianne, I . . . I'm really grateful for . . . for your hospitality."

His words tore at her heart. Was that all the last few days had meant to him? Hospitality? Like a bed and breakfast? Stay a while with strangers then leave without a backward glance, without regret. Live together for a few precious days, sharing meals, dreams, kisses . . . her son . . . then part strangers.

It didn't matter, she reminded herself. He had to go. For her sake, for Cody's sake, she needed him to go, and soon.

But her contrary heart wanted him to at least regret the necessity.

She held on to Cody tightly and refused to look at Ben. "You're welcome," she said.

He stood still a moment longer, then strode from the room. She listened to his footsteps going down the stairs, heard Gramma and Gramps wish him a good trip . . . and heard the door close.

He was gone.

She hugged Cody fiercely. Her son was safe. Their life was just the way it had always been. She had him, and he had her, and that was enough.

Except it wasn't anymore. Ben had changed that.

Chapter Twelve

Arianne stood in the bathroom, brushing her hair in slow, halfhearted strokes. The room was uncomfortably chilly in spite of the small space heater, and she was well aware that she could stop and go downstairs at any time. Her hair was long and straight and, beyond the rudimentary process of getting out the tangles, brushing it all day wasn't going to change anything. She was stalling, and she knew it. To say she was unenthusiastic about her plans for the evening would be a gross understatement.

A heavy sigh escaped her lips as she laid the brush down on the dressing table.

She and Cody were scheduled to meet a fellow teacher, Fred, and his six-year-old nephew, Zack, then drive to Goodland for a Saturday afternoon of eating pizza and playing video games. It wasn't really a date; that's why she'd insisted on meeting them in town and going from there. Only if Fred picked her up would it be a date.

She squared her shoulders, looking herself in the eye in the mirror on the medicine cabinet. Well, looking as clearly as she could. The glass was old, her reflection mottled.

Okay, she forced herself to admit, it was a date. Kind of, anyway. After her experience with Ben, she'd decided that both she and Cody needed male companionship. She'd decided that on an intellectual level. Now, faced with putting that thought into action, she wasn't so sure.

Fred was nice, and Cody would enjoy the pizza, the games and being with another child.

So why wasn't she more enthusiastic?

Because, intellectual level be damned, she didn't want to be with Fred. This man she'd known for years seemed more a stranger than the man she'd spent four days with. Like it or not, approve of it or not, she wanted to be with Ben.

He'd been gone a little over a week, and in some ways, it felt like an eternity since they'd sat in front of the fire together, walked through the snow together, since he'd kissed her. Yet in other ways, she could feel his presence still there; he seemed to be looking over her shoulder hungrily as she cooked an omelet or smiling in his teasing way when Cody unplugged his video game and it took her half an hour to figure out how to reattach it to the television.

It didn't help that he kept sending her things—two electric blankets, a new generator, a cord of firewood, a small television set for Cody's room so he could play with his video game any time and a portable telephone-answering machine combination. Not romantic gifts; only practical repayment for the time he'd spent here. She'd use the wood, but the other items were stored in the basement until she could make some phone calls, get an address for Ben and return everything.

As if that could get him out of her thoughts.

She turned on her heel, whirled out of the bathroom and marched determinedly downstairs. Maybe she couldn't get him out of her thoughts, but she could and would do whatever was necessary to keep her son's life happy and normal.

"Cody, are you ready to go?"

He stood up, his coat buttoned askew. "I'm ready."

She smiled at his eager face above the misaligned garment. He looked so darned cute. Ben should be here to see this.

And that was something else she kept doing... wanting to share Cody with Ben. Well, not share *him;* just his actions, his expressions—

She bit her lip as the question that always seemed to be lurking around the corners of her mind burst into the forefront again. No matter what she might or might not feel for Ben, if there was any chance the man was Cody's father, did she have the right to deny him the opportunity to know his son, especially when that child happened to be the greatest kid in the world?

She rebuttoned Cody's coat and hustled him out the door. The snow had partially melted, leaving muddy spots to alternate with the patches of slush. As they made their way to the garage, she tried to steer Cody around the worst of the mud.

The sun was probably shining in Dallas.

When Arianne and Cody got to the drugstore in downtown Silver Creek, Fred and Zack were waiting at the counter, drinking sodas. Fred stood to greet her, and Zack slid down from his stool, running over to Cody. "Santa Claus brought me a new bicycle!" Zack bragged.

"Me, too," Cody countered. "A red one. And a daddy."

Any remnants of hope she might have had for the success of the outing disappeared.

"Did not," Zack argued.

"Did too."

"Where is he?"

Cody hesitated.

"I think—" Arianne began in an attempt to interrupt the discussion.

"He had to go to Dallas to get my baby brother 'cause that's where I was born."

"Did not." But Zack's retort was weak. Cody had him convinced.

Fred looked at Arianne with unabashed curiosity. She shook her head, not wanting to expose Cody's fantasy in front of his little friend. "It's a long story," she said. "I'll tell you when we get to the pizza place."

Cody hadn't mentioned Ben in several days, and she'd begun to hope he'd forgotten. Obviously he hadn't.

Of course, she herself hadn't mentioned him— aloud—in several days. And she certainly hadn't forgotten.

Ben stared out the window of his fifth-floor office. He paid extra rent for the spectacular view of Turtle Creek, but winter in Dallas wasn't spectacular. The grass and trees were bare and brown with no white blanket of snow. The Texas sun shone brightly—too brightly—as if it were trying too hard to compensate for the bleak desolation of the landscape. It was a deceitful sun.

The snow at Arianne's house had been cold and terrifying, but honest as well as beautiful and even cozy...as long as you were safely inside in front of the fire.

Immediately upon his arrival home, he'd made arrangements to have several gifts delivered to Arianne that he knew she could use. He knew she could buy them herself, if she wanted to, but for whatever reasons she hadn't. It was the only way he could think of to repay her. Still, he didn't feel that he'd evened things up. If only he could do that, he was sure he could get her out of his mind.

But it hadn't happened yet. A hundred times he'd reached for the phone to call her. A hundred times he hadn't followed through. He had no idea what he'd say to her.

"Ben?"

He jumped at the sound of the voice and looked up to see a tall blond man standing in the doorway. "Oh, hi, Frank. I didn't hear you come in."

His vice president and longtime friend sat down in one of Ben's client chairs and propped his feet on Ben's desk. "I don't think I've ever seen you daydreaming before. Or were you cooking up some new deal while pretending to admire the scenery?"

"You're married, Frank."

Frank lifted an eyebrow quizzically, looking a little confused at the abrupt change of subject. "Last time I checked," he finally answered.

Ben strained to remember Frank's wife. He knew he must have met her at office parties and dinners, but he drew a blank. "And kids. I seem to recall…" He didn't really. His almost-photographic memory for business tidbits had earned him quite a reputation. So why couldn't he remember the family of this man who was probably the closest thing to a friend that he had?

"Two girls," Frank said proudly. "Seven and ten."

Ben frowned. "It's Saturday afternoon. How come you're not home with your family?"

Frank gave a half laugh, as though he wasn't quite sure whether Ben was joking or not. "Because Saturday is the best day to work. No interruptions. We get more work done. Any of these quotes sound familiar?"

Ben grinned ruefully. "Nothing like being slapped in the face with your own words."

"Are you feeling okay?" Frank asked.

No, Ben thought. *I am definitely not feeling okay. About as far from okay as I can ever remember being.* But of course he couldn't say that. "I'm fine. Why?"

"I don't know. Ever since you came back from being trapped in that snowstorm, you've been kind of distracted, and that's not like you. You're usually the most focused person I've ever met. I'd even go so far as to say you were driven and obsessed . . . but I'd only say that behind your back, of course."

It took Ben a couple of seconds to register that his friend was making a joke, a couple of seconds before he fashioned the appropriate smile.

"See what I mean?" Frank asked. "Are you sure you didn't pick up a bug or something in that cold farmhouse?"

"Or something," Ben mumbled.

"Huh?"

"I'm not sick. I'm just . . . I don't know what I am. Reevaluating my life, I guess."

"Whoa! Heavy-duty stuff here. What's wrong with your life? I thought you finally had things going just the way you wanted them."

"I did. I do." *Like hell.* Ben rose abruptly, shoving his chair back. "Go home, Frank. Take your wife out to dinner and your kids to a movie, or however you work those things."

Frank stood with him, walked around the desk and clapped a hand on his shoulder. "Why don't you come with me? Linda's got a roast in the oven. We could play a little three-handed spades after dinner."

"Do you ever make molasses taffy after dinner?" Ben heard himself asking.

"No-o-o," Frank drawled uncertainly. "But I imagine Linda could find a recipe for it. So . . . can we count on you for dinner?"

Dinner with Frank and his family. Three-handed spades. Odd man out. Was he still the little boy who didn't quite fit in?

"Thanks, I appreciate the offer, but . . ." He could see Frank's expression closing, withdrawing. And he could hear himself rejecting such offers of friendship in the past. "I really would like to, but I guess you're right. I seem to have picked up something. I'm going to go straight home to bed."

But he remained in his office for a long time after Frank left. He felt no compelling need to go home. His condo was a good investment, it was a place where he could sleep, shower, shave and change clothes. But it really wasn't a home, not in the same sense as that ramshackle farmhouse of Arianne's.

There she came, intruding into his life again. What was going on with him? He drummed his fingers on his desk—his solid walnut desk.

He'd achieved what he'd set out to do. He was successful. He had a closet full of the right clothes, went to the right restaurants, belonged to the right country club, drove an expensive car. And a few minutes ago, he'd once again felt he didn't fit in.

It would seem there was more to this business of being successful than what took place in offices and conference rooms. For the first time, he missed having a family. Though not just any family. His idea of finding a woman as career-obsessed as he was wouldn't cut it. The woman he wanted—the only woman he wanted—was completely home-and-family-obsessed.

Just because he wanted her, missed her, thought about her constantly, didn't mean he could sustain any sort of normal relationship with her. Hadn't he already proven he couldn't? He hadn't been able to spare enough of himself from his first love, his work, to make his marriage a success. He couldn't even spare enough of himself to be upset that his marriage had failed.

But, he had to admit, something had changed. Work seemed to be taking second place to thoughts of Arianne.

Was she displacing work as his primary obsession?

He took a deep breath and faced that question head-on. Not that he had much choice. If he didn't, he'd never be able to get on with his life.

He had to make some hard decisions as to exactly what *getting on with his life* meant.

He needed to see Arianne again, try to figure out where they'd go from here... and where Cody fit into the equation. Arianne came with a ready-made family and, cute as Cody was, he would never be his flesh-and-blood son. The boy wanted a father badly, but could he ever fill that role? He didn't know. What did that do to any prospects of a long-term relationship between Arianne and him?

Of course, Arianne had made it clear what she thought about Dallas, about men like him and her father. Maybe all this soul-searching was moot. Maybe she wouldn't want to see him again. He knew she was as attracted to him as he to her, but that wasn't the issue. The issue was whether they dared risk further entanglement, the possibility of having to blend their lifestyles.

So he'd better find out. Pick up the phone and call her. If she wanted nothing more to do with him, then he should finally be able to put her out of his mind and get back to his former life.

Far from being comforting, that thought drew a black pall over him. He stared at the phone, afraid to pick up the receiver, afraid to call, afraid of what Arianne might say.

That's ridiculous, he chided himself. *You've got to know. Just pretend you're calling a CEO of a large company who can make or break you with his decision. That way, it won't seem so important. It won't be as intimidating as calling Arianne.* He tried to smile at his own joke, but he wasn't sure it was a joke.

He snatched up the phone before he could change his mind and dialed her number. And listened for ten rings. She wasn't home and she hadn't hooked up the answering machine he'd sent her.

He realized there were beads of perspiration on his upper lip.

Get a grip, he ordered himself. It was Saturday. She was probably shopping. *Except Arianne didn't seem like the shopping type.* So maybe she'd taken Cody to a movie or whatever kids did on Saturday afternoons.

As for the answering machine, with her dubious mechanical ability, she likely wasn't able to figure out how to hook it up. He smiled at that thought, at the prospect of helping her with it.

That smile faded as the cloud of suspicion he couldn't seem to avoid washed over him again. Was she merely out for the evening? Or was she avoiding him so she wouldn't have to tell him...what?

He slapped one hand on the desk, irritated with himself. He was being unduly cynical. Just because she hadn't told him every detail about her ex-husband didn't mean she was hiding something. Could be, the problem was entirely his, that he was looking for reasons not to want her, not to be forced to compromise his life-style.

Well, he'd go home and call her again. And again. And again. Until he reached her. Until he got a handle on this thing.

Arianne pulled up to her garage and got out to open the door. For some reason, the place seemed spooky and deserted tonight...as though the sun, along with the rest of the world, had vanished, leaving them alone. With the early onset of darkness in the winter, she usually came home in the dark, and it had never bothered her before.

She opened the garage door and wished she'd gone to the extra expense of having electricity run to the old structure. She'd like to be able to light the cavernous depths that loomed before her and made her feel very alone, surrounded by nothingness.

Which was nonsense. A few feet behind her, Cody slept in the car. Across the yard, her home waited for her.

Her empty home.

She ought to be glad to be alone. The day had been exhausting. She'd enjoyed watching Cody and Zack have fun, but being in a one-on-one situation with Fred had been a strain. Not that there was anything wrong with Fred. No, the only problem was that he wasn't Ben. Somehow, in his short time with her, Ben had managed to infiltrate her heart, her very being. Never mind that she knew all the reasons she could never be with him. His leaving had left a big, ragged hole.

She hurried back to the car, to Cody. But even Cody's warm, cuddly love couldn't fill that gaping hole in her heart.

She parked the car in the garage and carried Cody to the house. As she struggled to unlock the front door, she could hear the phone ringing. By the time she got inside, it would have stopped. Briefly she wished she'd set up the telephone-answering machine Ben had sent her. Maybe she ought to buy one.

The phone was still ringing when she laid Cody on the sofa.

She lifted the receiver. "Hello?"

"Arianne, it's Ben."

Well, damn. Her heart didn't have to do flip-flops at the sound of his voice.

"Ben, I'm glad you called."

"You are?"

"Yes, I need to get your address so I can send all these things back to you. I appreciate the gesture, but it's not necessary."

He was silent for a moment. "Then I won't give you my address. I don't want them back. I'm planning another trip to Denver, and I sure would like you to have those electric blankets if I get snowed in at your place again."

She caught her breath. Was he teasing or was he planning another visit? Of course he was teasing. She gave a brief laugh to show she understood that. "It'll never happen," she said. "The snow's melting."

"Good. I'm glad to hear it. It's been sunny all day here."

"Really? That's great." She felt heavy all at once, full of lead. Surely after all that had happened and almost happened between them, they couldn't be reduced to discussing the weather, could they?

"Arianne, we need to talk," he said, his voice suddenly firm.

She looked at Cody lying on the sofa, one lock of hair falling over his forehead, one small hand fisted under his chin, eyes closed in sleep.

"Yes," she agreed, "we do." And she knew in that instant that she was going to tell him the truth. The thought filled her with dread, but it had to be done.

"I've missed you," he said, and the words took away the leaden weight, sent her spirit soaring, light as a spring breeze.

"I've missed you, too," she whispered.

"I need to see you."

Let's don't start something we can't finish, she wanted to say. But it was too late. The *something* had started the moment she'd dragged him through the snow to her house. It was already too late when he'd kissed her in front of the fireplace.

She took a deep breath. If nothing else, she could tell him about Cody in person rather than over the phone. She could prevail on him not to do anything that would disturb her son's happiness, his security.

"Yes," she said, excited and fearful at the same time. "When and where?"

"Tomorrow at your house."

"Tomorrow?" Her head whirled. This was too soon. She needed time to prepare herself, to sort things out.

"I've already checked. I can get a late flight to Denver, connect with a commuter airline to Goodland in the morning, rent a car there and be at your place by noon."

She gulped, suddenly overwhelmed.

"I can't wait to see you and Cody," he said.

After he hung up, she stood looking at her sleeping son. *I can't wait to see you and Cody,* he'd said. He cared about Cody. It would be all right. He wouldn't do anything to upset him. Surely he wouldn't.

As for herself, she had no idea what she was going to do. Did he care for her, too? As much as she cared for him? Did it matter? He was still the quintessential businessman. She couldn't risk any real involvement with him.

But she couldn't deny that she was totally intoxicated at the thought of seeing Ben again, that she would put her own emotional well-being in jeopardy to be with him again, to touch him again.

Ben sped along the highway, trying to keep his concentration focused on the road, on looking for the turnoff that would take him to Arianne's house. His thoughts kept drifting, anticipating the way she'd look, the way she'd feel in his arms. She'd said she missed him, too.

The morning was cloudy, gray and cold, but it seemed brighter than yesterday in the Dallas sunshine.

Sometime on the flight to Denver, it had dawned on him that he was in love with her. He wanted all of her, her vibrant smile, her musical laughter, her fierce determination. Maybe he should have figured it out earlier, but it was a totally new thing. No wonder his first marriage hadn't worked out. He'd never felt like this about his ex.

He was going to ask Arianne to marry him. He had to. He had no choice. He wanted to come home to her every night, to wake up with her every morning. If he couldn't pry her out of that old house, he'd…well, he didn't know exactly what he'd do.

For the first time in his life, he was rushing headlong into something without having every step planned out. If she loved him as much as he loved her—and she had to, he couldn't live with anything else—somehow they'd work things out.

His thoughts drifted again from the road ahead to her bedroom, to the big quilt that showed the date of her grandparents' wedding. That's what he wanted. Over fifty years with the same woman. Fifty years of growing old together and knowing the wrinkles and gray hair didn't matter to the person you loved.

He could still see that heart in his mind's eye, Cody's small finger tracing the date. June 4, 1943. And the names above it, Samuel Lawton and Margaret Landis.

He frowned. No, that couldn't be right. He must be confused. Landis was Arianne's name. That would be too much of a coincidence that she had married a man with her grandmother's maiden name.

But he wasn't confused. He remembered it quite clearly. *Samuel Lawton and Margaret Landis.*

And he remembered another name from Arianne's house. Samuel Landis. The man listed on Cody's birth certificate as Cody's father. A man with Arianne's grandfather's first name and her grandmother's maiden name.

He jerked the car to the right, barely making the turnoff to Arianne's.

His blood pounded loudly in his ears. He had to calm down. He was about to jump to conclusions. So Arianne had made up a name for Cody's father. So she hadn't been married to the man and didn't want anyone to know. That would be like her. Her values were kind of old-fashioned. That didn't mean anything. It didn't mean he could possibly be Cody's father, that Julia had told the truth.

But there was more. There was his feeling that she was keeping something from him. With that same technique of recall that enabled him to keep track of all the facts in every business deal, he replayed in his mind the things she'd said that had jarred, that had brought him up short though he hadn't been able to find anything really wrong.

Like her reluctance to talk about Cody's birth or his father, the nervous way she'd picked at the sofa cushion then changed the subject when he'd pushed her.

Cody's father was consumed by his work. That was all that mattered to him. He was no more ready to be a father than mine was. Had she been describing him?

Then there was the time she'd told him that, after the water-skiing accident, the doctor had said she'd have trouble getting pregnant, that he didn't think she'd ever be able to. So the doctor had been wrong, he'd thought. That happened.

But when they'd come so close to making love, and he'd asked her if she was protected, she'd replied, "It's okay. I told you what the doctor said." She hadn't been worried about getting pregnant. He'd thought that strange at the time since she obviously had become pregnant at least once, had proven the doctor wrong.

Or maybe she hadn't.

She and Julia looked enough alike that Julia could have passed for her in a hospital environment with strangers around.

Ahead of Ben, the narrow two-lane road stretched straight and flat. He wanted to focus on that road, on the asphalt, away from the stained, ugly direction his thoughts had taken, from the fierce anger building inside him. He could be wrong. It could be that he'd seen too much deceit—from his mother's lies to the perpetual lies known as everyday business negotiations—and now he expected to find it everywhere.

He clenched his jaw and tried to stop thinking about it. Soon he'd be at Arianne's house. Then he could ask her.

But the questions wouldn't stop bombarding him. Had Julia told the truth? Was Cody his son? Had Arianne lied to him? Was she keeping his son away from him the way his own mother had kept him and his father apart?

No. Arianne wouldn't do something like that. At least, the Arianne he loved wouldn't.

Chapter Thirteen

"There he is! There he is!" Cody bounced into the kitchen, eyes shining, face aglow.

He didn't need to announce it. Although Arianne was putting away the last of the dishes from lunch, keeping herself busy and away from windows, she'd heard the sound of a car approaching, slowing and turning into her driveway.

Ben had arrived.

She went to the door with Cody, trying to keep her steps even and unhurried. It was hard to do. She'd been awake most of the night, anticipating and dreading this moment. Ben hadn't really said much on the telephone—just that he missed her and they needed to talk. But his voice had caressed her. Against all common sense and logic, even with the knowledge that she had to tell him about Cody, she was thrilled at his arrival.

With Cody beside her, she opened the door. Ben, wearing a ski jacket and blue jeans, climbed out of his

car and started across the yard, coming toward her with
his long-legged stride. The sight filled her with summer, made the gray sky, the mud and the snow disap-
pear. She wanted to run to him, fall into his arms, savor
the bliss of being with him again for one sweet moment before she came to her senses, before she told him
about Cody.

But something was wrong. She could tell it in his
walk, in his stance, in the way he held his head.

The brief spurt of summer was gone. The dreary
landscape returned.

Cody burst from the house and ran to Ben.

Ben cast her a dark, scowling look, then knelt to
embrace Cody briefly.

"I knew you'd get here soon," Cody exclaimed. "I
told Zack you would. Pretty soon we can play base-
ball 'cause the snow's all melted, almost."

As Ben stood and approached the porch, Cody bab-
bled happily beside him, but Ben's attention—his
glowering attention—was focused on her.

"Come in," she said, holding the door open.

"Thank you," he said, his voice and his eyes so cold
her heart shriveled to the size and texture of a hickory
nut.

She closed the door behind him, but her action
didn't shut out the chill that had entered the house with
him.

Turning around, she found him standing in the entry
hall, his expression the same as the night they'd
brought him in from the snow—cold and distant. Cody
hung on to his arm, looking up adoringly, and Ben
neither acknowledged nor ignored him.

"Did you have a good trip?" she asked, the question sounding impossibly inane.

"Can we go somewhere private to talk?" His words fell between them like icicles.

"Of course." She dropped to her knees in front of Cody, her action as much a response to the oppressive atmosphere that pushed her downward as a desire to be on her son's level. "Cody, can you stay down here while Ben and I go upstairs to talk? We won't be gone long."

Cody heaved a monumental sigh, but he didn't argue. "Okay, Mommy."

She stood, crossed the room and climbed the stairs to her bedroom with Ben following behind—a scene that had often teased her fantasies, but not like this, not with apprehension dragging at her every step.

Inside her bedroom, Ben closed the door and she turned to face him.

His gaze was no longer cold; it blazed with white-hot fury. "Is Cody my son?" he demanded.

She backed away from him and sank onto her bed, wrapping her arms around herself as much for protection from the scorching rage that blasted from Ben in waves as from the cold in the unheated room. So this was it. Cody's fate was on the line.

"I don't know," she said. "Maybe."

"Maybe," he repeated, folding his arms across his chest. "Did you give birth to Cody?"

She took a deep breath. "No. Julia did."

"So you lied to me. You tried to keep me from my own son."

She shot up from the bed. "No! I mean . . . I only wanted what was best for him."

"And that didn't include me."

"I didn't want him to be hurt."

She hadn't thought his expression could become any darker, any fiercer, but it did. "What sort of man do you think I am that I would hurt my own son?"

Her anger rose, mingling with her fear. This was a question she could answer. "A busy man. A man, by his own admission, married to his work. Cody deserves better than that. Anyway, there's no proof you're his father. Even Julia isn't positive."

"He looks like me."

"He's a little boy. He looks like himself." But her argument was weak. Ben was right on that count. "Julia's lover, the one we always thought was Cody's father, has the same build and coloring you do."

"Is he left-handed?"

"I don't know."

"I want DNA testing."

She sagged onto the bed again. "Cody has a good life here. Everybody believes his father died in a car wreck. If people knew the truth about his birth, there would be talk. He'd never be treated the same again. If you care about him, don't do this to him."

Ben's eyes narrowed. "Are you that concerned about his reputation, or are you just afraid to share him?"

Arianne stared at him for a moment, then looked away. His poison dart had hit home. "Both," she said quietly. "I love that little boy more than life itself. I'll do anything to keep him from getting hurt. And, yes, I'm terrified of losing him. I know I have no legal right to him."

"You knew that when you took him to raise."

"But I didn't love him then the way I do now. At first, I loved him because he was a baby, a human being, Julia's child. Now I love him because he's Cody, a very special person. He's not the son of my body, but he's the son of my heart. Can you say that?''

Ben didn't respond by word or expression.

"Do you love Cody or is this strictly a macho 'child of my loins' thing?'' she demanded, pursuing her momentary advantage. "If he's not your son, can you just walk away from him? If you can, then he's not your son, no matter what the DNA shows.''

He didn't say anything for a long moment. Her grandmother's clock on the dresser ticked loudly in the silence, and she dared to hope.

"I want to know," he finally said. "If you don't agree to it, I'll petition the court to force you. Then the whole town will find out.''

Her hopes died. "What happens if the test is positive?" She couldn't bring herself to say *if you're Cody's father.*

He ran a hand distractedly through his hair. "I don't know.''

She nodded. "I see. You haven't given any thought to the effects of your actions.'' Anger that more than matched his coursed through her, anger spawned by anxiety about Cody's well-being along with alarm that she might lose him.

She rose slowly from the bed, and moved close to him, invading his space. "You just want to satisfy your ego,'' she accused. "You think donating a sperm makes you a father. Well, it doesn't.'' She leaned toward him, her face inches from his. "You don't have room in your life for a son. You have your damn company, and that's all you need. That's your offspring, your life. Go back to it and leave us alone.''

His eyes narrowed. She'd touched a nerve. He grabbed both her arms and held her immobile. "I came here because I couldn't stop thinking about you, not even long enough to run what you refer to as my 'damn company.' I came here because I thought you were more important than my work. But that was before I figured out that you lied to me, that you hid my son from me."

She tried to jerk away, but he held her firmly. "I'll lie, cheat or steal to protect him," she threatened through gritted teeth. "That's what love's all about, not DNA molecules."

"Are you going to agree to the test or do I go to court?"

Nothing she'd said had mattered. She had failed at changing his mind. Her gaze darted around the room as if frantically searching for a way out. There was none.

"All right," she whispered. "But I can't guarantee that Julia will agree. You'll need her consent. She *is* Cody's biological mother." She grabbed at the last wisp of hope.

"She'll give her consent," he said flatly. "I'll pay her."

There was no way she could argue with that. Julia's greed had started all this in the first place. She nodded, and he released her. He'd won. She'd lost... not just the argument but maybe Cody and certainly this man who'd come into her life and awakened her emotions then turned them upside down. Even though she'd known that both losses were inevitable, the pain sliced through her, hard and deep.

"Don't say anything to him," she begged. "Let me handle the explanations. Please."

Ben watched Arianne's face, her whole body, sag in defeat, heard her pleading words. And his victory was bitter.

He turned away from her, not wanting to see any more. His gaze fell on the quilt, her grandparents' wedding quilt, and he ached for his own loss. Not an hour ago, he'd planned—hoped—to have with Arianne what her grandparents had. That could never happen now. If Cody was his son, they'd have to work out something, but they'd always be enemies. He'd always resent her for lying to him. If Cody wasn't his son, he'd walk away, just as she'd accused him. Arianne had lied to him; if Cody wasn't his son, he had no attachment to either of them.

"You have my word," he promised her. "Handle it however you think best."

She didn't answer, but he heard her soft footsteps leaving the room and going downstairs. Was she going to talk to Cody so soon?

Suddenly he panicked. What *would* he do if Cody was his son? What did he know about being a father?

As much as any new father, he told himself. As much as Arianne knew about being a mother when she took possession of Cody, and she'd turned out to be a damn good mother.

He'd done the right thing. If Cody was his son, they both had a right to know.

He ran one hand over the quilt that promised so much, and snatched it away at the same time.

From below he could hear Arianne calling for Cody. He ought to go down. He couldn't stay in Arianne's bedroom forever.

The door slammed downstairs and Arianne's voice grew fainter. Cody must have gone outside. He walked over to the window. He watched Arianne as she slogged through the mud and the slush, over to the barn.

He couldn't deny a feeling of admiration for her. Living in this old house, raising a child alone—she did it all and did it well.

In spite of his anger, he admired her.

And he loved her. Somehow, that hadn't changed.

She emerged from the barn, running now, over to the old shed she called a garage. Was she still looking for Cody? Why would she think he'd be in the garage?

He hurried downstairs and looked around, checked the basement then the other bedrooms upstairs. The house was empty.

Arianne burst through the door just as he came into the living room, her face flushed from the cold, her eyes wide with panic.

"Cody's gone!" she exclaimed.

"Gone where?"

"I don't know! His coat and bicycle are both missing."

"Don't worry," he said, talking to himself as much as to her. Her fear was contagious. Cody was so little, so helpless. "He's around here someplace. Where could he go?"

"I don't know, but he's not here. I found bicycle tracks through the mud out to the road."

"Well, that's it. He's just gone for a bicycle ride."

She glared at him. "He's five years old. He doesn't go for a bicycle ride without asking me. Anyway, he wouldn't go anywhere since you're here. He's been as excited about your coming back as he was about Christmas."

Her words swelled Ben's heart. Cody had been looking forward to seeing him. And, he realized, before he got sidetracked with the issue of whether or not Cody was his son, he'd been looking forward to seeing the boy. Arianne wasn't the only person he'd missed.

Arianne crossed the room and snatched up her purse. "I'm going to look for him."

"I'll go with you. We'll take my car, and I'll drive while you look."

She seemed about to argue, then nodded. "Okay, but let's take both cars. You go west, and I'll go east."

"No. He can't have gone far, and he'll be easy to spot in this flat land. We should be able to see him from pretty far away. If we don't see him after five minutes in one direction, we'll go the other." She needed him to be with her, he told himself, then admitted that he needed her to be with him. He knew Cody was all right, and they'd find him soon. But he couldn't dismiss a nagging worry, and he didn't want to be alone with that worry. He needed to share it with someone who understood, someone who cared about Cody, too.

And she was right. He didn't know the first thing about being a father. He needed her to be with him when they found Cody.

They hurried out to his car.

"Go east first, toward town. He might be heading for Gramma's."

He followed her direction.

She chewed on one fingernail. "He must have heard us arguing."

Ben tried to remember exactly what they'd said, but for once his memory failed him. Even so, he didn't think it was the kind of conversation a five-year-old child should hear. Guilt flooded over him at the thought that he might have hurt the boy. Cody had given his love freely, without question or reservation, and Ben had repaid it with pain.

"There he is!" She pointed ahead.

In the distance he could see a tiny figure.

The surge of joy that shot through Ben told him how concerned he had been. "Are you sure that's him?"

"Of course I'm sure. I'm his mother."

"Yes," he agreed. "You are."

Even as they approached Cody, the boy still seemed impossibly small against the vast landscape. He steered his bicycle off the road as the car came up behind him.

"Cody!" Arianne called, tugging on the door handle before Ben could bring the car to a complete stop.

Cody looked up and smiled. He braked and climbed off the bike.

Arianne got to Cody just ahead of Ben. She knelt and pulled the boy into her arms, and Ben stooped to wrap one arm around each of them.

"Cody, I love you," he blurted out. "I didn't mean what I said to your mommy when we went upstairs. We don't need any test to prove I'm your daddy."

Cody disentangled himself from the two adults and looked up at Ben. "I know that," he said calmly. "You're going to marry my mommy and then I'll have a baby brother."

And a little child shall lead you. Cody had had it right all along, Ben realized as the boy's words registered. Cody had never had doubts. He'd been able to cut through the garbage, through all the layers of trivia adults surrounded themselves with, and get to the core of things, to the important part...to the loving part. That was, in the end, the only part that mattered.

"I'd like that," Ben said simply, turning his gaze to Arianne. "I'd like to marry your mommy. If she'd like to marry me."

Arianne gaped at Ben in astonishment. Was he proposing to her? Right here in the middle of the mud and slush? And if he was, what was she going to do about it?

Ignore it for the moment. That was all she could do right now.

"Cody, did you hear Ben and me arguing? Is that why you ran away?" she asked, determined to handle one crisis at a time.

Cody rolled his eyes to Ben as though marveling at her stupidity. "I didn't run away. Daddy came back, so I was going to the hospital to get my baby brother."

"Oh." She straightened and took a deep breath. "I see." Her relief that he hadn't heard anything to upset him was tempered with distress over his continuing fixation on this baby brother business.

"Well," Ben said, obviously determined to ignore the subject, "let's get this muddy bike into the trunk of this nice clean rental car and head home."

Cody protested. "What about—"

"Your baby brother's not at the hospital," Arianne said.

"Where is he?"

She looked to Ben for help, but he picked up the bicycle and moved away—hastily, she thought. That was just great. One minute he wanted to marry her, and the next he deserted her when she needed him.

"In heaven," she told Cody. "Your baby brother's still in heaven with Jesus."

"But you said after you and Daddy got married, we'd get him."

"Your daddy—that is, *Ben* and I are not married. Get in the car. We'll talk about this later."

He looked at the ground and kicked at an imaginary rock with his muddy shoe. "Okay," he agreed grudgingly.

Not bad. She'd managed to successfully evade uncomfortable questions from both Ben and Cody. For the moment, at least.

Arianne finally got Cody settled on the sofa with his video game. She wasn't sure she'd convinced him there was no baby brother waiting at the hospital, all alone and wondering what was taking his mommy and daddy and big brother so long to get there. Cody was one stubborn kid when he made up his mind to something. Nevertheless, he was distracted for the moment, and she was counting on the noise of the television to cover the sounds of anything she and Ben might have to say to each other.

"Let's go in the kitchen," she said.

He nodded and followed her in. She headed toward the table, but he stopped her, pulling her into his arms.

"I meant what I said, Arianne. I love you, and I want to marry you."

Before she could protest, he covered her lips with his...and she couldn't remember what she'd been about to say. His touch set her blood laughing and singing. She slid her arms around his back, pulling herself closer to him, responding to his kiss with a pent-up fervor she hadn't realized she possessed.

She wanted to go on kissing him mindlessly forever.

No, that wasn't quite true. Kissing Ben was wonderful, but other parts of her body ached for his touch. She wanted all of him. Only Cody's presence in the next room kept her from offering herself to him completely.

He pulled back from her. "Do I take that as a yes?"

She blinked in confusion and tried to get her thought processes going again. "No," she finally whispered and tried to extricate herself from his embrace.

He held her tightly and started to kiss her again, but she turned away.

"Ben, there's got to be more of a basis for marriage than . . . than—"

"Arianne, I love you. Yes, I want to make love to you. I won't even try to deny that. But that's not all. I want to come home at night to you and wake up in the mornings with you and hold your hand when you're sick and watch Cody grow up. I want to grow old beside you. I want us to have what your grandparents have."

His words were hypnotic. She wanted to close her eyes to reality and dive in head first, indulge this overpowering desire she had for this man. But she couldn't. If for no other reason than Cody, she couldn't. "You've already admitted that's not possible. Your first love is your career. Cody and I would always come second."

"That's not true. You've already shoved all that to the rear. I haven't been able to keep my mind on my work for thinking about you."

"And how long do you think that will last?"

"As long as I have you. Believe me, Arianne, the last couple of weeks have been a real shock to my priority system. My company, money, none of that matters if I can't have you to share things with. You and Cody."

"You told him there wouldn't be any DNA test," she accused, remembering what he'd said to Cody when they'd found him.

"And I meant it. It doesn't matter. All that matters is when you love somebody. Do you love me, Arianne?"

"Yes," she admitted. "I do. But—"

"That's all we need to know. We can work the rest out. I'll come home after work every evening, spend the weekends and holidays with you and Cody. I'll even come here to live in this—" He swallowed and grimaced. "This lovely old house. I could get a small plane and commute. Heaven knows, there wouldn't be any problem making a landing strip in the backyard."

She laughed and allowed herself to cuddle closer to him, to believe it might work, she might have Ben in her life. "That sounds really serious. But you wouldn't have to go that far. I confess, I wouldn't mind living somewhere with central heating and air-conditioning, appliances that work and neighbors close enough to wave to once in a while. Maybe we could just come back here on vacations."

"And Christmas. I want to spend every Christmas here."

That reminded her of Cody's Christmas wish—his obsession.

"Ben, now you know I didn't give birth to Cody, that I've never been pregnant. And the doctor said I probably never will be. Cody will never have that baby brother."

"We can always adopt. To quote somebody we all know, 'Love makes a parent, not DNA.' And who knows? Miracles happen. My finding you and Cody—

and you and Cody finding me in that blasted snow-storm—all that has to be classified as a miracle.''

"What about—" She swallowed hard and tried to pull away from him. "What about the fact that I lied to you about Cody?''

He held her more tightly, refusing to let her go, even though the lines around his mouth tensed. "You did it because you love him. I understand that.''

"But it still bothers you.'' Was it, after all, too late for them? she wondered.

He tugged her over to the door and nodded toward Cody sitting on the sofa, engrossed in his video game. "That little boy has taught me an awful lot about love. He recognizes it even when we stubborn adults don't, he values it above all else and he gives and accepts it without question. Between the two of us, we've pro-duced one heck of a kid. Now it's time we learn what he can teach us. Maybe you've done some things that upset me at the time, and maybe I have, too. I'd say sleeping with Julia was not one of my finer moments. But if we hadn't both done exactly what we did, right now wouldn't be happening. I love you, and I accept you unreservedly.''

Cody looked up from his game and saw them watching him. His eyes widened happily, expectantly.

"Not yet,'' she called, and he shrugged then went back to his game.

"Not yet what? How did you know what he wanted?''

"It had to be either his baby brother or our mar-riage. The answer's the same for both.''

"So tell him in two weeks we'll be married. That should satisfy him.'' His eyes were warm and smoky now, like twilight in summer.

"Okay," she agreed, grinning at him. "You can tell your son we're going to make it official in two weeks."

He claimed her lips just as he'd claimed her heart, and she gave both willingly and happily.

After a long, delicious kiss, he gazed at her. "Let's tell our son together."

Epilogue

Ben lifted Cody so he could put the star on top of the Christmas tree. The ornament looked mundane as the boy's small hands adjusted it. But he was reminded anew that this piece of tinsel and glass had guided him a year ago today to his wife and son.

"There," Cody said. "That's just right. Turn it on so Santa can see it."

Ben set the boy on the floor and plugged in the lights.

"Next year, I'll be tall enough to put up the star all by myself."

"Well, maybe. If we get a shorter tree."

Cody giggled. "You're silly, Daddy. I'm going to call Mommy in to see our tree." He scampered to the kitchen doorway. "Mommy, we're ready! You can come in now."

Silence answered them.

"Arianne? Sweetheart, do you need some help with dinner?"

"No," she answered. "I'm almost finished."

She didn't sound quite right, and Ben started toward the kitchen.

"Maybe we better put some blankets outside in case Santa Claus leaves my baby brother out there like he left you last year," Cody said anxiously, darting over to peer around the Christmas tree, out the black window. "Even if it's not snowing, it's real cold out there."

Ben went over and wrapped his arms around the boy. "Trust me. Santa won't leave your baby brother outside. In a week or two, Mommy will go to the hospital and bring him home with her." Which only went to prove his son had been smarter than the doctor who'd predicted Arianne would probably never have a child.

Cody shook his head stubbornly. "Not in a week. Santa Claus only comes on Christmas. Listen. I hear his sleigh bells."

Ben frowned. The power of suggestion was great. He did seem to hear a tinkling noise, but it could be anything in the old house. "Maybe your brother will get here for New Year's. Wouldn't that be exciting? Having a new baby brother and a new year at the same time?"

"No." Cody lifted his square jaw obstinately. "Santa Claus only comes on Christmas." He repeated the information slowly as though Ben were slightly obtuse.

Arianne waddled into the room, clutching her rounded stomach, ripe with the miracle of the new life their love had created. "Cody," she said with a grimace, "do me a favor and check with me next year before you make your Christmas list. You seem to have an in with Santa Claus. I believe you're going to have a new baby brother for Christmas."

Somehow, Ben wasn't even surprised. With the eyes of love, Cody had known all along that Ben was his father, that Ben should marry his mother and that, against all odds, he would have a baby brother. Getting the arrival date of that baby brother advanced a few days was nothing to someone with that kind of power.

*   *   *   *   *

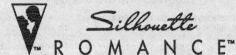

Silhouette ROMANCE™

COMING NEXT MONTH

#1126 A FATHER'S VOW—Elizabeth August
Fabulous Fathers/Smytheshire, Massachusetts
When Lucas Carver's little boy picked the lovely Felicity Burrow as his mother, Lucas knew she was perfect. For Felicity touched his heart and mind in ways neither of them had dreamed possible.

#1127 THE BABY FACTOR—Carolyn Zane
Bundles of Joy
Elaine Lewis *would* keep custody of her baby—even if it meant a temporary marriage to her employee Brent Clark. But leaning on Brent's loving strength soon had this independent lady thinking of a ready-made family!

#1128 SHANE'S BRIDE—Karen Rose Smith
Hope Franklin left Shane Walker years ago to avoid tying him down with a child. But now Hope knew their son needed a father, and she owed Shane the truth....

**#1129 THE MAVERICK TAKES A WIFE—
Charlotte Moore**
Logan Spurwood had enough problems without falling for Marilee Haggerty. He had nothing to offer her; his past had made sure of that. But Logan couldn't stay away or stop dreaming of a happy future with Marilee.

#1130 THE MARRIAGE CHASE—Natalie Patrick
When heiress Felicia Grantham decided on a convenient marriage, no one could stop her—not even dashing Ethan Bradshaw. But Ethan's bold manner took her breath away, and soon Felicia was determined to follow her plan—with Ethan as the groom!

#1131 HIS SECRET SON—Betty Jane Sanders
Amy Sutherland traveled to the wilderness to find Matt Gray. He certainly wasn't the man she'd imagined as her nephew's father, but she hoped to persuade this rugged loner to accept the boy she loved.

MILLION DOLLAR SWEEPSTAKES (III)

No purchase necessary. To enter the sweepstakes and receive the Free Books and Surprise Gift, follow the directions published and complete and mail your "Win A Fortune" Game Card. If not taking advantage of the book and gift offer or if the "Win A Fortune" Game Card is missing, you may enter by hand-printing your name and address on a 3" X 5" card and mailing it (limit: one entry per envelope) via First Class Mail to: Million Dollar Sweepstakes (III) "Win A Fortune" Game, P.O. Box 1867, Buffalo, NY 14269-1867, or Million Dollar Sweepstakes (III) "Win A Fortune" Game, P.O. Box 609, Fort Erie, Ontario L2A 5X3. When your entry is received, you will be assigned sweepstakes numbers. To be eligible entries must be received no later than March 31, 1996. No liability is assumed for printing errors or lost, late or misdirected entries. Odds of winning are determined by the number of eligible entries distributed and received.

Sweepstakes open to residents of the U.S. (except Puerto Rico), Canada, Europe and Taiwan who are 18 years of age or older. All applicable laws and regulations apply. Sweepstakes offer void wherever prohibited by law. Values of all prizes are in U.S. currency. This sweepstakes is presented by Torstar Corp, its subsidiaries and affiliates, in conjunction with book, merchandise and/or product offerings. For a copy of the official rules governing this sweepstakes offer, send a self-addressed, stamped envelope (WA residents need not affix return postage) to: MILLION DOLLAR SWEEPSTAKES (III) Rules, P.O. Box 4573, Blair, NE 68009, USA.

SWP-S1295

It's our 1000th Special Edition and we're celebrating!

Join us these coming months for some wonderful stories in a special celebration of our 1000th book with some of your favorite authors!

Diana Palmer	**Nora Roberts**
Debbie Macomber	**Christine Flynn**
Phyllis Halldorson	**Lisa Jackson**

Plus miniseries by:

Lindsay McKenna, Marie Ferrarella, Sherryl Woods and Gina Ferris Wilkins.

And many more books by special writers!

And as a special bonus, all Silhouette Special Edition titles published during Celebration 1000! will have **_double_** Pages & Privileges proofs of purchase!

Silhouette Special Edition...heartwarming stories packed with emotion, just for you! You'll fall in love with our next 1000 special stories!

INTRODUCING...

A collection of award-winning books by award-winning authors! From Harlequin and Silhouette.

Falling Angel
by Anne Stuart

WINNER OF THE RITA AWARD
FOR BEST ROMANCE!

Falling Angel by Anne Stuart is a RITA Award winner, voted Best Romance. A truly wonderful story, *Falling Angel* will transport you into a world of hidden identities, second chances and the magic of falling in love.

"Ms. Stuart's talent shines like the brightest of stars, making it very obvious that her ultimate destiny is to be the next romance author at the top of the best-seller charts."
—*Affaire de Coeur*

A heartwarming story for the holidays. You won't want to miss award-winning *Falling Angel*, available this January wherever Harlequin and Silhouette books are sold.

You're About to Become a *Privileged Woman*

Reap the rewards of fabulous free gifts and benefits with proofs-of-purchase from Silhouette and Harlequin books

Pages & Privileges™

It's our way of thanking you for buying our books at your favorite retail stores.

PROOF OF PURCHASE
SR-PP88
Offer expires October 31, 1996

**Harlequin and Silhouette—
the most privileged readers in the world!**

For more information about Harlequin and Silhouette's PAGES & PRIVILEGES program call the Pages & Privileges Benefits Desk: 1-503-794-2499

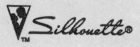